Undressing Lavinia

Also by George Rabasa

Glass Houses
Stories

Floating Kingdom
A novel

The Cleansing
A novel

The Wonder Singer
A novel

Miss Entropia and the Adam Bomb
A novel

Undressing Lavinia

≈ by ≈

George Rabasa

The Fiction Factory

Tasora

COVER CREDITS
Photo: Holly Wilmeth
Art: Ruthann Godollei
Ink: Leviticus Tattoo and Body Piercing
Design: Kyle Hunter

Interior design, typesetting, and printing: Bookmobile

Tasora Books
5120 Cedar Lake Road S
Minneapolis, MN 55416
(952) 345-4488
Distributed by Itasca Books

Undressing Lavinia

Jordi

Lavinia has been going fast. Months, weeks, days. I'm entrusted with the care of the Snake, the Puma, the Cheshire, the Owl, the Rabbit. All the living things in her dying head. Such vital alertness, luminous even as she fades. I wonder if she can hear their growls and howls as she sleeps and drifts. I'm here, I say. Yes, she says. Letting me know that she is also here, present. Her hand stirs under the taped IV, skin bruised after so many stabs, dragging her intubation along the side of the bed, fingers feeling out, seeking my touch. Finally, her hand closing on mine, a strong grip that surprises me even as I respond with a squeeze. It's so familiar, the skin on the back of her hand. Under the punctures and remnants of adhesive, a map of islands in freckles, brown sunspots and faint down. I lean down to touch the skin with my lips, and marvel that it's so dry and cold, evidence that life is seeping out with every short breath. Her fingernails have grown brittle, etched with striations that culminate in jagged tips. Then in a moment of anxiety, she digs into the back of my hand, leaving a grouping of half-moons. Her hand falls limp, spent from the effort, and I pull back my own, rubbing my thumb at the sweet pain of her nail tracks, all the while knowing that the memory of her touch will follow me always.

She is happy these days. The glory of her head taking shape, the confidence that Xeloda is not too crippling in its side effects, and might do some good. Arrest the advance of the shit in her lungs, prevent it from going elsewhere. The knowledge that we will travel well into the magnificence of the west, the holy places where our joined psyches have in the past experienced such earthshaking beauty. How do bliss and mourning coexist? Her head is beautiful. When she goes, it will be like autumn, one last blast of color before the leaves fall.

Lavinia

Again, as I have waited night after night, I yearn for the snake. It clings to the top of my head, motionless for now, but its slithery, almost liquid motion reveals its gift of life. Vibora, viborita. I am the soul snake, the pulsing, breathing core of the dried, wasted body. There is no I but I, at the intersection of mind and heart, no longer waiting but at peace with the unfolding that I know is happening, the shutting of light, the descending of outer darkness, the ghost of inner glow, faint and distant, but somehow inevitable.

Are you with me, Jordi? Are you there still? Somehow, against everything I believe to be true, I want to take you with me, as ghoulish as that sounds, because this thing needs company, a witness. And after thirty years you have been the watcher of all I am, the depths of anger and sadness, courage and fear, the joys and ecstasies, the delights of desire and fulfillment, pain and orgasm.

I awake and feel your breath on my face. I whisper "blue" and then again, wondering why you are not understanding, it is frustrating to have your ears deaf to me. Blue, blue, blue. And then, out of the blue, you understand me.

An hour later, a day later, a week later, you hover by my bed and raise a small crystal bowl of perfect blueberries up to my eyes. Dark as midnight, opaque, almost lightless, their skin tight and seamless to enclose the burst of flesh within. I inhale a scent that rises improbably from the fog of piss and shit and baby wipes, manifesting somehow subtly and elusively, to herald the gift to follow. You put one to my mouth and I part my lips to hold it in a kiss. I open my mouth to take it inside and the berry drops to my chest. You place another and another and every time I'm unable to eat it. Finally, you push the berry past my lips onto my tongue. I work it around until it finds my teeth and bite on it, a break through the tight skin makes a snap that only I hear. A gift.

But you have understood me. Always, my love, my keeper, my champion. From the time you became my friend and called me the sanest woman you had ever known. That was a gift too, because you didn't know how not-sane I was, how afraid I was. Of myself. Not of the world, or of criminals, or of my father (that sanctimonious judge of everything I am), or easy lovers, or wild dogs. It was my own tendency to anger and hate that scared me.

My pride in the righteousness that I saw myself embodying was a drain. The shame of my face, my flesh, my hunger, my smells and fluids and excretions. I never knew when my need for spiritual uplift became greed for God. Because I was a deserving vessel of his goodness, and he was the father who would indulge me with gifts of peace and health, to loosen the vise around my head and the fire in my belly. All I had to do was ring his bell and wait, the good Lord's spoiled brat. In response, I vowed to sing his praises, preach his truth.

And how I love the theater of ritual—baptism, communion, marriage, funeral. Ritual awakens a response from within, connecting me to the mechanics of a hermetic universe. God is not love, its realm is a soup, of tears, semen, blood, saliva, sweat, vaginal nectar. Ritual plunges me in the stew and I am the priestess of incantations. This is my flesh. This is my blood. From this cup I drink your truth. With this mouth, its thirst slaked, I speak your truth.

Now when I reach for the truth that I thought I owned, I find only darkness, a well of solitude, a frictionless plunge into nothingness. But my fall is broken by voices around me, the silence I yearn for is not yet within reach. I'm lifted by the rattle of wind, the hum of machines, the chimes that tether me to the bed, to the tubes that keep me here, swollen in my bladder and my feet and my brain. I know this because I hear voices when people think I'm gone, and they whisper about me as if I'm not present, they poke and needle me mercilessly. Violence.

Make them stop.

Jordi

I tell Ysbel when she calls me that she will need to take a taxi to Shanti House after she lands at MSP. No big deal. It will cost her about $50. And it's the best option with the roads being iced over and a new blizzard on the way. She complains that at age seventy she is in no shape to be traveling by herself. I'm a shitty winter driver, which is why Lavinia and I have lived for the past twenty years in a two-bedroom condo above the river on the edge of downtown. Besides, I don't dare separate myself from her. In truth, I hardly take the time to eat, bathe, sleep out of hearing of her voice, the faint moans that accompany her wakefulness, her labored breathing.

It has been several years since Ysbel and Vin were last together. She has many questions that I assure her will be answered once she is here. As it is, it took me several weeks to locate her, first through the International School in the Lomas district of Mexico City, then following the links to retired teachers and students of Lavinia's generation. Clearly, after the way things turned out with her most gifted and challenging classmate, Ysbel was happy to disappear from that insular expat community. I couldn't blame her. Not that I knew many details. Only that the events of a single week had left a residue of guilt and silence, of a hanging apology and delayed forgiveness.

But Lavinia had insisted that I find Ysbel. Now, she's just a couple of hours from reuniting with her.

"She's on her way," I say loudly, my mouth grazing Lavinia's ear. I believe she has heard me, though she doesn't react because the drip has her fading in and out of alertness. As it is, I feel we're betraying her wishes with the medication because she had insisted that life's great transitions should be faced with clarity. An infant is born with glaring consciousness. This is why I often take it upon myself to shut off the flow, let a measure of pain sharpen Vin's awareness. I do so now, knowing that she will want to look into Ysbel's eyes.

No other visitors are expected. I keep a closed system where friends and relatives call ahead and see if she has good energy for a visit. There are people whose idle conversation and fidgeting exhaust her after a few minutes; she closes her eyes with a sigh. Others, she has already dismissed, affectionately parted from them, allowed them to weep their goodbyes. No names necessary; you know who you are. No explanations are available, and you may not know why you've been shut out. I'm the gatekeeper and filter of phone and mail. I watch over her, cradling her heart and psyche, a treasure to be guarded from scavengers and looters gunning for one last piece of Lavinia. But you can ask me anything. I will tell you her numbers, her prognosis, the state of her emotions—which range from grief to anger to serenity to sparks of joy. Vin holds no secrets now.

As Ysbel approaches I work to make Vin's room warm and bright. This has been my role ever since I quit my job almost two years ago. She is regal in her hospital bed, usually during the day tilted at a 45-degree angle that helps her breathe. Shanti House staff keep the linens fresh, pillows fluffed, the commode clean, her meds labeled and arranged in coded multicolored cases. Close at hand, there are tangerine slices in a crystal bowl, ice crystals sweetened with honey, a small speaker piping Philip Glass, Cohen, the Doors, Caballé. Books to read aloud—T.S. Eliot, though much of his poetry she can recite from memory. Moby Dick because she's in love with Queequeg, *The Tibetan Book of the Dead—just in case,* she says—and Ionesco's Death of the King. When I read to her I keep my voice even, without particular emphasis but striving for clarity, sometimes lulling her to sleep. Other times, to her amusement, I myself start to doze as the words turn to mush in my mouth.

Read that part again, she says.

Except for the point, the still point, there would be no dance.

Again.

And I read the lines for as long as she wants to hear them, after a while our voices, hers and mine, murmur in unison.

And there is always dance for you and me, I say after she has gone asleep.

Jordi

Nothing about Shanti House hospice signals despair. At one time a large family home in the southern suburbs of Minneapolis, it has been converted into a gracious space for the terminally ill and their families. The rooms are spacious and cheerful, with large windows overlooking a garden, a hospital bed softened with a colorful bedspread, a recliner upholstered in bright patterns. There are twelve rooms for patients, each paired with a connecting bathroom. There are also three bedrooms for visitors. A quiet room is reserved for reflection, meditation, prayer, whatever.

And best of all, a basement features games, exercise equipment, and vending machines with candy and soft drinks. No coins required. Punch a selection and out come the treats. My favorites are peanut

M&Ms. Vin likes Reese's peanut butter cups. Can't underestimate the therapeutic effect of free candy.

There is a door for the living and one for the dead. Patients, usually on wheelchairs, are welcomed through the front entrance and into the reception hall. They are greeted by a director, a nurse, and various volunteers. They are handed a small bouquet.

On opposite sides of an entrance hall, there are two parlors, appointed with fireplaces and comfy chairs and big TVs, their screens like aquariums with silent pictures that nobody pays attention to. Small groups of friends and relatives huddle and murmur conversations around constant themes. How far did you travel to get here? Your mother, father, spouse? How many days? Any pain? Any conversations?

After death, the body is collected by funeral home staff and pushed out on a gurney through the room's side door, wheeled down a corridor along the garden, out of a back gate to be loaded onto a hearse. So begins the private, solitary journey of the newly deceased.

Outside room 41 at Shanti House, buttery light streams through the window slats creating zebra striping the length of her bed covers. A deep blue blanket has been laid over the sheets and pulled to just below her chin. Outside it's a bright fall day, warm for the season, but Vin has been shivering since awakening just before dawn. Her hands and face are cold and clammy to the touch. She keeps falling asleep as if to escape the chill.

Before she awakes again, I drive home and retrieve a pair of mittens with snowflake designs and a white knit cap with a red pompom. She is alert when I enter the room and place them on her lap and she touches them, admiring how soft as silk the cashmere is. When she complains that her feet are cold, I fold the covers first off one leg then the other and slide socks on her feet.

She lies on her back, head propped up at the nape to facilitate her breathing. Her eyes are closed, and the nurse assumes she's asleep. But I can tell the difference in her breath between sleep and meditation. She is spending more time meditating now, letting the barely realized thought kernel of the mantra lead her beyond the fear and the restlessness of her body resisting surrender. Sitting on a chair by the bed, I meditate with her. She smiles when she senses me close by, the two of us joined in silence. Then, in a blink, she is asleep again, the mantra abandoned. This is how she will go, says Nurse Jill, deeper and deeper sleep until she breathes her last. No pain. No fear. No anger. She is a good soul, she says, she has earned the gift of an easy death.

But her death will not be easy for me. I leave Shanti House for short periods to run errands, change clothes, walk in sunshine. I feel like I'm wearing a sign pinned to my back that reads "Carrying Death." Not my death but the death of my beloved. I'm so stumped by grief that I feel everyone knows. I'm like the bearer of the plague, a man to be avoided lest you catch his misery. Just a look into my eyes reveals the prospect of impending loss.

On my way to Surdyk's to pick up the fruit tarts that Vin loves, I'm abruptly gripped by pain at the center of my chest that seizes up as if the muscles had contracted to protect from some outer threat. I get off the freeway and park in a residential street under a tree's leafy canopy.

Gradually, as my breath settles down from its initial gasps, the circle of pain narrows until it's focused on my heart. I panic that I'm having cardiac failure, and that by some nasty whim of the gods I will die of a heart attack before Vin dies of cancer, and that she will be left alone through the torment of treatment and dissolution. This brings a mix of anger and sorrow. And the pain in my heart is a fist, gripping it so that it can hardly pulse its life blood. Even as I rest my head back and close my eyes and feel a return to serenity, the pain continues unabated. A broken heart. I always felt it was a metaphor for the disappointments of failed romance. I realize my heart will not physically break with grief, only that it will ache and ache, relentlessly.

Ysbel

My friend, my sister, my beloved. Under the hammering Mexican sun, our skinny bodies in matching yellow suits, chosen by our mothers so we would stand out on the crowded beach. Playa Caleta in Acapulco: its warm, gentle motion, safe for ten-year-olds discovering their ability to swim. Shrieking with delight as the sand washed beneath our feet with the pull of the surf, clinging to each other's hand, with the unspoken vow that if we were pulled by the undertoad (thanks, John Irving) and drowned we would drown together, a pair of Annabel Lees in our kingdom.

That day marked our first kiss. Our mothers became friends because we were friends, though there was no way they could inhibit the kind of intensity that ruled us, sharing reveries, inhabiting each other's dreams, somehow connected through sleep. The stuff of the night became our waking reality, the fear of the old priest with the stains on his surplice, who we knew had it in for girls because we were not boys. It was hard to tell which dream belonged to whom, the rub of yellow teeth, the breath of wet cigar, an oily head staining our pillow, Padre Anselmo haunted our beds. His image so vivid it brought out a stream of nervous giggles.

At the height of our fun in the water, a dance with waves and slithery sand, our mothers pulled us out and slathered sunscreen lest our faces age into prunes. We were then exiled to a shady spot under a low umbrella, where we built a private fort with big bright towels draped over upturned beach chairs. We dabbed lotion on our cheeks, ears and forehead, buttery dots of coconut oil, shiny like caramel to make our mouths water. I was the first, even then the subversive, spreading the lotion with my fingertips, making spirals and streaks, then lying still for you to do the same for me.

We kissed, putting your mouth to mine with more confidence than I felt, grazing at first, then pressing insistently, finally tonguing your lips open. Dear, dear Lavinia, ten years old and had never been kissed, not like that, like a big girl. I helped you rest back on the beach towel as you shuddered, stretching your little legs out, back arching under my fingers on the nubs of breasts, then spreading lotion down your belly, past your jutting hip bones, and below the elastic waist of your bikini. A sweet slit, smooth as peach, even then moistening under the magic of the lotion

After a moment, when you had fallen into a kind of drowse, I took your hand, or rather the index and middle fingers, and rubbed myself with them, allowing you to learn what to do in your own good time, even as I used them like a tool disconnected from the rest of the hand.

We didn't speak of our discovery after that first time. Only occasionally, during sleepovers or playful wrestling on the lawn where, without acknowledging their purpose, our fingers would find their spot with an intelligence of their own.

The results of this play brought such pleasure that we knew it had to be forbidden. As we grew into adolescence, the original sense of play became tainted by guilt. Neither had conviction to accept our transgressions, though I can't remember who of the two of us one night pushed away the hand that had crept under the elastic band of our panties. It had been a quiet, wordless rejection, like the brushing away of an insect. After that, we did allow boys to touch us. If we'd had the courage, we would've admitted to each other that their clumsy groping was not in any way equal to our early explorations. It would take years before we eventually found men that could love us with the same delicacy and tenderness. Or at least you found Jordi. There was never a good man for me. Years after we lost contact, I kept searching my way back to someone's hand, always trying to recover the sensation of that first touch.

Lavinia

Oh, Ysbel, we were such urchins, skinny and fidgety. One look and we despised each other. Eight years old and chosen for some obscure reason to sit side by side in class. Miss Christine thought we looked alike and therefore we were going to be sisters.

From the first days in Mexico you had noticed that many Spanish words were similar to English but with an O added to the end: bank-o, telephone-o, disc-o plus all the other words like gato, auto, perro, libro and so on. In the playground you boldly introduced yourself to a group of kids: "Hio, myo, nameo iso Ysbelo."

I thought that was so tonto!

There was to be no talk or smiles or play with you, the new girl, recently arrived from the US. You wore fancy dresses as if your mother was using you to make a good impression. You had blond hair, pale skin, crooked teeth. And you didn't speak Spanish, which gave me a clear edge because I could talk around your face, above your head, past your ears.

Even your name was dumb. I mean Isabel is not spelled Ysbel. It was obviously some weird made-up thing that nobody had ever heard of. Which made you a freak, so I was not going to be your friend no matter who said I would.

Every day I sat stiffly, not showing the faintest awareness of your presence at the desk beside mine. When by chance our eyes met, there was a squint and pursing of the mouth into a scrunched grimace because such a creature was beyond comprehension. I couldn't believe you were human. But as we practiced our cursive, I could tell you had nice handwriting. Almost as pretty as mine.

Then one day I dropped a pencil and we both bent down to pick it up. It was so sweet that after all those days of ignoring each other, you wanted to help me. We bumped heads as we reached down and broke into a sudden fit of giggling that wouldn't stop even after Miss Christine fixed us with her icy glare. We were friends from that moment.

Mother

I tried to like your new friend, but she was not going to be a good influence on you. Of all the girls in the International School you had to make friends with a weird little urchin. Still, I welcomed her into our home. I thought I could have a civilizing influence on her, and she started staying for supper most nights when you and she studied together. I let it be known that she was welcome in our home, but that I preferred you did not go to hers. I don't think it mattered to her parents one way or another.

It was clear her family life was not happy because she seemed to need the orderliness of a well-organized household. It was up to me to cure her of her bad habits, sloppy table manners, careless hygiene. I remember one afternoon when you two came in all grubby after playing outside, I sent her into the bath after you. It was such a change to see her clean and well-scrubbed, her hair shiny and smelling fresh. I swear, her parents must've been hippies. Then, once she had dried off, I lent her your clothes. You looked like sisters in matching sun dresses, yellow with blue flowers for you, and for her, a blue one with daisies. Like the halves of an apple, you two.

She was so pleased with her dress that she kept glancing at her reflection in mirrors and windows around the house. I threw her dirty shorts and T-shirt in the wash with the intention of getting them dry before she left that evening after your study time. But she left early, still wearing your blue dress.

She never did return the dress, as you know. And you started wearing her shorts and Batgirl T-shirt. In the years since, I still marvel how you influenced each other.

Ysbel

Oh Vin, years ago you tried to lead me towards the spirit. You were the priest and I was the acolyte, subverting the catholic strictures against the female role in the liturgy. In the empty church I followed you down the middle of the dark nave, a procession of two, climbing the three steps to the altar and then spreading your arms in an echo of the crucifixion, an invitation to be entered by the mighty mystery.

For a time you stood still, mumbling Latin mumbo jumbo, *introit ad alterei dei.* . . . Unto the altar of God I will go, naked of pretension and cleansed of sin, like the first woman before she became the instrument of the fall.

I watched from a couple of steps back as you began to shake from your shoulders to your legs, then before I could let out a yelp, Padre Anselmo, stealing from the wings like a giant black crow, swooped down and laid a meaty hand on the top of your head, as if to bless but really to freeze the motion of the spirit coursing up the spine to your neck.

He ordered us to leave. He said, "a girl can't be a priest."

You knew he was watching us.

He doesn't understand the spirit. You directed me to kneel at the pew. You whispered that he couldn't kick us out while we were at prayer. It's called sanctuary. That's how criminals evade arrest.

I could sense Padre Anselmo standing behind us, his breath perfumed by Sen-Sen licorice lozenges to hide the smell of booze.

You whispered, just loud enough for him to hear, "he can't touch us. We're girls."

I wonder how long it took him to reach the same conclusion, the reality of handling us physically bringing on the wrath of parents, church authorities, God Himself. He crept out without a sound, but we held our breath until the shutting of the sacristy door confirmed his exit. Glorying in our victory, we leaned back on the pew, in a darkness relieved only by the flickering red votives in the prayer chapels.

It took less than an hour before our mothers, joined in a fierce mission of salvation, followed Padre Anselmo into the church. He switched on the glaring overhead lights, revealing us still kneeling side by side before the altar.

After that, you decided you'd be a priest, not a catholic one of course, but surely some religion would offer women a function as ministers with their own quality of truth, closer in spirit to Mother Earth or Guadalupe or Kali with her garland of skulls. You invented rituals involving communion with Twinkies and Coca Cola. And I was the faithful acolyte, ringing bells and waving incense sticks, sandalwood wafting about. Over the next couple of years as we entered puberty, you developed your own rituals. A smear of blood from your very first period on a postcard of the ascended Jesus, a blush on his cheek, became a sacred offering, a message to the rulers of the universe that you were presenting yourself as a lamb for sacrifice. Somehow, I knew we were messing around with mysteries better left undisturbed. But while I was cautious, you plunged ahead with blind confidence, fully trusting in the forces at the heart of creation. I was afraid of the devil, you were convinced that in the face of love, Satan was helpless, irrelevant, and he would revert to his status before the fall.

"Where do you get this stuff?" I asked.

"It just comes."

"In dreams?"

"No. In the moment."

"Like right now?"

"Yes. I don't know what I'm going to say until I say it."

"You don't remember everything, do you?"

"I do. At some level."

"What level would that be?"

"Blood. Marrow. Spit. Sweat."

"But you can't tell me what you said the last time."

"When my body shakes, twitches, pants like a thirsty dog, I know what I know."

"And what do you know?"

The Gospel According to Vin:
Know your song well before you sing.
I'm older than God, but nicer.
My face before I was born was not this face.
The love than can be uttered is not the true love.
Hate moves mountains.
All lies contain truth.
All truth contains a lie.
Silence isn't always golden.
All gold is fool's gold.

I don't think we would still be friends if I hadn't followed you wherever you went. You walked barefoot all over our wealthy neighborhood, steep circular streets surrounding the deep ravines separating the fine houses and gardens from the shanties in the village below. The soles, which at first blistered and cracked, eventually calloused to the consistency of leather. It was a point of pride for you, to identify with those children from the pueblo whose parents could not afford to buy them shoes.

Now, years after we last saw each other, I travel to Minneapolis for the first time. Mexico City is in the distant past. Our brief meetings in Cambridge, Barcelona, Oaxaca, only served to tantalize and reawaken. And now Minneapolis where you have lived the last thirty years is such an unlikely place to grow old in, with its blizzards and prairie winds. Its wide river connecting you to the gulf of your original home.

Jordi
It's Luis again.

He calls several times a day and won't accept that every time I explain that you are sleeping, that it would be better not to wake you,

I'm blocking his intrusion at your request. Your brother's voice alone is enough to exhaust you with its endless questions and challenges.

"Her numbers, I want to know my sis' numbers."

"She doesn't like you calling her sis."

"That's what I've always called her. She's my older sister."

"She doesn't like it."

"She never complained before, not when we were children or teenagers or ever."

"She's complaining now."

"She can tell me personally."

"I will relay the message."

"Hand her the phone."

"Sorry, she's resting."

Such fury at your resistance, which has taken you to this place with your lungs riddled with globules, slippery marbles, eerily translucent under the lens of the roaming biopsy camera, your mind growing unreliable with brain swelling. In the face of dissolution your anger makes you fearless. Typically Mexican, men thinking that they know better than the women in their life. And as you weaken, disruption from old friends, tired flames, your brother and father, all fuel your resolve to wither in peace.

Luis

Hermanita, I don't know what possessed you to marry such a bully. What does Jordi think he is? Warden, keeper, cop? He thinks he owns you and I imagine that he has bound you to the bed with ropes and cuffs for wrists and ankles, strapped duct tape across your mouth, placed a blinder over your eyes. Because that is the only way you would not respond to my desire to help. And you know I can help.

I've been in touch with doctors here in Mexico. A close personal friend of a dear friend is a world-famous oncologist specializing in your specific condition, if that is in fact what you have, because the numbers I'm getting from Jordi are inconclusive. Don't believe everything you are told. Obviously, it's in the interests of doctors to squeeze you out of every dime. I had a friend who was told she had cancer so advanced she had only four months to live before dying in horrible pain and she visited this oncologist friend who, as I said before, is one of the best in the world and he gave her a treatment that totally eradicated the tumors. That was six years ago. Total remission! I will send you a picture; she is now the embodiment of health.

But meanwhile, Señor Jordi keeps blocking all communications from your family who loves you, your mom, your father, and above all me, your brother who knows what is best for his sister. Trust me.

We all think you should move to Mexico to be taken care of by those who are available for you around the clock. You will have your old room back with a view of the garden and the flowering jacaranda tree. Everything is as you left it years ago to marry Jordi. The embroidered huichol bedspread, the writing table with a tulip lamp, your collection of Dias de Muertos skulls.

We will hire a dedicated muchacha to look after you. To cook and clean and run errands and answer the phone. Our driver Miguel can take you shopping or to the movies or the doctor whenever you need. One of our friends is the best masseuse in Mexico City, healing hands and vibrating fingers. Another is the best nurse at the Hospital General and will be on call for all your treatments. Señora Erminia specializes in herb healings for hopeless cases, so-called "hopeless" that is, until her teas and tonics work their magic. Can Jordi give you that in Minneapolis?

I think not.

And best of all, you can get away from the harsh freezing weather of the Midwest which has to be injurious to your lungs. Maybe that's the reason you got sick in the first place. People say the air here is polluted, but we don't have as much cancer as the US has. Think of smog as a kind of inoculation. The chilango vaccine. Building immunity with every breath you take! I'll propose that idea to the tourism department.

Just brilliant, if I say so myself. Because you see, you're not the only creative one in the family. Sure, you're a poet and an artist and a musician. And Jordi scribbles books that no one buys. My kind of creativity is the sort that makes money. Just ask Coca Cola, Bacardi, Marlboro, Corona. One little idea of mine can mean millions in sales. And big bonuses for me.

I'm not the only one that knows that if you want to get healthy again, you need to come home. I took a poll of your father and cousins, former teachers at the Universidad along with prestigious doctors and other experts in the field, and they all agree with me. You belong with us. And if you don't come back home it's because Jordi has brainwashed you, manipulated your love for him into inertia, bound to a mechanical bed, where he sits at the door like a dog, day and night with nothing better to do than keep those of us who love you away.

It's good thing I'm not a violent man, dear hermanita. I choose the path of reason. But Jordi must know what I'm capable of. You think he's protective of you? See how he behaves if I come by with a team to give him a bit of persuasion. My belief is that he would crumple. I'd walk right in and roll you out in your wheelchair straight to the airport and a flight to CDMX. You are a citizen of our country and you have a right to return home for your health.

This is not an actual threat. I'm just thinking out loud, contemplating what the last resort might be if Jordi won't be rational about you. I don't have high hopes. He is not a reasonable person. He is arrogant and stubborn and narcissistic. I wouldn't be surprised if he wants to keep you in the death spiral so he'll get money after you're gone.

Lavinia

No, little brother. I feel you nearby, breathing at my door. I can smell you. It's hard to figure out where your tongue has been, the breath exhaling tequila and cigarettes. You claim to love me with a higher status than that of a mere husband.

I did love you once, dear hermanito, and love you still when I remember your skinny frame at six years old in your orange swimsuit at Caleta beach, the little brother I was to care for and keep from drowning. That's when you learned to swim, with me holding you up by your belly so you could splash and kick with hands and feet. I gradually let you go and you were gliding on the water by yourself. You were a natural athlete even then, and you stroked through the surf with great form. Such a triumph that day. "I can swim, I can swim," you exclaimed at the dinner table until our parents stopped talking to each other and paused to listen and acknowledge your great achievement. "Vin taught me." You made sure I got credit.

I also taught you to play chopsticks, blow Bazooka bubbles, make origami birds, and then to read when the teachers said you were too stupid to learn. We knew better. You weren't reading because you wouldn't concentrate. But I introduced you to stories that pulled you in. Robin Hood, Tom Sawyer, The Odyssey. You couldn't get enough, and I dutifully sat with you on opposite ends of the fat velvet sofa, slurping hot chocolate with marshmallows, the two of us reading and reading until our mother grew worried that we would burn our eyes out, that we weren't getting any fresh air, that we were turning into moles. Nothing outside the house could compete with the wild flashes of our inner worlds. You became the star of the third grade. I knew then that I would grow up to be a teacher. You were my first pupil and your accomplishments thrilled me. Even now, a hundred years later, when I encounter a beautiful boy with a scattered mind that can be harnessed by the power of stories, I think of you, hermanito.

Then, at age twelve, you turned on me. You little shit. You were too busy making jokes, farts and burps. The louder the better so that the class would be disrupted and you would be a hero to the other boys. That was always important to you, to be a boy's boy, a man's man.

And then you were gone. From one moment to the next, as sudden as a bucket of ice water on my head, you rebuffed my invitations to read, my suggestions for books, my offers to show you my poems.

You were thirteen and I was sixteen when, as if by accident, the back of your hand brushed my breast for the first time. It was a touch as light as a breeze, barely a whisper on my silk blouse, a slight bump on the nipple, then a glide to the under slope of the breast. I challenged you with an angry look, but you simply gazed back as if wondering what my reaction had to do with you. I grabbed your hand and sank my teeth on the fleshy pad by the thumb.

Marcial

He was a boy. Too young to have meant anything by touching you. So, it was not worth mentioning. And certainly not to your mother.

Women are ignorant in the ways of men. We can't help reaching out, even as children, to express our maleness. In any case, you have to learn to let things pass when no real harm is intended, merely a game, a tease. You, on the other hand, meant harm with your teeth.

I have had my eye on you, dear, since you were a child, because you are willful like your mother. I insisted on meeting any boys that wanted your company. They were to be of a proper class. That is why my children attended the International School. Not so much for the education, as for the network you would build over time.

What did you think I would say when you started seeing Jordi? Middle aged, divorced, an aspiring writer. There is nothing that spells defeat with greater clarity than a writer still unpublished at forty. And not respectful at all. He swooped into your life and claimed you like some kind of raptor's prize. And what a find you were for him. He had to scrape the wax out of his hairy ears to hear your laughter, rub the crust from his eyes to see your natural beauty. Couldn't you see that he had all the suppleness of an old shoe? And on top of everything he was bent on taking you away from your home, from your country, to be more like a nanny, to be sure, to his children from his broken marriage. We did not raise you for domestic servitude.

And now you seem to be stuck in a cage to await your end in isolation, while Jordi takes it on himself to determine who can come to show you love and who can't. Does he think he owns you? It's gotten to the point that we can't talk on the phone, or be sure you read our emails and texts. Well, we, your brother, your sister, and your father, who have loved you all your life, are not going to take this. We are flying to Minneapolis and, if we have to, we will camp outside your door and wait Jordi out until he opens the gate.

Jordi

Luis and Marcial have a fantasy that they will come to Minneapolis to rescue and spirit you back to Mexico City. While neither of us grew up here, in this shimmering oasis in the prairie, we have over the course of over thirty years established our bond with this land.

Mexico City with its stifling haze, relentless clamor, and gridlock, pales in comparison to our spectacle of seasons. The mighty cloud formations in a sky of pristine blueness which can change in a blink with the rage of westerly winds driving a blizzard of alarming fury. Weeks of heat and months of deadly freeze remind us of our vulnerability. We cope with whatever is thrown at us and this makes for a lively dance.

Through the expanse of glass, our condo overlooked the Mississippi River below, a mighty force from the northern headwaters down to the Gulf of Mexico. The sculptural city rose ahead, its buildings of glass and steel and Kasota stone ignite with the dawn. The banks, the insurance companies, grain merchants, the temples of greed you call them, all promise wealth within everyone's reach. It's a lie of course, since the bounty of capitalism is not shared equally. A hopeful myth nevertheless.

Of course, we're believers. I became a writer here, from early stories written in the early hours before punching into my marketing day job to a couple of novels that were commercial failures but modest literary successes.

And you, dear Vin, take the prize, growing majestically from your adjunct job teaching composition to earning a PhD in comparative literature and a tenured chair at the University. You still had time to be a poet.

When I think of our time here, our friends and colleagues, we are filled with gratitude for this city, and cannot think of a better place to end the life we began thirty years ago.

At our spot on the edge of downtown, the river broadens to actually accommodate two small islands that serve as neighborhood parks, both part of a running path along the banks. We often took a breather on Boom Island with its steps leading to the water, reminiscent of the ghats in Varanasi that take mourners down to the Ganges. As you've reminded me, years ago we decided that if death found us here, we wanted our ashes cast from that spot.

Lavinia

Daddy, I'm at a loss why you feel you know what's best for my life, even now that it's coming to an end. No, I will not go back to our home in Mexico City as you and Luis demand.

I stopped being your obedient daughter once I grew to tell the difference between love and control. I started pushing you away when I was not to have suitors without your permission, because you claimed to protect me. And naturally you approved of no one. I had to leave for Harvard before I was able to get away from you, far enough so that a man knocking at my door would not meet with scowls. I had been reduced to permanent childhood under your power. You were the opposite of Jordi once he came into my life.

There were other men before him, of course, and some were your brothers in spirit and loin. Truth is, I had trouble trusting any man. Only Jordi came to provide the antidote to your bullying. Hard to know what sort of serum flows through the veins of your ilk, the macho camachos of my birth country, following the tradition of men all over the world who fear women—our pleasure, our sexuality, our intellect, our energy, the monthly blood that makes you nauseous. Our capacity for repeated orgasms as we pleasure ourselves when you are soft and spent is a threat to you. Our excitement in the embrace of other women is a threat to you. Our ability to control the progeny that proves your virility is a threat to you. Nevertheless, whether you are fathers, husbands, lovers, brothers, you claim to know what is best for the fragile creatures that God has burdened you with.

Mother

Don't pay attention to your father and Luis insisting that you come back home for whatever treatment options they claim would be best for you. You belong where you feel most loved and cared for.

It didn't take long for Marcial to show his true nature after his old-fashioned Latin courtship. Mexican men at the time were skilled at charming American girls and then, once the honeymoon was over, reverting to the ways of their fathers.

It became clear to me since you were a child that he would impose his macho will on you. His authority over women was something he took for granted, never a question or a hesitation if it came to deciding whom you would befriend and how you would conduct your social life. His rules were clear. Home by ten, hems below the knee, weight controlled, makeup forbidden, music and movies and books strictly censored. It's no wonder you developed a secret life from an early age. And I covered for you as best I could. In that sense we were partners in crime.

But when you complained, all I could do was back him up. It was hard because as an American woman I had grown up, if not a feminist, at least a believer in equality inside the home. That was not how marriage worked, I was quick to learn.

I will spare you complaints. But now as I feel compelled to step in and defend your decision to stay in Minneapolis, I realize that for all these years I was never able to talk to you and your brother freely. Minnesotans are notoriously inhibited. My main goal in the years we were married was to maintain the peace. It's not that he was physically abusive. He didn't need to be. But he was dismissive and patronizing.

I was docile until I left him, which must've come as a shock to you and your brother. And certainly as a shock to Marcial. Later, the opinions of friends and family peppered me with accusations that I should've done something to negotiate his tyranny. That may have occurred to me at the start of our marriage, but after twelve years, I simply wanted out. My main regret is that I left you to fend for yourself under your father's grip. I'm grateful that you never held that against me. But I wasn't so much escaping as rushing to recapture a part of me that I had thought dead for years. Before meeting your father, I'd been going steady (that was the term then) with Stuart Iverson since the sixth grade. We broke up in the last year of college, just when we had anticipated we'd marry.

I met your father during a senior trip to Mexico, The Mexican Discovery Adventure, and Marcial was a handsome athletic fellow who followed our tour bus throughout the country. There were tame little parties at every stop from Puebla to Veracruz so we could meet and mingle with the local young people. I noticed your father from the first gathering in Mexico City, and then realized he was inviting himself and a couple of his friends to every party along the route. It took him a while to concentrate on me. It was a game for him to flirt with the gringas, until the last stop of the tour back in Mexico City when he cut in on the fellow I was dancing with. He spoke words that sounded rude to me and sent him slinking.

I asked him what he'd said, because I felt sorry for the boy.

"I told him to get lost because he doesn't speak English. And you don't speak Spanish, so he was just wasting your time."

He was forceful that way. And he talked me into jumping off the bus and staying in Mexico City. Professor Colson who was in charge of the tour was furious. I was old enough to do what I wanted. My explanation was that I would enroll in summer language courses and really learn Spanish. My parents went along when I pointed out that by staying in Mexico, we were saving on tuition.

It wasn't hard to leave Minnesota behind. College friends went in different directions after graduation. The kids I grew up with in Farmington were outgrown. My boyfriend since high school was Stu Iverson, and I had already planned to break up with him, for no reason except that he had no ambition and no sense of a world beyond Minnesota. I broke his heart, but I bear no responsibility for him becoming an alcoholic.

It was only later, after Marcial became unbearable that I harbored the illusion that if I had stayed, I might have fixed Stu. I realize that was a fantasy later when after a few years I kept finding ways to be with him, time after time during trips back to Minnesota.

There was a limit to how long Marcial could play the role of a patient husband. When he finally settled into macho mode, he went at it with a vengeance. By then I was pregnant with you, and no longer the young, flirty gringa he had chased after. I gained weight. I had asthma attacks. The altitude of Mexico City had me gasping for air after just a small effort. It came rather suddenly.

During the first years I was happy to party with Marcial, as if a few drinks and clumsy sex could forestall the looming rift. One night we were out dancing and in the middle of a cha-cha I found myself struggling to breathe. It didn't help that in those days clubs in Mexico allowed smoking and were often thick with a smelly fog. I barely made it to our table before I found myself in a panic. It was a revelation that instead of being sympathetic my husband was embarrassed. He couldn't wait to drag me out of the club. He consented to stop at a pharmacy so I could buy an inhaler.

That was the end of the honeymoon. It was only when I would leave him for Stu time and time again, that he would decide he couldn't let me go. Too big a blow to his pride, I believe. He would coax and plead and promise things would be different. The good behavior would last a few weeks. And I would wait another few months before running away again. Finally, it was better to be with a drunk who valued me.

I'm nearing eighty now and if confession is good for the soul, I don't want my rambling about the past to be a burden to you. Mainly, I urge you to stand firm. Be strong, my girl.

Lavinia

Am I becoming a werewolf, Jordi? When you said that perhaps the meds are making my face downy, I looked in the mirror and I swear I couldn't see anything different. Maybe I've always had a hairy face and now you have an excuse to mention it. In any case, I'm worried that you might be ashamed of me when we go out together, even for a stroll, pushing my wheels, what with my bloated body and my bald head and my uncertain balance. My legs give out at the oddest moments and I've fallen more than once out in the street. And then you have to lift me and support me like you would a drunk. People do stare and I wonder how that makes you look, you who walked so proudly with me, because we were a fucking beautiful couple, slim and athletic and just fashionably odd.

But now, I have a furry face. I asked Ysbel and she said not to worry, that most women who can afford it wax their faces, unless they are old or solitary or queer, or all of the above.

So, I made a deal with you Jordi. I made two appointments at the salon. One for me to get my incipient whiskers pulled off and another to wax your hairy back, which always struck me gorilla-like but which I never in our thirty years mentioned.

Jordi

No, my love, you are not a monster or a monkey or a werewolf. What I saw in your face was a tender down, a silky patina invisible except when our faces leaned into each other for a kiss or a whisper.

And, yes, yanking hair off my back is torture, but the results seemed to please you, skin baby soft and blushed pink. The women at the salon were amused to high hell. They called us "tit for tat."

You also had your head shaved smooth by Kyle with his straight razor. The result is a shiny pate where the ink pops like neon. You may be dying my love. Of that there is no doubt; you were declared incurable from the moment you were diagnosed. And even as you go toward death, you have the joy of vanity. You will be beautiful for the journey.

Meanwhile, I mourn the death of sex. It's been over two years now. Your vagina sealing up frightens me. I touch the folds of your labia gone dry and papery, hermetic to any potential thrust I can muster from my tired old pud. The times we recently used our hands and mouths gave me the feeling that my tongue was not particularly effective, and manual ministrations seemed to be perfunctory even if determinedly generous in their intent. Toys might have been a solution, but we made no real attempt to find anything helpful. As your libido has faded, I am left to find my way to the fetish of choice, sometimes over an hour of titillation over web or phone, and either an explosion or a dribble to leave me sated but also ashamed and remorseful.

And all the time I wish I had it in my power to arouse you, like, perhaps, I was able to do at one time. I know that we both often look back with nostalgia to that time in our life together when we fucked with abandon, allowing ourselves to dabble in kink, you watching yourself in a mirror while engulfing my cock.

Still, we cling to each other through the night, our bodies touching, legs embracing, kisses soft and earnest. With a love that feels unbounded, deeper now than during the naïve time of unshakeable health.

Lavinia

Days of fury, nights of despair. What is this shit that is pumped into my vein that has such emotional consequences? All in an effort to keep my brain from bleeding into the prison cell of my skull, to keep the glistening lung marbles from swelling and multiplying. I hear myself exploding in anger, sarcasm slithering out of my mouth like a snake's tongue. I snap out at ladies wearing pink ribbons who with well-meaning sentiment shove me back into the realization that I'm dying of cancer. And, how is your treatment going, dear?

Jordi

Her head is beautiful. When she goes, it will be like autumn, one ecstatic surge of color before the leaves fall.

Marcial

If you don't answer the phone I must resort to email. I have erased photos you sent of your head. People like us do not tattoo. We are not gangsters, convicts, perverts, primitive tribesmen. These people deface their body to signal to others of their ilk. You were brought up to take a place among the gifted and the decent. You come from a family that has taken great responsibility in defending the civilized order of our country for generations. We help the needy and prosecute those that undermine the social contract. You come from a line of thinkers, teachers, poets and artists. You have no right to betray their legacy with your subversive behavior.

As a spiritual person, you must know that the bible prohibits tattooing. Leviticus 19:28 "Do not cut your bodies for the dead or put tattoo marks on yourselves. I am the LORD."

My suggestion is that you get a wig in a flattering style. You're a pretty girl and there is no need to go around looking like a freak, just because you are battling a health challenge. I will be glad to pay for a hairpiece if Jordi won't.

Lavinia

Papito, here's more nonsense from Leviticus (19:27). "Do not cut the hair at the sides of your head or clip off the edges of your beard."

Luis

Do you really want to spend these last few days of your life going against your family? You have hurt father's feelings by defying his standards. Is this how you want to be remembered? You are making it very hard for us to show you love and sympathy in your battle as you persist in denying our role in your life. That said, everything would be fine if Jordi, who I blame for your aggressive avoidance, did not insist on standing in our way. Just the other day, I tried phoning you three times at different hours of the afternoon and evening. On each occasion he insisted that you were either tired or asleep or getting therapy, and that he would call me back when you were available to talk. I am waiting.

Jordi

On the road again. On impulse we packed a bag and headed north as far as Grand Marais, on the north shore of Lake Superior. I've learned that when we're traveling, we're happy, distracted from the coming horrors. The chemicals are working, but there has also been a slow creeping of the cancer in the lungs and the brain. Not enough to cause new symptoms, but hard to ignore the cold numbers.

You're hungry at unpredictable times, so we packed some nuts and crackers that you kept in your pocket. Mostly you napped in the car, and then, suddenly renewed, you stirred into bright wakefulness. The woods around us exploded with summer greenery, and a fawn stood on rickety legs on the side of the road and you exclaimed with delight.

"Slow down, Jordi. I want to get a look at it. So sweet."

I stopped the car beside it and the creature held its ground fearlessly. It stared at us with soft eyes, as if to acknowledge the wonder that you expressed with a sudden bated breath.

Lavinia

The creature knew me to my very depths. This meeting had been long in the making and we recognized each other immediately. Her eyes soft as with tears fixed on mine in an unwavering gaze. I couldn't look away.

Jordi started to drive off after breathing a sigh of relief that he did not hit the fawn. I told him to wait with words that blurted out with sudden urgency. He said he couldn't just stop in the middle of the road, so I told him to drive to the shoulder. He parked a few feet ahead of the deer. I got out, leaving the door open so as not to make any noise, and walked toward her, taking one tentative step at a time, so she would know I meant no harm.

I knew somehow that it was female. Those were the eyes of a girl child, and I sensed that she was me when I was so much younger than today, a time when I felt myself to be immortal. She waited.

The air felt cool north of the city, and a brisk wind stirred the leaves of the surrounding poplars, their spindly white trunks mirroring the fawn's unsteady posture. As I came closer, I reached into my pocket and pulled out a handful of almonds and put my palm out as an offering.

As the creature leaned down towards my hand and gathered the nuts with her wet tongue somewhere behind me a burst of gunfire shattered the stillness. I saw her head explode in a shrapnel of blood and brains and skull fragments.

Jordi

You let out a cry and told me to drive off, that the fawn had been murdered and that there were killers all around us. I said the deer was fine, that it simply scampered across the road. I am frequently wary of my tone as the slightest sign of irritation becomes a personal injury. You slouched down in a sulk for the next several miles.

This weekend I felt frustrated because you got some driving directions mixed up which took us on a long detour. I called you a dingbat in fun. I spent the weekend working to assuage your feelings.

Since the brain metastasis and the subsequent radiation, lapses of memory and attention cause you anxiety. Added to this are the mood swings that are the consequence of medication.

Overall, we are happy. But I know that things are going to get worse and I fear I'm not up to expectations. This brings about a measure of guilt and frustration. I'm prey to periods of anger and grief. I sometimes feel weary that much of my life is basically dedicated to keeping you happy. The headaches, dizziness, fatigue are mine to worry about and try to alleviate. I am the consoler, cheerleader, helper of whatever you want to do—eat, travel, movies, socializing. Reassuring you that your unsuccessful efforts to get poetry published, in spite of it being mostly quite good, are part of the drill. Our sex life, once joyous and unrestrained, has gone dormant, even as we find comfort in close physical communion.

Lavinia

A day of rage. Dilantin level low and so it's time to increase the dosage. I rail against the idea of more pills, greater disturbance in my system. The increase brings in more nasty side turbulence—dizziness, fainting, headache, insomnia, confusion.

And finally, I'm overwhelmed with the breakdown of the body. The breast cancer metastasis to lung and brain, with nodules agitating like crazy, a little larger here, smaller there. The waiting game is resumed with scans every three months or so. The Decadron for brain swelling has continued to soften my bones, so that an infusion of Reclast was prescribed causing extreme flu-like symptoms, exhaustion, muscular pain. And the fear that brittle bones can crack with a fall. Then, migraines every night for two weeks or more, treated with sumatriptan which raises the possibility of damage to the heart with repeated, prolonged use. And there's the busted toe from working out.

I don't like being on a first-name basis with so many doctors—Bruce, Dave, Greg, Sarah, Joseph.

Why not just stop all these drugs and die?

Jordi

Her friend Janice asks if the C on my bumper sticker stands for Catalunya.

Actually, I say, it's for Cunt.

A faint attempt at humor that masks my anger. I wasn't calling her such a thing. Only, that in a stream of free association, that's what blurted out. I might have said Cancer, or Chaos, or Cock. Go figure.

I'm angry at old women, healthy women, couples who live without this thing hanging over their heads. I'm angry at living in the constant shadow of disease. At my life no longer being mine.

Lavinia is sick and I'm not sure I'm mustering the proper amount of patience and equanimity. So I get cranky. I feel like my whole life revolves around her needs, wants, whims. My writing has not gone well since Vin's diagnosis.

I'm ashamed of my thoughts: I will get pity blowjobs from her friends. I will move to CA to be near my kids. I will be able to get a reverse mortgage loan after she's gone. I fear going broke with the weak stock market and increased, uninsured expenses like hospice, more travel, in-home care.

I'm afraid of her pain, her dying.

And we continue to mourn the coming dissolution. You will go with a whisper and a sigh, without a cry or a curse. You have always said you want to be fully awake when death happens, yet nothing disturbs the mind like pain. Fire in the brain and ice in the lungs, blood in the eyes and bile in the throat. All these conspire to shake and rock the still flame of pure awareness. Allow me, dear soul, to relieve your pain.

Luis

Your husband is killing you. I'm convinced of this, and I will have my friend the oncologist confirm it from your lab reports and medical protocols. While my requests for information have been denied, my friend can exercise professional standing to evaluate your treatment by the team of hacks that have been assembled in your city. They are content to tinker with your failing health, rather than aggressively pursue a cure. How else can they explain that they have suspended treatment so that you and Jordi can go on a trip to Machu Picchu? There is no vacation from disease. It will advance relentlessly when left on its own. Meanwhile, there are tools that my friend the oncologist has told me about—hormones, genetic manipulation, radiation directly to the source.

For all this neglect I blame Jordi. I have tried to talk to you, my sister, but Jordi refuses to let you speak with me. He answers the phone and tells me you are tired and don't want to talk—not to me, your brother, or to father. That is not like you, always so loving to the family, and now refusing our calls.

Or he whispers dramatically, "Lavinia is asleep, and I cannot disturb her rest." Or he simply doesn't pick up, and lets our connection languish until the line goes dead. I will on the legal front challenge his authority and remove him from unilaterally directing your care, or lack of. If you die I will hold him directly responsible. I don't know what his motivation is, to collect on life insurance, your retirement savings, or who knows what financial manipulations he has found to profit from your death. But I will find out, I have friends who can audit his accounts and get at the hidden motivation for his ongoing criminal exploitation of my sister's life.

Jordi

Mi borrachita. During an easy walk by the river outside our apartment on the way to Wilde's for a sweet treat of milk and caffeine, you weaved and stumbled as the walker with its six-inch wheels escaped your hands during a brief incline, rolled away and crashed into a clump of bushes. You chased after it, teetering on weak legs, your hands grasping for a hold, arms flailing as you realized you were folding, and I was too far to hold you up.

Such fury. Legs splayed on the ground, you let loose a stream of fucks that drew the attention of passersby. A woman in tight jeans pulled a toddler out of your way and jogged down the sidewalk with the child on her arm. I got to you in seconds and put out my hands for you to pull yourself up, but it was only by embracing you around the waist and lifting you that you managed to stay upright, unsteady and precarious. As I held you, we stepped haltingly to the walker. I locked the wheels in place and you stood by, leaning on the handles.

Lavinia

Falling is for children. When a grown woman falls it's fucking ridiculous, and the people around me stare and wonder if I'm a drunk, which is better than having cancer. At least a drunk is partying, whereas my condition is no party at all. I tried to stand on my own, but my legs had gone to rubber. What is in my cancer makeup that makes my legs weak? Breast, lung, brain.

Jordi rushed to lift me. I was dead weight in his arms and I was a baby when he lifted me to my feet. I felt like a woman who is loved.

Jordi

I grew annoyed with your dumb prediction that you would die before me. You started with this when you were around 40, and there was no way you would know that cancer would hit you at 56. You said that I was healthier than you, because of your migraines. Nobody dies of migraines, though they might wish they had. But you seemed so certain that the possibility frightened me. I was ten years older than you. Women statistically outlive men, and, of course, you were supposed to take care of me, change my diapers, count my pills, give me hand jobs under the sheets. I don't think you had any dreams or visions about an early exit. It was something you would blurt out on occasion, out of nowhere with no deliberation or context, as casually as a comment that you're going to bed early while I sit up and watch gangsters on TV.

And now here we are.

Lavinia

Pay attention, Ysbel my friend. You will need to be strong for Jordi. On the next Nov 1 and 2 Dias de muertos celebration after my death, you will build the ofrenda with him. It doesn't matter where you are living, there will be enough money in my account for you to fly to Minneapolis. Jordi knows what to do; he has set up ofrendas with me every year since before we were married.

Here's a drawing I made in the doctor's office the day I was given the shitty news, no operation, no cure, no recourse. But, hurray, two and half years, with good quality of life, thanks to modern chemistry and electricity. So keep those drips and zaps going. Keeping me alive while killing me softly.

Ysbel

I treasure the doodles and notes on every scrap and page you have given me since we were girls. Your handwriting, a hybrid of cursive and print, always its own look, speaks to your quirky sensibility. Even now, fifty-some years later, the letters remain distinctively yours whether in a poem or a recipe, interesting enough that a typeface company bought the rights to offer it as a font.

The simple sketch of the ofrenda speaks volumes. The three levels of the altar which is more of a pyramid than something you might find in a church, rising from the earth to the heavens, from remembrance to tribute to sacrifice.

At the center is the photograph you have chosen, serene in profile, communing with a life-sized sugar skull enhanced with your name in a sweet filigree across the forehead. Your hair is cut short, but lush and abundant, no hint of the hair loss that would make room for the dome tattoos. Very much you, that picture, so that you will recognize your-self as you visit the living, accept the offering of chocolate, lavender, bread, mole, candy from our childhood, the paletones and tamarindos and caramels that filled your mouth with heaven.

But the journey is long and arduous. There are candles in votive glasses to light your way from the darkness. There is a dog, an es-cuintle, to guide your way. Water for the dry desert crossing and a book for company. Your beloved Don Quijote, a manual for the traveler on the road of madness. And the cempazuchitl flowers that maintain their color against all odds, a bright orange beacon.

Things you loved are the magnets that draw you home. The Grateful Dead on the system. An earring with a single perfect pearl. Whimsical figurines of skeletons cooking, writing, dancing. Match-books from hotels and cafes around the world. A skeletal mariachi with a huge sombrero and a mocking grin blowing away on a trumpet. The small universe of your life in life, living on for you after death.

Marcial

I never understood your morbid obsession. This whole thing about the ofrenda and the visits from the dead is a ritual of heresy and super-stition. How did you manage to reject Christian customs from early adolescence? This stuff comes from the Indians and their misunderstanding of the doctrines brought over by the priests during the colony. It's pure ancestor worship. And now you, educated at Harvard, manage to devote your life to this mumbo jumbo. I've seen the pictures year after year featuring images of your abuela Luci and your grandfather Poncho. Do you think it would make them happy to be seen in the company of grinning skeletons and clouds of incense and smelly flowers? I wager not.

So, now that you have decided that you are going to die, you are letting the world know that you want the family to gather at the first opportunity after you pass for a reunion on November first and second. Hosted by your husband Jordi and crazy friend Ysbel. Well, I don't think your brother Luis and I can in good conscience join. I hesitate telling you that now, because I realize you are in a fragile state, so I'm letting Jordi know that he can't expect us to participate. It's up to him to deal with you.

Lavinia

Back from the road trip up north. Exhausted. I was glad to cut it short as I experienced such a range of troubles that made me always alert to my helplessness. A fall in the bathroom brought on sudden panic. It bruised my rib cage, caused pain getting in and out of the car and sleeping on my side. The side effects from Xeloda and Tykerb seem relentless and cumulative: edema from feet to knees that makes walking painful. Fatigue causing extreme drowsiness and long periods of sleep both on the road and late in the morning. Then dizziness and unbalance, mostly at night. Jordi gets up to help me to the bathroom, but now, at home, with the aid of a walker I can manage on my own. I find the walker a shameful contraption, the evidence of a feeble body. I've decorated it with a dangling skeleton and some tinsel.

I'm like a dizzy drunk during the day. Diarrhea somewhat controlled with Lomotil. Nausea giving in to sudden bouts of vomiting. On the drive home Jordi had to stop the car so I could open the door and throw up on the side of the highway. Fucking migraines give me no relief as if the cancer were not enough.

Sudden confusion about meds took us to pharmacies along the way for refills and clarification. Sudden weight gain from the Decadron puffs up my face and neck with pockets of fat. My belly is large and ungainly, so that eating is both compulsive and guilt-provoking. I feel like I'm feeding a beached whale. Is this what the future holds? Ill effects from meds until they stop working or I say fuck them and quit cold turkey? The latter seems unlikely, as I am quite attached to life on almost any terms. This all makes me so sad.

Jordi

I've started managing refills because you run out without anticipating it. This morning you cut your finger while slicing an apple. Another moment of panic from me. You control these cuts with Band-Aids, though this one seemed worse than most, yet not bad enough to go to the ER.

I try to be helpful and supportive. I will learn to manage the meds. I will help you move your body. Drive and run errands. Talk to you, help you sort out your feelings, let you know I love you.

Now is the time to seek absolution. Not from a priest or God or society, but from you, my beloved of over thirty years.

I have much to atone for.

During our first years, I didn't love you as deeply as you thought I did. Not as strongly as you loved me. Yet, day by day, I knew I was good for you. And if at times I felt your closeness to be suffocating, I tried not to show it. I found some relief in infatuations that were fortunately unresolved. I was never good at infidelity, a logistical nightmare with all that work, lying, expense. Except when I hired professionals for my rituals of perversion. No guilt there.

You only had a vague inkling into the darkness of my heart. I would return from a business trip feeling purified by the excesses of my unbridled psyche. New York and Los Angeles were prized destinations for cheap thrills.

Remorse was more about padding my expense account to cover the $200 dollar session at The Chateau with Mistress Lotus, a popular moniker in the genre. I always wondered why some clerk in accounting didn't raise questions about my clumsy fudging of restaurant checks, adding a digit here and there, sometimes not even matching the color of the ink.

I counted on the boredom involved in sifting through hundreds of receipts and credit card slips, knowing that the effort of busting some vice president's travel shenanigans would be shrugged away. Unless, of course, some sap was marked for removal due to incompetence or bad chemistry. That would have been my case. I was not a brilliant ad guy and my chemistry with clients and superiors was chancy. The results of getting caught would have been devastating. I would have been shamed before you, Lavinia, the truest, most ethical person I know. Fired for stealing would be the least of it. Judicial charges would ruin me. Yet, I did not worry. Everybody at the agency cheated on their per diem. I was doing it for mental health.

Lavinia

You never believed me when I said in all seriousness that I would die before you, even when you had ten years on me. I was assaulted by headaches so severe they made me want to die. Not in order to leave you, or this beautiful world, but to escape the pain. Surely there had to be something wrong with my brain to cause me such misery. I pictured microscopic larval cysts nestling into the folds, confusing the neurons so that the messages transmitted from one cell to another become unreliable. This short-circuiting results in pain. Also, confusion, amnesia, seizures, vertigo. And underlying the physical distress are mental quirks that I own as my fingerprints.

My dearest, you're inheriting the life's work of the ultimate letter writer. I have carbons from back in the days when I wrote lengthy missives on my little Lettera 22, typing as fast as I could think, single-spaced with minimal margins on onion skin paper to reduce postage. I corresponded with my parents, childhood friends, lovers, teachers, mentors, students, and total strangers who seemed interesting because of the books they'd written or the music they played. Then I stapled the replies to the carbon of my letter. I have boxes of this correspondence that I cannot toss. What you do with them after I'm dead is up to you. My apologies in advance.

Jordi

Lavinia, the ultimate collector verging on hoarder, sits at a table with some dozen glass jars of different sizes spread out before her. She has spent the past hour matching lids to jars. Eventually, containers without a lid will be discarded, and the remaining ones are placed in a dedicated cabinet. I'm touched by the effort to minimize the chaos that is sure to follow her death.

It's gotten so that when we're traveling we're okay, emotionally, distracted, I imagine, from the coming horrors. The drugs are working, but there has also been a slow creeping of the cancer in the lungs and the brain. Not enough to cause symptoms, but hard to ignore.

I have to be careful with my language as the slightest sign of irritation from me becomes a personal injury. This weekend I got frustrated because she got some driving directions wrong, which took us on a long goose chase. Once we discovered the problem, I called her a "dingbat." This affected her so violently I spent all weekend working to assuage her feelings.

She has grown sensitive, since the brain metastasis and the radiation, to lapses of memory or attention, which I don't usually see as much different from the signs of my own shriveling brain cells, but which worry her. Added to this are the mood swings from one of her meds.

And yet, I know that things are going to get worse. I wonder if I'm going to rise to the task. I love her so much and I want to be as good for her as she thinks I am. She is very appreciative of my attention and care. So that sometimes I fear I'm not up to expectations. And this brings about a measure of guilt and frustration. I have nobody I can talk about this with. Our friends and their partners are all part of her support system and it would be impossible for me to confide.

Ysbel

In the mail today, a box of your schoolwork from grades three to six. Drawings, poems, assignments with a big A+ in red. There must be over a hundred pieces, all bearing your name in distinctive printing, all lower case, on the top left corner. And how I love to see your face shining and to hear your voice singing and to feel your touch. From the start you were obsessed with rainbows. Every drawing of a horse or a dog or your family complete with mom, dad, little brother, had a rainbow arcing at the top of the page. Never the pot of gold though, as the harbinger of happiness and good fortune was enough. I wish I had saved my own schoolwork from those years. It would've been a nice companion to your memories, my beautiful friend.

I spent all day Sunday sifting through the magical contents inside the shoebox. I even found a note from me. I had a neat, round cursive hand in those days, which I know you admired. I wrote it in lavender ink because it was my favorite color and your favorite scent. Not much has changed, has it? Anyway, I remember it clearly even today. There had been a moment during Mr. Roberts' sixth grade history class when he described how boys in ancient Greece would form friendships that were very intense and close, but not physical. This was called Platonic love in honor of the philosopher Plato who said that such affection honors and uplifts. He never mentioned if it applied to girls too. I think not. Girls were meant to always treat each other like sisters or daughters or mothers. Or maybe, the special love between girls would be physical, with touching and smooching and deep kissing. There was an island in the Aegean, I now know though not at eleven, called Lesbos. Ha, so there!

"Dear Vin, Can I be your special friend forever and ever? With oodles of platonic love, your best friend, Ysbel, aka Dizzy Yzzie."

I don't recall if you wrote back, but on the back of the paper you scribbled a note, which you may have intended to slip back to me across the aisle out of sight of the watchful Mr. Roberts. "Platonic love is for smelly Greek boys. I kiss you everywhere!!!!! In Sin, Vin."

Lavinia

I remember that time in Acapulco when our parents took us to the same resort for a whole week of running and screaming like maniacs, skirting the lapping waves at our feet and then rushing into the gentle surf of Caleta beach. At night we had the Hotel La Selva to explore, sneaking into secret passages, pantries and storerooms, the ballroom with a bandstand and dance floor, and the leather and oak men's club with billiard tables and games, and big chairs, always stinking of cigars and farts. We had it to ourselves until guests would call the front desk and ask for someone to come and usher us out.

It was during that trip that we spotted Mr. Roberts. Oh, how different he looked out of the classroom and on vacation. Gone was the same tweedy sport coat that he wore with either tan or gray trousers. We were so used to that daily uniform that we hardly recognized him in a flappy green shirt with parrots and pineapples, Bermuda shorts with a washed-out madras plaid showing off his chubby pink legs, and a straw panama hat with a polka dotted band. He was standing in line by himself to check in. Among all the kids and parents, it was odd that he was without a companion.

La Selva had a big lobby with palms, plastic flamingos, huge ceramic pots with flowers and throne-like chairs made of rattan. After two days at the resort we knew our way around. We saw Mr. Roberts get in the elevator and then watched the lighted numbers stop at the ninth floor. We took the next elevator up and when we got out at nine, the hallway was deserted. At first I thought it would be fun to ring doorbells until we hit his room and surprised him. Then, we thought that it would be way more fun to follow him. And see what he was up to. The plan made my heart beat like crazy, so we went back down before he emerged from his room.

We figured he would hit the pool soon after arriving, and by early afternoon he had staked out a lounge chair. He still wore the parrot and pineapple shirt but had changed into a Speedo that nearly disappeared under his belly. A straw panama with a rainbow hatband shaded him. He bantered with the poolside waiter out of our hearing, sharing soft chuckles and winks. He ordered a beer and chips with salsa.

After draping his towel on the chair, he strolled around the pool, as if surveying the crowd in search of a familiar face. I thought he looked silly in his colorful getup, but he conducted himself with confidence. It was much as his style in the classroom where, draping himself with a kind of regal dignity, he held us in thrall to his easy authority. We were close enough to speak to him, but unrecognizable in our little one-piece suits, big sunglasses, sunblock on our noses, floppy hats. It was a fun challenge to see how close we could get without him noticing us.

Finally he tossed off his shirt and sandals and lowered himself into the water. He swam like a whale, with slow breaststrokes and leisurely frog kicks. It was a huge pool with the shallow end reserved for kids. There was so much splashing and fooling that adults doing serious swimming stopped well short of the dividing rope that marked the children's territory. We watched Mr. Roberts do a few laps, each time coming closer to the kids' section, until he found himself, in the midst of a foursome of boys playing some improvised water polo game that involved more splashing and horsing around than anything to do with a ball. They were lean sun-browned boys around my age, not yet in middle school. Yzzie was quick to point out that one of the boys was my little brother Luis, who was studiously ignoring us. For our part, boys were not a species that we wanted to be associated with.

Mr. Roberts joined their fun. They might have been shocked to see that the grown man scrambling for the ball was actually a teacher, known for his strict classroom style and easy way with the paddle on rowdy boys. A ball, perhaps errant or maybe aimed at him, smacked him on the side of the head. He grabbed the ball and held it high above his head in triumph, while the boys crowded around him jumping to snatch it from his hand.

He finally let one boy reach it, and then went on to join them in the improvised round robin. He played with them for twenty minutes while Yzzie and I watched, holding on to the side of the pool as we practiced our flutter kicks. When he finally gave up, pleading exhaustion, it was clear he had made friends with the boys who called out after him, "Goodbye, Mr. Bob. See ya later, Mr. Bob."

I didn't realize at that young age that what had appeared to be spontaneous fun, an adult fooling with some kids, was a maneuver to insert himself into the confidence of the boys.

The next morning we spotted Mr. Roberts sitting by himself at a table under a beach umbrella with a tray of paletas, the icy popsicles made of fruit pulp from lime to guava. He had changed out of the speedo and back into his madras shorts, but instead of the pineapple shirt, he had on a tank top that showed off his beefy arms and hairy back. Yzzie and I rolled our eyes. He looked disgusting. He started juggling three paletas, just a simple roll which he made look easy and which drew the attention of the people nearby, along with scattered applause and groans when one of the paletas would hit the ground. It only took about three minutes before he was surrounded by some of the boys he'd met in the pool.

"Who wants a popsicle?" He taunted them. "Grab one if you can."

And that became the game, each boy in turn snatching a paleta in the air, which would not faze Mr. Roberts, who would take another one from the tray and keep on juggling.

Yzzie thought we should get our share of treats, but I held her back. Our fun was to spy on Mr. Roberts, not give in and reveal our identities. Our success in prying into the secret Mr. Roberts depended on our invisibility. We would lurk about as silent as fairy ghosts. Even when Luis joined the fun with the flying paletas we managed to spy unseen.

Ysbel

Acapulco was a blast. It was all the fun we could manage to fit into every day. We were as light as fish in the water, as fast as rabbits racing along the beach. Then curling up at night in front of a firepit until we were drowsy, and our mothers bundled us up in bed.

But things changed after we spotted our teacher Mr. Roberts and we decided we would spy on him. It was a game that you devised on the fly without much planning, and I went along. There would be no harm in snooping. We didn't think he had anything to hide. There was just the fun in watching our teacher being himself out of the classroom.

By afternoon he was the pied piper. A group of boys followed him and took his lead at whatever games he cooked up in the pool or the beach. Luis was among them, so we had to be careful in our spying because he was apt to recognize us, even if Mr. Roberts was oblivious to our stalking.

At night, sitting on the beach, watching the stars, no one was surprised when Mr. Roberts brought out a set of bongos and drummed away, improvising intricate rhythms that had the boys dancing around manically until they would collapse in fits of laughter. That led to wrestling on the beach as he challenged all comers to pin him down. Even as they piled on him, he managed to twist his way out of their clutches, choosing instead one of the boys to toss on the sand. Luis was a wiry little guy at the time, stronger than his skinny frame might indicate. Somehow it became clear that he was becoming a favorite of Mr. Bob's.

Before the week was over, Mr. Roberts had established a pattern. He didn't make friends with adults, but the parents liked him and appreciated him entertaining their kids, channeling their energy with pool games and races and impromptu juggling. He was generous with treats, sometimes paletas, or platters of sliced jicama with lime and salt and chile powder and pitchers of lemonade. He would play with a group of boys for a while, then send them away.

Luis would scatter with the group, but then after a few minutes, as if already arranged, he would sidle back to Mr. Roberts.

Lavinia

Yzzie didn't miss a detail at that age, so observant, so intelligent. My parents were not aware that Mr. Roberts was spending so much time with Luis, but Yzzie made sure I noticed. The main thing was the fun we were having, sleuthing like Nancy Drew and her sidekick Bess, sneaking around, observing without being seen. We liked that the characters in the books were older than us, so emulating them made it seem that chasing after the solution of a mystery was a worthwhile pastime. We grew bolder, so it was inevitable that we would push the invasion of Mr. Roberts' privacy to revelations beyond the limits of our understanding.

As we roamed the hallways of the La Selva it was easy during the day to peer into people's rooms while the housekeepers were making beds, vacuuming, cleaning the bathrooms that we left in a state of chaos, with towels and wet swimsuits flung about. We usually wandered in as if entering someone else's room by mistake. Such interesting worlds we discovered, suitcases with clothes spilling out, bathrooms with collections of strange shampoos and conditioners and soaps, all of which we would examine and smell, but never steal. The stacks of books and magazines, the paperbacks with lurid covers, and the newspapers from distant cities, their headlines in foreign languages added to the mystery.

We ended up, not by accident, in Mr. Roberts' room. The housekeeper was finishing up with the vacuuming and so didn't hear us as we snuck into the bathroom, muffling our laughs into bursts of barely contained mirth behind the closed door. We heard the housekeeper leave, and found ourselves alone in the room, so neat and orderly after the place had been cleaned that we knew to be careful not to disrupt anything that might reveal intruders. It was close to noon, so we assumed that Mr. Roberts would be at the pool playing with the boys. Three days into our weeklong spring break, routines had been set.

There was nothing particularly revealing about Mr. Roberts' closet, suitcase, nightstand. We opened drawers, careful not to disrupt the contents, and closed them right away. And then, tucked under a pile of socks, shorts, shirts, a thick brown envelope. Yzzie placed it neatly on the bed. She opened it by carefully lifting the metal clasp and withdrew a sheaf of Polaroids. They were pictures of boys against a plain wall, bare chested or in swimsuits, unsmiling and staring straight at the camera. There was something distant about them, the kids not reacting in any way to the photographer, no grins, no poses, as if the shots had been taken for a school ID, or a wanted poster.

Ysbel

I figured then and there that Mr. Bob was a pervert, although I'm not sure I would've used that word. Weirdo was my favored term, and weirdos were part of the human landscape, even if we didn't know what made them such. As I recall now, the photos were not obviously sexual. But even at that age I could see there was something creepy about his hobby, a secret stash of boys not yet in their teens collected like baseball cards. These were not vacation snapshots that he could've taken by the pool.

What innocents we were. There was no widespread knowledge of pedophiles in those days. They led shadowy lives behind the doors of churches and schools. In our wildest imaginings I don't think we could've pictured any shenanigans, although girls were warned about strangers touching us. But even that was beyond our experience. Girls were more innocent in those days, before the full oddness of the world could be perused in clicks and streams. I knew weird when I saw weird.

I wonder if Vin's heart was racing like mine as we spread the pics on the bedspread. She shuffled through them and rescued four of Luis from the pile. He was standing in his blue trunks with a goldfish pattern, bare chested, almost defiant with fists on his hips. Each shot practically the same, with only the slight variations that could occur with a breath or a tilt of the head in response to the photographer's instruction. He was such a serious boy, his gaze fixed lazily on some point beyond the camera, reluctantly humoring the person behind the lens but unwilling to engage him with even a hint of a smile.

Vin grabbed the four and stuffed the rest back into the envelope, which we placed carefully in the drawer where we found it. We were out of the door and bounding down the hallway and up the stairs, slipping quickly into the safety of her room.

Lavinia

I tucked the Polaroids of Luis inside the pages of my copy of *The Grapes of Wrath* (on my third reading already!). I wondered how long it would take for Mr. Roberts to realize they were gone. He acted completely normal until the next day when I saw him pull Luis out of the pool with a scowl. He wrapped his hand around the back of his neck and marched him to a corner of the terrace where he towered over him all the time speaking harshly. We couldn't hear the words, but Luis kept on shaking his head in denial.

I guessed that Mr. Roberts had discovered that pics were missing and assumed my brother had taken them. Luis broke down sobbing until the teacher pulled his hand from his neck and spoke to him earnestly, as if trying to persuade him of something. He kept on talking, pleading it seemed, until Luis nodded his head, turned away, and jogged back to the pool. He joined the other boys in their rough-housing without apparently being missed.

After that, Mr. Roberts kept to himself. He settled down with a book, taking the sun, first prone then supine, carefully dosing out the rays to get an overall tan. Occasionally, he would put the book down and look around, surveying the people by the pool. He ate snacks at the bar, talking to no one in particular, and already distant from the groups of boys he had courted. By evening he seemed to relax after a few drinks, and would join some of the other men at the bar in easy conversation. Occasionally he borrowed limes and oranges from the bartender and juggled for the guys' amusement.

Yzzie wanted me to question Luis about the pictures. She was intrigued and full of curiosity, feeling that whatever strange doings had been going on, it was our duty to find out. I demanded she back off. Instead, we would watch and wait and try to understand. We didn't have the words for the thoughts that teased our brains.

Ysbel

I knew what I knew, even if Vin did not want to know of the dirty things grown men did with kids. In those days, we were not brought up to distrust adults on sight. Stranger danger was not part of our lexicon. In Mexico adults were to be respected and obeyed. We were taught to speak only when spoken to.

Mr. Roberts knew what people would think of the pictures. It showed in his nervous eyes as he looked around, clearly perusing the faces of people around the pool or in the dining room. He was a man with a secret. I didn't know at the time how much that would weigh on him over time. Now, with many years' perspective I can identify. I have kept my own share of secrets and wondered who knows what I hide. Often, inevitably, where there is a secret there is shame, which eats and eats at you until your heart withers.

Mr. Roberts must've been haunted by the four missing Polaroids, especially after he was persuaded that Luis had not taken them. It was the last official day of the Easter break, when the whole of Mexico City would start packing up from the beaches to return to classes and jobs, when he recognized Vin and me. She had no idea that I had manipulated the encounter. After the disappearance of the Polaroids Mr. Roberts had kept his distance from Luis, and also from the other boys. That's not to say that he didn't continue to stalk Vin's little brother, our pet boy. He was this huge pink shape drifting in and out of view trailing him from the pool to the volleyball court to the beach to the children's table in the restaurant.

I deliberately chose a moment when Luis was the object of Mr. Roberts' attention, showing off by jumping in and out of the pool and doing cannonballs. Luis was standing on the edge waiting to jump, when I came up beside him and pushed him in. Then I glanced back in time to see Mr. Roberts turn away to hide a look of recognition.

Lavinia

I remember that year. I was eleven and finishing my last year of elementary school and I knew something about our teacher Mr. Roberts. I could not describe what I knew, only that he had pictures of boys and that was definitely suspicious behavior. I also knew that Mr. Roberts knew that we knew.

Yzzie and I continued to sit together, but instead of staying on the front row like before, we moved to the back of the room. We noticed that he avoided meeting our gaze, especially Yzzie's, who took to staring at him with the barest hint of a smirk. He no longer called on us or scolded us for whispering across the aisle. He collected tests with a blank expression and then returned them by piling them on the edge of his desk for each of us to take. The first time I got a test back from him, I thought for sure he had made a mistake. Math was not my best subject. I was used to As in history and English and biology. Then I got a test paper back and I had scored an A in math, solving five word problems of the kind where two cars are having a race at different speeds and leaving at different times and we had to figure out who would get to the finish line first and by how much time to spare.

I got twenty points in each problem for a total of 100! The same score as Yzzie who was better at math than I was, but no genius. It went like that for the next two months until the end of the school year. Straight As for the nosy girls in the back row.

We had a secret, and Mr. Roberts was making sure we kept our mouths shut. Really? I knew we were eventually going to tell, the only question was to whom. It all started with vague bragging about the adventure we had in Acapulco over Easter break. And the mystery about a certain teacher we would never, ever reveal.

The pressure was seductive. Here we were, Ysbel and I, the keepers of embarrassing knowledge, never mind, we were not about to name names. But the more we teased out crumbs of information—we have pictures, they involve a third-grade boy—the more attention we got. Our fame grew across the lunchroom and I gloried in being popular in school for the first time in my life. We had to keep the suspense going, so that every day we had to resist accusations that we were just making a lot of crap up.

One day, after fanning the flames of our adventure for a week, I took the pictures to school. I intended to show them to only a couple of special girls, ring leaders in the public approval circus of middle school. They followed Ysbel and me to a distant corner of the lunchroom. I took out *The Grapes of Wrath* and opened it to where the Polaroids were nestled. Methodically, like a card dealer, I placed them one by one on the table before the two girls.

As word spread about a teacher taking these pictures, a queasy feeling took over me when I realized I could not pull the Polaroids back and pretend they did not exist. Word spread, and before long our remote table had become the eye of a storm. What had been until then a quiet rumor about Mr. Roberts, conducted in stealth, exploded in a small frenzy which drew the attention of Mrs. Nesbitt, the strict lunchroom supervisor. She swept the pictures up in her chubby fingers, and before the final bell, Ysbel and I were standing outside the principal's office.

In the summer there was talk that Mr. Roberts had swallowed a bottle of sleeping pills. Yzzie and I did not talk about what we had known and whispered, but I was certain that in some clear way we had caused his death. The images of Mr. Roberts' face, eyes shut, mouth sadly drooping, pink skin faded to gray, haunted me in wordless dreams and imagined glimpses in crowds. For years I was gripped with regret, a bitter sadness poisoned with guilt. Yzzie's point when I brought it up years later was that if he hadn't been abusing boys, he wouldn't have taken a hundred pills. We didn't know exactly what he did. Only he and the kids knew. Luis, claiming ignorance of Mr. Roberts' death, refused to say anything.

Mr. Roberts

Oh, I did not commit suicide. Heavens, I'm not even now ready to die. What you and your friend Ysbel did with your snickers and whispers was to scandalize me out of a job, a career, a life. Luis was one of several boys that I photographed. That's all I did. But when Ysbel started whispering with the other students, eventually the kids' vague notions of perversity got to the parents. They in turn got the school administration involved. An investigation was started.

The girls had to explain how they took the Polaroids from my hotel room. And based on that, I had to agree to a thorough investigation. Apparently, a detective was hired, first to follow me and make a record of anything incriminating I did, and later to search my desk at work, my car and finally my apartment.

They found things—photos and magazines and drawings. But my point is that there was nothing immoral in any of it. The demons that possessed me were held captive inside my mind. I loved children. That's why I taught school. I would never do anything that could harm them.

I was told I was lucky. That the school would not report me to the police because there would be so much bad publicity; the students and the other faculty would be permanently harmed. In return, I would go. After I quit, no other school in Mexico would hire me. My references were a blank. It was as if I had never existed, worked, lived among decent people for twelve years. I moved back to the US and eventually changed my name and carved out another life as an SAT tutor for slackers. It was still teaching, of course, and I had my favorites among the students. But I will never forget the two girls who so drastically

changed the course of my life. My God, you were such evil little innocents. No idea what you were letting loose with your blabby mouths.
Do you even now feel remorse?

Ysbel

Oh, Vin, remember how we waited for news of Mr. Roberts' death?
Everyone assumed he had done himself in, for reasons that we even-
tually sorted out from whispers and speculation from the older kids.
But he didn't die, did he? And now it turns out he's been living in
Minneapolis.

I knew it was our old teacher, the moment I spotted him in line
for his latte at Wilde Café. A cloud of something ripe and fruity followed the man as he took his coffee to a nearby table. I may have actually recognized the scent from his days at the head of the class,
strangely familiar fragrance of aftershave and chalk. I actually smelled
him before I saw him. But then there was no mistaking him, now close
to seventy, overweight in a square and frumpy way in his loose slacks
and wrinkled linen jacket.

It's a wonder that you never crossed paths. I'm sure you can't miss
him with that freckled face and big head of orange hair. So much like
a clown. A sad clown: we never thought he was funny.

Lavinia

Mr. Roberts, you have not died, you have not left my mind, the stain
in my heart remains undisturbed. I should feel some relief that you
are alive and walking my own neighborhood streets, less than a mile
from here, hanging out at Wilde Café for happy hour, Lourdes for mass,
Surdyk's for cheese and wine. We might have brushed shoulders on
the bus, our eyes met as we crossed the street. All that proximity and
never having spotted each other. Hard to believe. Perhaps you recognized me and chose not to acknowledge me. Did you feel that I had
perhaps continued to terrorize you? The girl that once ruined you has
now come back as a dying woman, determined to take you down. I
wish we had met before now. You would have understood that I was

eleven years old and had no idea what those pictures of Luis said about you. Or of him. He was a beautiful kid, I knew that much. That was why you wanted his picture. Of course, I knew the Polaroids were a secret, which is why they were concealed in your room.

And now as I limp in and out of a medical fog, I need to see you. Yzzie thinks you are living under another name, that "Mr. Roberts" is forever damned to a solitary exile, dead even if the body and mind that once owned that personality continues to exist. I will ask Jordi to locate you and bring you here.

Jordi

It didn't take long to find him. Even a twenty-year-old picture of Mr. Roberts showed up on an image search. It identified him as Jeffrey Garrison on the Testing Doctors website. "The coaches that get results. SAT scores in the 500s guaranteed. Or half your money back." Mr. Garrison was one of the star tutors available to help high school slackers on a variety of subjects, from math to composition. More browsing revealed a phone number and an address in an old apartment building off University in the NE neighborhood. Three days of roaming east Hennepin, from the grocery store to the liquor store to the sandwich store paid off. He is seventy-five, oddly boyish with a head full of hair still rusty with some gray, an easy gait, a toothy smile for clerks and cashiers and neighbors. Once I recognized him, I managed to stalk him, not quite sure when and how to approach him. He has learned to appear guileless. He has escaped a miserable fate by dodging the legal system and hiding his original identity. A more careless lifestyle might have landed him in eternal therapy, sex offender's status, a leper relegated to a double-wide in a trailer park, constantly on the move away from schools, parks, churches, playgrounds.

That's not to say that he doesn't need to tread gently. Especially once he learns that you are here, have been living a couple of miles away and I tell him that you would like to see him. I still think it's a dumb idea, but if you need to set things aright, I'm not going to argue. I accept that time is running out and you are revisiting the past with a need to cleanse.

I thought I was a pretty good gumshoe as I followed him around, but it didn't take him long to confront me. He liked to spend his evenings at the public library and I found it easy to sit near him on an adjacent worktable. He read Mexican newspapers, Excelsior, El Heraldo, Novedades, as if he were homesick for his adopted country after so many years away. Clearly, Mexico City had been home, and the International School had been his family until he was violently uprooted. I hid my face behind random books. The evening in question, a large-type version of *Middlemarch* was a fortress.

One problem is that the book was so tall that to observe my quarry I had to stretch my neck and lift my head over a veritable parapet. It was during a covert glance that I found myself facing Mr. Roberts' steady gaze, though more of an inquisitive stare if the truth be told. I ducked immediately. And waited a minute or two before looking again. He was still staring in my direction, as if expecting me to look again.

Mr. Roberts

Even thirty years after being shamed out of my job as a teacher at the International School, the past has come back to haunt me. A man has been following me at unpredictable times, and I've come to recognize his face as he hovers close by, fixes me with a neutral gaze, then glances away when he realizes I've noticed him. This time in the library he is ducking behind a book, which he is not reading.

I would like to march up to him and ask him who he is and why is he stalking me. Because that's what this is, stalking, and there are laws against tormenting a person with this passive aggressive stance. There is an implicit threat in his behavior, but I can't muster anything concrete. And I cannot complain to the law. There is too much about me that would make for a conversation with unpleasant fallout. In the past thirty years I have lived in four different cities under three names, originally Mr. Roberts back in Mexico. Since then, I have become Michael O'Herlihy in Boston, and now Jeffrey Garrison here in Minneapolis, fortunate to make a living by tutoring for SATs. An occupation some consider questionable, if my ability to provide answers to anticipated questions based on my experience is cheating.

Let the man watch me. I have nothing to be ashamed of and I will not change my behavior. Even after dark with the curtains of my apartment drawn and the laptop screen glowing with images there is nothing that would get me in trouble. Some embarrassment, yes. That's an unavoidable consequence of being solitary, bored, restless.

On the day that my stalker finally spoke to me, I left the tutoring center a few minutes after 9:00, what 5:00 means for normal people. Most of my work is in the evenings and weekends as that's when the students are available for tutoring after school.

It was a cool September night, toward the start of fall with October's chill looming. I walked to Whole Foods to find a dinner that I would microwave, world cuisine in under 5 minutes. This time kofta balls with basmati rice by Tandoor Chef. I also got a pint of Talenti gelato, Mediterranean Mint. Finally, a bottle of Pinot Grigio. I anticipated a relaxing evening with my music, my TV shows, and finally by two am, if I couldn't sleep, my photos.

There are nearly a thousand of them in my computer under the password-protected file "Fresas." Cute, no? It's the Spanish word for strawberry, which in Mexico also means innocent—chica fresa, niño fresa—meaning sexually inexperienced. These are the faces of boys between the ages of nine and thirteen, just their faces and sometimes their torso, but never so much as a penis or a buttock or even a navel. I don't collect child porn. I think it's an evil hobby that needs to be prosecuted and punished. I collect expressions, personalities, attitudes. I used to take my own pictures of boys I knew from school or the boy scouts or little league. I was involved in all these fine organizations during my years in Mexico City.

Now, my contact with boys is limited to my tutoring and occasional college counseling for the older ones. Some of them are real fresas of course, and I sometimes catch myself gazing at them a little too insistently, and looking away when I realize my interest beyond the assignment at hand has been noticed. These moments cause me some anxiety. The thought that one of them might comment to a parent or a teacher or even a classmate that Mr. Garrison is weird. Weird how? He stares. Just that? No touching? One look could unleash a whole bag of worms. But, hey, I'm innocent, not a pedophile, not a molester, not a child porn addict. The law can't touch me, although in the court of community opinion I'm guilty. Fit to be shunned, shamed without a trial.

When I noticed the man I later met as Jordi, I was not unduly worried. If anything, his behavior was just as questionable as my interest in boys. Why stalk a solitary geezer? I actually wondered if he had a homoerotic interest in old men, their wrinkled puds peeking out of a forest of white pubes. Unlikely, but there is a thrill for everyone. In my case, the faces of boys engage me, captivate me. But not all. I avoid the impudent, the snarly, the bully. I gravitate to young poets in the making. Pensive faces, a little old for their age, somewhat confused about their role in life, lost in dreams too compelling to surface for the school tasks at hand. These are the boys with few friends, reclusive little monks, apprentice hermits. They are me at one time.

I do have my favorites. And I go back to them time and time again. Fortunately, in their digital realm, they don't show smudges from continual fingering. My eyeballs can rub their features at length with no wear. Most of the boys have no names attached to their pics, especially those that come from stock photo services. Some that I pull from Facebook, from birthday parties and family outings, have names and parents and siblings. I like them the best because they are more alive than images in settings suitable for advertising, generally mugging for the camera, eating soup, cereal, ice cream, going *yum yum*.

Tonight, sleepless and restless, I settle on little Carlos. Carlitos. About twelve, skinny, black hair, olive skin, serious of expression, large dark eyes, glistening as if about to weep, lips pressed to keep from trembling, perhaps in shame or remorse. I can tell the image dates from the fifties because of the school uniform, a pressed white shirt with a dark tie and probably, though not visible, shorts. Clearly a nice boy who's being blamed for doing a bad thing. I can't figure out the context of the photo, he is sitting in a chair and next to him I can see the waist and upper legs of a standing woman, her hand resting on the boy's shoulder as if to comfort, or perhaps restrain him.

Then, unable to will myself away from temptation, I surrender to my secret moment. The effect is immediate, tension flows from my arms and legs, a warmth invades my belly, I melt. My head falls to my chest and I am suddenly sleepy.

The next morning, I go for coffee and while I wait in line, the man who has been following me stands behind me, his breath on my neck and the rustle of his clothes audible. I get my coffee and sit at a corner table. He sneaks around with his phone and I can hear the click of the camera function as loud as a gunshot. There. He has my picture, although I try to act as if I'm not aware of it. The hunt is over, and he is about to speak to me.

Jordi

The cafe is crowded and I move easily to the vacant chair at the table where Mr. Roberts has settled, a steaming mug and a scone before him, clearly a pleasant routine for him. I indicate the chair with a nod and he nods in response.

In truth, I don't know what to say to him, and at that point I'm content to establish a visual connection between us, an acknowledgement that the pursuit of the previous days has reached a point of no return. I distract myself by fiddling with my phone, scrolling down a row of messages as if looking for something in particular. When I click off a photo, the snap of the electronic shutter is hardly audible, muffled by the chatter from surrounding tables and the hissing from the espresso machine. I put the phone back inside my shirt pocket and I'm relieved when his attention stays fixed on the plate in front of him, as he pinches off bites from the scone.

I finally get a good look at him. He is another older man grown soft, slouching in a rumpled suit jacket, white shirt, and a tie with a knot greasy from being habitually slipped up and down without being redone. He keeps his gaze lowered to the mug before him as if studying the loss of steam that will reveal that his latte has cooled enough to drink.

He takes a pinch from a corner of the scone and washes it down with a sip of coffee. It is then that I see in his pale blue eyes a dullness, which might be cataracts, or perhaps a deep sadness that has clouded his vision. I take out my phone and study it as if scrolling for some elusive message. He on the other hand does not distract himself with anything, not a phone, a newspaper, or a book. He is waiting me out.

Yet, I think it's up to him to speak first, to confront me, even if not aggressively. To ask what I want, and why I follow him. But after a few minutes I realize that is not going to happen. So I toss down my espresso, nod in thanks for sharing the table, and leave. It's enough that we have acknowledged each other. I will continue to be a presence in his life, a face in the crowd when he least expects me, a voice nearby, an inquisitive glance. We will speak eventually. He will hear Lavinia's name for the first time in forty some years.

Lavinia

Jordi has found Mr. Roberts and shows me the picture he took in the café after days of following him around. He doesn't look unhappy, an old and solitary man, finding comfort in the routines of work and the small pleasures of morning coffee, shopping at Surdyk's for wine and cheese, long walks to accomplish small errands. I imagine he went through some dark period after Yzzie and I damn near ruined his life, but somewhere along that time he resolved to survive. I had imagined him a lost soul for all these years, possibly in prison and further shamed for his secret, perhaps numbed with alcohol and loveless sex. The thought of his demise was a worm of remorse that has eaten at me every time I thought of Mr. Roberts and remembered those pictures of Luis, the beautiful little brother that I had also embarrassed. So, I breathed a sigh that he was alive. And yet, there were reparations in order. I needed for the eleven-year-old me to be understood and therefore forgiven.

I don't recall why I'd been uneasy about Mr. Roberts' pictures of Luis. All I knew at the time that they felt like a secret, a violation of my little brother that neither of us had a name for, but which made us squirm. I never brought up Mr. Roberts with Luis even as I remained curious about their odd friendship. When news of his forced departure spread in the school, I asked Luis what he thought about all the buzz, but he just shrugged as if the likelihood of this friendly teacher being in trouble were of no consequence. I don't think he has ever acknowledged my role in the destruction of the man's life. Exiled from the school and the students he loved, from his role in the society where his place was stable and respected; disgraced by his friends and colleagues; all had the potential to kill him. And I do believe he might have died, either of drink or pills or by the hand of those forces that felt entitled to persecute and torment his ilk. I heard he had left, disappeared without a forwarding address, or a word of goodbye or a small gesture by the school to acknowledge his contribution.

I don't know if Luis has thought about Mr. Roberts all these years. Whenever Yzzie and I reminisce, our conversation sometimes drifts to Mr. Roberts. We don't stay on the subject longer than the moment it takes to wonder what happened to him and to recall some incident we can smile about, but never a word about the reason his remembered face brings a twist of anxiety.

One fear that continues to haunt me is that he might have somehow damaged Luis. My little brother grew into a bully, a teenage creep to me and Yzzie, and later a martinet to his wife and two children.

Luis has come to Minneapolis on a rare visit and keeps me company for a short time during the four hours I have to sit and take my medicine. A chair is placed near my throne so that I can enjoy conversations with visitors without straining.

I mentioned that Mr. Roberts has been living just a few blocks away from my condo, but he expressed no interest. He closed his eyes as if in deep thought and waited a couple of minutes before speaking. When I asked him if he remembers the popular teacher who had befriended him during that spring vacation in Acapulco, he shrugged off my question as if to imply that his recollection is vague and, in any case, of no consequence. If I bring up the matter of the pictures he flinches in anger.

I settled back in the big green chair that tilts back sometimes suddenly without warning, so I can be hooked up to the dripping Taxol and Herceptin. The end of the IV is hooked up into the port in my chest, which has been surgically attached so that I can be connected to the chemicals without further punishing my veins, swollen and sensitive after a couple of years of infusions.

Luis wants to address another issue. His tone is measured but tense. He reminds me that I am very sick and under a cloud of poisonous infusions and nuclear zaps and dripping opioids. How could I be thinking clearly? He accuses Jordi of enabling my delusions and not forcing me to face reality. Thank God he is here to remind me of that. And the subject comes up again of my being moved to Mexico City to end my days in comfort and security. While I'm still strong enough to get on a plane, flying first class of course.

I wish I had enough strength to laugh.

I cough instead, and he wants to know if I'm Ok. I wait a moment to catch my breath and tell him that I was trying to laugh. And then of course, he wants to know what is funny. I have no idea.

There is very little that is funny at the end of my life. There are moments, of course, when Yzzie feeds me some of her brownies and I reel under the effects of the medical grade cannabis, smuggled from Berkeley. She brings it already infused in butter inside a jar that she wraps in her dirty undies. That thought makes me laugh, the DEA opening her suitcase and recoiling from the lady smells that waft upward.

There is nothing in this conversation with Luis that is funny. My mind keeps coming back to Mr. Roberts, just blocks away from where I've been living for the past many years. I try to probe him some more about whether he thinks that his expulsion and banishment were justified. He acts dumb. He says he doesn't know what I'm talking about.

Luis

Of course Mr. Roberts was a homosexual. Still is, since it's known to be an incurable condition. But he didn't turn me into one, even if he took all those pictures and tried to flatter me that I was the best-looking boy he knew. He never touched me. If he had, you can bet I would have fought him off.

Everyone needs to know that. Whatever happened, he had it coming to him, whether it was Vin and Yzzie who did the gossiping, or his stash of pictures was discovered by accident. There was no way he could explain those away as a hobby or art or research.

I was eight years old and being as pretty as a girl detracted from how I saw myself. Looks had nothing to do with being in a gang, learning how to dribble from one end to the other and kick goals, building spaceships out of Legos. In fact I worked at not being good looking, not washing my hair unless I was coerced by Mother, wearing the same clothes day after day, getting into scrapes so that I could show bruises proudly.

In fact, even as a kid I was known as the grabby kind. Ha! Ask Lavinia. There was even an occasion when I was thirteen and she was a junior in high school that I took advantage of an opportunity to touch her small breast. We were at the breakfast table on Sunday, and then, as if it had been without intention, I reached across her chest to grab a platter of eggs and the back of my hand pushed against the gentle yielding of her boob. I didn't immediately pull back.

She went bananas. You'd think I had assaulted her instead of just copped a feel. She went right to Father with her complaint because Mother was fairly passive about the squabbles between us. Father was the ultimate authority, the judge, the executioner. He took me into his study and sat me down across from his desk. He kept shaking his head and grinning, so I knew I was not in a whole lot of trouble. He said that I was showing natural male impulses as I entered puberty, an explosive time, when our instincts can take over without warning. So it was up to me to be vigilant and control my impulses, even when urges come without warning. One of the controls is that we don't touch family. Lavinia was declared to be off limits. He said he would talk to my sister and calm her down. He ordered me to apologize. And I assured him I would, but I kept putting it off until the apology never took place.

Ysbel

Please Vin, just let this thing about Mr. Roberts go. His life was derailed after Mexico, but it was not our doing. Everyone thought he was creepy and he kept taking all those pictures of the boys. I feel no guilt if at the age of eleven we thought it was exciting to speculate and whisper. I don't know what happened to those pictures of Luis, but it would be nice to find them again in a corner of some drawer or at the bottom of a box from your various moves. He was so pretty! And if you take them out of the Mr. Roberts' context, they are sweet.

So please, please dear friend, don't expect me to be here when you meet with Mr. Roberts. I don't want to see the man's face again, and unlike you I feel no need to ask for his absolution. I know I sound hard but that's just the way it is. You are my friend and I want to comfort and amuse you in equal measure. There is such a bond between us from the time we were kids which makes my heart full.

Unearned guilt should not cloud your experience at this moment. You are facing your end with courage and serenity, and your drifting in and out of wakefulness should allow the peace you deserve. You must always know that during those moments when you are awake, I am here, Jordi is here. And where we are, there is love. Mighty waves of it that will lift you from pain and fear into a sea of tranquility.

Also, you must know that this need for Mr. Roberts' absolution is about your peace of mind, not his. He has probably long forgotten the little vixens that derailed his life without a clear idea of what they were gossiping about. Do you really think he will get some satisfaction from your guilt? That he will be ready to forgive you? If nothing else, your contacting him will bring back the anger and frustration of having had to explain himself to an ignorant jury. He was not quite thirty at the time, a cheerful teacher who entertained as well as educated. He wore bow ties, fancy silk confections of paisley and flowers. And he juggled apples that we placed on his desk. He brought all kinds of energy to the classroom so that even the most distracted among us settled and focused.

And then he had to explain himself to the school board for taking pictures of boys. He said it was a hobby as a portrait photographer. He planned to make a little extra cash by offering them to parents for purchase. He wanted them as memories.

In the end he was encouraged to seek counseling, and to submit his resignation. He could reapply in the future if he completed treatment. It was all ostensibly amicable. But he never returned. There were rumors that he had been sent to prison. That he had committed suicide. That he had been beaten up by a gang of concerned parents. All we knew is that he left the city without a word of farewell or apology. Adios, Mr. Roberts. Your fifth-grade class misses you.

Lavinia

I insisted to Jordi that he talk to Mr. Roberts. He and Yzzie thought that there was no point in dredging up such an old incident, one that I have no reason to be tormented by. It is not so much a matter of asking for forgiveness, but to reassure myself that he has been able to have a decent life and that his old age is gentle. Surely, whatever demons tormented him in his younger days have now grown dormant, rising only occasionally as the dregs of past obsessions.

In truth, my sense of obligation and responsibility for what has likely been a sad lonely life means that however late I can come to his aid, there is still time to ease his days. Jordi and I have been fortunate. Wealth has accrued through our good luck in work and in family. We have no children, so after I die Jordi inherits half of what I have. The other half goes to Yzzie, my dearest friend and sister, who has managed to squander a couple of divorce settlements. And who is now broke.

I have good days and shitty days. I am filled with gratitude to the hospice nurses that come to visit with their vials and needles. I asked the grouchy one, Jill, with the smoker's voice and the spiky haircut, how she can do this work. And she said, "just because I can." All her patients are dying, some slowly and painfully, others, like myself, in a cloud of lavender mist. Yet she gives love and then accepts the need to detach. That's true caritas. No questions asked, nothing required in return. Clearly not something an ordinary person, even one trained in nursing, could handle.

Today I awoke with a surge of energy such that I couldn't stop talking, even after Yzzie and I got thoroughly baked on her signature brownies. It may help that I've taken up coffee, after a lifetime of Darjeeling. Espresso is best.

I have so much to say suddenly and I asked Jordi to take down some notes that could become a letter to give to Mr. Roberts. He agreed reluctantly to record what I say and then shape it into some kind of written communication. I tell him to do what I say because when I wake up tomorrow, if indeed I wake up, I may only drool and moan. I have a clear sense of my failing energy, so that I can observe myself and know at any given moment how close I am to fading totally. Even when numbed with morphine I am curiously awake in-side. Jordi wants to argue. Yzzie tells him to shut up and help me write the letter.

Mr. Roberts

I have a clear recollection of the two monsters who upended my life with whispers and snickers. They were students in my fifth-grade class, the two of them friends, so intertwined with each other that it was hard to distinguish one from the other. They were diligent in their schoolwork and attentive in class, quick to catch on to the intricacies of geometry and the details of history.

Of the two, the Aguilar girl, the girl who stole the Polaroids from my hotel room, was the more dangerous one. I had no idea that the boy I'd photographed, was her younger brother. Even now, as I remember, I can't see the resemblance. Luis was dark and thin, with black eyes that sparkled as if with fever, hair long almost like a girl's, and so serious I couldn't even coax a smile out of him with my jokes and juggling tricks. He's the kind of boy I've always found compelling, a kind of melancholy urchin that seemed too fragile to touch. To be sure, I never placed a hand on him, not his shoul-der or his back, even when I was getting him posed for the photos. Something about his quiet energy made me fear his skin would burn my hand.

Lavinia, his sister, remains clear in my mind. Everyone called her Vin and the nickname fit because she was a bit of a tomboy, complete with scuffed knees and hair cut blunt to stay out of her eyes. She was fair in contrast to her brother, blond as opposed to his black hair, quick to laugh, always in motion, twitching and stretching and leaning from her chair to whisper to her friend Ysbel. I tolerated their quiet unrest because they were two of the brightest students I had. Even when I thought they were distracted, they surprised me by participating in the class discussion when I called on them. Their giggling would stop instantly upon one of them hearing her name, just when I thought I was about to spring a trap.

"Perhaps," I said on one occasion, "Miss Aguilar would like to shed some light on what Robert Frost is intending to communicate with his poem 'Stopping by Woods on a Snowy Evening?'"

She stood by her chair as I had trained my students to do when addressing the class, and in a voice of quiet authority she quoted the last few lines from memory.

> *The woods are lovely, dark and deep.*
> *But I have promises to keep,*
> *And miles to go before I sleep,*
> *And miles to go before I sleep.*

She went on to explain that the poem was a contemplation of mortality. Or rather, postponing the peace that death delivers because there are still obligations to be met in life.

I was fairly stunned, and complimented her on remembering the ending. She said that she had memorized the whole thing, and started again, right from the beginning to those last moving lines. I thanked her and said she could sit.

She went back to her whispering with her friend Ysbel, not showing that she was proud of that moment. Or even that she understood it had been in any way remarkable. The rest of the class shrugged her off; they were used to brilliance from their classmate.

I hadn't thought of her more than a passing recollection until her husband Jordi brought me the letter. I finally understood who he was and why he'd been hovering about me for days.

It was the second time he had approached me at Dunn's while I was facing the morning with my triple latte, a scone, and my phone. This is a quiet hour for me, and I'm not up for conversation. On the previous occasion, we had shared the table because the place was crowded. Now there were seats available elsewhere so when he asked if he could join me, I wondered what he had in mind. I gestured toward the rest of the café to indicate other options, but he had already placed his cup on the table and was pulling out a chair. I continued scrolling through my phone.

Without a word he took an envelope from his pocket and slid it across the table with his index. I did not reach out to touch it. He waited as if expecting me to open it. He tossed back his coffee and left with a shrug. Apparently, he was just the mailman, not caring one way or another whether I read the letter.

I was mildly curious, but had refrained from asking questions, and he hadn't volunteered any explanations. It was all contained inside the blank white envelope, which I stuffed inside the briefcase. There, crammed with workbooks and manuals and tests to be graded, it sat for days. Then, one evening, while organizing myself for the following week, the envelope fell out. I plead guilty to not so much a lack of interest as a reluctance to complicate my life. A hand-delivered envelope promised complications.

My first thought was that a student's parents were unhappy with SAT scores that had fallen short of expectations. It wouldn't have been the first time complaints had been lodged and lawsuits threatened. This was not the case.

> Dear Mr. Roberts, We are acquainted from your time in
> Mexico City and I now realize we have been neighbors
> for years.

That got my attention. I hadn't been Mr. Roberts for a hundred years. Not since teaching at the International School in Mexico City, a period in my life that had unfortunate consequences, and which haunts me to this day. I was not yet thirty and this was my first time outside of the country, a good job with my newly minted MA in education and a couple years of teaching experience. I was not prepared for the onslaught that was released on me.

The sixties were a glorious time to be an expat, an ambassador of contemporary American culture to the more conservative Mexico. My hair, ginger at the time, was down to my shoulders. In my free time away from school, I wore bell-bottoms, I got into bullfighting, I smoked pot, loved Credence Clearwater Revival, joined Democrats Abroad, I learned to juggle.

I used a Polaroid camera to take pictures of interesting faces, which meant I didn't have to take the photos to a lab. They were of boys, only their faces and torsos. I liked serious expressions. I didn't like kids with easy charm or pleasing smiles. I was drawn to the melancholic, the restless, the timid. This was a hobby that I kept to myself; I knew how easily it could be misinterpreted.

Even at that age, I had grown accustomed to being alone. Outside of the school, I had no real social life. Mexico City was an easy place to find quick release with a faceless partner. I had a nice apartment in the Cuahutemoc neighborhood right off Reforma Avenue. All I had to do when desire raised its head was step out the front door and walk a block or two before some man in a car would roll down the window and ask if I wanted conversation. "Quieres platicar?" Do you want to chat? No names, no details, and precious little conversation. Mexican men thought they maintained their macho status of not being homosexual if they were the aggressive partner in the exchange. A mouth is a mouth and all that. I felt some shame, but it faded until I went out again, after a week or a month.

This was not what my boys' faces were about. Instead, they brought me to a place in my own childhood, before I was old enough to realize how warped I would become. A time when my sadness seemed to rise from inside me without any tangible source, and my differences from other children went unexplored.

It's no longer acceptable to feel guilt. Never homosexual. Gay is a sweet, non-threatening label. And how being happy or at least cheerful became the designation for a deviation from the norm is an admirable example of language's adaptability. I teach English and to me language is a reliable thing, it has constant values that generations of writers and readers have relied on for understanding the world and the self. Otherwise, it's all footnotes. "Homosexuality" has been banned to a time when craving someone of your own sex was a distortion and a malfunction and a disturbance.

Now, I'm expected to be gay and proud, to march in a sea of rainbows and shout out cheers. I'm supposed to happily accept what I am. Queer, strange, odd. Well, I can't. I may be the last homo willing to take the term to the grave.

You may not remember my name. But even if you don't, you surely recall that a pair of stupid girls sneaked into your hotel room and swiped the pictures you had taken of a boy named Luis.

Lavinia. I have never forgotten you. You and your little friend Ysbel managed to have me tarred and feathered out of the International School and Mexico City. You know what "tarred and feathered" refers to, don't you? Google it:

> Tarring and feathering is a form of public humiliation used to enforce unofficial justice or revenge. It was used in feudal Europe and its colonies, as well as the early American frontier, mostly as a type of mob vengeance.
>
> In a typical tar-and-feathers attack, the mob's victim was stripped to the waist. Liquid tar was either poured or painted onto the person while he was immobilized. Then the victim either had feathers thrown on him or was rolled around on a pile of feathers so that they stuck to the tar. Often, the victim was then paraded around town on a cart or wooden rail. The aim was to inflict enough pain and humiliation on a person to make him either conform his behavior to the mob's demands or be driven from town.

It didn't take me long to move away. My one-bedroom apartment in Colonia Cuahutemoc came furnished and equipped with linens, pots and pans, even a black and white TV. I didn't own much beyond books and clothes and a cassette player.

When I got wind that Maurice Mendota, the assistant principal, had been investigating me, my best pictures of boys went up in flames one at a time over the stove burners. So search me, I thought, and good luck pinning perversities on me.

Still, the rules of judicial evidence did not apply at the International School. Even after I was handed a letter of resignation to sign, I had to show up to get my last paycheck. I was kept outside the administration office for almost half an hour, like some errant pupil waiting to be disciplined.

During that time the recess bell rang, and the halls were suddenly streaming with kids on their way to lunch, some of them slowing for a moment to give me a wide berth as if to grant me the respect of a leper. I think that last bit of theater had been planned from the moment I was invited to pick up my pay. Well, I wasn't going to skulk around. I stood up from the chair outside the principal's closed door and held my head high, countering the stares of the kids bold enough to meet my gaze. I kept an eye out for you and Ysbel, but you were not among the throng. I don't know what I would've said to you, a bit of sarcasm wouldn't have done the trick, a challenge to confront you inside Gleason's office. Not that you had accused me of anything. My crimes had been inferred by the powers that be based on thin evidence beyond your understanding. Still, you knew you were stirring up some shit. Didn't you?

> *My name is Lavinia Aguilar. Luis is my younger brother.*
> *I was in your sixth-grade class. And the purpose of this*
> *letter is not to remind you of a painful episode, but to ask*
> *forgiveness for the harm that I have caused you.*

OK, little Miss Cruella. You are forgiven. You need me to reply to this letter? Maybe your furtive messenger, whom I take to be your husband, will cease stalking me and we can lay the whole thing to rest. Children, as I have learned in a hundred years of teaching, are capable of spontaneous malice with no thought of the consequences. They are little forces of nature, pointed thunderbolts that strike the innocent and the guilty alike. I imagine in the past years you have given me scant thought until you realized that I'd been living right here, in your city, in your neighborhood, a few blocks away.

And yes, I do recall Luis.

Lavinia

I do have some good days in our lovely condo by the river. Today is not one of them. I sit with the drip in my arm for four hours and during that time I'm gripped by bouts of nausea and itching, from the soles of my feet to my scalp. Jordi has sat with me the whole time. He has been neglecting his work to the point that he's about to get fired. He's not saying anything so as not to worry me.

On other days, I'm living my most gorgeous time—head shaved for Ruthie Lee's fine hand, bright laughing with friends, with all my staff-of-life music and song always winging inside my head, with the planet's most loved lovely man in my bed. I fear no night noise, no nightmare, fear nothing and nobody living or dead. A sword-swinging angel in flight, I surf, as long as the curl can hold, the wave that will glide my sun, moon, and stars, my foam and my light through my stellar life to galactical night.

I asked Jordi if he had delivered my letter to Mr. Roberts and he assured me he had, but that there had been no conversation. I wait for him to contact us.

Ysbel

I don't want to be here when Mr. Roberts shows up, as I know he must. I've seen the picture that Jordi took surreptitiously, and he looks like a ghost. The once charming popular teacher is now a sad man in a rumpled jacket and crooked tie. I can't believe that two gossipy kids were the cause of his decay. I will not accept responsibility. He has his own demons to thank. I have tried to persuade Vin that she should leave well enough alone.

It's been forty years since that time when we showed the pictures to the kids in the lunchroom. The principal at the International School made sure they got to Luis' parents. Don Marcial, as I liked to call him, summoned Vin and me to his study.

We were subjected to insistent interrogation as her father tried to find out what exactly had happened between Luis and Mr. Roberts. It didn't matter that we didn't understand what the fuss was about. The teacher had simply taken pictures. Yet, there was an undertone of perversity that we sensed but which we could not put a name to. It's that whiff of the forbidden that made Vin hide the pictures at first, then engage in a suspenseful reveal. If only she had just thrown them out, so much pain would have been avoided.

He wanted to know everything from the beginning. He clutched the pictures as if to obliterate the images. Shaking them at us, he asked who had taken the pics, the meaning of which we barely intuited. Where had we found them? Why were we in this man's room? Did he know we were in it? What classes did this Mr. Roberts teach? The questions were barked out so fast we hardly had time to answer them. And so it went, on and on with the pictures, until we admitted everything. Yes, we were a pair of snoops and sneaks and thieves and we regretted the prank.

Then Luis was called in. It was obvious that his father indulged Lavinia, and leaned on him, as if a boy needed a stricter rule simply because males had to develop a specific kind of backbone.

I was sent home, glad not to be part of the family drama about to unfold.

Lavinia

I waited for about an hour outside Father's closed door while he questioned Luis, the child's keen and the man's bark, the words muddled, rising and falling in counterpoint. I had settled into a comfy chair near the phone in the hallway. I didn't want to seem like I was eavesdropping, but about to call my one and true friend, my loyal partner in shenanigans, Yzzie.

I have never forgotten Luis's expression as he left the room, his eyes glistening as if he'd been refusing to cry but had finally surrendered his tears. It wasn't just his face that revealed the pain and humiliation he'd been subjected to. His skinny frame looked hurt and exhausted, his shoulders sloped, as he shuffled past me bent over like an old man without meeting my gaze.

I tried for days to talk to him, about the usual things like school and the TV shows we liked, but he refused to give me more than a brusque acknowledgement. I wanted to tell him that I was sick to my stomach with worry, that I missed the happy kid brother that I loved. But he never stood still long enough for me to get the words out, and when he finally appeared to have gone back to his normal self, it seemed ill advised to bring up the situation.

It took weeks before he seemed to have thrown off the cloud that had settled over him. I was once again the big sister that looked after him and helped him with homework and interceded with Mother and Father for more TV and later bedtimes.

Even now, when he has grown into a typical Mexican male, a little machito in his father's image, I find that I can't judge him. And when he attempts to question the care I'm getting from Dr. Dave and the rest of the kind people at the Cancer Center, I try not to show my irritation. He turned out the way he did in part because of two girls who stumbled into a teacher's secret hobby. Still, when I've tried to bring up the situation he found himself at the age of eight, and what my role had been and how sorry I was, he acts as if he doesn't know what I'm talking about. He does know, of course, and that is why he shrugs off the subject with a curse and a threat that I should mind my own business. Really? His sister is fucking dying and he doesn't cut me any slack?

Jordi

When I hear about Mr. Roberts and his harmless photography, I am certain that Vin needs to let the whole thing rest. If her old teacher's life was messed up, it's too late for her to do anything about it. I tried to bring it up with her but she was not responsive. She did say I had no understanding of the restorative power of forgiveness, that this is something she needs to obtain. And time, as I should well know, is running out. As usual, I'm stymied by the tyranny of the dying.

No sleep. Lavinia is awake. Eats when she is hungry. Goes where she wants to go, but can't on her own. So it's up to me to lift her. I'm to be close, always close by. Vin calls Ysbel and leaves a message saying that she wants to say goodbye because she expects to die tomorrow.

This creates fear and sorrow, and I end up having to talk Ysbel down from her panic. Was this the cannabis brownie talking? Or is Vin coming to terms with the possibility that death could come without warning? I know she wants to talk to Dr. Dave about reducing the Decadron. I.e.: fewer side effects, more cancer. Damned if you do, fucked if you don't.

Dr. Dave said the weakness comes from nodules swelling in her brain. Stopping Decadron could provoke a seizure which might be more violent than the gradual deterioration she is experiencing now. The predictable course is increasing weakness until she is too exhausted to move from her chair or bed. Then what? New symptom: unprovoked choking, even in her sleep or simply sitting. So far she eventually catches her breath without any help.

I ache to watch her fading every night. We are talking more and more about the end, the love for life that she has, the sadness that pains her to let go. I tell her that the way she has lived, without shame in her work, without flagging in her love for me, she will go with a clear conscience, a rare condition considering the frailties of humans.

Tonight I massaged her feet and back with lotion. She is more unsteady every day, so that bathing and changing clothes are major undertakings. I felt as if I was worshipping her body, touching divinity in her flesh.

At night the reality of this thing hits me and I'm appalled about what lies ahead. Then I get on with the tasks at hand. I'm enjoying cooking under her supervision. Our spirits are high during these tasks, especially in the preparation of magic brownies. I mash the pastries into a mug of milk, heat it in the microwave, then stir the treat into a kind of toddy.

I'm uneasy with weepy expressions of praise from Vin's friends. The only gratitude that matters is Lavinia's, which is unnecessary because I know she would do the same, and more, for me.

And when she wakes, at whatever time of day or night, she asks if I have given her letter to Mr. Roberts. She wants to know if he read it in front of me, and what his expression was, and if he said anything. I'm sorry to disappoint her.

Luis

Sure, Mr. Roberts took my picture. He took pictures of many of the boys at the International School. And for this the parents and the administrators decided that he was a threat to us? So, he was tainted as a perv and run out of town. I didn't have a problem with that, except I was branded as the perv's victim. When whispers and speculation swirled about what Mr. Roberts had done and with whom, everyone assumed that he was a homo and had somehow turned me into one. He had it easy. All he had to do was leave town and find a new life somewhere. I had to stick around.

Until I graduated from high school, I was looked at with suspicion. I went out of my way to show the world that I was a regular guy. I was the first kid in high school to find a prostitute and go to a hotel with her. I made sure everyone knew.

We were a group of boys out in Chapultepec Park improvising a basketball game. After dusk when the streetlights came on the women would cruise the neighborhood in taxis. It was a smooth routine. The cab slowed down and the girls rolled down the window as if to ask directions, but instead asked us if we were looking for a date. Vamos?

I got inside the cab dense with the women's fragrance, which smelled vaguely of bubble gum. I sat close to one of the women who claimed her turn and pretty much established that I was to go with her. She said her name was Chantal, so French, maybe thirty which was old for me, with black hair and white skin, her sequined mini skirt hiked up mid-thigh. Her mouth and eyes, overly expressive with red and blue and black enhancements, promised an experience beyond my daydreams.

I followed her into a courtyard surrounded by black metal doors with white numbers. One of the doors was marked Oficina with a thin wormy man behind a counter using a tortilla to scoop up black beans and chicken in a green sauce. He took a long swallow from a bottle of Pacifico and scowled. I counted out the precise fee for one hour with Chantal, three hundred pesos in fifties. She pushed a few bills across the counter and tucked the rest into her purse. The clerk slid a metal ring with a key dangling number six.

She instructed me to drop my pants and underwear and jerked my dangling penis with her index and thumb in order to inspect it from all sides. She guided me to a sink in the corner of the room and washed me with soap. She handed me a towel and told me to hurry and take my clothes off as we now had less than an hour left on our session. She kicked off her panties, pulled up her dress and lay on the bed. The sight of her black bush and gaping slit froze my resolve. She pulled me on top of her and even after a few minutes of her undulating beneath me it became clear even the slightest stirring of an erection was not happening.

She pushed me to my back and caressed my penis until it became hard and, for the first time, I felt a bit of sympathy from her. She pumped with no result and finally took my hand in hers and together we masturbated me to an abundant ejaculation. "No te preocupes," she said. "Asi pasa." It happens.

Afterwards, I met my buddies later at VIPS restaurant where about half a dozen of them were squeezed into a booth smoking and drinking coffee. I smiled bravely at their good-natured applause.

Fantastic, I said. They challenged me. How many times? I lifted my hand and splayed all five fingers. They laughed uproariously as their celebration turned to mockery. I learned soon enough, not even Superman comes five times in an hour.

Four years went by before I dared to try again. Sally Blanchard was as inexperienced as I was, so whatever attitude I could muster was enough to impress her. I was so grateful that I fell in love and married her as soon as I was out of college.

Mr. Roberts

In those days Mexico City was an international playground. There was opera, symphony, ballet, even theater in English and French. The bars were special, with all manner of jazz and pop. And in Plaza Garibaldi, a square near the Centro, mariachi bands vied to give personal serenades at twenty pesos a song. It was a wonderful place to get drunk on tequila with beer chasers, the cleverly named submarino with a pony glass sitting at the bottom of a chilled mug. There was the Hotel Victoria nearby where a room could be had for an hour of fun.

At 2:00 am Garibaldi fostered anonymity. The respected teacher at the International School was free to slither and roam at El Gallo with its meandering mariachis and free-flowing drinks.

Memory is a chancy thing. I can't remember how I managed to be sharing drinks at a small table with Hermano Alonso, a young seminarian, smooth of complexion and lithe of form in his black trousers and shirt with a white starched collar. I was surprised that he didn't make any attempt to disguise his clerical persona.

"Are you really a priest?" I said, when he politely asked if he might join me.

"Not yet," he displayed the whitest toothy grin. "I'm in seminario. So I can still go out and be sociable. Libertad, until I get ordained."

"So, this is what you do with your freedom? Tequila and mariachis?"

"I go where I'm needed."

"And you think I need you?"

"I'm here. It's for you to decide if I should stay."

After a moment, he rose as if to leave the table. I tugged at his sleeve to coax him back down.

"I don't need religion."

"People don't need God. God needs us. We testify to his reality and that keeps Him going."

"Do they know you believe this at the seminary?" I was relieved when he laughed along with me.

"I would be burned at the stake."

"They still do that?"

"At night, when nobody is looking."

"Well relax, your secret is safe with me."

"And yours with me."

"So you know something about me? Some terrible, forbidden thing?"

"Forbidden, maybe."

"Yes, I'm a schoolteacher."

"God forgives."

"I thought you said there was no God."

"If you need God to forgive you, God will exist for that purpose."

"Repent, repeat?"

"As often as it takes. God is patient. God is kind."

"Sounds like you have put Him to the test."

"Love God and do as you please."

"How can you love what doesn't exist?"

"That is a problem, my friend."

I never saw Hermano Alonso again. I kept going to Plaza Garibaldi, usually on payday, when the International School's pesos burned a hole, for drinks and the company of the crowd, pressing against me as I stood with them in the plaza, following the groups of mariachis, and later sitting at a table in El Gallo. The rub and breath of strangers brought relief. I developed a routine. I prayed in secret and waited. Always in the dark, in my room before dreams replaced the day's visions, before the body found rest, and the heart slowed down, and the soul found stillness.

Mornings were grim, when God's presence would leave me, and I wrestled with the worms of guilt and sadness. Washing and dressing were a struggle, the clothes abraded my skin, soap burned my eyes and the toothbrush made me gag.

Then when the International School learned of my photos and they searched my apartment and questioned the neighbors about my comings and goings, I knew that I had not been forgiven.

Those days would become a blot on my history. A page had to be turned and a new life invented. It was easy enough to cook up a couple of letters and invent a list of references. I don't know if any of those were checked, but calling Mexico in those days was expensive, and sending letters by mail erratic at best. Naturally, I didn't apply to mainstream schools, which would have procedures in place to check out applicants. The test prep services where I was a freelance instructor, not an employee, were more likely to save themselves time and money by skipping the vetting.

So, in a sense I feel forgiven, the anticipated beating turned out to be a slap, and I'd been left to go forth and sin no more. As a result, I've grown to believe that I'm not a sinner. I try not to injure or cheat or betray others. I encounter men with sins and assure them that they are safe with me, that I do not reveal their secrets. I have nothing but compassion for those that share my frailties, truly my brothers in arms.

Now, with the resurgence of my child nemesis, I confront again the problem of forgiveness. This time Lavinia, the more interesting of the Vin/Ysbel team of urchins, now a middle-aged woman in the last stages of breast cancer, needs to seek forgiveness. Not God's, mine.

Ysbel

I am sorry, dearest friend, I do not need forgiveness from Mr. Roberts. We may have been clueless at age eleven of the true import of his shenanigans. But he knew damn well that taking Polaroids of boys for a private photo album hidden at the bottom of a closet was compromising.

And now it seems he has rebounded, working with boys again, but he's probably too old and depleted in the libido department to be of much harm to them. I say we need to leave him alone to enjoy his golden years, touching no one but himself as he remembers the faces that brought him low. Luis among others, but so many others, because the man had an insatiable appetite for the disdain and arrogance and petulance of children. Is there a name for a Lolita-type among boys? Lo-li-to.

Mr. Roberts

11:00 PM and I'm alone with the mirror. I search my image for the boy I was. I have always been pulled by the faces and expressions of confidence, even impudence. Those pictures of boys were me. Surely, somewhere hidden under the puffy pouches under my eyes, the pocket of fat under my chin, the thinning hair revealing a latticework of scalp, there is a face worthy of Narcissus' love. The skin in my face remains pocked from the acne that assailed me through my adolescence. Then there are the moles and spots and crusts that punctuate my cheeks and forehead, a scattering of red and brown without logic. I shower and shampoo and start with a close shave, using a new blade that delicately scrapes away two days' growth, going over the same surfaces until my face is as smooth as the proverbial baby's bottom.

I move to the small table I've set on a corner of the bedroom, the mirror circled by lights that can be dimmed or brightened for the best effect. On the black marble surface, placed with orderly precision as if for surgery, are my colors, brushes, sponges, powders and oils. First step, so much to conceal. I like the Mediterranean skin tones, the look of a man who's been at a resort or a cruise, so much more flattering than my reddish, cratered face. I use the pads of my fingers, soft from never having done manual labor, to smooth out and camouflage the puffs and crow's-feet and around my eyes and the corners of my mouth. Then it takes just a dab or two to fill the deeper acne scars. I'm a scary pumpkin face with beige spots, but I can see progress almost immediately. Such magic from Shiseido and Lauder.

I use a sponge to lay on a foundation of Arizona Sunset by Makena, at forty dollars for a small jar, a serious expense destined only for special occasions when I need my soul to gaze out of a serene expression. A fine powder completes the look and takes the shine out of the finish. And so the acne scars and the gaping pores are smoothed out as if a second silken skin had been laid over my features. I do have good bone structure underlying the puffy pockets and jowls.

I've always thought my eyes are small and beady, giving me a shifty evasive look. So I use pencil and mascara judiciously to give myself a more engaging gaze. Not so much that I will look effeminate or clownish, barely enough so the cosmetic doesn't call attention to itself. And I can face the world with confidence.

I avoid the gay bars, not for me the anxious rub and leer of The Gay 90's or the Bolt. There is a stink to those places, the air heavy with sweat trying to hide under the faint perfume of latex and lube and breath mints. I like the finer traditional places, oak bars with dim lights that bring a glow to the hues of whiskeys and wines and gin cocktails, from golden to ruby to silvery. With $15 cocktails and little plates of scallops or lobster cakes my budget does not tolerate more than a couple of these nights out in a month.

Oh, but I am a handsome man! I think, as I go on the prowl. I am nicely put together with black pants and a white silk shirt, blowsy and loose and buttoned to show off a little bit of chest hair which I trim for subtlety and stain dark to project virility.

Tonight, Manny's. I couldn't afford to eat here if I blew a year's entertainment budget in one night. At $69 for prime rib and $89 for lobster tail, the place is obscene. But for a single man at the bar with an $18 cabernet and an appetizer consisting of three perfect scallops on little toasts, I enjoy the access to a better class of folks. And Jocko the bartender tops off the glass with a complimentary splash when I'm two thirds down. He's a kind man, who's been behind the bar at Manny's for twenty-four years. He has seen the rich and powerful fall off his radar, the young and lovely grow old, and the old die. He's kind to me because he knows I'm a harmless loiterer, one of the few who drink alone at Manny's. It's mostly couples and corporate groups and teams of women on the prowl for younger men. Cougars is the current label, which I find hilarious.

In the dim light a woman sitting nearby comments, "It's a nice evening, isn't it?"

I treat it as a rhetorical question that requires little more than a nod of acknowledgement. I turn to look at her. She's a petite doll, would seem almost frail if she wasn't all dolled up in a little dress with big orange and blue and yellow flowers, something like giant poppies on steroids. I guess she's somewhere under eighty. She fixes me with the sparkling blue eyes of a girl as if waiting for me to acknowledge her, to examine her, to gauge her desirability. I smile, a slight gift that costs me nothing. But when she smiles back to show her interest I look away.

"What? You think you're going to get someone younger."

I give a small shrug. "I'm just here to get a drink and a bite."

"Well, I will buy you a drink." She signals to Jocko to refill my glass. "And I won't bite."

"Thank you." I move to the stool beside her.

"Good. You're not a solitary drunk after all."

"Actually, not a drunk. Just solitary."

"Worst thing in a man is whiskey-dick. That's why all these old women are here, to find the company of younger men." She pauses for a moment as if to rethink her words. "You barely qualify as young."

I'm afraid that close up, even in the kind, dim light of Manny's bar, she has seen through my cosmetic camouflage.

"You, on the other hand, are beautiful. Ageless. Ethereal. Vital. Angelic," I say.

"That's the best you can do?"

"I'm at a loss for more words."

"My name is Marjorie." She reaches out with a thin hand to clasp mine. Chunky rings on three of her fingers sparkle furiously.

"Severin."

"Pleased to meet you, young Severin." Her hand is dry and delicate. "I get the feeling that our best days are behind us."

"In my case. My best and my worst."

"That's good. A sketchy resume makes for interesting company."

"You have a scary past, Marjorie?"

"I do."

"You first."

"Such a gentleman. So eager to have a woman reveal her shame. Well, sorry to disappoint you, but I have none. No shame at all."

"You are free, then." I took a breath to steady my nerve. "Whereas I'm haunted by shame, past and present."

She toyed with the rim of her glass, absently wiping off traces of lipstick. "I miss smoking. Before it became another object of shame, one could sit in a bar and light a cigarette, inhale, flick ashes, and not have to say a word for a minute or two while contemplating a conversational gambit."

"There is shame in smoking. Dirty habit. I was fired for improprieties with students."

"You had sex with kids?"

"It just seemed that way."

"I can beat that. Twelve years ago, I murdered my husband. Charged with first degree. Acquitted."

"That's a shameful thing."

"Not the murder. The shame is that I waited six years before killing the creep."

"You had to kill him, not just divorce him?"

"He was rich, with mean lawyers."

"But you got away with it."

"Yep. Here I am. And I haven't been beaten up in twelve years. I kept walking into doors and falling down stairs until I grew so ashamed of taking it that I stabbed him in his sleep. He was so drunk he didn't feel a thing."

"No pain. That was kind."

"I think so."

"What did it feel like for you?"

"The knife slid into his gut like butter. Seven times, I was told. I used a very sharp Wusthof."

"Better than those Japanese Ginsus."

"It was all so messy. The sheets were soaked and he was flat on his back in a lake of blood. I froze and just closed the door. I slept on the living room sofa because I wanted to be close to the door when Clarissa the housekeeper arrived. I woke up when she came in at eight. I told her not to bother with the bedroom yet. She wanted to know if she should make breakfast for my husband and me. I asked for her special eggs Benedict but said that the man of the house was indisposed and not to be disturbed. She makes the best hollandaise, like silk on the tongue."

"And then you called 911?"

"Not right away. I took my time putting on my face and dressing for drama. All in black, you know. It's not my best color. I do better in pastels, but I thought that the situation called for seriousness."

"And you got away with it? No shame in that."

"I posted a huge bail with the stipulation that I did not leave the country. So I went to Hawaii. They'd never even heard of Minnesota. Much less follow our local news. I enrolled in hula dancing classes and played with a cabana boy. Best three months of my life. It was winter by the time I came back to stand trial."

"But you got off?"

"Without even a slap on the wrist. The DA tried to nail me for first degree. Saying I had premeditated the act. Really? If I'd thought of it first I would've hired a professional. But then I would have missed out on the satisfaction of watching him bleed."

"Marjorie, you're dangerous."

"Yep, I'm a merry widow. Want to come home with me?"

"I don't function well with women."

"Not for sex, dummy. We're both past our expiration dates. For tea and sympathy. You still haven't told me your story."

Outside Manny's while Marjorie waits for the Uber I say that my story will have to wait for another time. I lean in to give her a peck on the cheek, but she pushes me away. She calls me a coward. And then, to my surprise, through the passenger window of the black town car, she playfully gives me a girlish finger wave.

She's right, of course. I am a coward. I'm scared of myself, of what I look like, of what other men will assume about me in the clubs that cater to unhappy deviants as far from gay as you can get in the spectrum of moods and attitudes. I keep my story well hidden, which is why it makes me uneasy that the girls that tormented me so many years ago at the Mexico International School are now such a threat.

Lavinia

I anticipate a time when I won't awake from the continuous napping, like a cat's as they say, by the disturbances of catheter adjustments, meals of soup and mush, vital signs, and words of cheer and comfort. I surrender to sleep with sadness at odd times of the day and night. I feel I'm missing out on life.

That this is how the end comes, not with a bang but with a sigh. I so want to be conscious when I die. To be fully awake for the mystery. And even in moments of slumber I get hints of what is to come, nothing so flashy as the light at the end of the tunnel and the sight of ancestors smiling and beckoning forward.

Even in sleep I'm aware of my feet and hands growing cold. I awake to Jill rubbing the blood flow back into my legs and arms. It's a small miracle to be looked after while asleep, even when I don't complain of thirst or swelling or pain. How thoroughly loved I feel.

I fall asleep again, this time without anxiety at the cold horizon I face, the purple drapes of lent and a deepening fog that obscures my ability to see more than an inch or two past my nose, the darkness indivisible, the rarified air unbreathable. But this is not the end. According to the Bardo, the end will come as I face light going to dark, in the transition from one realm to the other.

Meanwhile, I cling to my need for forgiveness. I want to die with a clean slate, if that is at all possible in this world of contradictions and compromises. Of course, I can't contact every single person I might have slighted in the past. I can think of colleagues and casual acquaintances that I brushed aside without justification because of their patronizing aggression, sometimes camouflaged with a sort of sentimental kindness. I resented their well-meaning invasions and gossip mongering.

Yes, Lavinia has cancer, so advanced and so metastasized and so crippling in its treatments. So pitiful. So fascinating. I bristle at their attention. Clearly, I can't just go through my address book and beg forgiveness of a hundred people. That would put them in an uncomfortable situation and, rather than eliciting their understanding, would most likely make them resent my using them to rub purity onto my soul.

Mr. Roberts is different. The harm done derailed a promising career, a place in a community where he was appreciated and admired. His whole life was in tatters. I would not have followed my path in literature and philosophy if not for his teaching. He made me feel that my gifts of insight and expression were special, that they deserved nurturing.

I insist again that Jordi must connect with Mr. Roberts, or whatever his name is these days, and persuade him to come here for a visit. I wish I had known of his proximity just weeks ago. I would have gone to him. I don't kid myself that this will appear onerous to the man, and more easily avoided than agreed. In fact, insisting on my asking for his forgiveness is more about my peace of mind than his wellbeing. I even question if Luis was important to him, rather than one more boy to photograph for his collection. I don't know if he continues to harbor resentment for the thoughtless girl I was, he may not even remember Ysbel and me from a happier time in Mexico City as the instrument of his downfall and shame.

In a sense we were unwitting villains. Our actions and our words were not born of malice, but of delight in the taboo we had perceived, though not yet understood. Those pictures in my drawer were like an itch that nagged and begged to be relieved by exposure. The odor of the Polaroid chemicals begged for ventilation.

I wait for Jordi to come and sit by my bed with a bottle of lotion to rub into my dry skin, my hands and feet and legs, and as he works his hands gliding them over the reddened joints, I remind him. Bring me Mr. Roberts.

Marcial

There was a time when you stood up for good and exposed evil. You were eleven when I saw the pictures that pervert had taken of Luis during spring vacation in Acapulco. I always wondered how many other children had been caught in his net. Even after his apartment was searched, I believed that much remained hidden. Luis served as the tip of the iceberg, and other parents were quick to join in the effort for the International School to purge this virus.

You were shocked at how much importance was given to your

small discovery. You and your crazy friend Ysbel could only stand aside and watch the wheels of my indignation take their course. No matter that you both pleaded for me to let the thing rest, that Luis didn't care. Even your mother asked that the crime such as it was should be forgotten and Mr. Roberts let off with a reprimand. What you had considered a prank had resulted in a trial. A lynching, as you later recalled, when the full import of his actions was exposed.

You stood before me, trembling because as much as I tried to reassure you that I loved you and wanted only what is best for all my children, you were never able to face me without fear. I didn't know how to explain that this monster masquerading as a teacher had exercised his power over a child in order to derive some dark satisfaction. Those photos were not just trivial images, they were intrusions into a boy's innocence, the work of a rapist. It doesn't matter if he never physically touched the boys and that the pictures were innocent portraits, his intent was clearly invasive.

I made you tell me over and over all the details you had observed of Mr. Roberts before filching the pictures from his room. How he juggled popsicles and played water polo and showed off doing splashy cannonballs into the pool. Did he touch any of the boys while playing in the water? You accurately observed that there was no way you could know that. Did any of the boys seem scared or shy around him? Yes, he was a teacher. Kids were not used to playing with teachers.

And yes, you were shocked at the tempest your schoolgirl gossip unleashed. You and Ysbel retreated to sulk in your room while I gathered with other parents who'd been identified by their children's pictures and we stormed the principal's office at the school to demand that Mr. Roberts be expunged from our system, like a wart that had to be carved out before it could do further harm. There were six of us whose children remembered being photographed. There could be a hundred pictures of boys' faces that remained anonymous.

I was glad other parents would not suffer the anguish that we did. The problem of Mr. Roberts would be solved without them having any knowledge that safety had been restored to our community. It was up to six of us to act as a unified phalanx, storming the gates of the spineless administration.

At first I thought we would have no problem motivating the school. A kind of trial was to be held before a committee including a psychologist and a representative from the teachers' association. And the children would have to be interviewed. But then the other parents decided they did not want to expose their sons to the stress of facing their abuser. So it was just you and Luis joining me at the meeting.

Unfortunately, Luis became hysterical that morning, just as I was waiting for his mother to dress him in pressed flannel slacks and a white shirt, his black shoes polished to a gloss. I had never seen him like that, gripped by anxiety at the prospect of facing the man that was his friend. So I left him home.

But you were going to help me, niña. By telling the adults what you had seen during those vacation days in Acapulco.

Lavinia

I adored my father. I was his girl and I wanted to please him. When he told me he was driving me to school, I felt privileged. He had also planned to take Luis but when my brother started bawling that he didn't want to go, I was happy to leave him behind and have Father to myself.

I realized that I was to attend a meeting at the administration office to tell some people about Mr. Roberts during that time in Acapulco. I was afraid of being put on the spot. After all, Yzzie and I, after sneaking into Mr. Roberts' room, had swiped those pictures from one of the drawers. That made us snoops and thieves. More me than Yzzie because I had kept the pictures. I was entitled since they were of my little brother Luis.

Father noticed how silent I became as I rode beside him, glum and unresponsive to his banter about the nice sunny day and how maybe we should play hooky and escape to the zoo. He said I shouldn't be nervous, that all I had to do is tell the truth because nobody was out to punish me. I didn't believe that. I had gotten myself in trouble and I didn't see how adults would let me off the hook. Luis had done nothing wrong by getting his picture taken. I didn't understand why they wanted to talk to him.

Just tell the principal and other parents what I saw. What could be simpler than that?

Was Mr. Roberts angry at me? I liked him and I was sorry I had stolen his pictures. Maybe all I had to do was apologize and that would be the end of that. Or I could say that it had all been Yzzie's idea. I didn't see her being dragged to the principal's office. To this day, I'm ashamed that the thought crossed my mind, as brief as the temptation to blame someone else had been. I took a deep breath as we drove the familiar avenue leading to the school, every familiar landmark bringing me closer to my reckoning.

I had to wait outside the principal's office while the adults gathered inside. I was left sitting erect, my fingers gripping the edge of the bench, pulling down the hem of my dress over my knees, scuffing the toes of my shoes on the floor as I swung my legs back and forth. And all I could think of is that I had to pee. But I didn't dare leave my assigned spot outside the principal's office.

The shame started when Father stepped out and signaled with a nod that I was to go in. I walked with a shuffle with my legs so tightly squeezed together. And when I whispered that I had to go, he said that I would be done in five minutes and that everyone was waiting for me. There must've been eight people in front of the principal's desk. As clear as that day is still in my memory, I can't remember his name. Only the troublemakers, mostly boys, had a close acquaintance with that office; I was not one of the bad kids. I was a goody-goody girl back then, not at all like the rebel I eventually became. That day may have been the turning point when I saw that obeying orders and rules did not carry any reward.

I didn't recognize any of the adults, except for Mr. Roberts. He was like a child being disciplined, but instead of looking humbled he was sitting quite erect, his head high, his face expressionless except for his pursed lips as if struggling to keep silent. He looked at me when I entered the room, his eyes shutting and opening in a slow blink, as if to acknowledge that he knew who I was and why I was there.

The principal smiled to let me believe that I was not to be afraid, that I was under the protection of powerful adults, who would ask just a few questions about what I had seen in the La Selva hotel during that vacation. I kept my head down, my eyes fixed on the geometric pattern of the parquet flooring. The words came as if disembodied so I couldn't tell who was speaking among the faces staring at me.

I said I had seen nothing.

"Not Mr. Roberts fooling around with some of the boys?"

"Fooling around?"

"Bad choice of words. I meant playing with the children."

"Yes."

"Playing games?"

"Yes, in the pool, keep-away with a ball, then on the lawn juggling, just clowning around."

"You didn't join in?"

"It was only boys."

"Also taking their pictures?"

"Not outside."

"In his room?"

"I don't know."

"But you found the pictures in his room."

"Yes."

"Were you searching for them?"

"Yzzie and I, we found them by accident."

I heard Mr. Roberts clear his throat as if preparing to speak. There was a sudden silence in the room, and I lifted my eyes for the first time since the interrogation began. His face had taken on a sad expression, not as if he were judging me, but feeling sorry for me.

"You were snooping," he said softly. It was not a question.

I couldn't pull my gaze away from his eyes. It was at that moment that I felt the warm stream running down my legs, and looking down in surprise, could see the puddle growing at my feet. I tried vainly to hold it back in as if to minimize the damage, but I could only wait in fascination as piss poured out of me. The meeting was over and I was excused.

Father took me home so I could shower and change into clean clothes. Later I learned that Mr. Roberts was blamed for my "accident" and accused of intimidating me. Well, it wasn't his doing, was it? The problem was Father, who would not let me go to the toilet when I was twitching and dancing in place.

Mr. Roberts was allowed to resign voluntarily rather than be fired. He went home that morning and never came back. He was never seen or heard of again, just totally disappeared, erased from the International School's memory.

The truth is I missed him, his charm and energy in the classroom, and wished I'd had nothing to do with his downfall. I would have liked the opportunity to explain myself.

For a time, Yzzie and I talked about what had happened and speculated within our limited appreciation for human perversity. It was only a couple of years later when I was thirteen that I learned about men who prey on boys and girls. But the idea that Mr. Roberts had somehow abused Luis was hard to accept. Eventually, unable to forget Mr. Roberts and the terrible moment when I last saw him in the principal's office, I asked Luis what had happened besides getting his picture taken.

"Nothing," he insisted. And I believed him.

Luis

Vin must've thought I was some kind of queer after word got out that my face was among a hundred polaroid pictures taken by that teacher who was fired years ago. She'd started all sweet and big sisterly with me, she and Ysbel, trying to coax some kind of confession out of me.

"Little brother," she whispered years later, "you can tell me the truth. I promise I won't tell; it will be our secret. And if you tell me I will tell you a secret of my own." I'm not sure what she wanted me to admit to.

So that's when I grabbed her little boob, to show her that I liked girls and was not going to take insults from her or anyone else. I was surprised when she cried out. I hadn't meant to hurt her.

And then she went and told Father.

Well, I wasn't sorry, even though I didn't realize that at her age her breasts could be sensitive. And the sweet softness on my palm and underneath the racing of her heartbeat, remained as a kind of revelation, that simple flesh could be such a lovely thing to hold.

Father had me close the door to his study and I stood in almost military attention before him. Show me the hand that you used to touch your sister. I extended it to him. As punishment that I had crossed a serious line, Father took my fingers and bent them back until I thought they would break. I didn't cry out so Vin wouldn't know that I was being punished.

While I cradled the bruised fingers in the palm of my other hand, Father explained that men who were real men were expected to abide by a code in their behavior with women. Most women were to be respected and at the top of the hierarchy was my sister. After that, women got the respect they deserved. Decent girls from good families were to be handled with discretion. Girls who displayed their sexuality with immodest dress and language were making themselves available, and men were expected to give them what they wanted. I was too young to know what that was, but the truth of men and women in society would be revealed over time.

In the end, Father walked over to me and offered me his hand. I stood up to reach for his, but I winced in pain when he clasped it. He laughed even as he tightened his grip. Still, I felt we had reached a new chapter as father and son, that I had been initiated into some realm of truth.

Don't say anything to Vin, he said. Not even to apologize. As far as you are concerned you never touched her. It had been an accidental brush of your hand.

Marcial

So the boy grabbed his sister's chichi! I mentioned it to his mother and she was appalled and insisted that I had to punish him. I said I would definitely speak with him, but I was laughing all the time. Not because I found the situation funny, but in relief that the boy even before puberty was giving a sign that he was a regular healthy boy.

I had a talk with Lavinia. I explained to her that in this world, men act according to their nature. And even at a young age, the tiger will show his stripes. It was hard to see how this explanation was sitting with the girl. She sat still and stared straight ahead with that fixed expression of hers, one that I had grown familiar with from the time she was a toddler, a kind of impassivity that revealed little of the emotions she was feeling.

This was a child who did not cry or scream, but left it to me to figure out what was in her head. Still, I rambled on about the need to be tolerant and understanding of her little brother until I realized I was repeating myself, unsure whether I was making an impact or not. So I waited for her to say something.

"May I go now?"

Mother

I never got over the way Marcial dealt with Luis's groping of your breast. I tried to intervene with the boy and let him know that men must respect women, and not take advantage of their strength or the power that Mexican society bestows on them. But your father told me to stay out of the business of men. And I kept my mouth shut, even after you pleaded with your eyes for some guidance. I shrugged in helplessness. You were learning.

Lavinia

I love Father. And I don't love him. He's my judge. My cheerleader. My warden. My coach. My boss. My preacher. When he said I could have any friends I wanted, I believed him. That's the kind of family we are, he bragged. We love all mankind in the Christian way.

When I was fourteen, I had a brown-like-coffee boyfriend, and at sixteen another one as black as coal and at eighteen an Indian who was gold like tea. I loved the lovely shades of skin that were different from my washed-out whiteness. Father exploded. They were not allowed in the house to visit, or to call me on the phone. No private lines or cell phones for teenagers in those days. Thank god for the back of the school bus where Miguel and Brandon and Mahesh and I could canoodle to our heart's content.

When I started in with Jordi I was thirty years old and still Father disapproved. Too old. Married. Jobless. Bohemian. A failure as a writer.

"What on earth do you see in him?"

"It's what he sees in me."

"So, he tells you that you are beautiful."

"He tells me I am the sanest woman he knows. I have to love a man who sees sanity in me."

But of course, I was far from sane. I was easy to anger, to sulk, to judge. After all those years of obeying Father, I resented authority. And when the snake rose within me, Jordi was patient and would wait for the thing to coil back down and calm itself.

He taught me to breathe. He would have me sit beside him, and then placing a hand on top of my head as if to press down his love into the center of my brain, we would start with long slow breaths and gradually allow them to grown thinner and fainter until I seemed to be taking in a finer kind of air through the pores of my skin.

To this day, only by sitting with Jordi can I attain a stillness that cancels fear. I call to him, and, whether he's in the next room or across town, he will come to me. I will confess to him that I'm unhappy, not with tears and curses but in whispers, that the idea of being sick and helpless, more so day by day, makes me so sad, and there's no medication that can lighten the weight of this profound melancholy. Jordi, with his breath and the nearness of his skin, brings me relief, touching me with a kind of energy that sends a tingle along my arms and shoulders.

When I first became Jordi's friend, back in my twenties before we became lovers, our connection even then was a mix of the ethereal and the mundane. Claire, his wife at the time, was an anthropologist and was attending a conference in Oaxaca. I knew Jordi was alone in the city because of work and most likely spending the evening by himself.

I may have been looking for an excuse to offer my company. He was older and smarter than the rest of us, and his tolerance for me was uncertain. But then I had the ideal magnet to draw him. Mother Theresa was giving a talk at the school, mainly fundraising among the international community. Yes, that Mother Teresa, the one who ministered to the dying in Calcutta.

There we were in the front row of the auditorium, early because that was Jordi's habit, never to rush and be late, but to own the evening by being present. She was scheduled for 8:00, and by 7:30 the hall was packed, with every seat taken and people standing in the aisles, gently jostling to get close to the podium. Even with the excitement of the event, it was a quiet crowd, speaking in whispers. I reached for Jordi and at first his hand felt inert in mine. But as we grew closer to the appointed hour, his grasp became firm and certain.

Then she appeared on the stage, just her, walking resolutely to the podium. A tiny figure in the white and blue habit of her order, her serious face, brown and wrinkled as a raisin, peeking out from under the cowl, her black eyes glistening under the lights as if moist with tears. There was no word of introduction. We all knew who she was and why we were there.

She spoke for about twenty minutes in English inflected by her Eastern-European background, and I can barely remember all she said. Just a reminder that we in the audience represented the wealthiest of the wealthy and it was our obligation to give to the poorest of the poor. I had on me only a few pesos, less than ten dollars, and I was of course going to give it all to her. I wanted more, to learn about the guidance and comfort of those who would otherwise die alone.

I thought that she would have some insight into the mystery of death, the passage from one state to another, the revelations of the soul in transit. I raised my hand high to catch her attention, to ask a question that was nevertheless unformed in my mind. When she called on me, I couldn't speak a word. She fixed me with her brilliant black eyes and smiled in encouragement. She finally said, It's all about love, the expression of love with no hope of reciprocity, judgment, or reward in heaven or earth. That's the connection between souls.

After the talk, I waited with others to greet Mother Teresa. Jordi, never fond of standing in line, hovered a few steps to the side. He knew this was important for me. When my turn came, I stood in front of her, speechless, and reflexively reached for her hand. She clasped mine in hers, strong and bony, but instead of releasing it after a perfunctory shake, held on for over a minute. Even after she slid her hand from mine and I was encouraged to move on and let someone else greet her, I felt the power of her gaze drilling through me. Someone handed me a card with her picture on one side and a brief text on the back, which I tucked into my pocket without a glance.

Later, still shaken by the encounter, I sat with Jordi at a café with a mug of tea, the two of us just being there with each other, without much conversation. I tried to hide the tremor in my hands by holding on to the sides of the mug. When I finally let go, I rested my hands on the table, and Jordi slid his hand to rest his fingers on mine. I became immediately calm, even though in some corner of my mind I sensed a clear line had been crossed.

"She didn't want to let you go," he said.

I handed Jordi the card.

> Informational meeting tonight at 8:00 for the Missionaries of Charity, Mexico City chapter.

"I get it now. I'm supposed to follow her and minister to the dying."

"Are you tempted?"

"Yes. But I'm not going."

Even then, while in school, I was aware of my vulnerability to people who exercised their spirituality like a hammer, to get their way or to gain control of others. Priests, roshis, swamis, nuns, all thought I was fair game. So, instead of going to the Mother Teresa meeting, Jordi and I ended up at his house.

He cranked up the Grateful Dead; even back then we shared some hippie obsessions. We drank red wine and smoked pot and made love on the couch. I appreciated not being taken to Claire's bed. The door to their room remained closed.

I lay awake most of the night, gripped by slow remorse that was unusual for me, as I enjoyed sex with some abandon. Friends, classmates, and even the occasional teacher were all fair game. What made Jordi different was his seriousness. This was not a trivial thing for him. My knowing Claire, who had always been nice to me, put a wrinkle in things.

The next morning, Jordi gave me a ride home, early because I had to shower and be ready for work. We hugged without words. I felt awkward and I was not sure when we would see each other again. To this day, when Mother Teresa comes to mind, I relive the mix of flesh and spirit that drives me.

Jordi

She has good days and miserable days. Today is not good. Six months into treatment she seems light as smoke as she hovers above the bed, shakily grasping the corners of furniture, walls, counters, finally kneeling over the toilet to vomit. The drip drip of poison takes its toll. It's become a ritual. She's strong when her infusions come due at the end of the two-week break. We're cheerful as we settle in for the four hours of medication. The treatment room is austere, without a picture or a plant to soften the white walls.

I pull a chair to be close beside her. The only improvement I can make is to turn off the fluorescent lights and rely on a reading lamp over the treatment chair to illuminate our conversation.

Today, a dim gray sunlight suffuses the winter gloom through the one window that gives off to a small green area surrounding the clinic, a still-green lawn and a leafy poplar. From her chair Vin only sees sky out the window, so I describe the scene to her.

I mention a man on a powered wheelchair traveling along the path. Hyacinths and irises in a flower bed. A teenage boy in shorts and a white T-shirt maneuvering the mower, as he cuts even stripes on the fresh grass, sending a lively fragrance through the window. Eventually she loses interest in my narration of the outside world. And I grow quiet, holding her hand as if to communicate through the shared silence. On clear days, she enjoys watching the clouds drift across a blue sky.

First Taxol then Herceptin. I bring candy and books and earphones for music. It's a retreat. She has a good appetite and the Davani's veggie hoagie with extra cheese is a feast. There is ice cream too, Cherry Garcia.

Nurse Ronda is a cheerful, plump presence and hooks up the IV needle. No pain anymore; a port implanted under Lavinia's skin takes in the poison. The implantation of this device was a shock, but after her veins became sensitive to needles, connecting the IV became torture. Admitting the need for the port meant that this was to be her treatment delivery for the rest of her life. If there was a cure the port could be removed, leaving only a small scar on her chest.

Four hours grind on. We read, we talk, we meditate, we doze. When

I'm awake, I watch the bubble travel the length of plastic tubing, so maddeningly slow, as if by the force of my attention I could quicken the flow, hasten her cure. Because in the end, through the torture, there is a shred of belief that Taxol and Herceptin can reverse the dying, prolong the living. Or at least make the remaining life more enjoyable. In that sense, chemo is a discipline, you don't do it for the joy, but for the results. And the results are revealed by numbers and pictures.

And we talk while she is able to stay awake.

She is so fragile, so vulnerable that I find myself being very careful with anything I say. For the last several weeks her face had grown downy. I waited for her to notice it. Finally, I mentioned it and said it might be due to simple aging or the Decadron. It became such a big deal. She felt ashamed, said she looked like a werewolf or a monkey. The problem, which seems to be common in some women, was easily solved with waxing. Fortunately it had nothing to do with the cancer or treatment. In reciprocity I had my back waxed, which she appreciated and found amusing.

Weight has become an issue. Weight loss, weight gain. Nothing extreme, actually. But she is eating somewhat unbalanced meals, large pieces of cake, cereal with extra sugar, cookies. Small portions of savory food which she often does not like. If I eat what she eats, I'll blimp out. But she is also cooking enthusiastically, lovely dinners which she prefers to eating out. If there comes a time when I need to cook for her, I don't think I will be able to please her.

Lavinia

"I'm so grateful to you, darling, for staying with me. Someone else would have farmed me off. Where do you get the patience?"

"You would have done the same for me. I know that."

"Yes, yes, that was the plan, as you grew older, for me to take care of you."

"We don't choose our moments. Life turns and slips in a blink."

"You are teaching me love and all I can do is accept gracefully."

"This moment with you is a privilege. To ease your discomfort, to accompany you in this journey is my role."

We had a cat we loved some years ago. Deva. She died in my arms, the same way I expect I will die in yours, Jordi. I still remember her breath growing short, quick little pants until then there was no breath at all.

After a minute I realized she was gone. I held her out and you lifted her from my arms. You said she was as light as air.

At the end of the chemo session, we walked the mile home from the clinic, braced against the wind and drizzle that stings our faces, but with a sense of accomplishment. Another hurdle cleared. Every step toward home is one of vitality and power. Even as we know that I will die in less than two years.

It's a privilege knowing how I will go. And when. It's no longer possible to live with the sense of immortality, blindly sipping at life as if it had no bottom. My senses have never been more awake to the world. Every breath I take is loaded with sensation, the acute beauty of a star, a flower, a taste. All this loss that looms over me makes me sad. And also happy to savor. Even with my lungs riddled with the tapestry of slippery nodules every sweet breath brings me life.

And you repeat your formula for balance and peace. Where I am, death is not. Where death is, I am not.

Jordi

The attack to the brain came as a shock. An errand to the post office, to buy stamps and mail books to your niece Anna had you twisting your head in a spasm that made no return possible. It was a crowded day, with several people in line, and someone had the presence of mind to place a coat on the floor and lay you on it. Someone called 911. You spoke of confusion and blurred vision and nausea. But not even a headache.

A call with your name came in and I picked up.

"Hola, baby."

I expected your voice. Instead, a man spoke in my ear. "Is this Jordi?"

Confusion again. "Who are you? What are you doing with my wife's phone?"

There was a siren in the background. And then his voice again, calm and collected. "My name is Bill. I'm an EMS tech, and we're riding to Hennepin County General with your wife. She may have had a stroke. She's stable right now."

"That's all you're going to tell me?"

"She'll be checked in at the emergency room in a few minutes. You can visit her any time."

5:37. I'm always checking. It's a habit from childhood when my father gave me my first watch in middle school. Timex, a beautiful intricate thing with luminous numbers, and a second hand I used to measure how long I could hold my breath. To this day, there is not a moment in my life when I don't know what time it is. I got to the hospital at 6:18 and the knowledge seemed to ground me, dispel the fear and helplessness that possessed me as I tried to assimilate the possibility that Lavinia had suffered a stroke on top of the cancer.

County General has the most frantic emergency clinic in Minneapolis. On the edge of downtown, they get all the stabbings, gunshots, rapes, car wrecks, and domestic mayhem. And yet when I get to the reception desk to ask about my wife, I'm greeted with courtesy and even a measure of empathy. But when they look up her name she hasn't been officially admitted yet.

"What does that mean?"

"They're working on her."

"What does that mean?"

The guy's name badge identified him as Joe, so simple and to the point I imagined he had a better name outside of work. He shrugged in ignorance. His expertise was paperwork. How doctors worked was beyond his area of competence. But he was sympathetic and I liked him, found comfort in his quiet way of dealing with anxiety and ignorance.

Emergency rooms are chaos, he explained. A bunch of people are right now jostling over your wife, trying to stabilize her. Believe me, it won't take an hour. They'll move her to either an ICU or a room. If they take her to a room, that's a good sign.

And then he gave me some forms requesting insurance info, advance directives on when and how to pull plugs, a credit card number for incidentals. It was all so mundane; I was glad to have busy work to keep me occupied. It was like checking in at a hotel. By the time I was done signing, Joe signaled that he was ready with news.

There is drama in a patient being rolled along, wheels squeaking on the shiny linoleum floor. They speed by so fast you know there's life-and-death shit going on. I followed a gurney pushed by two nurses down the hall and into a large bright room. Lavinia seemed so small and frail in a medical gown done up with pink bears, as if meant for a child. Inside the room were at least four doctors hovering above her—one Dr. Elise Halvorson with short graying hair, the other three fresh-faced and wide-eyed. Vin seemed intimidated by the attention, almost on the verge of tearing up, until she caught sight of me at the foot of her bed. She reached out her hand, and when I took it, she pulled me closer. She had two paper bracelets on her wrists, a yellow one and a purple one. They meant something—about resuscitation, hydration, oxygenation, nutrition. I edged up along the side of the bed and a couple of the young medical types respectfully got out of the way.

"Baby, you have more doctors messing with you than anyone else in this hospital."

"Like a celebrity."

Dr. Elise met my gaze and without my having to ask, said, "Not a stroke. Probably mets in her brain."

"What the hell is a met?"

"Metastasis."

"Oh, sure. Mets. Not the baseball team." An invasion of giant tapioca-like nodules filling her skull.

"We have an MRI scheduled in an hour."

"Fuck."

"There are things we can do. It's not the end of the world."

From this, I understood she meant a longer life through radiation.

Meanwhile, we were talking around Vin as if she wasn't there. But she knew it was the end of the world, had known since she was diagnosed with stage four from the start, less than two years ago.

Her only reaction was to ask for another helping of dessert, from the strange hospital lunch of chicken breast, mashed potatoes, a mix of peas and carrots. And chocolate pudding, the only edible thing on the tray. For the vegetarian condemned to die it's a shitty last meal.

I took the tray out into the hallway and placed it on the counter of the nurses' station, which earned me a stinky eye but no word of censure. I was a husband-whose-wife-is-dying, which put me in a privileged class. And got me another pudding for Vin.

Lavinia

I can't walk straight. I mix up my pills. I slur, I shuffle, I totter. I am lost in my dreams, wandering mazes of dark, winding streets. I grope for my glasses, my books, my pens, my words. I used to type at the speed of thought, now my damaged skill reflects my thinking: muddled, erratic, repetitious, obsessive. I make a hundred typos.

Jordi drives me to a center for radiation. We park in spaces reserved exclusively for patients, which makes me feel special. Every day at 3:00 for six weeks. I'm treated with gentle concern. The center employs delicate young women to prep and set up, lovely as angels in their powder blue smocks. They are not really nurses or technicians, more like spa hostesses.

The hard part is lying perfectly still for less than ten minutes, even though I don't feel anything, not pain or even a buzz. Just knowing that the ray gun is firing bullets through my skull into my brain makes me jerk. I'm reminded to be still, be a corpse ahead of my time. I join the legions of the walking dead, the zombies from radiation and chemo and surgery. Floating in clouds from morphine and fentanyl. Blissed with the lucky ones from ecstasy or acid or shrooms. Ysbel keeps me steady with pot brownies. Jordi is in charge of ice cream. And sex: tentative, easy going, unhurried. I'm a lucky girl.

I'm in and out of radiation in less than fifteen minutes. Hard to accept that even a brief time of that shit can so mess what's left of my life. On the drive home we stop at Keys Café for a caramel roll, the famous gooey monster packed with frosting and pecans. I gaze at it on the plate before me and tear a piece from the spiral wrap and fold it into my mouth. I chew on it until it becomes a wet pulpy thing, and still, I can't swallow it down. It sticks in my throat until I wash it down with coffee.

I push the plate toward Jordi for him to finish the roll, which he does eagerly. I am envious of his appetite, his energy, his ability to enjoy the mundane pleasures of our life. Nothing gets in the way. Even when we get home and I plead exhaustion and beg for a nap, he lies beside me, wide awake, his even breaths undisturbed by my shallow panting. Eventually, as if my own breathing could mirror his, I settle into a relaxed state, comforted by the press of his arms around my chest, the warmth of his body. Moments later the stirring of his penis sends a current of sadness through me. I reach down to touch myself and find that I'm dry as paper. He slides his hand under mine and he whispers that he loves me, his breath moist on my face.

Jordi

They are frying my love's brain, in ten-minute zaps, day after day, for thirty days, shrinking the grape-sized nodules to tapioca. But at what cost? The hair that was sparsely growing back has been reduced to fuzz, finer than what you would feel on a newborn's head. Her skin has grown flaky, her face puffy, her mouth dry. The point is not that this might extend her life a few months. The expectation is that she will not lose her mind before she runs out of breath. My love wants to be fully conscious to the end. She will witness the mystery in its splendor.

Lavinia

i.

When I was eight

I had a vocation.

Scribbling under the covers
while my morning brother slept,
very close, in his own bed,

I was no longer tongue-tied,
having become, pronounced I,
with the authority that only a child

should be allowed,
a Poet.

Absent my pen I was incomplete
without Brother and Yzzie,
blissful bitter three.

I was not
as comfortable feet on the ground
as I was with a notebook up in a tree.

ii.

When I was nine

serious face shadowed eyes,

was I in love with my lithe best friend,
long-limbed Yzzie whose sleeping hair
smelled warm and rich in our shared rest?

I had no words for the bonheur I touched.

Did she love me as much?

iii.

> *When I was fourteen,*
> *I married, my lord, you.*
>   «The river-merchant's wife, a letter»
>   —Ezra Pound / Li Po

No, no, I did not, at fourteen

marry anyone, nor did I marry, at sixteen,
the single most-loved man on planet earth.
But I was sixteen when I met him.

A poor actor with a good voice,
I did not get leading roles,
but I did kiss Jordi on stage in a mad play,
tongue and all,
his first wife (a half-dozen years my senior
and just delivered of their second child) in the front row.

How our parts would change! Little did we know
as our tongues converged.

iv.

> *Blown hair is sweet*
> *Brown hair over the mouth blown*
> *Lilacs and brown hair*
> —T.S. Eliot

At seventeen I turned my back

on my hard-won cool
for ecstatic love with a boy my age.
He would leave my country in one short year.

I wore no color but white white white
to celebrate the purity of repudiated virginity.

I did not fear my megacity but walked
on strong feet, bare,
with a fleshy white carnation
in my heavy long brown hair.

v.

Close close to sixty

(devoutly desired) I'm living my most gorgeous time—
head shaved for Ruthie Lee's fine hand,

under constellcancer, bright laughing with friends,

with all my staff-of-life music and song
always winging inside my head,
with the planet's most loved lovely man in my bed

I fear no night noise, no nightmare,
fear nothing and nobody living or dead,
but needles and seizures and medical glare
curdle my calmness now and again.

A sword-swinging singing angel in flight
I surf, as long as the curl can hold,
the wave that will glide my
sun, moon, and stars, my foam and my light
through my stellar life
to galactical night.

Marcial

She's obsessed with dying. And Jordi is to blame because he humors her and applauds her morbid poetry. She should be praying for life instead of romanticizing death. Since she would not answer our phone calls, it was time her brother and I paid her a visit. We would not be pushed away at the door if we came to wish her well.

I thought she would be glad to see us, but instead she acted as if she didn't know why we were there. And then she fell asleep. Jordi tried to explain that she slept much of the time, that her body required it. He tried to explain that when she declined our calls it was because conversation and visits proved to be exhausting. She was marshaling her strength by avoiding a drain on her reserves. How could the people that she loved be a drag on her vitality? Quite the opposite I would think.

Still, we were not about to give up. We landed in Minneapolis around 6:00 and it was already dark as midnight, cold and with snow flurries swirling in the wind. We were not dressed for winter in this tundra, a strange place for her to make her home for the past twenty some years, and we shivered in our light jackets until we climbed into the back seat of an overheated taxi driven by a negro man with an accent. An African, not an American, and he had no idea where he was going after we gave him the address of the Shanti House Hospice. Luis had to relay the directions from his phone GPS. Imagine that, a cab driver without a map.

Shanti House is a dull place, all blonde woods and muted tones on walls, carpeting, furniture, and art. Lavinia's kind of environment. Nothing that would shout or moan or wail. It was not, however, a welcoming place for us. The resident in room 108 was not receiving visitors without prior approval.

After we persuaded the head nurse to let us in because we had come all the way from Mexico, her father and brother—not casual visitors— we found ourselves in a stifling room where the heat had been turned up to compensate for the chilling of the patient's body. Skeptical of this explanation, I placed my hand over hers to send my warmth through her skin. Reacting to my touch, she exhaled as if to release a long-held breath and opened her eyes. I was uncertain during those first moments if she was seeing anything. But gradually she seemed to recognize me, not with a smile as I would have liked but with a focusing of her gaze, no expression beyond a quizzical blinking as if questioning that she was seeing clearly, wondering why I was hovering at the side of her bed.

My son Luis stood beside me, but I could feel him shuffling his feet as if all the effort to make it to this room, to this bed, had been wasted and there was no reason for us to be here. He wanted a reaction from his sister, an acknowledgement that we were there for her, and that she welcomed our presence. I knew this because I wanted the same thing. If not gratitude, at least a faint smile. And I found myself resenting this lack of generosity, as if the dying could afford to be cold and unforgiving.

Not that I need your forgiveness, you sanctimonious child of mine. It was your mother who left me. Many times over the years, to go back to her former lover in Minnesota. And then when things with that unhappy drunk grew difficult, she would return to me, exhausted. In those cases I was always the forgiver.

Unlike your brother, who resented her frequent absences and was threatening to cut out his navel in denial of his birth by her, you somehow seemed to blame me, even though I was clearly the innocent one. And when I tried to explain my side to you, thinking that even at age fifteen you would understand, your reaction was to run off and disappear into friends' houses.

Other families were eager to draw you in, so admired for your maturity and intelligence. You started seeing boys I did not approve of, not because they were brown and from humble origins, that was not it at all. They were not the sort of companions who deserved your finer qualities. The idea of their hands over you was revolting, especially when a housekeeper discovered condoms in your dresser while she was putting away your laundry. No, she was not snooping, but I did reward her with a few pesos when she brought the things to my attention. She started spying when she realized that your shabby little secrets were valued. Even while I was away during the day, and sometimes even for a week on business trips, I had a report of your visitors, phone calls, late nights.

And the more you retreated the more urgently I tried to defend myself against your mother's actions. How could you not see that I was able to hold on to my dignity in spite of being played a fool? Not an easy role for a man in our country.

And then, you went to your English teacher, Miss Delius. Your mother was on one of her escapades to Minnesota and you found in Esther Delius a refuge. Her apartment was your home after school, her company a source of sympathy. You were hardly around after you two became friends, always phoning at the last minute that you were staying at Esther's for dinner, that you were going to a movie and that you'd be late, that she was tutoring you on the weekend in preparation for Monday classes. I knew about women like Esther Delius, even if you didn't because, frankly, you hadn't been exposed to some of the marginal predators in our midst. Unmarried, childless, plain in dress and appearance, and with a haircut that looked chopped with garden shears, she was clearly warped.

Then, you came home one night and announced that henceforth you were to be called Vin, her preferred nickname for you.

II

Lavinia

Oh, Father. I know you are here before you speak, that particular smell of yours, the Brut cologne, as if by endowing it with a French name it could achieve a higher level of sophistication. A fragrance so old-fashioned nobody in the US uses it anymore but which is still popular in Mexico, a cloying blend of overripe citrus and clove. A recipe for headache. But a scent familiar to me from the tin medallions that dangled from the rearview mirrors in taxicabs.

And so I keep my eyes shut, my breathing even, feigning sleep, although that is close to reality as I'm often too exhausted to rise to the social demands of my father hovering by the bed. If I did not want to speak, I would not. As simple as that. Those that are about to die need not salute you. Uninvited means unwelcome, so dear Daddy, please go.

And as if to make the point I must've drifted off again. For a minute or an hour, hard to tell in my present state. And here you are again, silent and persistent, knowing that eventually I will have to acknowledge you. Truly, you suck the air out of my space. I can barely muster the breath I need to whisper a greeting.

"Pa-pá," pops across my lips.

You reply with my name and some pleasantry, which I cannot hear. These days people need to shout in my ear to break through, as I rise in awareness through the dream and reverie of pharmaceutical fog. I no longer know how they are doping me, drips to relax and muffle anxiety and push pain away toward a distant shore, medicine that numbs my mouth and chokes my words with cotton.

I want to please you, as I always did through my life at home, even when Mother kept leaving, time and again, and I was the number one female in the family, outranking the housekeeper or the occasional friend you invited over as if to audition for a role. I can even now remember the names of a few who were clearly finalists and who went out of their way to befriend me.

There was Sarah-Jean with her southern ways and steely heart, quick to sing my praises and eager to disparage Mother—no self-respecting woman abandons her children to such an incompetent father. She taught me to make cornbread. I remember other things about her, that she shopped for your clothes and had you wearing wide ties with prints of petunias on steroids. And for every tie she bought you, there had to be a little something for her, maybe shoes or a blouse. I could see you behaving like a silly man with a prize to show off.

She liked white wine, but it had to be "Blanc de Blancs," though it wasn't really French, and you gave up rum and Cokes to keep up with her. She came over for dinner every day, sometimes to eat at home, at others you two went out on the town. She eventually left after you argued with her about money, that she was costing a fortune. I think you resented that she never spent the night. Of course, she was taking advantage of you. I could've told you that, but I was only sixteen, not qualified to offer such opinions.

Mother left five times before she was gone for good. And each time you moped around the house, feeling sorry for yourself at the huge injustice that was being done to you. I wanted to sympathize, but the anger that simmered underneath your sense of victimhood found a target in me and Luis. We weren't to blame, but you resented that she burdened you with us when you were woefully incapable of dealing with our assertive personalities. What to do with Luis's smoking? His borderline academics? His pathetic hygiene, so that at thirteen he smelled like a dog? And green moss grew on his teeth from lack of brushing.

I, on the other hand, was the perfect daughter. I was a poet, an artist, a compulsive reader, a budding guitar player, a playwright and actor. I was the organizer of the school's creative festivals. Unelected, because I cared about art more than anyone else. The teachers at the International School loved me. Particularly, Miss Delius. Esther as I called her, at her insistence, during our get-togethers after school. Our teatime conversations, our visits to galleries, concerts, movies, and lectures, all sparked a deepening friendship.

It's hard to tell who chose whom, who was the seducer and who the victim, if I can use that word, for want of one that would define the passive recipient of pleasure and friendship. To this day, I know that I used every opportunity to attract Miss Delius's attention. I focused my attention on her lectures, responding with quick nods to every point she made, smiling at her quiet jokes, raising my hand to answer a question directed to the class. I was her star pupil. She was my star teacher. We fed on Earl Grey tea and butter cookies and soft cheeses. I fell in love with Shakespeare, Leonard Cohen, Mary Shelley, T.S. Elliot, Sylvia Plath, and with Esther Delius.

I admired Esther's sense of style and started dressing like her. I chopped off my hair into a spiky punk look. One time, when she was dropping me off at the house after a late concert downtown, my father noticed our Grateful Dead T-shirts, but he said nothing at first. She had walked me to the door but instead of shaking my hand like she usually did, she bowed to kiss me on the cheek. The sensation of her cool lips pressing on my face brought out a small gasp.

The next morning was a Saturday. Over breakfast, Father let me know that our friendship was problematic. There are boundaries between adults and teenagers, between teacher and student, which Miss Delius had obviously crossed. He wanted to know if she always kissed me. I said that was the first time, but after that she continued, just a peck goodnight after our dates, as I called our get togethers. And sometimes during the weekend, if we hadn't seen each other in class since Friday, a light hug and a kiss, that was all. I didn't see the problem; women in Mexico kissed hello and goodbye all the time.

If I insisted on seeing Esther Delius outside of class, Father would need to inquire with the school principal if such a relationship was allowed, a personal friendship with romantic overtones. I pleaded with him to stay out of my life. I was scared for Esther because I had seen what happened to teachers when the administrators decided to persecute them. But the more I argued with father that Esther was my friend and that was all, the more persistent his dislike.

I think he resented her because she became a replacement for Mother, my clinging to her instead of growing closer to him. At first I was so taken with her, the things she said in class, her encouraging comments on the margins of my papers, that I kept bringing her up. Miss Delius this and Miss Delius that. And then, after the semester was half over, he told me he was tired of hearing about her. He refused to even use her name, calling her instead *that teacher.* Her name is Miss Delius, I insisted, and she's OK with my calling her Esther, outside of class.

If Father had visions of us rolling around on the couch, he was seriously misguided. Esther was too much in control to give in to such idiocy. I was seventeen, and soon we had an unspoken understanding, we would be platonic friends until I graduated. There was no denying the energy that coursed between us, but there would be no harm in our being friends. I believed that. She wasn't so sure. She started to pull away when she became aware of my father's disapproval.

She set out to explain calmly and objectively that people would judge our friendship according to their own perverse natures and that there was nothing we could do to show that they were wrong. You can prove that something is, but not that something is not.

I remember our last meeting. There was a show of pre-Raphaelites at one of the museums and I had insisted that we see it because the women in those portraits reminded me of her, the melancholy eyes, and the pallid, almost translucent skin. I was looking forward to later stopping at her apartment for tea and conversation, but she insisted on driving me straight home. It was in the car, when she parked a block from my house and shut off the engine, that she informed me we would not be seeing each other again. Not outside the classroom. I was hearing her words but hardly registering the full impact of their meaning. It all seemed to be part of a lovers' routine, the ebb and flow of a relationship, the cold and hot, the push and pull.

It took a while for reality to sink in, especially after exams when we were not meeting as a class anymore. School let out a week later and she was gone, without a word or a glance, back to Boston for the summer. Not a note or a call or a letter. And I was sick with a queasy feeling in my stomach and a pain in my chest that saw no relief for days.

I was a senior in September and I harbored the illusion that in just nine months I would graduate and Esther and I could get together. I was not scheduled for any of her classes, so it took a few days to realize she was not back at the International School. The administration would not give me any information beyond that she had decided to stay in the US and continue with grad school. I had not heard from her during the summer and now she was fading without a word.

I had hoped that with the return to classes, Esther would at least be part of my life, even if at a distance. Meanwhile, as I faced the reality of her absence in the new term, I retreated into a dark and airless place. I slept for hours during the day, waking only to attend classes and grind my way through the minimum required to keep up. As a senior my class load was light. I spent my waking hours writing poetry, filling tiny black notebooks with my tight, nearly illegible handwriting in a kind of code for my eyes only. The pain at the center of my chest made every breath painful, words choked at the source.

Still, I managed to put up a front for my father and for Luis. Only Paquita, the housekeeper, knew that I hardly ate, unable to hide the revulsion that meat of any kind caused me. I successfully hid my distaste for food by feeding pieces from my plate to our dog Lobo who quickly learned to wait under the table for the tidbits he knew were coming his way. And that's how I became a lifelong vegetarian, not out of health or humanitarian reasons at first, but as the result of a broken heart.

Knowing that Esther had most likely stayed on the East Coast, I applied to colleges in New England. I was accepted at Harvard and my father couldn't argue with a member of the family attending a prestigious university, even though he suspected I was fleeing east to pursue Esther. I did not imagine at the time, when we eventually reconnected, that my relationship with Esther would have a violent end that to this day, forty years later, causes me grief and horror and unabated remorse.

It's easier now to locate someone. Scroll, click, and bang! In those days it took poring through phone books and University rosters plus many dead-end phone calls, my search stymied because no one by the name Esther Delius existed. There were over a hundred women called Esther, so I was forced to narrow down the search through her first name. All those Esthers in Boston and surrounding towns made for slow going.

Through considerable sleuthing, I did find her in the English department at Lesley College right in Cambridge where E. Greenwood, once Esther Delius, taught in the English Department.

It took several weeks before we met. I recognized her right away. I guessed she couldn't see my face as I huddled inside a hooded parka. Meanwhile, I spied, figured out her route on the red line, timed my walks across the square with her own, sometimes actually passing close enough to whisper to her as she went one way and I walked in the opposite direction.

She was consistently on campus three times a week on an identical schedule, and so I organized my life around her morning routine. For a while I was content to be secretly aware of her presence and found in my stealth a sense of power. By observing her without her knowledge I gloried in a kind of dominance I had never enjoyed over her.

She had changed her appearance, no longer bohemian, more stylish in the conventional sense, with a tailored coat that came to her mid-calf, and a matching knit scarf and tam that framed her face, allowing a few burnished curls to spill out. I so wished I could see her with long hair, but the context in which I observed her was limited. She carried a stuffed messenger bag slung from one shoulder and walked with purposeful strides, never in a hurry, but always with the sense that she had no time to waste. I recognized that look on her face, the furrowed brow, the pursed lips, her mind churning in preparation for the day's lectures.

I grew bolder as weeks passed. I neglected my own studies in order to be in the vicinity of Lesley College, hoping to catch sight of her as she went out for lunch or headed to the train at the end of the day. Her life was orderly, with no hint of the spontaneity that had guided her days and nights in Mexico.

I intuited that she could not be happy. I pictured Dr. Greenwood, a gynecologist according to my research, a puffy-faced scold in a lab coat, older and humorless and perhaps unable to look upon his wife with any kind of sensuality. I recoiled at the thought of his fingers itching for the speculum he used to peer into vaginas.

As luck would have it, I grew careless in my quest to know more about dear Esther Delius, now Professor E. Greenwood.

Esther

What had I created? This smart, spirited girl had been hovering on the edges of my awareness at every turn. It took a couple of sightings before I was certain that the young woman that made me think of Vin was indeed her. I might have guessed that, from the first time I became aware of her, sitting on a bench outside Crimson Café near Harvard Square. Her head was buried in a hoodie. But she was holding a copy of Virginia Woolf's *The Waves* as if to flag my attention.

I resisted my initial impulse to run to her. I wondered how long she'd been near me, stalking me actually, rather than simply announcing her presence. Certainly, she had put in some effort in locating me. Well, if she was playing a game, I would play as well.

I made a note of every time I spotted her. In our game, I made believe I didn't see her, just concentrating on class notes or the pages of some journal, and she made believe she was not shadowing me. We kept this up for weeks. Occasionally, some days would go by and I would think that she had gone, her curiosity satisfied. Then, unexpectedly, she would be riding the red line a few seats behind me, following me all the way to Summerville. But staying put, not getting off at my stop.

Her following me was frustrating because she was out of my range of vision, and I couldn't get a good look at her. If I caught a glimpse, then I had to rely on my memory to fill in the details of her face—a serious expression, pursed lips as if always in deep thought, considering and weighing grave matters of ethics and morality. I like to think that being with me released a happier side of her, allowing a sparkle in her green eyes, and in an explosion of mirth, a loud laugh.

It was her complex personality that first attracted me, even more than her incisive wit and sensitivity to language and ideas. She had this curious ability to find depth in the mundane, in the glimpse of a bird's flight or a phrase in a pop song. And there was her response to my hand, so that even the lightest touch would elicit a small gasp hardly louder than a whisper.

At first I was determined to wait her out. I would not say anything to her until she spoke to me. I expected that she would give up chasing me and settle into the everyday life of an undergraduate, find friends, a society of poets or musicians, maybe romance.

But then, on a winter evening, already dark by six, I was on the train home when she got on board. She must've walked the length of several cars until she found my row and sat beside me, her head still buried inside the hoodie that had become her uniform. As soon as I spotted her walking toward me I slouched down on my seat and concentrated on a book. I barely stirred when I felt her near me, pulling my arm close to my side. I was going to read until she decided to break the silence she had cultivated for the past few weeks.

"It's me," she murmured.

"I know."

"You've known for a while?"

"Yes."

"So, will you pretend to keep reading?"

I closed the book and for the first time turned to her. She lifted the hood off her face. We looked at each other with something like wonder, as if facing a friend that we had thought absent from our lives.

"Now what?" I said.

"You disappeared without a word. Did you mean to stay gone forever?"

"Forever is a long time."

"Till when, then?"

"I knew you would find me when you wanted to. And now here you are."

"I can go, if that's what you want." Her hands rested on her lap, and I reached over and placed my own over hers.

"Don't go."

We rode the rest of the trip in silence, our breaths short at first then gradually lengthening as a sense of peace came over us.

"We'll have tea. Like old times."

Lavinia

Sinking into the cushions of a blue velvet sofa I was content again. In the home that was rich with her presence. I had missed the sound of her voice, a deep and silky murmur that was like singing in my ears. Her husband worked late hours and was not expected back soon.

I listened as Esther moved about in the adjacent kitchen, catching glimpses of her as she filled the kettle then carried it to the stove, reached for the matching mugs with the Picasso dove drawings, and scooped tea into a blue pot. So much of Esther's world was blue.

The kettle whistled and Esther poured the water over the loose leaves. She placed a crocheted cozy over the pot and carried it to the parlor. She sat close beside me and we both stared at the pot as if willing the Earl Grey to steep faster. She was particular about tea but rather than rely on a timer she let her inner clock signal readiness.

The quiet of our meeting was animated with her many questions. I had Esther's undivided attention. I rushed to tell her that I was at Harvard majoring in English. Her hum of approval made me happy; I was still her student. I held the mug in both hands, letting its warmth radiate up my arms and, very precisely, right to my heart.

She wanted to know how my senior year had gone, whether I had continued to write and perform, if I had made peace with my father, if Luis had straightened out. I gloried in her interest, gave reports and relayed news, promised to show her my new poems.

And I asked about her life. She seemed reticent, unwilling to reveal more than superficial details. Yes, she'd been married about a year, having met Larry Greenwood soon after she returned from Mexico. He worked in Boston, was kind and generous, if not with his time, certainly with his wealth. He was often away for conferences and such.

"He's good friend," she said.

"And husband?"

"Well, yes, of course."

"A good one?" I insisted.

"Sure. He's attentive, and sweet. He's my husband."

And suddenly, in her quiet, uncommitted reply I sensed an opening. If she had been the instigator of our relationship back on Mexico, I could now take the lead.

"Do you have a boyfriend, too?" I tried to make the question sound lighthearted, a gentle tease between friends. "Or maybe a girlfriend?" I felt gradually in control.

"Haven't you become the nosy one?" She tried to laugh off the subject, but I persisted.

"Seriously."

"Oh, no boyfriends or girlfriends. Does that answer your question?"

I was not about to let her loose. "Halfway, actually."

"Meaning?"

"That you don't have someone to play with, doesn't mean you wouldn't like to."

"You think intimacy is play?"

"You know what I meant."

She shrugged. "Anything else you want to know?"

"Oh, Miss Esther. We have so much catching up to do."

I placed the tips of my fingers lightly on her wrist and drew small circles with the index. She slipped off my touch by reaching for the cup, and held it with both hands, even though the tea had grown tepid. A faint but discernible line had been crossed, and I was content for both of us to sit in silence, our hands and lips occupied with the sipping of tea.

Outside, the sun had gone down and the glow from a streetlight was all that illuminated the room. She started to rise from the couch to switch on the adjacent floor lamp, but I reached for her hand and pulled her back down to sit beside me. She allowed her hand to remain lifeless in my grasp, unresponsive to a meaningful press of my fingers, letting their slight pressure whisper the question that was begging inside me.

Finally, the words choking in my throat, I broke the silence. "Can't we be friends like we used to be?"

"We were never friends like you thought."

"But only because I was your student. I loved you. Anyone could see that."

"That was a problem."

"And you loved me."

"I cared for you. I admired your talent."

"You know there was more to it than that."

"Yes, but what you thought would happen when we finally met, after stalking me for weeks, is not going to happen."

I went back to my room in the dorm and slept in the next day. It was a good space for sleep, with small windows and blinds to block out the light. When I finally rose in the evening, after twenty-four hours out, I ate three bowls of sugary cereal and went back to bed.

My roommates thought I had the flu and stayed out of my way. They were a studious bunch so I was able to sleep undisturbed. When I did occasionally wake up it was with a feeling of such sadness that my eyes were crusted it over with dried tears. The only relief was to curl up in the dark and wait for sleep again.

I kept this up for weeks, occasionally rousing myself for class and to study, but spending the time I would have enjoyed socializing, in sleep. I seemed to have forgotten to eat and the idea of food gagged me. I declined invitations to hang out with my house mates who quickly became bored with worrying about my health, even as the pounds melted away and I became a kind of waif.

Eventually I grew tired of my own grief. I felt as I'd suddenly woken up from a long sleep and decided to embrace life again. I studied, and ran, and shopped for new clothes. I'd had enough of pining over lost love like a pathetic drama queen. I decided I would become a boy.

Esther

The next time I saw Vin was a chance encounter during a Grateful Dead concert. She had cut her hair short, cute like a boy's, and I barely recognized her from the back of her head as we stood just a few feet from the stage.

My husband had gone to one of his conferences, and I was free to indulge my taste for rock 'n' roll without lying. My rigid routine of teaching and wifeing demanded release. I'd dug up a skirt and peasant blouse from my days in Mexico. The loose flow of the bright cotton felt liberating, unbound from the bra and pantyhose that I wore under my serious clothes.

It had been some weeks since I'd had tea with Vin, and that moment had stuck with me as some persistent dream that cannot be quite forgotten or dismissed. I kept the back of her head in sight even as she drifted along with the crowd. I wondered if she would sense my closeness. She had grown thin, and in her jeans and T-shirt she looked like a boy, except for her graceful dancing which was a kind of self-absorbed bobbing and twirling to the Dead.

I followed her into the crowd until I was dancing near her, close enough that I could feel her stirring my skirt. She must've felt it too because she stopped suddenly and turned toward me. She couldn't hear me above the music but could see me mouth her name, Lavinia. And she broke into a wide grin.

We tried to speak but the words were lost in the noise of the crowd and the band. We moved to the beat together in a kind of shuffling dance and eventually pushed our way through the massed crowd to one of the exits. We laughed with relief once we were out in the street.

Lavinia

I should've been born a boy. I envied their energy, their freedom to dress however they wanted, without trying to simultaneously hide and show off their vulnerability—breasts, pubis, ass. They could have hair all over their body. They were allowed to fart and curse and burp, and laugh about it as if they had displayed some clever trick. I wanted to emulate their rough physicality with each other, scuffling and rough-housing as part of the games they were learning. I too wanted to play soccer, wrestle, trade punches.

I looked at myself in the mirror and marveled at my slight body, tender breasts the shape and size of peach halves, my bubble butt, and legs firm from running. I finally felt happy with myself. I wore boy's shorts, snug bell bottoms, shirts unbuttoned down to my breastbone. And I let my underarms and my legs go feral, with hair so silky it was a revelation. I felt downright revolutionary. And free of an annoying obligation.

I was the most attractive I had ever been in my life. I embraced promiscuity. I gloried in the knowledge that I attracted men and women. I thrived in the novelty, the release and purging of my stagnant obsession with Esther Delius.

My seminar on modernist literature was a place of reliable delight, rejoicing in the ideas and shenanigans of the brilliant professor who made the Bloomsbury group come to life, especially Virginia and Vita. I envied and yearned for the power in their uncompromised passion for each other. "I am reduced to a thing that wants

Virginia . . . It is incredible how essential to me you have become," wrote Vita to Virginia Woolf.

The class was taught by an elfin professor, who looked too young to be already tenured at Harvard. He favored flowery shirts and green velvet pants and, fancying himself a kind of sage, would sit cross legged on the desktop and smoke cigarettes, blowing circles whenever one of the class struggled with the task of making some bit of analysis that failed to impress him. I almost made him choke on his smoke when I interrupted one of his meandering musings on Orlando with a crisp, "Excuse me!"

He fixed me with a steely gaze and waited for me to go on. "You were about to say something, Miss Aguilar?"

It was the custom for professors to address students by their last names, in the spirit of serious collegiality. But our professor encouraged us to call him Lonny. Loony, we used to refer to him among ourselves.

"Sorry, Dr. Evans, I was just thinking, and a thought spilled out."

"Must've been a deep thought."

"I do have them."

"Please share," he said, shaping a perfect smoke ring that traveled the still air of the room toward me.

"Only that I'm not sure a male can fully grasp the shading of love and physicality between two women."

"By physicality, of course, you must mean sex."

"Yes."

"Well, it's not a subject I want to fully amuse the group with at this time." He paused to blow another ring. "See me after class."

He was the first professor at Harvard that supposedly seduced me. I say supposedly because I'm not sure who had the upper hand in our shabby transgression. Lonny Evans thought he would prove something to me about the shadings of touch and breath. I had no trouble accepting his invitation that evening for dinner, an easy gambit for a student on a limited budget. I ordered lobster. And he instructed me on how to use nutcrackers to liberate the flesh inside the claws; it was my first. I thought it was rubbery, so I took some home in a bag and fed it to one of the cats that hung out by the dining hall. The white wine was good, and helped me relax once we ended up at his apartment off Brattle Square. And so Dr. Lonny Evans set out to disprove my point about men being incapable of making love like a girl.

I did have hopes for a good fuck. He was lean and smooth of skin and he smelled nice. His erect prick was not imposing, but still respectable. He started to entertain me with his tongue and kept it up, lapping as if upon a scoop of ice cream, without his tongue finding its way to my sweet spot. I grew impatient and pulled him on top of me.

"What's the matter?"

"Nothing. You're better off doing what a man does."

"I thought girls like oral."

"Oh, we do." I didn't tell him that he should figure out where the clitoris was. They have books with diagrams for that. Or to shave his face the next time.

"You did get wet."

"It's OK. I like dick."

He seemed grateful to get off the hook. And relieved that I declined his next dinner invitation after class the following week. I was not looking for a boyfriend. I was enjoying the spontaneity of the zipless fuck, as Erica Jong put it.

And what a time it was. The Pill innoculated us against the consequences of semen spurting like so much hot lava. And the mess that men made did not require much cleanup beyond a handful of Kleenex and a bath.

Occasionally a quick encounter after a concert would threaten to escalate, and some guy overpowered with gratitude and a taste for the androgynous would decide he was in love. I would find that funny, and a sarcastic cackle was enough to discourage even the most ardent courtship. It was different with women. It wasn't until I rediscovered Esther, that I experienced lust turning into worship.

In those days the Grateful Dead played Cambridge every month. Their meandering riffs punctuated by Jerry Garcia's sweet tenor were an ongoing soundtrack to life outside the classroom. It was easy on a whim to rustle ten dollars and find a kind of church in the massed bodies inside the Boston Garden. If the classroom was cold and competitive, there was a sense of the crowd pushing and drawing me like a warm bath. The closer to the stage the more engulfing the sensation of being unable to move or hardly breathe, a clear surrender to the consciousness of the herd. My words were unsung. I was Casey Jones watching my speed. I was Althea. I was not Vin. My heartbeat was in sync with the two hammering drum kits, a magical overkill pounding an ecstatic blood flow.

And then as the crowd swelled and flowed around me, I became aware of her. A swirl of pink and blue out of the corner of my eye. Then the brush of fabric on my bare arm. And a familiar scent. Esther Delius.

I turned and she raised her arms to embrace me, then withdrew them as if suddenly changing her mind. She tried to say something above the music, seeming suddenly agitated, speaking and gesturing as the words were lost in the noise. She tried yelling, but I could only make out one word on her mouth.

"Out," she repeated.

I nodded eagerly, then turned toward an exit sign to one side of the stage. She followed close behind as I pushed and nudged in front of her, getting swallowed up again by the audience. The crowd was a fleshy wall, a breathing barrier that pushed back, unwilling to let me pass, then closing and shutting Esther off behind me. I had to stop and reach out for her to grasp my hand so I could pull her toward me. I kept mumbling apologies but the press of bodies against me, a kind of massive stew, was unyielding. The close reek of sweat and patchouli and pot were making me gag. Finally, I put my arm around Esther's shoulders, hugging her close so that we could push a way through the crowd as one double-headed organism. Meanwhile the music banged on, the crowd singing along with the familiar lyrics, Jerry's lilting voice floating above the din.

And then, suddenly, I was breathing outside air. We had tumbled out of the hall into an alley, fragrant with the smells of garbage and tar and grease from the back of a fast-food place. Potatoes in boiling grease had never been so enticing.

This time Esther took the lead, taking my hand and guiding me to the corner of the alley. From there it would be a couple of blocks to the train. And still, we had not said a word. We stood on the platform facing the tracks, the bare moist skin on our upper arms touching, yet our hands loose by our sides.

I can't remember when we actually looked at each other, possibly once we left the station. The car was half empty and we were able to find seats facing each other. Her face glowed pink and glistened with sweat, and then her mouth shaped into a slight smile as her eyes finally locked with mine. As if on cue, we both made small shrugs as if to say: *well, here we are again.*

"You look good," I said.

"You look nice," she said. "Thinner. I miss your long hair. It took me a while to recognize you in the crowd. You looked like a boy. A cute boy."

"And you look like an earth mother, with the big skirt and the peasant blouse."

"It's my outfit for when the doctor is away."

"What do you wear when he's home?"

"Anything."

"So, I won't get to meet him?"

"You don't want that."

"You mean, you don't want him to meet me."

"Also true."

That was all the conversation until we got to her stop, and walked the six blocks to her house in Summerville. We avoided the chintzy living room and went right to the kitchen, all intimidating appliances, a hardwood floor, and bar stools at a granite counter.

"Iced tea? Coffee? Wine?"

"A shower maybe?"

"For sure."

Esther

It was past midnight by the time I sent her home in a taxi. After her shower she wrapped herself in one of my robes, a purple velvet number with a hood that engulfed her from head to toe. She sat on one end of the sofa and I on the other, our legs stretched out, feet touching at the center of an ottoman.

I waited some time before reaching to open the robe and reveal the waif she had become, almost too tender to touch. The truth is that we had never been sexual with each other, even as we were both aware of the undercurrent between us. Fear and caution had prevailed. As my student back in Mexico the consequences of a relationship would have been devastating for me. And as we grew closer, and our friendship became increasingly public, I got out in the nick of time, one whisper ahead of the lynch mob.

I feel guilty that I never tried to explain my sudden disappearance. I underestimated her attachment to our friendship. After all, she was well liked by all the teachers and had many friends her own age. She was the star of the literary salon, the theater workshop, the arts festival. Thinking back, I'm flattered that she chose me. It had been her decision, a kind of courtship where she adopted me as her favorite teacher.

I was proud of her getting into Harvard, and proud of myself, taking some credit for having nurtured her analytical talents. My first impulse was to contact her and welcome her to Cambridge, just as I would any former student. I held back, not sure I wanted to ignite that spark again. Still, the possibility of seeing her again itched in my brain. I rehearsed sending a cheerful note or bumping into her on campus. In the end I waited for her to find me.

And tonight, I was practically in tears as Vin released the belt on the robe. I sat on the edge of the sofa and helped her lie back, her skin so white almost translucent against the deep purple of the velvet. Her right palm covered her pubis with only a shadow of down visible between her thumb and index. I brushed my fingertips past her knuckles up to her wrist. I lowered my head and lightly kissed the back of her hand. It was only a matter of minutes, I knew, before she would move her hand.

Later, I pulled her clean jeans and T-shirt out of the drier, folded them and placed them at the foot of the sofa. She dressed quickly. And when the taxi honked outside, she kissed my lips, I squeezed her hand, and she was gone. We made no date as to when we would meet again.

Lavinia

Esther Delius brought me back from the realm of the sleeping dead. It was around one AM when I reached my dorm, and it took hours for me to fall asleep, I was so rattled. Still, I was up by 7:00 and ready for class by 8:30. I hadn't eaten anything at Esther's the previous night. We did have tea and she brought out some scones, but the tea went cold and the scones uneaten. Now, as I stacked my plate in the cafeteria with eggs and hash browns and pancakes and milky coffee, I was taking on fuel for the adventure ahead.

I took my place up front in Lonny Evans' class, as he embarked on another of his musings on the nature of poetic, platonic love. Such bullshit, I thought to myself. He must've read my face because he suddenly gifted me with a smirk. Of course, he added, sometimes the poetic bypasses Plato's ideal and skates right into the carnal.

"You wish," I murmured. But then the class spilled with light laughter and I realized my words had been overheard. I realized I must've embarrassed Dr. Evans because he changed the subject. We would now discuss the political climate surrounding the emergence of the Bloomsbury group. Yawn.

I rushed back to my room and checked my answering machine. I knew there would be a message from Esther, I just knew.

"Don't hide again. Husband still away, free tonight. I'm done with class at six. Be at Lesley?"

For the first time in recent memory I was at a loss, as the time approached for my first real date with Esther Delius. Maybe the previous night had been some kind of reckless impulse but whatever might happen between us tonight would be consciously deliberate. Previously, I had been content to lay back and let her take charge. This time I wanted, earnestly, to please her.

I skipped my next two classes and went back to my dorm. I kept looking at the clock and tried to will myself into taking a nap. I had barely slept the previous night and a snooze now would make the time go faster. Sleep had always been a good escape for me whenever I needed to check out. I set the alarm for five.

I showered. And I spent several minutes looking at my body in the mirror trying to decide whether to shave. Oh, such a momentous decision! I saw last night that Esther was carefully groomed. No hairy armpits, no furry legs. I wanted to be like her, as when I had first followed her intellectual lead in high school.

I looked through my closet and landed on my one dress, blue

high-buttoned, belted in back, that I wore at the occasional high tea the English faculty gave for students. I was a hippie throwback in those days, but I was also flexible when it came to future career recommendations. Yes, I could be a nice woman. In any case, with my slight body and short hair I looked like a boy in a dress, and that was surely a subversive look. And I did not wear panties. The brush of soft cotton fabric on my ass and pussy gave me a secret tingle that nobody could see. But that I knew Esther would sense.

By six I had been waiting for twenty minutes on a bench on the small green square beside the entrance to Lesley. I had Woolf's Mrs. Dalloway open but was not reading; it was more of a prop to keep me from looking like some lost waif. Cambridge is such a studious town that to be alone reading a book at a park or a coffee shop is an invitation to conversation. That's sometimes a good thing. And that's how I met Jason Loomis, who claimed to know the novel, even though the chemistry students at MIT were not known for their literary inclinations.

"You know, she kills herself."

"Another character does, a depressed war veteran."

"Some woman does, anyway."

"Not Mrs. Dalloway."

"Yes, she filled her dress with rocks and walked into the river."

I sighed and took a long look at this guy. He was handsome, with a head of unruly curly black hair. "Do you know how dumb you sound?"

"OK. Who killed herself?"

"The author."

"Really? Why?"

"Because not enough people read her books."

"OK, you got me. Why so dressed up sitting alone on a Saturday night?"

"I have an appointment with Dr. Delius, a professor at Lesley."

And, as if she had heard her name in cue, I felt Esther come up and sit beside me on the bench.

"Who's your friend?" And yes, I was pleased to hear an edge of jealousy in her voice.

"I'm Jason Loomis," he grinned in his vaguely awkward way.

"Jason is a student at MIT, chemistry," I said.

"And interested in literature too?" Esther said.

"Oh yes," I said, "starting about ten minutes ago."

"Must begin sometime," Jason stammered. "Can't just be practical all the time."

"So you know some practical things to do with chemistry?" Esther said.

"You'd be surprised, but that's a topic for another time."

"That means you're leaving us?"

"Yes, but I'll see you again," he said directly to me.

"Something you look forward to?" Esther murmured after he was gone.

"Not at all," I said. I meant it at the time.

Suddenly, she stood up and started briskly towards the train station. "Serious dress," she said when I caught up with her. I couldn't tell whether she was earnest or ironic. Often the case with Esther Delius. I was pleased she noticed. I craved her attention more than her approval.

We didn't speak much on the way to her house. And then we were very domestic. I helped with the salad while she taught me that it was not about the vinegar but the good olive oil and sea salt. Also to tear the lettuce in small pieces. That's how you can tell a woman made the salad not a man. She put out a cheese board: port salut, brie, drunken goat, and some nice crackers and berries scattered throughout. And a few pieces of dark chocolate. A bottle of pinot grigio stayed in the fridge.

This time we went to her bedroom. I felt I was intruding on some private space, not entirely hers, which was clearly shared with the absent man. From the open bathroom door, I smelled aftershave and some masculine deodorant, so I expected some naked guy to emerge any moment.

There were pictures on the dresser, an older woman, a boy and a girl not quite adolescent, and a man in his forties wearing shorts and a shirt with pineapples, chest out, in front of a sailboat. Clearly showing his pride, the boat as a marker of his accomplishments. I studied the pictures until Esther gently turned me around to face her.

She had taken her clothes off. And she was now unbuttoning my dress and pulling it above my head. I felt her suddenly catch her breath and then let out a sigh when she saw I was nude under the prim blue dress. She had pulled back the covers as I lay on top of the sheets. I reached out for her. I lay back, expectant, feeling her breath on my face. We kissed, slowly, tentatively. And I remembered hearing from authoritative sources that women kiss better than men. Men can learn, but with women it's instinctive. I was happy, patient, ready for whatever was going to happen to take its sweet time. I buried my face in her long hair and inhaled a heady counterpoint of clove, mint, lavender. Then, like a shout in the dark, I was struck with the intrusion of a foreign smell, sweat, and cigarettes.

"Does your husband smoke?"

She raised her face. "Yes. Sometimes, at night, while I'm in the study preparing classes."

"In bed?"

"He's supposed to go out on the porch. I tell him he's going to set us on fire."

Suddenly, I felt we were not alone. *The Husband*, not even *hubby*, his name unspoken during the time we were together, had somehow intruded into our intimacy like a prankster ghost. I had spotted E.L. Greenwood on some mail, and now I asked casually, "What time does E.L. get home?" She seemed at a loss for a reply, as if she didn't know who E.L. was. "Oh, my husband," she said after a moment.

I couldn't shake off the feeling of this man, while across the country at some conference, being present in the bedroom. I wondered if he had a peeping system over the bed.

Then I thought I could actually feel his presence on the sheets, as if flakes of his skin had rubbed off during previous nights. Within a few moments I was itching on my back and legs. I sat up and started slapping the sheets as if to drive invisible insects off the bed.

"I have to get out of this bed. I have bugs crawling all over me."

"No bugs. I put on clean sheets this morning." She reached for my shoulders and held me close. The contact of her skin on mine relieved the itching.

I stood from the bed. "Can you see anything on my back, legs? A rash, maybe?"

"You have such smooth skin, almost silky." She ran her hand over my back, and I felt an immediate cooling sensation. She started to pull me back to the bed. But I resisted.

"He's everywhere, isn't he?" I said.

"Close your eyes."

"I can smell him."

"Please, you're with me. We're alone."

"Not now. I need a shower."

She led me into the bathroom and hung her purple robe on a hook. I ran the water as hot as I could stand, lathered up with her lavender body wash. I must've stayed for several minutes, letting the water wash over me in a fragrant rain. By the time I joined Esther at the kitchen table, all cozy in the magical purple robe that smelled of her and only her, I was already feeling somewhat embarrassed. I started to apologize but Esther would have none of it.

"You sensed what you sensed. Nobody can dispute that."

"Sometimes my imagination gets the better of me."

"You weren't imagining anything. There was truth in what you felt."

"OK. Can I have some wine now?"

"Yes, darling. And we'll get good and tipsy."

"Not drunk, though."

"No, that's for sailors."

Esther

Vin and I never went back to my house. It's not something we talked about, but it was understood. We took drives along the coast, stayed in frumpy B and B's, weather-beaten cabins, crappy motels, and the occasional fancy hotel. We chose, almost at random, different places as if to juice up our sense of adventure. And we carried mostly empty suitcases to look like tourists. We would pack some cheese and fruit and a bottle of wine.

Husband's comings and goings dictated what I could get away with. It was not a regular thing, when I could arrive at home and mention to my husband that I had a late seminar. Usually, we checked in after class and left after a few hours. And precious hours they were.

Best was when he traveled on business and we could make a night or two of our escape. Even the most mundane motel room became sacred space where we were free to indulge ourselves at leisure, happily making love until we were exhausted and starving. I could rarely spend the night and I would leave around ten, but Vin would often stay until the next morning and take a bus back to Cambridge. It would give me tender pleasure to watch her drift off to sleep, and kiss her before stealing out. "Drive safely," she would murmur.

We had our favorites that eventually we came back to. Vin liked rooms with large mirrors. She liked to watch us. "We are so beautiful, so graceful, like art," she'd say. On one occasion on the highway west, where exits to towns thinned out to occasional truck stops and service stations, an exit indicated lodging ten miles along a county road. We cruised past a Motel Six and then we both let out a sudden laugh at the sight of the Little Angel Inn.

I slowed down so we could appreciate the sign of a cupid whose neon bow and arrow kept pointing up and down. I stopped in the parking area. It was not a busy place in the afternoon, just a half dozen widely spaced cars and a semi in back. The sign in front of the office announced a vacancy.

Inside, a motherly type in a pink sweatshirt with the Little Angel logo in front and Marla on a nameplate greeted us tentatively. She stood at a counter in front of a display of similarly branded mugs and T-shirts and frilly pillows. She did show mild surprise at a strait-laced academic type and her younger, more or less androgynous companion, but managed to keep a smile.

"Welcome to the Little Angel," she said. "We do share a parking area with the Motel Six next door."

She thought we might have been confused and I was quick to reassure her that we were not. "You have it all over Motel Six in the charm department."

"Yes, thank you. I totally agree, although there are people who get the wrong impression about our business."

"Well, you are a motel."

"Of course, just not one oriented toward families. Couples always, even guy couples, no lady couples as a rule."

"Well, here are two of us ladies."

"I have a room for you on the second floor which is quieter. You'll appreciate that once it gets late. King size bed OK?"

"Nothing with a queen?"

At that Marla burst out with a happy laugh. "Oh, yeah sure I get it. Queen bed. That's a good one." She slid a card across the counter. "I need a name on the register, no address needed."

I wrote in Gertrude Stein. And passed the card to Vin who, without missing a beat, wrote Alice B.

Marla examined the card, as if checking spelling. "Well, you really don't look like a Gertrude," she said. "Most guests, usually men, just write in John Smith. We get a lot of those. Occasionally an Elvis. Gertrude is creative. Unless your name is Gertrude. I do need ID."

I slipped her my driver's license, which she photocopied without looking at it. "Cash, OK?" I said, pulling some bills out of my wallet.

"Yep. $69 a night, check out at eleven."

She handed me a key. We stopped at the car to get our bags, and off we went up the stairs to room 22.

Lavinia

We almost changed our minds. Pink walls, pink bedspread, pink carpeting, pink towels in the bathroom.

"Please, not pink."

"Think of it as rose."

I drew the curtains and everything settled into a diffuse glow. We stood apart on either side of the bed, removed our clothes and hung them neatly. We kept the lights off in the bathroom and I turned the shower on. Then I held my hand to Esther so she could get in with me. Oh, weren't we fussy! We'd both been with men who smelled, a wonder they could stand their own bodies. And they had the nerve to complain about the scent of a vagina. We lingered under a good strong stream, and lathered up with Little Angel lavender body wash.

The towels, pink of course, were thick and fluffy. There was a nice moisturizer lotion and a hairdryer and robes. I carry on like this because Esther and I had stayed in at least a dozen different places, and

Little Angel was made for sensuality. If we'd died and gone to heaven, this was where we'd spend our first night. We'd thought we were in for a cheap thrill, instead the Little Angel offered comfort designed for lovers.

Clearly, the company of a man would be incidental to the whole experience. In most settings, getting naked in stark light made our bodies clinical rather than sensual. Now, with the blush of twilight in the room, the textures and folds of flesh, the occasional mole and scar, were all smoothed out and softened. The pink motif made sense. Good of you, Marla, sensitive to the insecurities of female modesty.

I pulled off the top cover and fell back on the bed. The sheets of cool and crisp cotton felt nice on my skin. Above me, a ceiling mirror rewarded me with my spread-legged reflection.

"Wow, look at me."

"The mother of all mirrors."

"Come, lay beside me."

I drew you close and felt blessed by the image of the two of us, alone in a dusky room, side by side, our skin lightly touching. When you turned to be above me, the sight of your strong back and glorious ass was so lovely and perfect. You slid lower and I gasped at the sight of your lush auburn hair between my thighs. I shut my eyes, but the afterimage of your body above mine continued as you persisted in your gift, sending a shudder that washed over me like surf, again and again, from my toes to my head.

"My turn," I whispered.

"Your turn, yes."

We dozed. Then awoke to the sounds of autos and voices coming from the parking area, steps and voices along the open hallway leading to the other rooms. The Little Angel was gearing up for a busy night. You rose from the bed and put on the robe.

"Time for wine?"

"No time like the present," I said.

We had a bottle of nice malbec and two wine glasses. Also cheese and crackers and grapes. And almonds too, because you said they were healthy. The cheese was a drunken goat from Murcia and the grapes were black and sweet. We ended with dark chocolate truffles.

Everything you offered me was perfection. We didn't want to eat much, because we would make love again, this time under the buzz of the wine.

We stretched out on the bed leaning against the padded head-board, our feet touching. You grabbed the remote and clicked on the TV which offered a variety of shows.

"You know what goes with wine?" you said.

"Porn."

"Yes, but I don't want to see women getting fucked."

"Or women fucking each other," I said. "They couldn't be having as much fun as we have."

"No way."

We scrolled through the list of titles until we hit *Ride Him, Cowboy*, Starring Bruce Buckaroo and Randy Rodeo.

"That sounds promising," you laughed.

"What the hell," I said, "only six dollars on the credit card."

"We'll put it on yours, Vin. No paper trail for me."

"I forget. I'm the other woman."

"You're the only woman."

"Does your husband cheat?"

"I imagine. He travels on business and doesn't want me as much as he used to."

"Maybe he's gay?"

"He'd deserve getting it in the ass. Look, just like Randy Rodeo! Who are those guys? From the '50s with those haircuts."

"Amazing how quiet they are. They're too good looking to have much to say."

"Not even dirty talk. Husband likes me to talk dirty."

"What do you say?"

"Too stupid to repeat."

"Oh, baby, baby. I'll fuck you silly."

"Stop it," you laughed.

We poured more wine and settled back to watch the two men grab and suck and fuck with abandon. It was all very educational. I don't think either of us had seen such large penises. Which they would pull out to unload spurts of semen on each other's ass cheeks.

"Too strange to be watching this," you said after another twenty minutes of the same exertions.

"Totally. It's time to click off Bruce and Randy."

Esther

As occasionally happened, we got somewhat punchy. We didn't always finish two bottles of wine, but we did that night. It was fun getting buzzed with Vin, and I was in no hurry to get back home with Husband out of town. Not that we were falling-down drunk. Just rowdy and silly as we made love again. The room had grown darker in the evening and we had not turned on the lights. After a while I watched Vin as she dozed off and I pulled the sheet over us. I liked watching her sleep as her breathing lengthened. If there were dreams, there was no sign. She was a typical sleep-deprived student; she relaxed with me, and drifting off came easily, while I was awake and alert and protective of her.

I was starting to fall asleep too when I heard steps along the hallway come to a stop outside our door. Tentative knocking jarred me awake. Someone was standing quietly on the other side. At first I thought it was the adjacent room. A few moments later whoever was at the door grew insistent, and rapped again, louder this time.

I figured it was someone confused and having the wrong room. Some people are like that with numbers, especially late at night, dyslexic after a few drinks. I wasn't about to ask who it was. I tried to see out of the peephole, but there didn't seem to be anyone outside the door. I tried the front desk but there was no answer after several rings. Marla had left a recorded answer, "Sorry we have no vacancies tonight."

The knocking had stopped. I assumed in time the mystery visitor would give up and try another door. But then, a small voice spoke, "Can you help me, please?"

I rushed to the door and a boy about ten years old stood before me. That's why I hadn't seen him when I peeked out; he was no more than three feet tall. His eyes looked up at me with a kind of muted desperation. I imagined he had gone to the vending machines and forgotten his room. With the office closed, he thought a neighbor might help.

He seemed relieved that I had opened but was nearly in tears. I wasn't about to question him out in the hallway. I grabbed him by the arm and pulled him inside and shut the door. It had grown cold in the night and he was shivering in his Spidey pajamas. I wrapped him in one of the huge pink robes and sat him on one of the chairs.

"What's up, buddy?"

He wrinkled his face as if giving the question deep thought. I guessed there was more to his problem than simply getting confused as to his room's location. In the back of my mind I had to question the presence of a kid at the Little Angel.

"Are you lost?" If that was the problem I might be able to help him find his way back.

This time his answer was several determined shakes of his head. No, he was not lost. He had a serious look and had pursed his lips as if weighing a decision to speak further. I set the other chair in front of him and waited for him to speak. He was a pretty boy, soft features and serious mouth, clear blue eyes and a shock of unruly blond hair, the tips of which had been tinted blue. After a while, he stopped shivering and his face relaxed as if finding comfort with me. He kept glancing at the bed and seemed interested to see another woman lying there.

"Is that your daughter?"

"She's my friend. Vin. My name is Esther. What's yours?"

"Peanut."

"Really? That's your name?"

"That's what they call me."

"Very cute." I was pleased that we had started a conversation. "Won't your parents worry if they don't see you in the room?"

He clammed up again, lowering his gaze, unable to meet my eyes.

Vin had quietly risen from the bed and put on shorts and a T-shirt. She stood by my side and smiled at the boy. "So, we have a visitor."

"Yes, that's Peanut. Peanut meet Vin."

"Well, if we have a guest, we need to show some hospitality. There's not much in the room, but the vending machines are just around the corner. What treats do you like, Peanut?"

That got his attention. "Raisinets, chocolate milk, spicy Doritos, Gummy bears, animal crackers."

"Well, that's quite a variety. How about you, Esther? Any cravings?"

"Peanut M&Ms. In honor of Peanut here."

"Yeah, I like those too, the boy chimed in."

We had a feast in the room that night. It was after eleven when Vin came back with a bountiful stash, and we dug in cheerfully. We still had no idea what the deal was with Peanut's late-night visit. The boy was relaxing and actually getting chatty. We turned the TV to cartoons, and he curled up on the carpet, supported by a couple of pillows from the bed.

"It's getting late," I said around midnight. "Won't your parents be worried if they don't know where you are?"

"I'm not here with my mom."

"Are you here with your dad?"

He was entranced with the cartoons and seemed too distracted to answer. The sugary treats had made him sleepy. I didn't want him to drift off without learning who might be missing him.

"Wake up, Peanut," I nudged him. I looked at Vin, who was dressed. "Do you remember your room number? Vin can walk you back to your room."

"No!" He sat up and seemed to suddenly wake up.

"You don't want to go to your room?" Vin said gently. I waited for an answer, but he became suddenly engrossed in the show. He didn't react when I snapped the TV off, his gaze focused on the blank screen as if waiting for the program to start up again.

"Sorry, kiddo, no TV until you tell us what's going on. You could be in trouble just disappearing like that."

"And we could be in trouble too," Vin added. "They may accuse us of kidnapping."

At that, Peanut let out a harsh laugh.

"I take it you don't want to go back to your room?"

He'd sat up cross-legged and finally focused on me, as if he had decided that it was time to cooperate with the interrogators who were not about to give up on quizzing him.

"Kidnapping is when you tie someone up and gag him."

"You seem to know all about it. Were you kidnapped?"

"No."

"But someone brought you here. Not your mom or your dad."

"Yeah."

He was a slippery kid. I kept circling and every time I got close to his mystery he would manage to wriggle out of answering.

Suddenly, Vin took on the role of bad cop. "OK, Peanut. None of us wants to get in trouble. But if you don't tell us what's going on, I'll just push you out and you can find your way anywhere you want. What do you think of that?"

At that his face scrunched up with pain and tears started rolling down his cheeks.

"Are you afraid to go back to your room?"

He nodded.

"Who's there?"

"Uncle Freddy."

"Your uncle bought you here?"

"He's not my real uncle. He's just a friend of my mom's."

"Why don't you want to go back?"

"I don't like him."

"Your mom likes him, though?"

"Well, he pays rent and groceries, so we're supposed to be nice to him."

"Your mom knows you're here?"

"I don't know. She told Uncle Freddy he had to have me back home in the morning."

Vin seemed to read the situation before I did. "Is Uncle Freddy nice to your mom and you?"

"Not to mom. He says he's being nice to me."

"Really?"

"Kind of. If I'm nice to him, he buys me stuff and takes me to movies and the mall."

I just had to interrupt. "OK, Peanut, that's enough. How did you manage to leave the room?"

"Uncle Freddy got drunk and fell asleep. So I snuck out."

"What made you come to us?"

"This was the farthest room from where I was, at the other end of the motel."

"That was smart."

"And lucky," Vin added. "We're not about to make you go back to Uncle Freddy."

"Yeah, you're nice."

Lavinia

Sometime after two am, we had stretched out on the big bed, Peanut between us, when from below in the parking lot, a soft coaxing call drifted into the room. "Peanut, Peanut . . ." And then, after a couple of minutes a sudden, explosive, "Peanut. You little shit!"

I felt the boy stiffen suddenly, his body suddenly alert, as if ready to leap off the bed. "Easy," I whispered. "It's OK. Nobody knows where you are."

Somebody shouted for the man to shut up. He answered, "Mind your own business," but the attention drove him back inside. And then all was quiet. Clearly, Uncle Freddy had a problem. He couldn't report to the police that a child was missing without having to explain what he was doing with a kid at the Little Angel.

Esther said, "We are so much smarter than that Uncle Freddy."

"Way smarter," I added. "Esther is a professor and I go to Harvard. You don't get smarter people than us. Let him huff and puff like the bad wolf."

There were footsteps out on the corridors, stopping outside our door, hovering outside other rooms and then making their way back.

It went on like that for hours, the man making the rounds like some sentry waiting for Peanut to give himself away with a word or a cry. We slept fitfully, the three of us, waking and turning restlessly, the footsteps out in the corridor breaking through the slumber.

Uncle Freddy wasn't sleeping. By six, it was foggy out and dark as night, but there was already the occasional whine of a car driving out of the parking lot. I pictured him waiting and watching for guests to check out. He likely figured out that Peanut had found refuge in one of the rooms and it was just a matter of narrowing down the possibilities. Still, he couldn't very well walk up to someone and claim the kid without arousing some resistance. He was in a bind, and that made me nervous. Traffic outside increased as more guests left, probably eager to beat the rain. Finally, Esther called down to the office to speak to Marla.

Esther

I read too many mysteries and I found that I was enjoying playing detective. Matching wits against an evildoer. A pervert no less.

"Hello, this is Gertrude Stein."

"I know who you are, dear. Room 22. But you'll have to speak up. I can hardly hear you. Checkout is at eleven, if that's why you're calling. You're Ok for another hour. But there's some nasty weather coming in."

"Actually, I'm wondering if one of your guests is searching for a lost boy."

"Why on earth? We're not kid friendly as you may guess."

"Did some man check in with a boy last night?"

"Not that I know. What are you getting at?"

"Do people check in by themselves?"

"Could be. Guys keep the lady in the car. To be discrete, you know. Or an occasional sad sack, to watch dirty movies and beat off."

"Ok, I think we'd like to stay for a while."

"No problem. You can get a late checkout for no charge."

"Great, call us when you want us out."

"Leave whenever you want. But, like I said, the drive will be nasty."

Eventually Uncle Freddy must've figured out that Peanut was with the only people who had not checked out yet. Our two cars, my silver Camry and his black SUV, were left outside. I stood at the edge of the corridor and got a good view of the man shuffling about as if uncertain as to how to deal with whoever was sheltering the kid. Maybe fifty, clean-shaven, pink scalp visible through thinning brown hair, soft verging on plump, in a tight rain jacket, and a mincing gait as he walked aimlessly around the parking area. He looked for the world, harmless. He didn't know our room number, so he wasn't focused on this end of the corridor. And he couldn't very well go into the office and quiz Marla.

After a while, he must've decided he was calling attention to himself, a single man outside a couples' motel wandering about as if waiting for someone who would not appear. He got into his car with a last sweeping look at the two rows of blank room doors. He started the engine, waited a few moments as if to decide his next move, then suddenly peeled out of the parking area with an angry screech.

"He's gone," I said, coming back into the room and closing the door behind me.

"Gone where, is the question," said Vin.

"Not very far, I imagine."

I tried to get into his head, wondering how he would solve the problem of the missing "nephew." He couldn't very well report a lost child to the police. He could go to Peanut's mom and admit that the kid had gotten away. Let the kid's mother deal with the problem. That would not work well for him. His only avenue was to take the kid away from whoever had sheltered him through the night. He could appeal to reason, kids being mischievous and all that. And Peanut was a liar, a rebel, a little shit if the truth be known.

That argument wouldn't work with Vin and me. We couldn't hand over Peanut to Uncle Freddy. Not a chance. And giving the kid to the cops without a plausible story would put us in an awkward situation. We couldn't hang on to him, like finding a stray puppy. About the only thing we could do, if we managed to avoid Uncle Freddy, was to take the kid to his mom, and hope for the best for him.

But where on earth could Uncle Freddy be? Even if we waited another hour before checking out, he could be just down the road in the nearby service station or parked at the edge of one of the other motels. In any case, we were eager to leave.

Peanut was having a breakfast of chocolate milk and candy. Seemingly without a care now, he was fully absorbed in the morning Sesame Street. At least, I figured, he was getting a bit of an education from Big Bird. Vin had started up the coffee maker and brewed us two cups of something wimpy but black. That and Oreos would keep us strong and resourceful for a while until we figured out our move. With Peanut cross-legged in front of the TV, and Vin and I on the bed, we made a sweet family picture.

"We have to go," I said finally.

Vin agreed. "Ok, Peanut we're off."

"Where are we going?"

"To find your Mom. Do you know your home phone number?"

"Yes, she made me memorize it. 651-389-1250."

"Smart kiddo." I wrote it down.

"We could call her from here," Vin said.

"And what? Tell her we're barricaded in some motel with her kid? Just have her look for the neon cupid. No, we need to be closer to the city and make sure we've lost Uncle Freddy."

"Damn, sweetheart. You've done this sort of thing before, Vin laughed."

"I watch too much bad TV."

Lavinia

I felt a surge of excitement watching Esther take charge. Peanut and I could only sit and follow her lead. Somehow, thanks to all those movies she claimed to have watched, she proceeded with coolheaded resolve. And in her prim professorial dress she made an unlikely action figure.

It took us all of five minutes to pack her suitcase and my back-pack. Peanut had only the Spidey pajamas he'd been wearing when he came to our room. It was cold outside so I lent him a sweatshirt, which swamped him down to his knees, and he pulled on my Red Sox cap over his ears. He was now shaking, realizing he was now part of an escape plan. He knew more about Uncle Freddy's potential for violence than we did. I knelt on the rug and held him. "You'll be Ok, Peanut, Esther is in charge and we'll have you with your mom by dinner time."

"That's right, kiddo," she reassured him. "Just do what I say and you'll be traveling invisible."

Suddenly I could read her intentions through nods and hand gestures. Esther pulled the pink quilted bedspread and a blanket from the bed and folded it into a thick square. We rushed down and put the two bags and the covers in the trunk. She smoothed them out to make a bed for Peanut. It had started to drizzle under a gray metallic sky; suddenly it was a good idea to take off as soon as we got Peanut packed up.

"Don't worry," she said, "we can pay Marla for the blankets once we get out of this mess. For now, we'll give Peanut a comfortable ride."

"You trust, me kiddo?"

The boy nodded.

We took a look around the room, shut the door behind us and walked down the corridor stairs, hugging Peanut close between us. It was a tense twenty steps to the car. For all we knew Uncle Freddy had found some vantage point over the parking area. Even so, we had moved smoothly so that he may have missed our, if I may say so, clever maneuver. The trunk lid had been left unlocked. Esther lifted it and Peanut quickly slipped inside. He gave her a wide-eyed look of alarm, and she managed to reassure him with gentle smile.

"You'll be all right kiddo." He nodded seriously. She shut it with a satisfying click.

"Seems dangerous, him bouncing around in the trunk."

"Should be fine. It's just for a bit until we get to the city."

"See you soon, Peanut." I gave the lid a couple of good-luck knocks.

Esther got behind the wheel and took a deep breath to steady her nerves.

"Buckle up, dear."

I tried to find the snap but the belt was stuck and I couldn't pull it past my chest. Esther started the engine and waved good-bye to Marla who was watching from inside the office. We rolled smoothly to the exit of the parking area and pulled into the service station down the road. I held my breath as we parked by the pump. The black SUV was parked in front of the convenience store. Uncle Freddy was coming out of the store eating a donut when he saw the Camry. It was the first time I got a good look at him, all rosy cheeked and plump in his snug coat. He walked all mincing pigeon-toed toward our car and greeted us with a slight smirk as if to acknowledge that he'd seen us leaving Little Angel. Yeah, he seemed to be thinking, a pair of dykes.

"Oh, shit," muttered Esther. "Just be cool."

"Drive safely, ladies." He glanced meaningfully at the sky. "Nasty weather on the way."

He had moved closer to the car and was peering into the back seat. He kept staring and seemed confused because, clearly, he'd been expecting to see Peanut.

"Looking for something?" Esther asked just as calm as could be.

"Just admiring how roomy this compact is. Two adults could ride comfortably back there."

"Yeah, but it's just us chickens."

"Roomy trunk too?" He rapped the lid with his knuckles. And I had a sudden cough when I anticipated Peanut might knock back.

Uncle Freddy nodded and pursed his lips tightly over his small mouth.

Esther replaced the pump and grabbed the receipt. She climbed back behind the wheel. "We'd better be going. Nice talking to you, sir," she sang.

As soon as we reached the road, she stepped on the gas and we took off fishtailing as fast as the little Camry could go.

"I just about had a heart attack when he knocked on the trunk."

"He'll probably go back to the motel and quiz Marla. Then, he'll figure it all out in the next couple of minutes. He's not stupid, but he is slow."

We were all alone going about seventy on the blacktop. I finally heard Esther release a long pent-up breath. And I breathed along with her. This had been almost too easy, but here we were, rolling along with our little passenger.

The road was empty of traffic and I felt exposed. It had kept drizzling a fine icy mist which cut visibility and made the pavement slick. The wipers beat steadily, barely clearing the windshield. Esther turned on the headlights but they hardly made a dent through the fog. We wouldn't stop until we got to Cambridge and, once in the safety of people, we would call Peanut's mom.

Oh, my god, I thought to myself. This is ridiculous and exciting and reckless and dangerous all at once. And I was more in love with Esther Delius than ever.

"So, you think we pulled this off?"

Esther

"Oh, yes dear. We're getting away with grabbing the kid off a kidnapper."

Vin smiled. "As they say in Spanish, ladrón que roba a ladrón, tiene cien años de perdón."

"Which means?" I said.

"The thief that steals from a thief gets a hundred years pass from hell."

"I thought hell was for all eternity," I said.

"My God is the God of second chances."

"That's nice of Him."

"Her," Vin said. "There's evidence."

I nodded, gripped the wheel until my knuckles were white and concentrated on going as fast as I dared.

I'd better take it easy. I'm finding it slippery in spots. I kept glancing from the road ahead to the reflection in the rearview mirror. Suddenly, I felt the Camry swerve erratically, crunching on the shoulder before I jerked the wheel back.

"You saw something?" Vin said. "I'm getting spooked by every little thing."

I glanced at the mirror and was able to make out a pair of headlights barely visible through the fogged up back window. "It's nothing. Another car in this wet mess. It's keeping its distance."

"No point trying to race him."

"Actually, I'm slowing down so he'll pass me."

We went from seventy to fifty but the lights following us did not come closer. I tapped the brakes and we were soon doing thirty-five.

"Ah, here he comes now."

It took less than a minute for the car to catch up with us, but instead of passing, it drove alongside on the narrow blacktop. I couldn't make out the driver, but the vehicle was Uncle Freddy's black SUV. He stayed there, until a truck ahead forced him to slow down and get behind us.

"It's him, isn't it?" Vin said.

"Yep."

"You don't sound worried."

"We should lose him once we get to town." I was more worried than I sounded. I wished I could talk to Peanut in the trunk and reassure him that all was going to be fine, that we were taking him to his mom.

The SUV followed us close, as if not quite making up his mind to bump us. I wanted to make out the driver, but he was invisible behind his wet windshield. I kept remembering what Uncle Freddy looked like in our brief conversation in the service station. He hadn't looked like a monster, just a soft, dumpy middle-aged man. But inside the protection of his large black car he came across as menacing. Still, I hoped he would get bored and figured he could just go to Peanut's mom, and claim the kid had been abducted by two wacko women. I slowed down to about thirty-five and suddenly realized he was riding our bumper again. I worried for Peanut. He must've been hearing the rumble of the big car on my tail, just inches away.

"Are you playing games with him?" Vin scowled. "Slow-fast, slow-fast."

"I wish he would pass us and leave us alone."

At that moment I sensed him swerving into the adjacent lane. The yellow striping on the pavement indicated a safe passing zone with no facing traffic as far as I could see. He rolled his passenger side window down and started waving his arm, directing us to pull over. I lowered my own window down and stuck out my hand to give him the finger. It's not a gesture that I use routinely, but this time the insult felt very eloquent.

"Jesus, Esther, are you trying to piss him off?"

"Oh, we've already done that." I let out a kind of witchy cackle that surfaced in moments of righteous anger. Then an oncoming truck forced him back, and when the truck went by he again sped up to be alongside us, once more motioning for me to stop on the side of the road. And again, I waved at him and went a little faster. The rain hadn't let up, and the windshield had fogged over because of my crappy defrost. Vin kept leaning forward and wiping the glass. I rolled the window down a crack and that helped clear the mist. The game kept repeating itself. Oncoming vehicles would force the SUV behind me, and then he'd speed up, and so on.

The traffic had increased as the hour grew late, oncoming headlights blinded me so that only by focusing on the shoulder markings could I get a sense of staying on the road. After a while I stopped thinking about Uncle Freddy and his menacing SUV. I knew he was close behind but there was not much I could do about that; I would make it to Boston and lose him in city traffic. Unless he pushed me to the side of the road first.

The thought came with a sudden jarring clarity, dazzling in its diamond hard concreteness. In an instant I knew what was going to happen and that I wouldn't be able to do a thing about it. I felt no fear but a determination to push the thought away with enough force that I could replace it with another. I pictured Vin, her playful smile and the touch of her hand on mine. I reached over and felt around for her hand. She gave me a good long squeeze and for a moment I felt we were going to be fine, that this was a passing moment of panic. Then, she pulled away and I was left holding empty space.

Lavinia

You ask me what I remember. Not much, but I will try to work with you. Obviously, you mean well, in your crisp medical style with more questions than answers. So, I will tell you one thing I know, and then you tell me something you know. And we can go like that back and forth. I'll start with an easy one.

"Are you a doctor?"

"A nurse."

"So, I'm sick?"

"No, not sick. Injured. My turn. Do you remember being in a car accident?"

"Is that why I hurt all over?"

"Yes."

"So, I was in a wreck. I don't remember. When did it happen?"

"Yesterday evening. It's been about 24 hours."

"I was out?"

"Like a light. You had a concussion."

"I remember being with my friend Esther. Is she in here too?"

"I just know about you. Highway patrol called the ambulance and they will come later to ask you more questions."

"And answers too?"

"Yes. I imagine they can explain stuff better than I can."

I liked her. And I wanted to tell her so, but I got sleepy and couldn't concentrate.

I slept another night between the crisp sheets of a hospital bed, passing into a fog off and on, awakening to beeps and smells of medicine at work. The next morning, a nurse woke me up to check my vitals as she called blood pressure and temperature and oxygen. I felt fine. No headache. Just pain all over my beat-up body. I got French toast for breakfast. And coffee. And Tylenol. And still no cops. I buzzed for the nurse, but it was a different one this time, and she was even more stingy with explanations. She was brisk and casual and the only thing she did that was helpful was to give me a plastic bag with my notepad, glasses, and wallet.

"This is what made it out of the wreck," she said.

"I had a suitcase in the trunk."

"The highway patrol is dealing with all that."

"Can you tell me if my friend is Ok? She was driving. Her name is Esther Delius. Maybe she's in another room here."

"Sorry, I haven't a clue."

"So how come the cops aren't here? Investigating, you know."

The nurse shook her head and smiled apologetically. "Did you enjoy your breakfast?"

"Yes, thank you."

"Any pain? You got beaten up quite a bit."

"Could you hand me a phone?"

I dialed Esther. "You've reached Professor Delius. Please leave a message. I'll get back to you soon.""

"Jesus, Esther." Call me. "Ooops, never mind the law is here."

And finally a cop, M. Vargas according to her name plate, a bit butch, showed up. She pulled a chair to the side of the bed and leaned toward me so we could talk as friends.

"Is my friend Esther Delius all right? She was the driver."

"Are you a relative?"

"We are friends." I hoped she could catch my drift, without having to wink.

"Sorry. I really can't tell you anything. Her husband has been notified."

"Notified of what?"

She let that pass without a reaction.

"Also, there was a boy, about 10."

"Are you a relative of the boy?"

"No."

"Do you know his name?"

"He said it was Peanut. That's all he told us. He knows his mom's phone number and the name of some Uncle . . . Freddy," I added, not knowing if that would help nail the pervert. "I wrote down his mom's phone. It should be with my stuff."

I dug my notepad. Inspector Vargas copied the number down and gave the pad back to me. She started to get up from the chair, but I reached to touch her hand and held her back.

"You have something to add?"

"Please, I don't know what the hell happened. One moment we were driving and the next, twenty-four hours later, I woke up here."

"You have no memory of the accident?"

"It was raining mixed with sleet. Esther was driving. She wasn't going fast."

"You're lucky," she said, "you weren't wearing your seatbelt. First time in twenty years that's good news."

"I remember I tried to attach it, but I couldn't pull it to reach the buckle. So I said to hell with it."

Oh, dear, dearest Esther, my love. Officer Vargas did not have the whole story, but the basics lead me to assume that you did not make it out alive. And Officer Vargas doesn't know the half of it. I will get the info out to her some time, but for now I have a slow time reconstructing what happened, even as my memory feels stubbornly locked in darkness. Still, I know what I know.

I remember Uncle Freddy playing games, speeding up to be next to us, signaling us to pull over, angrily because you were flipping him off in your best professorial style, then retreating when faced with oncoming vehicles. Then it happened.

Officer Vargas thinks he was trying to pass us when he faced an oncoming motorcycle. The SUV didn't have time to pull back but tried to move closer to us to give the cycle room. The result was that it side-swiped the lighter Camry and pushed us down a ravine at the side of the road. I was thrown off the vehicle (yay, no seat belt!). The impact on the gas tank caused it to explode, a nearly soundless whoosh of flames that quickly engulfed the whole vehicle. Meanwhile, I had been tossed several feet away and was blissfully passed out.

The guy on the motorcycle called 911, and stayed to tell the whole story. The black car took off. And here I am. And I grieve for you and Peanut, even though nobody will tell me anything. Uncle Freddy got away with murder by SUV.

III

Lavinia

I knew in my heart that I would never find another friend, teacher, lover like Esther. And I never felt so alone in my life. I was barely twenty and had never suffered a death before. I fantasized she could hear my thoughts, her presence following me even as I told myself that she was lost forever

The horror of that night stayed with me long after I was checked out of the hospital. I had no recollection of the actual collision, but in dreams the explosion haunted me with the stink and heat of burning plastic and melting steel. I had visions of Peanut being ejected from the trunk and landing by the road. Then standing up and brushing off tiny flames licking his arms and chest. All was well in spite of the idiotic suggestion by two supposedly intelligent women that he could be safe from Uncle Freddy in the trunk of the car.

Scarcely a week after the accident I was in bed on my sleeping binge for the third consecutive day when someone in the house handed me a message. Dr. E.L. Geenwood would like you to call him. The Husband.

I did not call him back, but he kept leaving messages. My housemates started showing their annoyance, playing secretary to a slugabed. After a week, realizing he was not about to give up, I forced myself to call him. I anticipated he was eager to unload his anger and recriminations, so I was prepared to withstand the storm. Instead, he invited me for coffee.

"I'm in midterms. Crazy busy."

"Ok, I don't imagine you're eager to meet me."

"Like I said, I'm swamped."

"Please make the time."

"I'm not sure what we need to talk about. You must know I'm devastated about Esther."

"You and me, both."

I spotted him in a secluded corner of Café Roma, one in fact that I favored for studying. If this was to be a confrontation of some sort, I was glad to be in my home turf.

I knew what he looked like from the photos in his home, close to fifty, rimless glasses, clean-shaven, thinning hair; the blue suit and white shirt made him stand out in Cambridge. His eyes kept darting nervously from behind thick lenses as he surveyed the crowd in the café, not sure who he was looking for. He had no way of recognizing me.

He was holding a mug as if to warm, or steady, his hand. I waited for my latte, not eager to confront him. Finally, I approached his table. I don't think he was expecting a scruffy undergraduate because I'd been standing in front of him for several moments before he might have suspected I was the woman he was meeting.

"Hello, Dr. Greenwood."

"Ah yes, Miss Aguilar. Larry."

"Vin," I said. Even though I couldn't imagine calling the Husband *Larry*.

"You're young," he murmured.

"So I've been told," I said.

"I'm sorry if I sound surprised. I didn't even know Esther had a friend, until the accident. But of course, you knew she had a husband."

"Yes."

"Well, now we're even."

"Is there something on your mind?"

"I'm not sure what I want to say to you. You must realize what a shock it was to find out about the accident. And you with her."

"I am so very sorry, sir."

"Larry."

"Yes, well. I guess you might be resenting me, having been part of Esther's life, and death."

"More confused than resentful."

"I'm not sure how I can help with the confusion."

"Esther and I had independent lives, medicine vs academia. They coexisted amiably enough."

"She never said anything negative about her marriage," I said with as much kindness as I could muster. "You know, I admired her greatly."

We talked for over an hour. My answers didn't really help clarify Dr. Greenwood's search for understanding. The details of that last night at the Little Angel Motel and the resulting mayhem with Peanut did not interest him much. And what he wanted to know about Esther's heart was beyond my explaining to her husband. I could barely describe the love that was in my own heart.

In the end we parted with a handshake, and a stated intention to chat another time. We never met again, and the end result of that first conversation was to leave me with a deep sense of unease. His presence in Esther's life had always felt invasive to me. Now, I couldn't shake the remorse at the knowledge that I had contributed to the suffering of this decent man.

Jason

I finally spotted Lavinia weeks after I met her in front of the Lesley English building. It had been an embarrassing moment for me, to be sure, confronted with the fact that I had not read a book since the seventh grade. Ray Bradbury, not Virginia Woolf. But I kept on thinking about her, even if she was already in a relationship with some professor from Lesley. Ha! A lezzie from Lesley, I easily amuse myself.

I saw her before she saw me at Café Roma, slouched in a corner chair, a steaming mug cradled in her hands, her nose in a book so that I considered not speaking to her, knowing she would not appreciate being interrupted by me. Again.

She was so small, barely five feet, with a pixie haircut and a serious expression. She practically disappeared into her corner of the café. It was chilly, late October, and she wore a big Mexican sweater, wool and hand-knit, of gray and white pre-Hispanic geometric motifs. It was to be her one reliable winter garment all the way through March.

I got a coffee and found a spot at a crowded long table more or less out of her visual range. I could not let the opportunity pass and wait for some other time I might run into her. I resolved to speak to her as soon as she turned the page. Then when that happened, I decided

I would approach her when she put the book down to sip her drink. After a few long minutes, she closed the book and placed it on her lap, as if to ponder what she had read. I made my move.

I left my coffee on the table and stepped to her chair. She looked up, but there was no sign she recognized me. She frowned and waited for me to explain why I was standing in front of her. In seconds the opportunity to say something charming would be lost and I would have to mumble something and move on. Fortunately, she saved my ass.

"Ah! The chemist. What are you doing so far from MIT?"

"Hoping to run into you."

"A stalker! I've done a little of it myself. She stood up and lifted the heavy backpack onto her shoulders. I have a class."

"I'll walk with you. I can help with the pack."

"No thanks, I bear my own baggage."

"Just wanting to be helpful. If your friend from Lesley doesn't mind." I heard myself being snarky and immediately regretted it.

"She won't mind. She's dead."

"Jesus, I'm sorry. How did she pass?"

"She didn't pass. She died last month. In a car accident."

"She seemed like a nice woman."

"Yep, but she didn't like you. She saw through your attempts to sound intelligent, though illiterate."

"I will read any book you prescribe."

"Let me think."

"Sure. And believe me I can return the favor, if you'll take whatever I prescribe."

And that's how Vin and I collaborated to expand each other's mind. I labored through Moby Dick, which she had every suspicion I would drop. She was wrong.

I fell in love with the harpooner Queequeg, that mysterious sea islander described as a savage, but in reality a cool observer, cast in the midst of a crew of New England whalers. He may be the only character who sees Captain Ahab for a deluded obsessive in his hunt for his mythic nemesis, the white whale.

Of course, I got swamped in the ins and outs of the whaling industry in the harvest of oil and flesh and bone. Hundreds of pages of it, so I resorted to a tried-and-true undergraduate gambit, Cliff's Notes. Still, the rough plot summary left me feeling unfulfilled. I missed the rhythm and cadence of the sea and the search and so I started with Queequeg and read on and on. I wept at the islander's death struggle and exulted in Ahab's final surrender to his prey. Vin changed my life with that story. I have learned compassion from novels and that has affected the way I deal with the world and its creatures.

Fall moved into a typical New England winter, wet and windy, and still Vin wore that Mexican sweater, which she said came from indigenous sheep herders and knitters in the Mexican village of Chiconcuac.

We became friends before we were lovers. She was a diligent student, so I was only occasionally able to pry her away from her work. During those precious rare hours we found refuge in Café Roma and the Film Arts theater, both places overheated and hazy with smoke and feverish with earnest conversations. We talked at length about the nature of obsession, about the pursuit of the unassailable adversary, the sacrifices victory entails. How choosing an unworthy adversary is defeat in itself. Moby Dick was not the monster, until Ahab created him. A force of nature is only to be reckoned with, not overcome. Typhoons, earthquakes, beasts, drought, require acceptance not resistance. We overcome by surrender. Let it rain, let it pour, let it bleed, let it go, let it die. The adversary shows the path to survival.

"Wow," Vin said one night. "You're becoming a deep thinker."

Of course she wasn't serious. It was her habit to jab me when she thought I was getting carried away with myself. And I took it, and learned from her. It was not to be a one-sided acceptance. I knew without revealing anything at first that I would have an equally powerful influence on her. My gift would go beyond her expectations. Even if she didn't realize it at the time, I would change her life as she had mine.

Lavinia

Thank you, Jason. For the gift of the blue dot. The quiet, dark room and the sitar music. The heady cloud of sandalwood. Suddenly, in an instant as long as a day, you became the priest and I the devotee.

Was it coincidence that we chose November 2, Mexico's Day of the Dead for my first trip? It didn't occur to me until I found myself in the high desert, maybe Oaxaca, under a rain of brilliant orange flowers falling from a dense black sky, cempazuchitl, the flower of muertos ofrendas because it retained its vivid color for days.

I was walking not quite touching the earth with my feet, feeling light and graceful, across the parched ground with no destiny in sight, lost but content to wait for an end point to be revealed. As the rain of flowers fell, they eventually covered the ground, until a path through them was revealed that led to the first of three stages up the side of a mound.

Burning votives illuminated the way along the path and circled along the sides of the mound, their little fires welcoming me in a flickering celebration. Thirteen skulls guarded the first level, white bone and hollow eyed, jaws gaping in an interrupted laugh. I was expected to kneel and offer reverence. This is what I had been moving toward.

I made it past the barrier to a long table set for a feast, a centerpiece of calla lilies, everything fresh and fragrant and ready for guests. Clay bowls of white viscous pulque, mugs of hot chocolate lively with the scent of cinnamon, platters of rice and beans and savory mole sauce, golden towers of flan topped with burnt sugar, tamales steaming in their corn husks, and loaves of sugary bread in the shapes of skulls and bones and mummies at rest, hands at peace over their chest. Cool water in a crystal bowl.

And everywhere a celebration of bones, skeletal figures come to life. Lustful skeletons dancing and flirting and smooching, studious skeletons bent over their books, a clown, a priest, a nun, a charro, a fine lady with a flowered hat and a skinny mariachi strumming away. All together, heads nodding, bones clacking, feet dancing and tapping. The ensemble led by a grinning skeleton guide dog. Ruling at the apex, a triptych of mothers: Guadalupe, Kali, Tonantzin.

And just below, as the pyramid narrowed, a picture frame ringed with silver filigree, lacking an image of a beloved, waited at the center for the expected visitor. Gradually, as if a photo was being processed and developed under the light of the votives and candles, your face, dear Esther, began to appear. I understood a living ofrenda was growing before me, not something that I created, but that emerged from a younger self in time, my childhood in Mexico, celebrating the Day of the Dead, a kind of reunion of love and memory, a festival of sticky sugar skulls with our names Lavinia, Luis, Marcial, Ysbel. All four laughing at death, celebrating life unending in spirit and dream. I picked up a skull, with green eyes of foil and your name on its forehead, Esther.

As your image took on life inside the frame, I knew that all I had to do was wait for your visit, that you would follow the guide dog from the dark to the dancing lights of the ofrenda, that you would recognize me by the scent of sandalwood, that there would be fresh water for your journey. I could meet the softness of your gaze, feel the whisper of your breath, sense the cool touch of your skin on mine.

Suddenly, Jason's voice intruded in the silence. "What are you seeing, Vin? Where are you?"

I opened my mouth as if to speak, but I couldn't summon the energy to describe the scene.

"How are you doing?" he asked. "Tears are running down your face."

I am so happy, I heard myself think. *I don't want to ever leave this place.*

And then I knew you were with me, dearest Esther. I couldn't see you beyond your image inside the picture frame, but your presence was everywhere inside the room. There were so many questions I wanted to ask you. I wanted to know where you were, if you were in pain, if you were sad to die, if you would come to me any time I needed you, if you would be my guardian.

Somehow, the answers came without your speaking, as if the knowledge of your presence was nestled inside me. I knew everything there was to know. That you did not suffer. That you went in an instant to a peaceful void, pure, undisturbed blackness to the farthest horizon.

That you lacked nothing. Except to communicate that you loved me. And that you would be with me any time I thought of you, that I would be able to summon you in my heart at the first beat of memory. Therefore I was not to say goodbye, not to grieve, not to lament that the happiness I had yearned for was not to be in the land of the living.

Look for me, you said, and I would feel your breath on my face, in signs and numbers and birds. The same three digits in a clock, a raven on a branch outside my window. In dark times and happy times, I will be close. But it will be our secret, you are not to speak about this or try to explain it or even write it in a private journal. You will know. And you alone will know.

Jason

Now, thirty years after meeting Lavinia, I ask, does everyone know she is dying? Bad news streaks through the networks until the knowledge sinks in without any trace of its source. Vin and I were together for a brief time, and when we separated it happened as something sleepy and anticlimactic. She graduated and went back to Mexico, I stayed to do a postdoc in Cambridge. She said she would come to visit. She didn't. I asked for her address so I could write. I didn't.

But when the reality of her condition hit me, the knowledge that she had just weeks left, I felt a clear calling to offer her one last dose. I could do this for her. No matter that she never tripped again after that first time in Cambridge. She said that she saw a deep truth about life and death and that she would wait until she died before she looked again. Maybe God had something to do with it, but he remained quite hidden from me. Beginner's luck! She insisted she had crossed a taboo and would not be forgiven if she crossed it again. I on the other hand saw no mysteries, just colors and melting faces. I have continued taking acid every few months through the years in the hopes that God will pity me and make an appearance. But many are called . . .

No worries. If I couldn't see God myself, I could at least deliver Him to Lavinia one more time. And, because I made the stuff myself, could vouch for its purity. It's not like the old days before we became criminals. I was at MIT and we had a reliable source of ergot and we could process the fungus in a dark room to keep it from decomposing.

But those days are gone and I am now at home near Phoenix, a handy dandy mixer and blender in the basement dark room. If my family and mentors and classmates had expected me to grow up into a research chemist, they would be disappointed that I am now an investment analyst specializing in big pharma. In the world of organic cuisine, I was always more gifted at following recipes than creating my own. Hence, my fame as a psychic chef.

It may be home cooking but that doesn't mean I can't be a perfectionist. Which means that I prefer Hawaiian rose seeds instead of morning glory. The former are complicated to get and the cost difference is substantial. Hawaiian roses don't thrive in the mainland, the seeds need to be acquired at the source. Big Kahuna Nursery and Flowers does a nice business via FedEx. Even if DEA suspects they might be prime ingredients for LSD, they're not worried because amateur chemists would not get close to producing anything that could provide a trip. Still, Harry Chang, aka Big Kahuna, knows what I'm about and therefore exacts a premium price for a small purchase of a thousand seeds. Sufficient, after complicated mumbo jumbo, to distill around fifty trips.

I'm at my happiest when I'm cooking. I get in a zone and perform magic. From soaking the seeds in petroleum ether, through filtering, scraping and soaking the mush again in alcohol. Four days pass between the first soak and the second. Finally, after the second filter, you dump the mush. Then pour the resulting liquid into a cookie tray and allow it to evaporate. The resulting yellow gum contains LSD. It goes into the purple capsules that identify my product, each good for six hours of transformative travel. But beware of imitations. Mine guarantees a princely experience. "Journeys by Jason." I personally test every batch before it goes to friends and family.

I hadn't much thought of Lavinia in years. But now, when I thought it was time to reconnect, she was not answering her phone and Jordi was evasive, to the point of not acknowledging that she was already in hospice and dying one gray day at a time. And so I waited in the sitting area outside her room, having forgotten what November in Minnesota was like, cheerfully incongruous in my Hawaiian shirt with big hibiscus flowers, madras shorts and my feet in sandals. It was hardly the look of a man on a serious mission. A nurse said that Vin was aware of my presence and that she would give word when she felt strong enough. That night I was encouraged to go get a bite and some sleep and come back in the morning. I decided to stay where I was, nibbling on peanut butter crackers and coffee. The Shanti House hospice is a restless place, where we wait and wait through the night, for the word, for the breath.

Finally, sometime around three AM, I was awoken by a hand pressing on my shoulder. Jordi whispered that Vin had suddenly popped awake, as if in a surge of energy, and wanted to know where I was, that she thought I was in the room.

I approached and when she finally recognized me, she patted the side of her bed and I sat on the edge. She reached out and felt around, brushing my leg and my arm until she touched my hand. I had closed my fist and she pried my fingers open one at a time to reveal the gleaming purple capsule resting like a jewel on the palm.

I'm here, my friend, sitting at your side in this dim room, the one window now black to the night. I bear a gift. You know what it is. Jordi and Ysbel have left us alone.

I push the control on the bed so that you are lifted to a sitting position. You will be alert and unencumbered by other drugs. Jordi has asked the nurse not to renew your Ativan and your morphine. Like a priest dispensing a communion wafer I ask that you show me your tongue. You try to speak but the words remain choked in your throat. I press on your shoulder and whisper that you need not say anything. The glimmer in your eyes tells me you are ready.

"Tongue." I whisper again.

And, finally, you obey. A blue capsule with measured grains. Two doses, actually. One for me. I will ride on the stream of your energy to take me along, dear companion. Through the years I've taken so much that tripping is my ordinary state. I depend on you to show me the mystery.

I pay attention to your breath. Shallow and barely audible until I focus on its music, in and out, like the rustle of a brush on a cymbal, smoothly underlying the thrum of your blood flow, a kind of syncopated dance music on a marimba.

Lavinia

In addition to being a grad student in chemistry at MIT, Jason Loomis was a dedicated dealer of LSD. He had a business card decorated with shooting stars: "Journeys by Jason."

Jason had opinions on everything, whether it related to organic chemistry or not. Or rather, everything in our beings was about chemistry, the ecstasy of mystics and athletes, the heartbreak of love lost and the bliss of love found, all resonated in the rub of one cell against another floating in their endorphin jelly.

Depression, paranoia, rage, anxiety—all were treatable with the magic potion he and his friends at MIT were cooking. And if you had no psychotic symptoms, so much the better. Surges of creativity and compassion could be sparked with a tasteless blue dot on a square of blotter paper. I followed him to his room one night off Brattle Street.

It was a clean, orderly space, sparsely furnished with a futon, a card table with two chairs, a kitchen counter with a sink, a toaster, and a two-burner stove with a vegetable stew simmering in a pot. And then there were science books stacked in towers on the floor. Seen from the door, the piles were as orderly as buildings in a grid, so that stepping around them made me feel as a giant in one of Gulliver's cities. He put on the kettle and he brewed me a cup of some bitter grassy tea.

And then we tripped. With no advance warning, he tore a square of blotter paper from a sheet identified with blue dots and placed it on my tongue like a communion wafer.

From that moment and for the next three years Jason was my guru, my priest and my occasional lover. I say occasional l because even while he was a steadfast friend, we both had an erratic time being sexually faithful. It was a heady time in Boston, with thousands of undergraduates from a half dozen universities running loose after the rigors of parental supervision. Those of us from outside the US found an unfettered hunting ground for experimentation. There was sex and art, sex and film, sex and theater, sex and rock 'n' roll. It was all such fun.

And now, so many years later, Jason hovers at my side. I know it's him even though I cannot make out his features in the dark room. He smells the way he used to, a combination of patchouli and weed and cigarettes. He's wearing an insanely cheerful shirt for winter, a print of hibiscus flowers on a blue field.

It's very quiet at Shanti House tonight, no coughs or rattles from the room next door. We don't get to see the comings and goings of residents, the nearly dying and the no longer living. So when Jason whispers my name I can hear him clearly. I part my lips and take a breath to speak, but no sound emerges.

Jordi leans over and tries to hear so that he can communicate my words to Jason, but I lift a hand to brush him away. I don't want any mediation between my old friend and me. I will muster the energy soon enough to communicate in words.

For now, I want Jason to feel unencumbered, uncensored. That's how my goodbyes have been. A private moment with a cousin or an old lover or a colleague, some of them close at one time, others superficial until this moment of reckoning when there's a bursting of pent-up intimacy. Some are uncomfortable with my hand, but still I insist on touching. I strive to establish a physical connection, so that love or guilt can pass between us. The stirring of a hand tells me they're eager to leave. I may allow them to go, or clasp my fingers around their wrist to hold them back. Until I let go or drift off to sleep.

Jason settles in on the chair beside the bed. I like that we are still comfortable with each other, sharing stillness in the middle of the night. No thought of where we've been or where we're going, the moment is sufficient unto itself.

I turn my head and get a good look at him, older now, his hair still long but gray and thinner, tied in a knot on top of his head. He's too old for a man bun. I want to laugh but I don't have the wind for it. I smile, and he nods appreciatively and smiles back his wide grin, baring uneven teeth, stained from a lifetime of coffee and cigarettes. He shows character, this scruffy shaman, his features vaguely Asian, with a wispy moustache and goatee. He seems to have come into his own, from the preppy undergraduate to this lovely incarnation.

"How are you feeling?" He asks.

"No pain. Swollen. Bloated. Exhausted. Sad. Happy. Angry. Anxious."

It takes me a long time and a big effort to get these words out, one by one, each a complex thought in itself, and Jason knows better than to interrupt. He has always been a good listener.

"I brought you a gift."

"Communion."

"Yes. But no confession or absolution necessary."

But he is mistaken. There is no peace without repentance. No bliss without absolution. Defiant, I accept the communion anyway. I gesture to my throat to indicate that it's difficult for me to swallow. He opens a capsule and squeezes the grains on my tongue. I close my eyes and his image remains ghostly on my eyelids.

Still, the middle lover who won't leave, the one after Esther and the one before Jordi, providing balance in my sentimental education. He was the funny one, a dancing, naked clown, with a lean body that seemed to duplicate my own slender one, more like twin siblings than lovers, delighting in our complementary instruments of pleasure, the pride of his cock and the eager symmetry of my vagina.

We took turns shaving each other's pubic hair, so that we were like naked children playing, glorying in the folds and knobs and veins, and finally in the wet blooming of our desire. It was all such fun. There had been a serious intensity with Esther, a tendency to glory in our subversiveness, breaking the rules of gender and marriage and power differentials, she always the teacher and I the student. Jason and I, were each other's guides and accomplices, secret cohorts in a self contained closed universe. Sure, we had friends, MIT nerds and Harvard poets, and we hung out at the Café Roma and bantered at a more refined level than the common herd, but throughout all, there was a shield to our intimacy that put it out of reach from even the most seductive interloper. We were so damn pretty, and happy in the knowledge that we were unavailable, sufficient unto ourselves.

I remember. I may have whispered aloud, but did not hear a reply. I wanted you to know that recovering stored memory was like splitting my skull and allowing me to pick out self-contained nuggets of experience. Not as clean as clicking on a computer hard drive. My life has been a messy thing. The lies I told would fill a cesspool. The promises I broke could be links in an endless chain. The resentments I've carried through life are like leg-irons. The people that have drifted in and out, some rejected without explanation, would make a chorus of dissonance. The fears that haunt me are shadows and sounds and faces that cling forever. Spiritual pride swells me like a blowfish. And yet I've been able to accept the blessings of a rich life, a loving marriage, service through good work, friendships that have endured, pleasures of the flesh and the mind, music and art that nourishes me, the bliss of a full heart. Oh, forgive this lucky girl.

I don't want to die. There, it's been said now, without apology. It's not because of fear. But rage. The crab that drives its pincers into my breast, my lungs, my brain, is a thing of the devil, a glutton for my soft flesh, a mindless creature that walks backwards from what had been health and peace. But still, I say: Listen. Let's negotiate. You can have my breast and one lung but not my brain. You can have my whole body, but not my brain. I could live with spare parts attached to a ventilator that would do my breathing, and a tube straight up my anus to feed me, as long as I had a working brain.

The scariest time during this whole ordeal has been the seizures that gave evidence of metastasis in the brain, the clusters of shiny tumors like grapes in a bunch that derailed the smooth interchange of thought and emotion and reflex.

The treatments with zaps to the brain made typing an impossible chore. For me a devastating handicap, I was once able to type as fast as I could think. Now my thoughts lined up clearly but the results on the screen were gibberish. I tried voice recognition on my laptop but struggling for breath produced an unintelligible series of gasps.

It's all been very frustrating, because as my body fails, my mind grows richer with unexpressed depth and mystery. Just my fate, that I would think like a genius but have to keep it all inside me. Poetry goes unspoken. Insights on the nature of the universe massaged to unexpressed perfection. The mathematics that had always eluded my understanding now shines with elegance. The sight of God awaits, ready to ripen into knowledge.

Maybe that will happen, dear Jason, with your latest sprinkle of fairy dust on my tongue. The possibility scares the hell out of me. I never thought of God as a generous being, quite the opposite. Not a being at all, just a kind of energy field. Not a God of love, but a God of strict discipline, a source of laws that human judges can bend and forgive but not God. Hell is not a fiery realm of eternal punishment; hell is God's rejection. Knocking on heaven's gate that doesn't crack for even a sliver of light to come through.

The other possibility is that God speaks without my knowing It has spoken, a voice of untranslated dialect. Its truth is out there for those who can hear. The name that can be spoken is not the eternal name. I know my work is clear now. Only in the depths of my stillness can It be understood.

The taste on my tongue lingers, a gem of intense sweetness, the soma of the vedas perhaps, or simply the crystallization of the last touch of the world, so that its intensity perseveres and clings, a memory of the senses that hampers stillness. Wanting it to soften and dim, forgotten momentarily but then reappearing over and over, like the theme in a larger piece of music.

Even as I try to discard it, I find that sweetness that had earlier seduced my senses is now treacly and revolting. The more I reject it, the more it fills my mouth with worms and maggots. I open my mouth to spit them out, but they keep emerging so that I vomit from the depths of my gut. And I know that God will retreat as long as my being is contaminated. Its brilliance grown opaque.

"Vin, Vin."

I hear my name coming softly from close by, from Jason sitting on the chair by the bed. "Get me out of this, please."

"You don't get out. You surrender."

"Fine. Show me how."

There is no answer from Jason, and I realize that my thoughts were stillborn, words choked in my throat so that I can only rasp a cough. And so I feel his energy fading and I have never felt so alone. With no star to guide, I wander across a tundra without paths or landmarks. Forward is the same as back, right and left are indistinguishable. I twirl in place like a dervish until I find myself weaving and stumbling, pulled by some invisible string, one step at time to what is neither ahead nor behind, towards an uncertain goal. This is hell. It is God.

Are you happy now, Lavinia? Is this what you wanted, what you thought you deserved? The revelation that hell and heaven are God, indistinguishable, the same place for saints and sinners. No reward or punishment, only an inexpressible void. It is not fair, God just is. So the point is pointlessness. We behave according to our nature, all is forgiven, nothing is punished. Individual will is an illusion, we evolve and act without a plan, feeling our way in the tundra, avoiding hurt and seeking well-being, each according to our nature. Trial and error give the illusion of free will, seeking safety and pleasure, eating and drinking from whatever feasts and fountains are within grasp. Finding teachers and guides along the way, according to our needs. And the journey of life is a shapeless desert, ours to walk along blindly, drunkenly, grateful if we can stay erect and not collapse with no one to help us rise. Because to make progress we must be standing on our own feet, and then the signs appear. Stop. Go. Yield. Slippery when wet. Pay toll.

The coin is tears. Tears for the pain of the earth, for the forgotten race, for the lost children, for the starving women in drought and famine, for the boys and girls lost in war. We are put in this realm to soften our heart, to make it sensitive to the all that is around us, to take us out of ourselves so that our tears can be proof that we are worthy of life.

Hello, I'm the Elephant Man. No longer the stuff of literature and drama, but now as real as shit. You avert your eyes, attempt to bypass me without a glance even as I limp after You. You recoil and evade responsibility for my horror. I stumble on the same path You're in. You can hear me following you. You did not cause my spine to twist and arch, my skin to fall in leathery folds, open sores weeping a rank fluid. My webbed fingers keep reaching to caress Your face. Listen to me, I speak Your language. My mouth without lips is no more than a gash unable to communicate beyond cackles and grunts and moans.

When You finally turn to face me, what swells your heart is not compassion. Instead, You are angry that I have been placed in Your way. An angry God for creating me with no purpose but to unbalance You. And how You hate the very sight of me, the smell of my breath, the stink of my sweat. You search your purse for a coin to bribe me into disappearing. But I'm not going anywhere, I was put on this very ground in order to stop You in Your tracks as You negotiate the price of my release. If You could, You would heal my wounds, bathe my sores, pay for my surgeries. Indeed, You are supposed to be a generous being. It's a pity that the solution to my misery is beyond Your capabilities. Not Your fault that the poor are hungry, that the homeless are left to wither in the cold and heat, that the sick take too long to just die. The horror that I am is not Your responsibility.

Come close. You will not escape me until You stand close enough to feel my presence in your space. You know You must. Look. I am Your mirror. Let me touch You, just a light brush of my fingers across Your face. Now, Your turn. Touch me, I'm ready.

My tears are the price of my freedom. I am paying my toll.

Lavinia

I will not die alone. Jordi will be at my side, and hovering nearby, the visitors from the past. Father and Luis, demanding to be seen, wait outside my room, their voices arguing to be admitted rumbling just beyond clear hearing. I recognize them even if I can't make out their words. Occasionally, a spike of clarity will break through the muddle.

"We have rights as the closest family."

And I have rights. Not to be disturbed, shaken, tired, invaded. I have the right to be comforted, fed, warmed, touched, amused, absolved, washed, relieved of pain and anxiety. Not much to ask for at this stage.

Twice a day, first thing in the morning and last thing at night, I'm asked if I wish to see a minister. Not a specific priest, just a generic type who will wash me with platitudes and bromides.

It's not that I'm lacking in spiritual comforts. Twice a day I meditate with Jordi, while he sits with his back against the door to keep out the nurses and hospice volunteers who, with well-meaning insistence, come to check for signs of life. Sorry to disappoint, blood pressure is normal, temperature on the cool side, oxygen levels hanging in.

The dying are waiting in line. One doesn't want to overstay her welcome at Shanti House. I was expected to go in four days. I've made myself comfortable for two weeks now. I enjoy the view from the window of a garden rich in flowers. Nothing fancy—roses, lantana, clumps of humble petunias and pansies. Nurses are bewildered as to what's keeping me going. They don't say that to me, but I overhear their conversations with Jordi.

Jordi

"Are there people she needs to separate from?" asks Nurse Jill.

"Yes."

163

"Well, make sure she does. She needs a clear heart and mind to go peacefully."

"I've been working on it."

"Also, you must give her permission to go. Tell her that you will be fine."

"But I won't be fine. She knows that."

"Think. You will know what to say."

I realize she is holding on to me. And that I'm clinging to her. When she dies, I will have died a little as well.

Lavinia

No fear. No pain. For the first time I'm resting on a cloud. My body weightless. My skin frictionless. From under the thin sheet covering me, a blue glow pulses from my right breast, expanding and contracting with the heartbeat. Through my skin within the folds of flesh I see the worm of a larva, curled up and asleep. When did it start? Before I had any sense of myself as a woman, barely beyond the child in me. I carried this incipient monster dormant through the years. I wonder if it was a witness to my years as a student, budding actor, passionate friend, bold lover, fearless poet, world traveler. All the time an incubator of my destruction, beyond imagining, intuiting, or fearing.

Looking back, there were signs, too faint for attention, too casual for serious consideration. There was Paquita. She was to me a mysterious presence, a woman of many talents. A gifted cook, a spinner of tales from her pueblo, an artist with a needle and thread for mending the blouses and jeans that I held too dearly to toss.

I stand close by, following the back-and-forth dance of her iron. Steam rises from the damp cotton fabric. I'm caught by the smells inside the laundry room in the basement of our house in the Lomas district. The room is unheated, made even colder by the masonry walls and the concrete floor.

There are no appliances, not necessary with such an abundance of domestic workers. Clothes are washed in a sink, scrubbed against a rippled surface tilted toward the drain. Paquita does most of our clothes, but Mother sends the finer ones to a professional laundry and dry cleaner.

From the nearness of Paquita's generous body there is the scent of her skin, the fragrance of beans and tortillas and green serrano peppers. She sweetens her mouth with fresh mint to disguise the mezcal on her breath. I know she drinks, all day, reaching for any of several bottles she has concealed in different spots around the house, at the bottom of the clothes basket and the trash cans and the water tank in the toilet. I keep this knowledge to myself. She doesn't think anyone knows. Anchored to her ironing board, sink, stove, mop, without a lurch or misstep, she does her work in the house from six in the morning to nine at night with steady resolve. This makes for a long day, which she lightens with frequent breaks to sit and sip straight from the bottle, and chat with me. These are precious moments.

On Sunday, Paquita's day off, Father takes the family to a restaurant. Occasionally, I'm allowed to stay home and go to mass with her. My parents are happy to delegate my religious training. I'm eleven and the mystery of the ritual captures me. It's the one day Paquita changes out of her blue smock and puts on her oaxaqueña attire, a long lace dress thickly embroidered with flowers and birds, and a rebozo for warmth. She washes her thick black hair and coils it above her head in a single braid. She walks like a queen and I hold on to her hand. Proud.

Later we return to an empty house, and we settle into the family's formal parlor, Paquita in my father's favorite wingback chair and me in an ottoman before her. I'm aware how subversive it is for me to lead her into this space, reserved for guests. It was the sort of transgression that would reveal Mother and Father's need to protect us all from the invasion of the Mexico they inhabited but not embraced. Outside our home, I was told there was resentment by brown throngs wallowing in poverty, ready to march from their pueblos against people like us, the wealthy, the educated, the white. So even as we feared them, we allowed a select few into our walled homes, past our gates and locked doors, to serve and ease the discomforts of ordinary living. It was a life of comfort that I took for granted.

Paquita and her sisters scrubbed and polished, cooked, ran errands, diapered and held and comforted babies. Paquita shined Father's shoes at night and put them outside the bedroom door. She washed his car first thing in the morning. She answered the phone and filtered calls for Mother. Served at parties, walking around in a crisp black uniform offering drinks and nibbles from an expertly balanced tray. She was not expected to complain if a male guest reached out to her rear or brushed her breast with a careless hand. Mother's friends were jealous because of Paquita. They called her a joya, a jewel. Not all servants were joyas.

I still remember the day Paquita finally read my palm after begging her many times to do so. She said that such witchcraft was not the play of young girls. She had promised to tell my future once I became a woman. I was twelve when I had my first period and I reminded her of her promise. Even so, she waited a year. My small breasts, tender and sensitive to the touch, were gaining their shape. She laid her hands on my chichitas, as she called them, and the press of her palms was a kind of blessing. The laying on of hands for the easing of pain. But then, abruptly, she pulled her left hand back which, I clearly remember to this day, had been pressing gently on my right breast. I touched the spot to see if I could feel what had startled her.

"Que pasa, Quita?"

"Nada, mi hija." That was her favorite term of endearment for me, Hija. I wasn't expected to think of her as my mother, of course. But I knew I was her daughter in a subtler sense.

"Don't say 'nada.' You felt something."

She lay her hand on my breast again and closed her eyes tightly. "Nada, she repeated."

"Nada bueno?" I said.

But she would not elaborate and stood abruptly from the big chair, smoothing out the seat with brisk movements. Something in the formal arrangements of cushions and the still air of the shuttered room had been disturbed. Later, when my parents arrived from their Sunday outing, Mother insisted she could sense Paquita's presence in the parlor.

Only now, years later, do I realize that Paquita must've perceived the curled larva inside my breast. It took over forty years for the sleeping incubus to mature into a fully-grown crab. And now, under the influence of Jason's truth serum, I raise my eyes to its presence crawling on the bed, the opening and closing of its claws taunting me with silent menace as it scampers down to my feet then back up past my chest along my shoulder until it sits triumphantly on top of my head.

I turn to Jason beside the bed, holding my hand, and ask him if he sees it too. But he doesn't seem to have heard me, and I try voicing the question louder and still he doesn't respond with even a look or a nod. I feel, then, that I'm screaming inside me with no one to hear. I want to call out to Jordi or Ysbel guarding the door just outside the room, but again no sound comes out of my throat. It's only when I say Paquita's name, which rings in my head, that I feel her presence near me, even though she has been dead for years. She is gazing at me, not smiling. Her serious brown face hovering above me, the Mexican smell of her taking me back to a time when she was dearer to me than anyone.

Paquita

There are gifts that are curses. I can't help seeing what I see, and that day you were begging me to see into your future. I had to place my palm on your budding breast to be certain. It felt like I had touched a hot coal. I jerked my hand away, surprised the skin hadn't blistered. And all the time you were insisting I tell you what I had seen. But I was silent, reluctantly adding to my store of secrets. So many secrets that crowded my heart and would only go silent with the balm that is mescal.

Mother

We are part of a strange tribe, Lavinia, you and me. We have the women's curses on our breasts and ovaries, and our ancient hurts and resentments are about to fade into the equalizing ether of sleep. I was never able to get over the perception that you loved your nanny, the drunk Paquita, more than me. But now as you fade I learn that we don't decide our heart's preferences. I tried to make you more mine than hers after I realized that she had taken over the colicky baby and was able to offer you comfort that I couldn't. It was a relief at first to hand over the screaming creature to a gifted surrogate, who would hold you in

her arms and hug you to her generous breasts. I knew that you preferred her to me but thought that would change over time. Surely, you
would know that I was your mother.

As you grew to become a spirited child, I organized kitchen sessions for Christmas cookies, apple pie (the secret of the perfect crust!),
meat loaf (which you hated once you decided you were vegetarian at
age eight), Texas chili, tuna casserole, cheese fondue. And still you preferred Paquita's black mole from her native Oaxaca, such a complex al-
chemy of chocolate, almonds, cumin and black chiles, thick and dark,
gleaming over the soft tortillas rolled into enchiladas.

Paquita is gone now too. I fired her as gently as I could after you
went to college. With you gone she felt free to drink herself to death.
So I sent her away with some cash that she could use to buy a little
house in Oaxaca. I don't know what she did with the money or if she
really went back to her pueblo. I know that I put off letting you know
that she was gone.

You came home after the school term and a summer in Spain and
she was not there anymore. You kept asking and demanding to know
what had happened to her. I couldn't tell you where she was. I now realize that sending her away without knowing what would become of
her was a thoughtless and cruel thing. I emptied her room, gave away
her work clothes, and threw out the pictures she had tacked on the
walls of saints and martyrs and virgins, and the crucifix above her bed.
It was as if I had killed her and discarded the body.

By then I harbored no hope that you and I would ever be close.

Lavinia

The room is so crowded. I see Mother standing like a sentry at the foot
of the bed. And hovering by the door, as if too fearful to step into the
room, there's Paquita. Mr. Roberts stands beside Jordi, waiting for me
to acknowledge him. Ysbel is here too. And Esther Delius. Father and
little brother too. I remember the baby Luis, just a week old, lying in
his crib in the privileged spot beside my parents' bed, a shriveled pink
monster, smelling of baby powder and shit.

It's a reunion of the living and the dead. I can't tell who is alive and who are ghosts. There are so many people around me, hovering, vying for attention, sucking the air out of the room. I can hardly breathe.

Jason sits by the side of the bed. I beg him to send them away.

"Only you can do that," he says.

"Please."

"I don't see anyone, Vin. It's just you and me inside the room."

"Ok, but why do I see them?"

"People are waiting for you to allow them in."

"Imaginings from the acid."

"I didn't say that. They are inside you and outside you, like the air and the light around you, like blood that courses through you. Even when you don't see them, everyone you've ever known is lodged in the cells of your body. All your words and deeds and feelings stream through your veins, carrying a load of debris and memory. What the mind forgets, the body remembers."

I need to be free of these ghosts. They are crowding me, holding me back, hindering my way. The train I ride has no room for stragglers and stowaways, only ticketed passengers can board. It's slow going at first, meandering through a lush countryside, locked to its destiny but in no rush to get there. The gentle rocking, the rhythmic percussion of the track, lull me to a gentle twilight.

The afternoon sun streams through the trees and strobes past my eyelids in patterns of shadow and pink, until during a pause I open my eyes and look upon a green expanse of prairie. After the mountains of Mexico, the flatness of this land is something exotic and mysterious, a still ocean of tender grasses barely stirred by the blowing rush of the train, and a distant horizon.

And suddenly I awake to signs of life, the outskirts of a town, farmhouses and granaries, towering silos vigilant over the John Deeres of cultivation and harvest, but at this moment idle. In driveways, pickups and vans, kids' toys, bikes and wagons, and sleeping dogs, the occasional horse. But never a stirring of a human life, as if men and women and children had been sequestered inside the pretty white houses with blue shutters and yellow doors, the stuff of memory and nostalgia.

Then, in a surprise, the village station, its turrets and arches harkening to a lost time of adventure and escape when the promises of the wider world beckoned. There is a sense of pride in these whimsical buildings, the importance of the railroad in the life of the townsfolk, the point of departure and return, to love and forgiveness. The train station is a monument to leaving and returning home, again and again, to rest and renewal, to making up for lost time, to picking up in midstream.

The station is quickly left behind. And the train forces a momentary pause in the life of the town when it halts traffic at railroad crossings to clanging chimes and barrier lights. The view from the car engages the passengers; the eyes of the drivers, paused at the crossing, glaze over with indifference. Nothing to see here but a clattering chain of boxes, its progress punctuated by the plaintive whistle, a signal that some lives move on while others slip.

For long spells under an overcast sky the plain stretches in monochromes of dun and gray, at times covered in snow, at others parched in a summer drought. It feels as if nothing will relieve the monotony, but then when least expected, the forgotten backs of towns, the dumping heaps of trash and rusting barrels of industrial waste too toxic to bury or burn or pour into waterways, serve as blunt reminders that no journey is without stress.

There is a fascination with the dismembered hulks of once-gleaming autos, the piles of iron girders, heaps of boxy electronics, their screens mute and cracked, cords curled like snakes.

And always dogs, rutting about the urban dumps, feral creatures surviving by luck and wile on fast food refuse and market trash. Occasionally, rats and cats and squirrels and various obese vermin as big as beavers, all locked in bloody struggles, frozen and gone in a blink as the train pushes on.

Then, when least expected in the bowels of the train depot, dark caverns that lead to the order and safety of the track berth, a single figure watches the wagons creep by, looking through the lit windows, fixing in its stare the passengers ensconced in the safety of their sleeper lounges. The skeletal silhouette shows no fleshy contours, but a ragged ball gown, in drapes and flounces of pink taffeta topped by a feathered chapeau, elicits shocked recognition. The train pauses as if to allow boarding.

I know you. Beautiful, beautiful Catrina.

And I know you, Lavinia.

Are you death, la muerte?

No, I am life, See how the dead live. Our bones shake and rattle. We dance, work, drink, fuck and feel, even after the flesh is gone. Take the brain out of a skull and we go on remembering. Shrink the heart to the size of an atom and it still loves. Look at us and marvel how our jaws perpetually laugh. Flesh, hair, blood, sinew, all decay and degrade. Long after you are forgotten, the bones live. You know the song: The backbone connected to the neck bone, The neck bone connected to the head bone, Oh, hear the word of the Lord!

The head bone is connected to the soul bone?

And that is the finest bone of all. As weightless as a single hair on your head, but holding the stream of all your thoughts, no matter how fleeting, your deeds, even the most trivial, the feelings that sparked in your heart and were stifled. Bones outlast memories. What lies buried is as alive as that which was nurtured. Shame and pride are traded in the same coin, of equal value in the reckoning. And the pleasure of your first orgasm will continue to ring in a single note for all time.

Magic fingers. Petals opening on the cusp of a flower. Touching dew. Exploring past parting lips, gliding along the pistil into the depths of a wellspring. Then the whole palm cupping the entrance to the cave, fingers strumming the guardian sentry. My leg muscles seize, and the insides of my thighs start a series of spasms. I lose control of my breath. I'm not focused on anything else except these rising waves of pleasure going through my entire body. It's so intense that sometimes all my muscles just surrender and feel as if I've been blessed to the core of my soul. At last, I'm stretched out on the burning sand of a deserted beach while cooling ocean waves wash over me. I understand that this is heaven, this the gift.

Jordi

I am the priest of pleasure, the shaman of surrender, the owner of her orgasms. My instrument is her instrument. It responds like a trained snake to the flute of a charmer, rising from the nest of my pubes to the sound of her voice, the murmurs and hums of her desire. She owns my love, my manhood. We surrender to each other, our powers in fine equilibrium, pushing and pulling against our need.

We came to each other long past adolescence, already scarred by betrayal and loss, ready to invent ourselves in our mirrored ideals. I saw in her sanity and she saw in me a protector. She was neither wholly sane nor was I much of a protector. I flattered her by telling her she was the sanest woman I knew, expecting her to rise to the challenge. For my part, I spent too much time complaining to her, about my conflicted work, about friends who came short of expectations. But we, nevertheless, became each other's spiritual companions and perplexed guides. What we lacked in certainty we made up with fervor.

If God is love, then I fell far short of the ideal. I had a wandering heart, prey to occasional crushes on coworkers and neighbors. In truth, our relationship was protected by my being an inept adulterer. I didn't have the patience to court and romance, manage the lies and logistics of the expert philanderer. Platonic teases and fantasies served a shabby purpose. I like to think that a vigilant censor at my core held me in check. And my potential accomplices in lust saw through me, an unreliable partner in conjugal hanky panky.

For years I denied myself the total surrender to her love, until she became ill. Suddenly I was able to step up to my true role, and the result provided the happiest three years of our marriage. The inevitability of her death freed us from wishful thinking and fantasies of future happiness. From moment to moment we followed our bliss to Italy, Spain, Peru.

We ventured to Machu Picchu, a city of sacred geometry on a plateau near the clouds, itself appointed by two peaks rising like sentries at either end of the site. A narrow path alongside an Inca temple invited exploration, yet I could not follow her. I was seized by sudden vertigo, and felt myself walking unsteadily while Lavinia followed a child, a girl no more than eleven years old that traipsed her way along the ledge that circled the face of the structure, gradually spiraling to the apex.

I was unable to shuffle one inching step after another as I touched the stone wall to my right searching for some small protrusion that would allow my hand to cling. Meanwhile, I was being left behind by Lavinia and the girl, while other visitors managed to saunter past me, leaving me in a state of near panic. I managed to shuffle back to the head of the trail. I stood in the safety of the clearing where guides waited, smoking and chatting beside their taxis and tourist vans.

"Peligroso," a man whispered near me. "Vertigo makes you walk like a borrachito, a drunk."

And sure enough, falling would have freed me from the burden of witnessing your slow fade into death, the years of scans and treatments, the false cheers of momentary remissions, the frequent drifting into sleep, naps that prolonged themselves into hours, the stone-cold stasis of recurring coma. Always waiting and watching and listening to the susurrus of your breath.

There are moments of energy, when some force within you would rise to the fore and beat back the encroaching grip of the tumors teaming up in their malice from your breast to your lung to your brain. Then, in the darkest hours, you nudge me awake, asking for the gift of cannabis in a brownie soaked in milk. You glow with pleasure.

"Read to me. One of your stories."

"*The drive back is uneventful once the evening rush has waned. As I turn off the freeway onto Springer Way, following the narrow road up the hills above Lake Minton, the sun, already behind the top branches of the oaks and maples, heralding Canaan Hills, its mosaic of tender green lawns, deserted save for perhaps a toppled tricycle, one wheel still spinning . . .*"

"Can't hear you."

I realize I've been falling asleep, my reading fading to a slur. I awaken for a few moments and turn on my side to embrace you, hoping to lull you to sleep. Our cycles are out of sync; you sleep while I fret and brood. I wrestle with the guilt of wishing for a swift end. A better man would pray for remission, cheer when the latest treatment nudges your numbers, exult when Dr. Dave congratulates you on your tumors shrinking. But after a moment he grows serious when he admonishes me for not efficiently keeping track of your meds and appointments. This is my role, all else fades in the background. The new novel is shelved. My body grows soft from lack of exercise. I neglect the occasional friend that is not part of our support cadre. There is no life outside of Lavinia.

You are the undiscovered country, the planet of lost souls, the funeral pyre of surrendered dreams. Instead, memories rule. The past rises to relevance. Do you recall when you first felt I was a lover and also a friend? Maybe a single moment, the weekend I invited you to my house in the hills near San Miguel, without your boyfriend Ted who was away, I made your bed in the room next to mine. It was to be a literary visit; you had read some of my stories and were tasked to offer a critique. But work would wait until the next morning. We went out and sat in the town square listening to birds teeming at dusk within the thick foliage of the laurels. So many all at once chirping with excitement at the approaching evening. We had ice cream for dinner, small cups of the famous exotic flavors from Dolores: elote, cajeta, guayaba, mamey. We kissed, only once, as if by agreement to taste each other's sweetness. Then we kissed again at the end of the day. And I wished you good night.

Hours later, before dawn, you crept into bed with me. You were nude, apologizing that you hadn't brought sleeping clothes. You encouraged me to take off my pajamas saying that I needed to awaken my skin to the wonders of touch.

Mr. Roberts

I was finally able to shake off this man who said he was the husband of my former student and tormentor. I juggled my routine, found a different coffee shop, switched my scheduled students, shopped at different stores. I'd been able to avoid him, until he confronted me on the street and moved to block my stride as I was walking to Lund's. When I tried to dance around him, he found a way to sidestep and continue to stand in my way. I felt threatened. The sidewalk was crowded and passersby were clearly anticipating some drama between two old men.

"Let me pass."

"My wife needs to see you."

"Who are you talking about?"

We finally stopped shuffling about and managed to exchange a few words.

"Sure, you know. Of course you do."

"She was a kid. I haven't thought of her in years. Why are you bringing this unhappy episode back?"

"She needs your forgiveness."

"She's forgiven. They were children, she and her bosom pal Ysbel."

"She's dying."

"I'm not a priest. I do not grant absolution."

"Are you going to be an asshole at your age?"

He finally got through to me. I stopped trying to circle him and stood for a moment, feet squarely planted on the ground, shoulders slumped in surrender, my chest heaving as I tried to regain my breath. We all have our sins, I thought, and I stood still as if waiting to be punched.

"Are you going to come with me?"

"Not today, not right now. I need time."

"There is no time."

"Tomorrow, then."

"Here's the address." He handed me the Shanti Hospice card. Come any time, night or day. The place never sleeps. She doesn't go anywhere.

I stared at the card, running one finger cross the edge, then with a start, I saw that its sharpness had cut into the skin. I tucked the card into my wallet. And wiped the blood off my finger on my trousers. I could tell from his smirk that he was amused.

"Don't be a coward," he said, by way of farewell.

But of course, I was a coward. I did not want to confront this woman who was once the instrument of my undoing. And if I hadn't thought of her in years, she had nevertheless for years remained ghost-like in the periphery of my spirit. As I search my heart for a hint of forgiveness, I find only indifference.

My unrest followed me to my apartment, and even after enough drinks to muddle my thinking, it stayed with me through the night, hovering unseen, a ghost at heart's edge.

I'm not a violent person. Quite the opposite, most people would concur. So when I decided that I would in fact pay Lavinia the visit she had requested, my intention was not to deny her the forgiveness she felt she needed on her deathbed. She was no longer the monster child that had haunted me for years. I would overcome my resentment with a small act of charity, even if not entirely sincere. I would sit by her bed and whisper some conciliatory word or other, and give her shoulder a squeeze.

Lavinia

Mr. Roberts is finally here. I have good days and bad days, the common refrain of terminal cases, days when I can barely focus my energy on anything so simple as a spoonful of ice cream. Today is better. I hear tentative knocking on the half-open door. Before I can answer, Jordi holds it wide open for a soft old man in rumpled Docker pants and a blue corduroy shirt under a maroon cardigan. I'm still a sharp observer and it's not the stylish look I remember from his high school teaching days. He seems shy, reluctant to step closer to the bed.

Don't worry, I won't bite. I consider that I might be some kind of threat to him. And then I do try a small chuckle, not a full-blown laugh. I don't think I'm capable of those anymore; anything beyond a snicker requires too much oxygen to pull off. But that's not to say that I've lost my sense of humor. Although, the truth is there's not much to laugh about in this visit from Mr. Roberts. He's not here happily, but dragged by the scruff by Jordi, who knows what I need.

Jordi has surrendered the chair nearest me, the privileged spot for visitors who require my close attention. I pat the side of the bed so Mr. Roberts will take the hint and sit there. He finally does at a slight prod from Jordi. He is stiffly erect, reminding me of his fifth graders who would sit in class attentive and fearful of drawing his corrective eye. Now, it seems I am the teacher and he is the student, as if I had a lesson to impart. Such is the power imbalance of the dying. I reach my hand out and signal for his.

Come on, I think. Don't run away.

He places his hand on mine and I marvel at its softness. Clearly not the hand of an athlete or a laborer. I wonder if his hands can still juggle. There's a tray on the other side of the bed containing a half dozen orange pill bottles. I pull my hand from his and reach to take three. I'm clumsy and I drop them on the bed, so I frantically search through the covers to retrieve them. Ever attentive, Jordi finds them.

He is silently questioning me, as if I thought it was time for my afternoon meds—Ativan, Oxy, Docusate. "No worries," I whisper. "No anxiety, no pain, no constipation. They are for Mr. Roberts."

One thing I love about Jordi is that he doesn't question my whims, gives me the benefit that I will make sense eventually. Mr. Roberts catches on. He smiles at me for the first time since entering the room and sitting at my bedside. He nods at Jordi and reaches for the bottles. He weighs them, tosses them from hand to hand.

"I'm out of practice," he says.

He leans forward on the chair, takes a deep breath. I can see his pale blue eyes look up toward the ceiling as if seeking inspiration. Then one bottle flies up and a second one and the third. Mr. Roberts is juggling.

Mr. Roberts

It's like riding a bicycle. One, two, three. I haven't juggled in a hundred years, no longer having kids to entertain, and my SAT students are basically slugs with little interest in me beyond getting the answers to the questions most likely to be on the SAT. For my generous fee, I'm happy to provide results without wasting each other's time. It is cheating, of course, but I'm not cheating the parents who hire me or the nationwide testing conglomerate. My real victims are Harvard, Yale, MIT, and all the rest, set on their elitist, racially-biased selection process.

That was not the case with Lavinia, my gifted fifth grader who grew up to be downright brilliant. At Harvard, no less. According to her husband, I'm here so she can beg forgiveness of me. A deathbed remorse, repentance before judgment.

I so remember her, no longer as the instrument of my lynching at the International School in Mexico City, but as a brilliant child who tormented me with her arrogant intellect. They are the bane of us mediocre teachers, these urchins who even at a young age know themselves to be smarter than us. I was in my twenties at the time, still emotionally an adolescent and resentful of intelligent children. I was unaware of how special they are, taking their gifts as unwelcome intrusions.

Now, as I observe Lavinia, I hardly recognize her from the restless sprite I remember hiding at the back of the class. Good students like to occupy the front rows, to be always in view of the teacher. The real smart ones don't need to curry favor or put on the eager beaver act. Lavinia was one of a thousand, and her act was to appear less than she was, not out of modesty, but to get some satisfaction out of effortlessly gaming the system. Of course, I see that now; I was clueless back then.

Even in her sixties, visibly dying, I see Lavinia's childhood face, a smile breaking through her pain. She has been propped up on the mechanical bed, experimenting with the controls that hum and whirr to adjust the back and knees until she finds the proper comfort level.

"There," she said, "I can see you better, Mr. Roberts. And you can see me."

The room itself is sunny, with walls painted a soft peach, with a big window facing a garden and a bounty of flowers in pots that have been set up on pedestals so they can be viewed from the bed.

She seems to have been dressed for the occasion, a pink pashmina shawl wrapped around her shoulders, the covers smoothed out on her legs, which are lifted slightly, and her head, shaved of growing fuzz after chemo, to reveal the bright colors of her tattoos. That was a shock, which I tried to face with a blank expression. I had never seen a tattooed head before. And yet there was nothing arbitrary about it, a way to face the destruction of her body with a defiant, triumphant shout. I recognize some of the designs, a Posada skull, the Cheshire cat from Alice, a spotted wildcat, an owl, a snake from Mexican mythology.

"Forgive me for staring," I finally mumble.

She smiles and nods as if to signal that it's all right to look. "Tattoos are spectator art," she finally says. "Do you like them?"

I'm not sure what to answer. Her head is beyond liking or not.

"Yes," I say.

"Good. Not everyone does, you know."

"Did they hurt?"

"Everyone asks that," she smiles. "Dr. Dave had me well stocked with Percocet."

"Aren't opiates addictive?" I put on my concerned adult face, until I realize how dumb I may have sounded to her.

"Different designs hurt more or less. Even now that everything has healed, I can touch the snake or the puma or the skull, and they have their own sensation. They all come through my fingertips. That's how I visit my head without looking at myself in a mirror."

A moment of silence prolongs itself and grows uncomfortable. But now I wait without any further prompting of conversation. Her husband said she wanted to revisit that episode back at the school when she and her friend Ysbel turned me on my head and left me without any defense, in a narrative of children as victims and the adult teacher as pervert. Such was the script, and I was more of a spectator than an actor. Also, there was no way she was responsible, but also a bit player in a traditional drama. I want to say this to her. There is nothing to forgive. I could break the silence with such a statement and set her mind at ease. But I don't.

"Has your life been good?" she says.

I shrug slowly, as of to convey that her question would necessitate a long answer.

"Thanks for asking." And right away I recoil from such a lame response. But I can't help but go on, "If I told you I was fine and better than ever and grateful that I left the International School, would that make you feel good?"

"I would be happy," she says. "If I believed you."

I keep on shrugging deeply into my shoulders. I don't know what to say to Lavinia. Instead, I let my mind run off in silent dialogue. But you don't believe me. What right do you have to question me? What my life has been like for the last forty years is sadly none of your business. I was twenty-six when the scandal broke, and for the rest of my life I have been a sexual suspect unfit for the classroom. Even after I changed my name and embroidered a convincing resume, the stink sticks beyond all cleansing. I would sit for interviews and I could tell the person evaluating me could see right into my eyes to the depth of my skull.

"I've had a great life," I say. "I'm still teaching, and mostly happy, with many friends." I'm not sure she's aware of the game I've embarked on. By not admitting suffering, I give her nothing to atone for. Nothing to beg forgiveness for. A small satisfaction on my part, to be sure.

"Speaking of ups and downs," she says, "would you juggle again?"

And that was the last word. With no harm done to me, there's nothing to beg forgiveness for. So, she lets me play the fool and entertain her. But she knows that I have not let her off the hook. That's my way of frustrating her expectation for forgiveness. Even on a deathbed there's no need to tie up every loose end.

Lavinia

I let Mr. Roberts leave without another word. In fact, I feigned sleep while he juggled, and realized he left without saying anything to close the visit, not even a wish good night. I have my good days and I have my bad days. Tonight I'm left without resolution, and that is not good.

What I wanted to say remains unsaid. Therefore, in spite of my expectation, I have not been absolved. And the frustration I feel is a poison I don't know how to purge.

At times, I wish I were Roman Catholic. So simple a mechanism—confession, repentance, and guaranteed absolution. With penance, of course, because nothing is free. That's the tricky part. How does the priest make the punishment fit the crime? A thousand Hail Marys, a hundred rosaries, a three-day fast, a week in a hair shirt, or, better still, a spiky cilice around my thigh. Such a clever institution. I would prefer its medieval techniques of punishment for sinners, quite willing to whip, yes flagellate is the word, myself to ecstasy. With my heretic orientation I would be a candidate for the rack and the water, stretch and dip, pull and choke, twist and gurgle. Slice off my nipples, make me walk on hot coals, hang me by my thumbs. None of that would be enough to earn forgiveness for my sins. Not just my one against Mr. Roberts, but the sins of spiritual pride, envy, anger, lust, and all the rest that have found targets along my way. Too many to atone one by one, so the result would be an unspecified sentence to purgatory.

I first learned of purgatorio at age seven from Paquita. A taste of hell without the eternal ticket. Again, genius doctrine from the church. Scary but not hopeless, tortured but unconsumed by the fire, able to pay my debt and enter the kingdom.

She reassured me, at my age a child would not enter hell or purgatory, but we would float in limbo. Not heaven, but also not bad, a kind of sweet morning slumber, dozing in a warm bath, swaddled in silk. All that would end by age thirteen, when baptized by blood I would learn to sin.

After that I would have to make confession and receive communion, which was the means to take Christ into my body to protect me from evil. All that seemed very complicated, dying before age thirteen would be just dandy. I prayed for death to come gently and deliver me to limbo.

I pictured myself laid to rest upon the church altar in a white silk gown, laid face up inside a tiny casket tufted in satin. Everything would be white to signify my innocence. There would be tears from Father and Mother and Luis who was only a toddler but who would grieve the sister he would never get to know. Looking back I marvel how much trouble that would have saved all of us. At the time, I only thought of how everyone would love me and weep and apologize for making me eat meat, which I hated. Dear God, who art up there and down here, in my house and in the sky, please take me.

And then I caught the measles. It started one morning when I discovered a cluster of red spots on my skin. They didn't itch at first and there were no more than a dozen spaced around my chest and belly. It was a Saturday so I had been allowed to sleep late instead of the usual rushing and nagging to get ready for school. It was to be a warm morning so I dressed in shorts and a light top. I didn't pay the red spots any attention for most of the day. Until they started to itch. I lifted my top to look at my belly and they had spread into red splotches. Still, I didn't say anything because they had turned ugly and the whole thing was embarrassing. It was only when Paquita had served me lunch in the kitchen that she asked why I was scratching over the fabric that I became the unwanted center of attention.

I can still see her expression when I showed her my chest, her eyes wide and her mouth agape, looking as if she had seen a monster. I didn't think I was capable of eliciting such a look of panicked anxiety. I tried to reassure her they didn't hurt, just itched, but she would not enter into a conversation about the problem. Instead, she ran off to the kitchen yelling for Mother.

"Señora! Señora!"

And then Mother was screaming. Father was shouting. Paquita was weeping and snuffling. I assumed that they thought the red splotches were her fault and that if she gave me a bath with plenty of soap they would go away.

I burst into tears that I was sorry to have caused such a problem, that Paquita had nothing to do with the splotches, that they were all my doing. I was expecting some kind of punishment but instead I was hurried into my prettiest pajamas, very soft flannel ones with butter-flies on a blue field, and tucked into bed.

Paquita brought a pitcher of lemonade and a plate of cookies, my favorites in animal shapes, and Mother sat on the side of the bed and kept placing her hand on my forehead. So far, I was reassured that I would be coddled rather than scolded. Through overheard agitated conversations, as Mother got on the phone and shared the news with friends and the family doctor, I picked up a new word—sarampión. It sounded important and somewhat dangerous, and I accepted it as a badge of honor.

Yes, I was the victim of sarampión. I repeated it like an incantation: Sa-ram-pión, over and over so I wouldn't forget the mysterious word. I didn't feel ill, so it was easy for me to enjoy the attention, once it was clear that I was not at fault but rather an innocent victim, propped up on extra pillows and nibbling on cookies. And reassuring Mother that I felt fine as she kept placing a thermometer under my tongue.

Around nine o'clock, early for me, Mother said I should get some rest and turned on the small bedside light, because I enjoyed even at that age reading myself to sleep. That night I was in the middle of Black Beauty, which I loved because it was about a girl and her wonderful horse and I loved anything to do with horses. I was a good reader at that age, but that night I had trouble concentrating even though it was the third time I had read the book. I kept losing track of what I was reading and had to keep going back to the previous paragraph or even earlier.

At first it was too hot in the room, then I would kick off the cov-ers and I would be shivering. I called out for Mother and said I was thirsty, so she brought me a glass of juice with a pill, and again stuck the thermometer under my tongue. This time she turned off the table lamp and said I had to sleep because that would be the way I would get well. I felt restless and had lost interest in the story but I wasn't at all sleepy between shivering and sweating. At one time I tossed off the covers and stripped off my pajama top. I called to Mother that I was too hot, so she came into the room and ran a cool sponge over my body.

I spent the long night between waking and sleeping, shaking off vivid dreams of bugs crawling all over me, spindly spiders with round bellies, that cast red spots as they moved on me. I kept trying to brush them away, but they would cling to my hands and I couldn't shake them off. My cries must've brought Mother into the room, because she was once again at my bedside with the moist sponge. She must've come in several times, because when I wasn't sleeping or dreaming there was Mother cooling my face and chest.

I must've finally fallen asleep because I woke up in the morning, my room bathed in sunlight through the curtains, my body heavy like stone on the bed, my arms like lead beside me, my hands as if encased in thick leather gloves, which I kept trying to yank off. I raised my hands before me and screamed in fright because they had become huge monstrous mitts, knuckles swollen and fingers twisted, nails black and broken, as if belonging to an old and gnarled witch.

It took a while for Mother to come into the room while all the time I was stretching my arms straight out and holding my hands up for her to see. At first she couldn't understand what was happening. I kept screaming, "my hands, my hands!" And finally, even if she couldn't see anything wrong with them, she took my hands in her soft warm ones. Gradually, I felt my fingers withdraw into my palms as they folded inside Mother's hands.

I was over the measles in about a week. The fever never came back and the spots gradually dried and faded. And all that time I breathed with relief that I had enjoyed a reprieve from an early death, and resolved that I wouldn't challenge God again. Even after I stopped believing in Him, I knew that you should not indulge fantasies involving the higher powers of the universe. There are forces out there that you don't fuck around with.

Jordi

Two months into the start of chemo, Lavinia's hair was falling in tufts, clinging to her fingers whenever she touched her head. It began one morning after her shower when I heard her cursing inside the bathroom. I rushed to her but the door was locked. I knocked and she told me in a voice choked with tears that I should go away and leave her alone.

I could hear the hair dryer buzzing and after a few minutes she came out to show me clumps of hair in her palm, a mute explanation of her distress. I didn't at first see much change in her head, she had always had thick brown hair cut to a boyish length and that morning she had styled it by tousling it in a kind of pixie. I reassured her that she looked fine. But she insisted that this was only the beginning. She had been warned at the start of treatment, and now this was evidence that hair loss had begun.

It was time to get in front of the problem. We went shopping for a wig. I tried to persuade her that it would be fun to experiment with her look. The nice woman at the wig store who was in fact wearing a riot of curls in a shoulder length platinum mane took on the project cheerfully.

"Trust me," the woman said, "you will look fabulous."

"I will look like I have cancer."

"Nonsense. Flight attendants and dancers and businesswomen all wear wigs because they want to look their best without fuss and bother."

We had fun. There were mirrors all around the shop for front and back and side looks. She tried bobs and page boys and perms with cascades of curls, from purple to platinum blonde to wild red. For a moment she saw that she could beat the side effects of the chemicals with a defiant attitude. She would look beautiful. And with every hair change different personalities revealed themselves, my lovely Vin as career girl, 1950s housewife, movie star. She could cheat death and be all things. And I would buy as many wigs as she wanted.

In the end, she chose a chestnut-brown bob with wispy bangs. I thought she looked cute in it, and best of all, nobody could tell it was a wig.

"Unless you know me," she said.

"Try it and wear it home," the wig lady suggested. "It will be your new you."

"I'll put it on when I have to."

We took it home in a wig box. And that's where it stayed. She never wore a wig even after she lost all her hair. Eventually, we donated it to the Cancer Center.

On one occasion, deep into her treatment, Vin was in the La-Z-Boy recliner in the treatment room, while a plastic bag on a pole with a clear liquid dripped into an IV. It was winter so she had been wearing a wool beany, but the room was warm and she had pulled it off. By then she had lost so much hair that her head was covered in nothing but fine black fuzz. I was on a chair beside her when I noticed that the solitary woman across from her was wearing the chestnut bob wig that we had donated.

Vin smiled at her and mentioned that it was nice she wasn't losing hair.

"Oh, but I have. I'm as bald as Mr. Clean. This is a wig."

"Well, I wouldn't know. You look good with it."

"Thank you." A moment later she nodded to me. "It's wonderful that your husband is here to keep you company. Mine would not come within a hundred feet of the Cancer Center."

"It is a freaky place," Vin agreed.

The woman directed the next comment to me. "You don't mind seeing your wife without hair?"

"I don't think about it anymore."

"My husband never sees me without the wig. I sleep in another room. Then I wear the wig for breakfast. And take it off after he goes to work."

"You should go without it some evening. He may accept the situation," Vin said.

"No, I'm too ashamed. At my age it's worse than being seen naked."

Lavinia

Hair comes and goes, with the switch in chemicals. Sometimes it looked like it was trying to grow back but the result was only a thin black fuzz that went nowhere. I decided to embrace the old noggin, and made an appointment at the Justin K. Salon in the neighborhood. I was already somewhat unsteady on my feet, so Jordi walked me the six blocks to the shop. It was slow going and I was exhausted by the time we got there. I asked Jordi to leave me and said that I would find a way home once I was done.

I was wearing the beanie down over my ears so I didn't attract much attention when I checked in. I hadn't been in for months, since the hair started falling, so when they asked me if I wanted to see Lisa, my usual stylist, I said that I would rather work with a guy, who would know what to do with a razor.

They booked me with Marcus. He is a tall, handsome Black man who specializes in elaborate styles for weddings and such. He came out to greet me and seemed somewhat confused to see me. He led me to the chair and stood behind me while he looked at my reflection on the mirror.

"So, what's the special occasion?"

"Oh, nothing right away. Getting ready for a future event." I enjoyed that moment of coyness.

"Something soon?"

"Maybe in a couple of years."

He was smart enough not to pursue details. "Take off your cap, and let's see what I have to work with."

"Not much, I'm afraid." I pulled the beanie off and watched his expression of barely contained shock in the mirror.

"I see."

"Can you shave it close? I don't like the fuzz."

Marcus had wonderful hands, so soft and tender as he lathered my head with a fragrant lavender lotion, smooth and silky, that lulled me into a contented reverie. It was reassuring to have the head that I was ashamed of be so gently caressed. Then he started working with a straight razor, tiny strokes flicking the fuzz away, making a scratching sound, a rhythmic dance of the blade against my skull. The process took longer than I expected, as he started in back, then moved around the side to the top, flick flick, back and forth until my head was a gleaming orb. He massaged the sensitive skin with a minty lotion that made my scalp tingle.

"All done," he said.

"Thank you. It feels nice," I said, as I ran my hand over my head. I started to put the beanie on when he stilled my hand.

You need something prettier on top. He went to the front of the salon and came back with some silk scarves. "You choose."

I picked an emerald-green print of abstract swirls in different shades.

"Good choice." Then he proceeded to show me how to wrap it pirate style around my head and knot it in back.

I must've literally sauntered on the way home, eager to show off my new look, feeling more confident and energetic than I had in weeks. I felt I had crossed some forbidden threshold and was ready to embrace the devastation that chemicals were having on my body.

"I have a surprise for you," I announced.

Jordi

I embraced Vin at the door. I'd been concerned over her walking the several blocks from the salon and was proud she had made it on her own. She withdrew from my embrace enough to show off the silk scarf that covered her head in a dashing pirate look.

"What do you think?"

"Take off the scarf," I suggested. "It covers you, but it screams bald lady."

"Well, surprise!" She took off the scarf and her beautiful, perfectly round head emerged in all its glory.

"I like it better naked."

"You sure?"

I bent down and kissed the top of her head by way of an answer. It was like Vin to transition from grief about her treatment side effects, to anger, to eventually owning her lot in the battle. From that time on she carried her head proudly. No matter that whenever we were out she attracted stares. More annoying were the occasional comments from well-meaning women who saw in her a sister in chemo.

"Oh, dear, and how is your treatment going?"

I felt Vin bristle. I touched her hand to calm her down, but she had to snap: "Thank you so much. I forgot I had cancer for two hours, and now you've reminded me. And, I have no fucking idea how my treatment is going."

And yet, Vin used her beautiful naked head as a symbol of defiance in her personal battle. She would not let the world forget her head. She went from shame to a kind of quiet pride, a vanity statement with her head at the center of attention.

Lavinia

I thought of my head as a blank canvas. I kept it closely shaven because the black fuzz that insisted on sprouting in spite of the chemo was not at all "sightly," as Marcus the hair guy put it. I rubbed a vegetable dye all over it so that it glowed with vibrant color, sometimes pink like a rose, at others orange as a harvest moon, yellow like the sun, purple like grape jelly. The stuff would wash out, so every day according to my mood, a new color would go on. Jordi loved the effect.

Sure, people still gave me looks, bewildered and inquisitive but not quite in the pity mode that had been prevalent when my head was bare except for the fuzz. And nice ladies with pink ribbons knew better than to ask me how my disease was progressing. Treatment, what treatment? There was something liberating in my owning my baldness and dressing it with color.

One time during one of my shaving sessions with Marcus, he drew a flower on my head with a green sharpie. I loved it, of course, and found that it brought a smile to the stylists in the salon, who had been reluctantly accommodating me as I shuffled in, clearly freaking out the rest of the clientele with the invasion of the cancer lady.

"It's great," I said to Marcus. "I wish it wouldn't wash out."

"Doesn't have to. Get a tattoo."

I took my head with the little flower home, and that night I had a dream that my whole skull was alive. Through a tropical mist, emerged colors and shapes that were both familiar and strange. It vibrated with jungle rhythms, the cry of birds and the roar of big cats, the slither of a snake, the clackety-clack of dancing skeletons. My skull would reflect the visions and dreams that had haunted me my whole life.

And that's how I ended up at Indelible Ink whose rules were listed on a sign up front: *No kids, no drunks, no sissies.* It was a magical place with a huge aquarium that went wall to wall with exotic tropical fish in every color imaginable. It was so relaxing to be on the cusp of having my skin altered for all time, and just take a breath and relax, gazing at the fish cavorting about. The place hummed with activity beyond the parlor, the buzz of needles, very little talk except for the occasional laugh or whimper, and on the sound system, drums, marimbas, flutes.

I would be in the hands of the brilliant Ruthie Lee, a true artist who could create tattoos freehand with the needle on skin rather than traced from a stencil. I liked that she worked dangerously, getting it right on the first pass of the buzzing needle without the possibility of erasures or hesitations. Other artists offered a selection of designs where a customer could pick something out of a sample book to put on their skin. I mean, do you want Daffy Duck on your breast quacking for all time?

Ruthie Lee was more than a tattoo artist, her whole person was art from her hennaed feet to her goth lipstick. I wanted to be like her. Purple hair cut close on the sides and fountaining on top, rings and studs on her lip and ears, tattooed swirls and mystical motifs on her arm from the wrist to the shoulder. And a variety of bracelets and bangles on her wrists and ankles that jingled with her every move. She was a vision and she was music.

Ruthie Lee didn't offer a sample book. "Tell me what you want and we'll work it out together. Are you looking to adorn a private place for special people to enjoy?"

"Nope," I had to laugh. "As public as it gets. My head."

"Oh, how glorious," she said. "I've never done a dome before. Do you have some design in mind already?"

"Many, all over my head. Top, sides, front to back."

"It will be a total honor to do your head."

"Will it hurt?"

"Yes, like hell. There will be beauty, but you will pay."

We met at her studio, a cluttered combination of bedroom and workshop, to plan our project. She offered me tea, wine, weed. And I accepted all three. I needed all the courage I could muster. Ruthie Lee sat at her drawing board and I watched. I had brought a folder of clippings showing some of the images I was after.

This would be my tree of life. A snake because it sheds its skin and grows a new one and is thereby reborn many times in one lifetime. A

Posada skull. A spotted puma. A rabbit in the moon. An owl reading a book, because he's wise. A peacock because Jordi. I delighted in watching Ruthie Lee's fine hand assemble the images on a round drawing of my head.

The snake went first, a slithery creature across the top, from rattles in the rear to its flat head up front. She experimented with colors. The snake was green. The rabbit white in the middle of a blue moon. The Puma with yellow and black spots. A black owl reading a red book. The skull bone-white. And throughout, the tree with fine spreading branches and tender leaves with brown roots all the way down the nape.

We must've sat for hours, sipping and smoking, with Ruthie Lee occasionally pulling away from the drawing board to take a close look at my head, holding it with her strong fingers and turning it this way and that toward the light.

"When will you start in earnest?"

"You mean with the needle and ink?"

"Yes. Soon?"

"We can start tomorrow and then go for once a week."

"It will take months at that rate," I sighed. "I want it done before I'm done."

"The images need to heal."

"You're in charge."

"No, you are. I'm the hired needle. We'll go as often as you feel up to it. It can be tiring."

We started with the snake bisecting my head. It was my first time, and I felt sharp pain under the buzzing needle, with only brief pauses for Ruthie Lee to wipe the ink. I tried to keep from even the slightest yelp so as not to alarm Jordi, who waited in the parlor. He was not particularly interested in watching Ruthie Lee at work, but he would pop in from time to time and make appreciative comments.

After about an hour, I asked him to go into my bag and pull out a Percocet. It helped. That session went on for three hours. He offered coffee to Ruthie Lee and she said she would love him like no other if he brought her some French roast from Dunn Brothers down the street. After that, he became coffee guy and general cheerleader. Meanwhile the buzzing went on like a bumble bee hovering over my head. The sound would stay with me even after I went home, all through sleep and meditation and reading.

I remember that first night when I went home and finally pulled off the film protecting the new work. I wept because I had never expected to see something so beautiful become a part of me. The brilliant green of the snake's body, tempered with darker shades for the scales, and a pair of red, glowing eyes in its head. I was going to have something fantastic for the world to see. Yeah, cool ink, lady.

Every session was new: new pain, new art. Some areas seemed to bring more pain than others. Different colors of my head vibrated in different ways under Ruthie Lee's insistent needle. And all the time I could feel her soft breath near my face, slow and even, not showing the least excitement. She hardly spoke beyond a soft word to herself, yes, good, more here, as if she was communicating with a part of her that was beyond the reach of the surroundings. I would have liked to follow her progress, but there was no way I could see the top of my head without a mirror positioned just right. So I trusted and surrendered.

Jordi

That's the happiest I had seen Vin since the diagnosis. Her head was the light of her life. She was the star of the Cancer Center, bathing in a constant stream of praise from nurses and techies, who would send word out when she was in the treatment room so others could come by to admire Ruthie Lee's fine work. When we were out, nobody would notice her halting progress down the street, leaning on the walker she eventually required to keep upright, but focused instead on her beautiful head. Instead of the well-meaning litany from concerned women, the comments came from rougher side of the street.

"Wow, nice ink, lady!" yelled a guy in leather chaps as he slowed his motorcycle to roll abreast of us for a block.

Oh, my Lavinia was so cool. And I was cool for walking beside her. Eighty percent of my coolness factor came from being with Vin. Without her at my side I was just another sad sack husband waiting for his wife to go to chemo, come back from chemo, go to radiation, come back from radiation, go to sleep, then wake up hungry in the middle of the night so I could heat a pot brownie soaked in milk. I had my roles, which I think I performed conscientiously.

After some weeks, the greater part of the head show was done, with only work remaining on the roots spreading down the back of her head to the nape. Sessions with Ruthie Lee became fewer when Vin pleaded exhaustion from the more intense treatment Dr. Dave had been prescribing as her numbers escalated. It became clear that there would not be many more remissions.

⚜ V ⚜

Lavinia

At one and a half years since my diagnosis, I reminded Jordi that I had been promised possibly three with decent quality of life. And that meant planned breaks from chemo and radiation so I didn't go around feeling all sick and depleted. That was the horror of cancer, that trying to do battle meant feeling sicker than surrendering. All along I knew that the battle we waged was a losing one. Dr. Dave persuaded me that it was my obligation as a human to pursue life even in the face of imminent death.

I knew that Jordi would be reluctant for us to embark on another travel adventure. But I also knew that he would not be able to refuse me, such is the tyranny of the dying, as I learned. Still, I didn't want him to indulge me out of obligation or guilt.

First step would be for Dr. Dave to taper off treatment so that I would feel more energy. One morning, I woke up with two words on my mind, Machu Picchu, and I kept repeating them like some magical incantation.

"What was that?" Jordi asked me to repeat myself.

"Oh, but darling, you heard me."

"That's all the fucking way to Peru."

"You looked it up on the map?"

"Everyone knows where Machu Picchu is."

"We can discuss it with Dr. Dave. I'm estimating a week off juice and another week off for travel."

"Maybe not great timing. Your numbers haven't been great."

"Two weeks rest from poison will not kill me."

"Ok, Machu Picchu."

Once Jordi was on board a project, he pursued the details with single-minded concentration.

Jordi

There was a whole breast cancer industry that Vin didn't buy into. The Cancer Society with their pink ribbons. The support groups. Internet cures with mystery herbs, almond extract, Haitian shamans. Tijuana clinics offering injections of hydrogen peroxide, coffee enemas, Laetrile infusions. People had a secret cure to share, the miracle of a friend's years of survival, stories of overnight remission. The dominant theme was that accepting the inevitability of death by tumors was tantamount to suicide.

Vin would subject herself to grueling radiation and chemo as long as they provided a good quality of life. The point was not to deny eventual death, but to enjoy whatever life she was given. Her resolve was a lesson to me.

And she became greedy to live, restless with the possibility of wasted time. Dr. Dave was an artist in the design of dosages that would allow for periods of rest between bouts of misery.

Machu Picchu came as a surprise. It had apparently been on Vin's radar for years without her mentioning it. You don't go to Peru on a whim. There was always travel that took on greater urgency. Machu Picchu was one of those adventures that you could put off indefinitely. After all, it had been around for five hundred years, now waiting for Vin to go there at the last moment.

I was worried about us being in Cusco, and then crossing the mountains to the site itself. With Vin's compromised lungs, even after radiation had shrunk the scattered tumors, she was often out of breath. Cusco is over 11,000 feet above sea level. Even after living in Mexico City, that was the highest we'd ever been. We would take it easy and acclimate for three days before traveling on to the ancient Incan citadel. Tea from the green coca leaves was supposed to help, and it explained how the ancient Incas were able to construct fortresses out of massive stone blocks transported for miles to the actual building site.

It was no secret that I disliked air travel, and Vin was always ready to hold my hand during the bumps and dips, the longer the flight, the more I anticipated crashing. I breathed a sigh when we landed in Lima. I was not ready for the leap onto Cusco in a bouncy two-engine turbo prop. There are no mountains like the Andes, especially when they are as close as your nose, dazzling, snow-capped, sculptural monuments stretching above and below us as far as I could see out of the passenger window. I was sure that the pilot enjoyed taking his rattling airplane roaring between peaks he could not surmount.

During a particularly nauseating lurch, Vin reached for my hand and held it to her breast. "Relax, Jordi. It's my turn, not yours."

Cusco was a revelation, the capital of Inca civilization, the navel of the world, at its center a fortress of massive stone, its walls over three feet thick winding around the town. Vin studied everything she could get her eyes on, from guidebooks to internet searches in her quest of details on the Inca. Travel with Vin was an education.

Mysterious in its origins, founded in 1100, it withstood centuries of internecine wars, until the Spanish conquistadors humbled it, building a Dominican convent and cathedral on top of the Incan Temple of the Sun. A main feature in a side chapel along the nave is a statue of St. James as a knight on horseback, the original Santiago the Moor killer, referenced by Shakespeare's Iago. In the Cusco church, instead of a black man being trampled under the horse's hoofs is a brown Inca, so Santiago goes from mata moros to mata indios.

We traveled from Cusco to Machu Picchu with a sense of increasing anticipation. Suddenly we were more pilgrims than tourists, and as such the journey would need to be complicated, and for Vin, especially, challenging physically. It was not hard to talk her out of taking the three-day Inca trail with camping along the way, with the added thrills of mule riding, rafting and zip lining. Even with guides and porters and cooks to help out, trekking along the Andes was a daunting adventure. Vin was disappointed until she learned that there would be ample opportunity for hiking on the way to the citadel. I would later encounter my limits for high places, while Vin found renewed energy and took to the trails like a mountain goat.

The first leg was by rail boarding at five am at the nearby village of Ollantaytambo where we joined about a dozen travelers of different ages and nationalities. Being the only one of the group that could pronounce the name of the village, Vin was much admired. For that and for her inked head.

Our first taste of luxury during the trip was traveling on the Hiram Bingham train named after the fabled explorer who discovered Machu

Picchu in 1911, a slow trip along the beat-up track. The first-class carriage dated from the forties, appointed with gleaming wood and brass fixtures and huge windows overlooking the steep canyons on either side of the tracks, craggy chasms with no bottom in sight, a constant spectacle during the four-hour journey.

The seats were upholstered in red velvet that was somewhat thinned in places but still retained a rich feel, reading lamps with amber glass shades cast a golden light on Vin's brilliant head. As the train clattered merrily along on the ancient track, we tried to hold on to our pisco sours while perched unsteadily on leather bar stools facing a beveled mirror and about a hundred backlit bottles featuring spirits from around the world.

We reached Aguas Calientes, the town nearest the site, around two. It's a shabby town with a couple of good restaurants and many shops. We ate a lunch of potatoes, the national food of Peru, different varieties from familiar russets to knobby tubers dipped in a fragrant sauce, washed down with more pisco. Vin bought a Peruvian knit cap with ear coverings that could be tied under the chin. I got one too, along with a T-shirt featuring a Llama spitting.

I was glad to have mellowed myself with alcohol by the time we got on the van that would take us to the Belmond Hotel at the entrance to the site. The trip took twenty eternal minutes while the vehicle teetered on the edge of the switchbacks taking us lower onto the plateau where the Incas had built Machu Picchu, a combination ceremonial center and fortress for the nobility. Vin gazed with wonder at the crevasses opening up beneath us, while I reassured myself that the drivers did this particular trip several times a day without incident. It would be just our luck that our man would slip up and send us down to join the Inca spirits who might be resentful of outsiders invading their sacred space. I felt a stab of shame at the realization that I had accepted Vin facing an early death but horrified with my own during this journey. This would be a recurrent theme: facing my mortality while watching Vin at peace with her own.

And we splurged. The Belmond Lodge at the gate of Machu Picchu welcomed us into a stately lobby, a welcome refuge after the van ride. Finally, my feet were touching solid ground. Beyond the building I could catch a glimpse of the arches and turrets with the solitary Huayna Picchu peak rising like a sentry over the architectural complex.

As we entered the lodge, we were greeted with smiles, offers of coca tea or pisco, all set to make us feel the special privilege of being here, at the very entrance of sacred Machu Picchu.

We had more potatoes for breakfast and by seven we were part of the small group of early risers entering Machu Picchu. A clerk at the gate congratulated us and stamped our passports with the honorary visa. As we took our first tentative steps into the fabled Inca space, the enchanted terraces and stone structures were enveloped in a mist that would slowly dissipate with the rising sun.

Vin set out with enthusiasm and I followed her. Without ever having been here, she had memorized maps and layouts for the trip and was suddenly at home climbing the terraced platforms through the narrow passageways set in the walls on the way to the Temple of the Sun. It was designed not so much for worship as for observations of the stars, with stone nooks aimed at capturing the sun's journey during the solstices.

Throughout, small buildings were divided into quarters for royalty and nobility, priests, and the secluded rooms for noble girls. We were not prepared for the nearby Inti Mach'ay cave, where festivals were conducted to initiate young nobles into manhood, their new status marked by fasting, visions, and an ear-piercing ceremony.

We ended up before a carved pillar that marked the entrance to the vaulted mausoleum with designs that spoke of rituals and sacrifices and ceremonies for the dead. As Vin pointed out during our travels to cathedrals and temples and catacombs, the dead are everywhere. Some of them are not even wholly dead.

By nine, the sun was in full splendor rising above the citadel and we made our way to a scheduled climb of Huayna Picchu, the daunting peak that loomed above the citadel.

Lavinia

I was so thrilled. We were going to climb Huayna Picchu, a hike limited to two hundred travelers at the ten AM start, all of us lined up around nine thirty, slapping our arms for warmth, twitching and dancing and stretching in place. I could feel the energy similar to the start of a race. I was well equipped: sun hat, Vasque hiking boots, no-blister socks and moleskin patches, a light backpack with water and energy bars. This would be a stroll in the park.

At the gate we showed our passports and signed in the start time. Someone joked that anyone not signing out at the end of their hike would be presumed missing in action. Not all of us thought that was funny, and I saw Jordi visibly pale. I was impressed that he had stuck with me this far.

For the first few minutes the trail was wide enough for two abreast, allowing the more energetic among us to jump to a head start. Then the trail narrowed at the cross leading to the right for the forty-five-minute shorter climb. And to the left for the longer circuit that would take about two hours around and up to the peak. Jordi and I had decided we would take the longer path which was also apt to be less crowded. And hopefully less steep than the shorter, more verti-cal crawl.

Ha, what fools. We started up single file, with the stronger climb-ers pushing against the slower ones, without many opportunities to pass along the narrow trail. And while the longer climb was supposed to be less crowded, the fact that we would be circling the mountain meant that for much of the time on the trail we had the side of the hill on one side and a steep drop on the other with occasional lengths of chain to grab for safety. The vistas of the surrounding mountains and the city below were magnificent, but I found it prudent to focus on the uneven, rocky trail as I walked. I had started out ahead of Jordi, so I figured he was following closely behind me, breathing hard, grunting and quietly cursing.

On steeper sections steps had actually been carved out that could only be climbed on hands and knees, but the other hikers were so close behind me that there was no chance to sit on a step and take a break. And when the path widened by even a few inches, a stronger hiker would lunge forward and pass. When I did get a chance to pause and look back, Jordi was nowhere to be seen. I was hoping to be able to rest at the top and wait for him there.

It took me nearly two hours to get to the top. The narrow plateau was crowded with hikers who had ascended from the earlier time slot and were milling around jostling each other to get out of the way to take pictures of the surrounding mountains and the spectacular geometry of Machu Picchu below.

I must've waited for half an hour, shoving and squeezing my way through the crowd, hoping to find Jordi. It seemed that wherever I stood I was in someone's way, getting cursed in different languages so that I quickly grew increasingly xenophobic. My hard-earned serenity was flying in in the face of pushy Germans, clumsy Americans, massed Asians, rude Russians, and of course the know-it-all French. Somewhere in the middle of the crowd was a small brown man in an army uniform, trying to keep order. I caught his eye and I think he could see the desperate look I gave him, because he edged his way toward me and clasped my wrist and started pulling me through the crowd.

"Way down?" He shouted.

"No," I answered. "Temple of the Moon."

"No, señora," he shook his head. "Muy dificil."

"Si. Templo de la Luna." I insisted.

He shrugged as if to let me know that it was my choice, then gently guided me by the hand toward a sign that pointed to the Templo de la Luna.

At that point there was nowhere to go but onward. Next possible stopping spot would be the Great Cavern where the temple itself was housed. I looked forward to the cave because I assumed it would be a cool restful space to catch my breath. But first the "stairs of death" awaited.

I was glad Jordi had not made it this far and hoped that he had found a gentle way to turn back. Built by the Incas out of stone hundreds of years ago, the stairs were another example of how a pilgrim to a sacred site had to earn the privilege. The favor of the gods does not come easily.

And so I climbed, sometimes on my knees, grasping my way from one step to the next, touching the wall to my right and looking below at the Urubamba river. Eventually stone steps gave way to a wooden ladder that had to be climbed, clutching and crawling rung by rung until I reached the opening of the cave. All the while I felt invincible. I would not die on the Stairs of Death.

Finally, I was there, breathing the cool air within the great cave, feeling for the first time that I was almost alone, not being pushed around by other tourists, who may have been discouraged by the climb.

Deeply beyond the opening was a massive boulder carved into a seat, described as throne. A couple of us took turns reclining for a bit of a rest. I felt like a priestess surveying her disciples. Several feet beyond that, under the vaulted ceiling of the cave, was the temple itself, a gracefully carved façade in the traditional Inca trapezoid with the upper level narrower than the bottom. I couldn't discern the purpose of this ceremonial building, since the Moon aspect seems to have been decided arbitrarily. It apparently predated Machu Picchu proper by around a thousand years. Whatever its purpose, it was deliberately a spiritual space, perhaps for invocations or sacrifice.

Even with the crowd milling around me I found myself settling into a deep sense of tranquility, the trials of my disease fading into irrelevance, and I thought this was perhaps a healing space, a kind of therapy for mental distress, a balm for the psychotic.

More likely this was a site for the common practice of child sacrifice among the Inca, usually to curry divine favor in times of famine or drought. Boys and girls between the ages of six and eight, of great beauty and of noble families, were selected to be sent to their reward in the heavenly realm, mercifully doped up with coca and chicha and placed in the mountain to freeze to death in their sleep.

Whatever the intent, it was impressive the punishing lengths to which the Inca went to create these massive constructs, perhaps as penance or the brokering of a compact with the gods, possibly for a personal blessing or, better still, for the good fortune of the community. As I stood at the opening of the cave to prepare my mind for the return hike, I was struck by the beauty of the surrounding mountains and, below, the majestic geometry of Machu Picchu.

I started down and thought of Jordi, wondering if we would meet going in opposite directions. Perhaps he had found a spot to rest and wait for me. Whatever the case, I prayed to some undefined Inca god that he was well, and that he had found some joy in the pilgrimage up to the Huayna Picchu.

Jordi

I froze. I did not have it in me to take one more step in my climb to Huayna Picchu. I'd been doing fine trying to stay close to Vin, watching her summon reserves of energy that enabled her to march resolutely up. And then the marching turned to climbing steps and the climbing occasionally shifted to crawling on hands and knees. I lost track of Vin. Around a bend where the path clung to the side of the mountain and provided only a chain as a guard rail between me and the chasm stretching down for hundreds of feet, I stopped..

Someone spoke to me, so close he could reach out to touch me. "Don't look down."

It was impossible not to look down. Down was all I could see.

"Keep your eyes on the path."

I tried to shuffle forward, a few inches at a time, until my feet refused to move, and I had to lean back against the wall of the mountain, my hands feeling behind me for some jutting rock to grasp.

"Oh, man. This is not the fucking place to stop, the voice said."

"Keep moving!" someone further back shouted.

My breath came in quick short pants and I was afraid I would faint.

"I told you not to look down," the man next to me muttered.

I shut my eyes. And that seemed to help steady my breath, although my head was spinning.

"Sorry to leave you like this, buddy."

I thought I heard a note of compassion in his voice. And then felt him push past me, shoving me back against the side of the mountain. Other hikers kept pushing on beside me, which actually made me feel safer, to know there was some large body between me and the edge, feeling supported by the crowd filing past me, feeling the rub of their clothes and the huff of their breathing, so close I could smell their skin, their clothes. Even the occasional word, spoken close to me, usually an insult—*idiot, chicken*—but also expressions of comfort, *take it easy, you'll be fine, breathe.*

I felt if I could gradually retreat to where the ledge started then I would be on solid ground. Even with my eyes closed I could let the hillside at my back keep me on the path. But I was unable to force myself to move an inch.

Eventually, the passing throng thinned out as the last of the scheduled hikers filed past me. And then I was by myself. I had never been so alone in my life. I kept my eyes closed tight but the memory of the drop filled my mind and took my breath. I was helpless, standing a couple of feet from the edge, not daring to open my eyes, yet feeling a pull and a temptation to just step forward and fall. I wondered how long I could stand in a state of hopelessness, even if no longer breathing the agitated panting of earlier. Trying to stay erect was straining my shoulders with sweat running down my back and legs, and I was trembling from my head to my knees, which felt as if they could buckle at any moment.

I was in such despair as never before, a feeling of hopelessness and shame, and the thought came that the only way out of misery was to step into the void which was now calling me, silently offering relief from the situation I was in. I recalled that the suicidal were not so much attracted to death as to freedom from an insufferable living cage. I had never before felt like killing myself until that moment. Certainly there would be no pain, just the stomach-churning sensation of falling, which would go on for a minute or more, including a comical attempt to change my mind and flap my arms for a way back up to the questionable safety of the ledge.

I was facing my death for the first time in memory with profound sorrow. I have always gloried in life's gifts, taking for granted the pleasures of music and art and opera and film, and the rich satisfaction of having written an elegant sentence. And more than that, the rarest gift of being loved by Lavinia. I clung to thoughts of her, my wife, my love for thirty years whom I had resolved to protect and nurture to the last of her days. That would certainly be a dirty trick to play on her, leaving her in the lurch to die by herself. Forgive me, darling, but I cannot stand on this spot for much longer.

The filing of hikers past me started up again, this time the early climbers who were working their way down Huayna Picchu, again rubbing against me, some silently, others with a word. It took me a moment to realize that someone had stopped to stand on my left with their back to the side of the mountain, followed by a similar sensation of another person on my right, both close enough so that their shoulders and arms touched mine. It occurred to me that I had been joined by other panicked hikers, but then I realized these exuded a rare kind of calm that was actually starting to wash over me, as my trembling abated, and my breath evened out. I was not alone with my fear. Their even breathing, their simple presence was giving me sudden rare comfort.

A male voice on my right murmured in my ear, "vertigo?"

"Afraid so."

"You're right to be anxious. Vertigo is dangerous."

"I see all kinds of people, all ages climbing this thing."

"Yes, but when you have vertigo you walk like a drunk."

"So I've heard. Sorry."

"Now, friend, take a couple breaths, slow in, and slow out."

I did as he said.

"See, how easy it is? Keep breathing like that."

"I'm doing it," I said.

"We can't solve your problem unless you breathe," a female voice on my left said.

"You're going to get me out of this?"

"Sure, but you have to do your part."

"I can't even walk."

"Oh, but you will. Just do as we say. But first we have to know and trust each other. What is your name?"

"Jordi," I said, my voice choking with emotion.

"I am Evan. And next to you is my sister, Drea."

"Hello, Jordi," said the female voice. I was struck by their steady tones.

"Ok, Jordi," said Evan, "I'm going to hold your shirt, and you are going to turn and face your left."

I forced myself to shuffle my feet inches at a time and turn.

"Put your hands out and touch me," said the woman. She seemed small and I reached out and found myself grasping her shoulders.

"Ok now," the man said, "you're holding on to Drea, and I'm holding on to you, and we are not going to fall together. I promise."

"And guess what, we're going to walk down the hill."

"Are your eyes open?"

"No, I panic when I look."

"Don't worry about the view, focus on the ground so you don't stumble or trip."

"All together now," the woman sang.

"Are your eyes open?"

"Yes." I stared at the woman's bright red hair tied in a ponytail shimmering under the sun. I focused on details, unwilling to look anywhere else, freckles dotted her arm raised to touch the side of the mountain and her legs visible below her shorts.

"Follow the Celtic goddess," her brother chuckled.

I shuffled forward, gradually feeling the safety of the siblings' sure-footed escort, my hands on Drea's shoulders and Evan's fists clutching the back of my T-shirt.

"Just trust," he said. "I'm sure there has never been a case of three people falling off the ledge at the same time."

And so I trusted, allowing myself to surrender to the three of us walking together like a six-legged scarab. Within minutes, the path had debouched from the ledge onto the steep descent of the trail. I felt Evan let go of my shirt, and Drea marched ahead so that I could no longer hold her shoulder.

"Okey dokey," the man said as he found a wide spot to pass me. "You can manage from here."

I watched their red heads bounce down the trail, and eventually lost them. I called out "thank you, thank you," but I'm not sure they heard. I slowed down by sitting on the ground and lowering myself on the stretch of stone steps. And I kept my gaze on the ground, skirting rocks and twists along the path until I stumbled down the last few feet to the entrance of the trail. I handed my passport to a guard and made sure he registered my exit. Vin would know I was Ok.

It felt so good to be on flat ground as I wandered around the perimeter of the site searching for two redheads. Surely they would be easy to spot. I needed to thank them again, and to see that they were real. Their presence had been something miraculous; I don't know how long I would've been able to stand at the ledge.

I looked up toward Huayna Picchu and started weeping. Suddenly I could not force my feet to walk another step, and I found a rock on the outside of the citadel and sat and sobbed. Crying, my whole body started to shake as if to purge myself of the experience. Mostly I was given a wide berth by passersby, though an occasional kind soul would ask if I was all right. I tried to smile and raise my hand and make a little wave, unable to explain that I was experiencing a profound sense of relief that I had not fallen to my death.

After some deep breaths I was able to still the shaking that rattled my body, and when I stood I walked with resolve, but not back to the citadel; to the lodge where I would find my spot at the bar and wait for Vin, with some pisco courage.

Lavinia

It took over two hours for me to crawl and slide my way back, sometimes climbing for a spell, and then finding the trail that led to the bottom. Suddenly I was in a hurry, eager to reconnect with Jordi, hoping to find him as I stumbled my way along the return. I grew careless as I hurried and banged up my knee and my ass and my arm trying to break a fall. And everything was hurting, from my lower back to my quads to my shoulders. Sweat streamed from my forehead and made my eyes burn. I was a mess with about an hour yet to go.

The glow I had felt in the cavern dissipated as I worried about Jordi. I would have preferred for him to sit out Huayna Picchu, but it was not in his nature to bail on me. I should've known better. And wondered what it was in my character to be so driven, that I would on a whim cause him distress.

So I'm back to the tyranny of the dying. When time is short only our living matters. We eat what we want, go where we want, sleep when we want. Time is short, darling, make the most of it. And if I want to climb a fucking mountain, that's what I do, knowing that Jordi will not dissuade me. Such is the punishment of the living, not to be

haunted by ghosts but by those of us in some in-between state, termi-
nals, not yet dead, not fully alive. Beware the hopeless when they have
given up hope.

I was often tempted to tell Dr. Dave to stop the torture of the poisons and zaps of last resort because they made me sicker while pro-
longing my half life. I was happier when we suspended treatment for a
while, even though I knew that by doing so I was shortening my time.
But no, there is another cocktail we can try, always another mix of
chemicals that kills the cancer and spares the host. Such a fantasy.
Hang in there because research is ongoing, and the miracle drug can
be found to cure. Immunotherapy coming soon! It will be my fate that
the cure is found after I'm dead. So, I agree to press on, attaching a
port to my vein to serve as the conduit for the progression of small,
hoped-for miracles. The idea that cancer is a battle is ridiculous. We
don't fight cancer, we find a way to negotiate, some of this in return for
a little of that. Not to fight is tantamount to suicide by surrender. And
yet it's the stance of surrender that keeps me sane.

I finally limped my way to the trailhead and stood in line so I could
sign out, take my place among the victors. Everything in my body hurt
from the various falls and scrapes and twists on the way back. I asked
the guard with the registry if I could look through it to see if my husband was down yet. I had to look back through several signatures before Jordi popped up. I could tell by the time he checked out that he
had retreated about an hour from starting. Which meant that he'd
been back at the site since around eleven. It was now almost two.

I went straight to the hotel and sighed with relief at the sight of
Jordi happily perched at the bar.

"Darling." We kissed.

"Darling," he echoed. He patted the stool beside him and ordered
me a pisco sour. It was getting to be my favorite remedy for the rigors of the adventure. That and the sacred infusion of fresh coca leaves.

"Salud," my love.

"Salud," we clinked glasses. "By the way, did you see a couple of tall
redheads, a man and a woman, on your way here?"

"They don't grow red hair in Peru."

"These were tourists."

"Well, there' a guy with red hair at the end of the bar." I gestured.

"Oh, man! I've been sitting here for two hours and I can't believe I didn't see him."

"Is this someone you met?"

"Briefly, on the trail. He and his sister saved my life."

I think Jordi was a little drunk the way he almost fell off the stool. He walked over to the red-haired man. "Hola," he said cheerfully, "how great to see you. Is your sister here too?"

The man turned to Jordi with a quizzical look. "I'm sorry, I don't think we've met. Do you know my sister? Here she is now."

The man stood to welcome the woman, both were tall and very slender and beautiful in white shorts and silk shirts. They didn't look particularly outfitted for hiking, in contrast to Jordi and me in our grubby clothes from the trail.

"Andrea, meet my new friend here. He thinks we met."

"Yes, I'm Jordi."

"Well, hi Jordi," she said. "Nice to meet you."

"I'm surprised you don't remember me," Jordi stammered. Were you on Huayna Picchu a while ago?

"No, not really. Heights freak me out. I wouldn't go on that mountain for anything."

Jordi seemed confused and at a loss for words. He kept shaking his head as if to clear some cobweb in his thinking, so with a smile of friendly apology to the two redheads, I gently pulled him back to our stools.

"That's just the weirdest thing, they acted as if they'd never seen me before."

"Maybe there's a redheads convention going on. We should've asked them. That would explain the confusion."

"I need another drink."

"And I need a bath. And a massage. They have a special for couples who are hurting all over from the strains of hiking Huayna Picchu. It's called El Vertigo."

"So funny."

Jordi

The glow of the piscos had worn off and was replaced by the soothing coca tea. The Belmond had a wonderful spa, and we were able to book our massage together after a prolonged soak in a hot tub scented with lavender.

The Jacuzzi soothed my aches and sent bubbles swirling and tickling all over and I could feel myself settling into a sweet drowse. Vin did not mention the matter of my two redheads who had rescued me off the mountain and I wasn't about to bring that up again. Whatever small mystery I had been a part of, I could wait before I sorted it all out enough to discuss it. I knew what I knew, and I was here inside a steaming tub, not at the bottom of a ravine, and talking about it would make me sound like an idiot.

I glanced at Vin and she had closed her eyes and was smiling, letting the bath soothe her bruises and twists. I reached out with my foot and touched hers, and we sat like that for several minutes playing footsie in the water. As the sage said, *to the clear mind all waters are Ganges waters.*

Later, we sat swaddled in fluffy white robes waiting for our massage artists to lead us to a room suffused in a golden glow with two beds overlooking the citadel. And more coca sent us into a mellow spin of well-being and gratitude, as helpless as infants waiting for their nurses. Only these nurses were two mighty indigenous Peruvians, easily descendants of the Incas that had built the citadel. I was expecting a couple of angelic women and instead got warriors to battle our sore muscles and aching joints.

"Hello, my name is Atahualpa," the biggest of the two introduced himself.

"Like the king, correct?"

"Yes, my friend is also named Atahualpa, like the emperor."

"And the singer," said Vin. "Atahualpa Yupanqui."

That elicited broad grins from the two. And I knew that at least for the next ninety minutes we would be friends.

They left us to remove our robes and get face down on the bed between two crisp white sheets. They entered the room quiet as shadows and my Atahualpa stood by my head and said softly, "A little pressure, or much?"

"Whatever you think is best."

"How are you doing, darling?" I said softly.

But her Atahualpa made a shushing sound. "No conversation during the treatment," he said.

"Usted es el jefe," chimed Vin.

"Silencio, por favor."

He spoke with quiet authority, so we were silent, with only the breathing of the two therapists and soft Inca flutes sounding faintly around us.

The two men had stood near me but out of sight, burning incense and waving the smoke around while they chanted a soft invocation, their voices cascading one on top of the other. Their full-throated chanting and the soft lights and the incense filled the room with the mystery of a ceremony. I realized Vin and I were the subjects of a ritual and the thought lulled me into a state of placid acceptance. We were in good hands.

Then, punctuating the beginning of our experience, a bell was stuck once, its resonance ringing for several seconds then growing fainter until there was nothing left but the memory of that single chime. Atahualpa proceeded to run his palms with warm lavender oil up and down my neck to the thighs down to the ankles. Whatever apprehension I had felt about being buff naked in the hands of an Inca warrior vanished.

Then the pain started, thumbs digging into the deep muscles of my back and legs and feet. But the man had ordered silencio, and so I refrained from even the weakest yelp. But Atahualpa was basically kind, and he knew what he was doing, after a spell of gouging and digging, he would press down with the palms and rub vigorously as you would to calm a child who has fallen.

"Pobrecito, mucha tension," he would murmur. And then he would apply pressure again.

I could feel the knots of stress along my body that he was dissolving with his magic thumbs, pushing down on a spot until the pain eased. Eventually, he mercifully finished with the torture, and started vigorously sweeping his hands in broad stokes from my neck to my feet sending a warm tingling sensation throughout my skin.

He told me to turn over and he worked on my chest and legs and arms, up and down in long rhythmic sweeps, and it occurred to me that this was the part where one might suggest a happy ending. The thought itself started to uncurl my penis. But, no, Atahualpa gave no sign that he was aware of my arousal even as he massaged my lower belly.

I had started to doze off when I felt my man's hands pressing the sides of my head while he stood very still behind me. The two men left the room quietly with a softly spoken word of gracias. We were done.

I started to move gradually and felt as if I'd been inside a warm bath, my muscles fluid and long as I sat on the edge of the bed. Vin went to a table and served us a couple of cups of coca.

Back in our room, Vin and I took off our fluffy white robes and lay down on the big bed, our bodies languid, our skin still tingling with the memory of being so intelligently touched.

"Are we going to nap before dinner?" I said.

"Maybe. Maybe not."

It had been nearly two years now. And all the time I wished I had it in my power to arouse her, as I was able to do at one time. I know that we both look back with nostalgia to that time in our life when we fucked with abandon, Vin watching herself in a mirror swallowing up my cock. And still, now we cling to each other through the night, our bodies touching, legs intertwined, kisses soft and earnest. With a love that feels unbounded, deeper now than at any time in our lives.

From a James Joyce letter to his wife:

There is also a wild beast-like craving for every inch of your body, for every secret and shameful part of it, for every odor and act of it.

I'm saddened that I will probably never feel this way again about a lover. I'm getting fucking old. There, the thought has been uttered, though perhaps not with great conviction.

Lavinia

It had been months since I'd been touched intimately. Not blaming Jordi for this, since I'd been unresponsive to his overtures. It seemed we had become reconciled to some appetites waning, you don't miss what you faintly remember but no longer want. Chemo had me craving sugar and salt but not sex. It had been satisfying to lie on my side and allow myself to push back and surrender into his generous enveloping body. Dusk comes quickly by the Andes since the mountains hide the sun as it sets, and with the curtains parted, the room settled into soft darkness with only a huge yellow moon faintly illuminating our bodies.

The massage, after getting myself beat up on the trail up and down Huayna Picchu, had left my muscles lax yet alert to the slight touch of Jordi's hand on my hip. For several moments it lay there, then, as I had hoped, he wandered across my leg to the inside of my thigh. Even that slight touch suddenly awakened a long-forgotten hunger, and I could feel my vagina swell in anticipation.

I released a long sigh. Jordi took this as a signal and let his hand cup my mound, before allowing a finger to rest between the dry labia. As I grew moist, he caressed me gently as he knew how, and then was able to easily slip first his index then the middle finger in as I tilted up to allow him easier entry. I held his face between my hands, gazed into his eyes and kissed him deeply. "More," I whispered.

Once on my back I guided him on top of me and reached down for his cock, delighting in its expectant swollen state. With his knees on either side and his elbows on the bed, I relished how he took control, first pushing the tip in, waiting and waiting, holding back as I bucked my pelvis, my body pleading for more. Finally he pushed in until he touched my uterus and then he withdrew a bit and started to slide in and out, in long strokes, slowly at first then quicker and deeper. And he felt so new inside me, as if the memory of a thousand previous fucks had receded to allow only the full experience of this one glorious time, the culmination of thirty years of loving this beautiful artist of my flesh and heart.

We lay back quite spent and content. I could feel Jordi starting to doze off as had been his habit. Sex had the opposite effect on me; I felt quickened and energized, maybe ready for another bout.

As I lay awake next to my sleeping darling, and in a twilight dream I saw my body etherized upon a table, cut open from head to belly—the red, slippery tumors exposed—it occurred to me that we just experienced our last hurrah. I'd be going back to Dr. Dave in a few days and the slow poisoning would resume.

Jordi

Back home, the routine resumed. A tough day yesterday, with symptoms of·dizziness, so an MRI was hastily arranged. Today, the news brings relief that the brain shows nothing new and even some slight improvement.

I had a dream last night:

Vin and I are in a taxi to the airport for some trip. I enjoy the ride and like the driver, so I give him a tip. He says that airline schedules are disrupted because of operating system problems. While I'm paying the driver, Vin goes on ahead.

I'm left in front of the terminal and don't know where the luggage is, either it stayed in the cab's trunk or Vin has it. But she is nowhere in sight. I expect that she will come back for me when she realizes I'm not with her. I stay in place thinking that if I go off on a search then we really won't find each other.

The real anxiety kicks in when I decide to call her on the cell, and all I get is a movie playing silently on the screen. I can't get her name or number to connect. I want to borrow a phone, but somebody says the whole phone system is down at the airport.

Is this what I'll feel like when she goes?

Lavinia

Yesterday: A day of rage. Dilantin level low and so it was time to increase the dose. I railed against the idea of more pills, more upheavals in my system. The increased dose brings the likelihood of dizziness, fainting, headaches, insomnia, confusion.

And meanwhile, I felt overwhelmed with the breakdown of the body. The breast cancer metastasis to lung and brain, with nodules showing signs of activity, a little larger here, smaller there. The waiting game was resumed with scans every three months or so. I don't like being on a first-name basis with so many doctors. Bruce, Dave, Greg, Sarah, Joseph. I wondered if it wouldn't be easier to just suspend treatment and die.

And there was the busted toe and the muscular aches from working out.

I was determined to keep running outside, through muscle pain and shin splints and exhaustion, to keep at bay the dulling, dizzying power of the meds. Keppra made me dizzy and unbalanced. Herceptin was an every-three-week, ninety-minute ritual in the clinic, my artery tethered through a port on my chest to a 250cc bag of medicine and saline solution. Decadron kept the swelling in my brain at bay, but increased my appetite, and caused me to gain about fifteen pounds and made my face reddish and puffy. I looked fat, not cute like Jordi insisted.

I summoned all the energy and cuteness I had in me to make the short flight to Chicago to meet with Ysbel and see a play. *Exit the King*, by Ionesco. I could identify. It's all about dying, the railing and eventual acceptance of the end. Jordi seemed glad to stay home.

Jordi

Lavinia left this morning at eight AM for Chicago and I couldn't wait for her to be gone so I could have a session with Miss Lotus. This is disloyal or what? But her cancer has become the overriding concern of my life and our relationship. Therefore, when she's gone it's like taking a breather, a chance to release some pent-up tension. This makes me feel guilty because I know that when she is in fact gone, I will be bereft and not know what to do with myself, being unattached for the first time in my life.

And yet in the last few weeks, under the influence of various medications, she has been by turns moody, often sarcastic. No point correcting her because I know that her anger is beyond her control. Yet, it takes an effort of will not to acknowledge a mean, dismissive remark. I will eventually ask her to watch her tongue for both our benefits.

It was so nice to indulge myself with Miss Lotus for an hour of sexual fun. I am now facing four more days without Vin, which will bring loneliness. Next week we have an appointment with Dr. Dave. We are braced for more chemotherapy, to arrest and delay this advancing creature that can only be temporarily stifled.

I have been saddest at night. Feeling her lie beside me, her soft breathing, snoring sometimes, reassures me that she is in a place of rest. Sometimes, when we are feeling close to each other, she talks about dying and apologizes for not having been a better partner. I find this annoying. We are for each other who we are, there are no conditions or rules or goals in the union. Otherwise, how could I live with my irritability, my unfaithfulness, my too-cool contemplation of life after Lavinia?

Lavinia

Bad news on Tuesday. Cancer was worse in brain and lungs. And yet, I have to roll with reality, that is the zen of the mortal. I'd known that the tumors were growing, even if slowly. Dr. Dave was coy about how bad this new development was, and I didn't press him. I reasoned that whether things are just bad or godawful, I will not live my life any differently. I do what I want, to the limits of the situation. He prescribed a new Herceptin type med, Lappatin, in a pill this time which will cross the blood/brain barrier and help shrink the tumors there. Ok, but I wasn't sure Herceptin had done much with the lung tumors so my expectations were low. And Xeloda again, which in the past was effective in restraining the lung invasion.

Meanwhile, I was tormented by fatigue, dizziness, daily migraines, cramps in hands and feet. According to Dr. Dave most of these symptoms were likely related to the spreading disease. Plus he stopped my driving, as the risk for seizure was increased due to the brain growths. This was such an affront and an insult to my dignity, to be reduced to a childlike status in the way that I manage my life.

I insisted we hit the road one last time. Jordi would do all the driving while I navigate. The plan was to head west until we made it to the ocean. California here we come.

Jordi

We packed the night before with the goal of getting on the road at first light. But we slept fitfully, too eager to get going, as if every static minute was time stolen from this, her final pilgrimage to our sacred places.

I did have my responsibilities, which kept me awake half the night thinking about them. I was the master of a dozen orange plastic bottles, all neatly tucked into a black zippered case. Once the tumors appeared in the brain she was now sometimes confused, so I managed the meds, the dosage and the timing. It would be nice if cannabis were part of the mix, but we haven't yet developed a source to outsmart the law. For now, Dr. Dave replaced the poison that would go into her vein with milder versions in tablets and capsules. Also Imitrex for migraines, Ativan for anxiety, Omeprazole for reflux, all on hand to take as needed. Vin teased me that I was her personal pill pusher. I embraced the job.

First, south to Iowa then west into Nebraska, as the prairie, a flat green sea, stretched ahead for unbroken hours under a luminous sky. I found the solidity of this landscape somehow reassuring, the occasional circling hawk an omen of a fortuitous journey.

A rest stop, providing an oasis in the middle of the summer tundra, offered fuel and a chance to piss. We sat at a picnic table shaded by generous trees. Vin was in charge of snacks and sandwiches which she prepared with care: ripe brie, avocados, and heirloom tomatoes to be sliced at the moment, and for sweets, dark chocolate truffles from Surdyk's. For this part of the journey, we picnicked and celebrated food on the road.

Later on the trip we were apt to stop for fast pizza or subs, and finer dining in whatever city the evening found us. There would always be a nice Italian place or a Chinese, we'd ask around and find out where local people went for a special date or a family gathering. Sometimes it was only Red Lobster or Olive Garden, and we were often hungry enough to be grateful for corporate cuisine.

After lunch, the hum of the road lulled Vin to sleep.

She is untroubled when she sleeps, her dreams sweet she tells me, images of childhood and visions of travel to magical realms, free from the chatter in her mind that shakes her ability to live with death. Her peace is my peace. The sun loomed ahead on a cloudless sky of such blue perfection that even Yves Klein could not improve on it. I nudge Vin so she'll wake up to this show.

Lavinia

I will go gentle into that good night. I will surrender my breath and heartbeat to a glorious end with all the spectacle of the dazzling sunset ahead. I would like for it to be possible to drive into the sun and sink beneath this fertile earth that has sustained me so generously, with gifts of love and art. Even if we are not getting closer to the sun, we are rewarded with a spreading bed of pink and orange darkening along the horizon. This spectacle connects me to every human of every age dating back to the beginning of time, when powerful cave dwellers and fire makers and wheel inventors gathered and hunted along these plains. Perhaps they were awed and likely fearful that the life-giving sun might be extinguished and not reappear at the end of the long cold night.

Damn right, the sun had to be worshipped. Its daily rebirth celebrated with feasts and sacrifices, a miracle acknowledged through every whim of the big star, from the occasional eclipse to its concealment during storms and fog. The ancients learned that the god traveled shorter days in winter then renewed itself during the summer, casting its shadows for study and manipulation by the priestly classes. If the sun was to be considered a god with will and whim to rule the order of life, it was thanks to the priests, who from times immemorial in different nations and tribes invented god to suit their own power. Salute the sun, the giver of life. Fear the sun, the glutton for human life and beauty. Feed it young blood, virgin blood, warrior blood, the reddest blood.

The Aztecs from the fourteenth century knew how to manipulate the faithful to participate in their hunger for conquest. It was what the sun god wanted, and so its power had to be purchased with a human heart carved out of the chest of a warrior, and held up still beating toward the warrior god. It is recorded in the annals of the conquest that on the occasion of a major battle, thousands were sacrificed and the steps to the base of the pyramid ran red with flowing blood. The naked dead warriors were left for days to stink and rot and feed the buzzards.

The highway was a straight shot to the sun that afternoon, aiming for the perfect fireball slowly sinking into the horizon, starting with a metallic blue, then plunging into a sea of pink deepening into bright orange as the sun set. I yearned to see the very moment it was swallowed by the earth, shimmering as its sank until all that remained was a golden rim, its fire continuing to rise into the sky long after it had faded from view. The sun's gift went on blessing us, as the sky

darkened from red into shades of crimson and purple, finally fading
to black.

Jordi

After a twelve-hour drive, we slept in South Dakota. There was a sense
of triumph in going past dark and stopping at the first place with a
VACANCY sign all lit up just when my eyes were smarting and the road
was a blur. We were not choosy on the first leg, glad for a big bed, a
shower, and free waffles for breakfast.

The receptionist at the Smoky Hills Motel couldn't help staring at Vin's colorful head, and spotted us for the Minnesota libs we
are. When asking for a non-smoking room she wrinkled her nose and
deepened her frown as if searching for something she doesn't believe
exists. I enjoy these thrusts into the heart of red America more than
Vin does. I marvel that such a combination of stupidity and mean-
ness exists in a people so blessed with natural beauty. They did fuck
up majestic Mount Rushmore with the giant heads, kind of a feat if
you think about it, but to such a shabby end. For the rest, they let the
beauty stand, with no more than a parking area and a gift shop to disturb the splendor of the Badlands, the Black Hills, Devil's Tower. Vin
nodded as I carried on my habitual screed, and humored me with her
sweet embrace.

We ate dinner at the Hunan Garden where the Chinese host
greeted us as long-lost relatives with tea and crispy noodles to munch
on. No need to look at the menu. There's a Buddha's Delight in every
Chinese restaurant in the country that happily piles on the vegetables
in a stir-fry. Everything is rich and spicy and crunchy, and Vin and
I celebrated our first night on the road with deep gratitude to the
Buddha and his incarnation in the wilds of South Dakota.

We were glad to take our happy Buddhist bellies to bed early and
waited for the busy motel to settle down. This took a while, as late ar-
rivals wheeled down the hallway and turned on TVs and calmed restless babies. One insistent guest kept trying our door with the wrong
key, softly cursing to himself until I managed to rouse myself from
twilight sleep to shout that he had the wrong room. He insisted we

were in his room until I persuaded the woman at the desk to come rescue him and lead him, still muttering curses, to #165, next door. But
the walls were cardboard thin, and his snores rumbled on through the
night.

I only recall this to take into account how differently Vin and I
react to the bumps on the road outside our comfort zone. I couldn't
ignore our neighbor who I imagined as some gun-carrying cowboy
now resentful of me because he thought I took his room. Vin thought it
was funny and told me to relax, and then fell asleep. I swiped an Ativan
from her stash.

She was still asleep the next morning when I awakened to bright
sunlight through our flimsy curtains. I stood at the window and parted
the drapes to get my first look at our surroundings. The parking area
was full, our silver BMW clearly out of place surrounded by minivans
and muscle cars and motorcycles and, right beside our car, a sinister
black pickup, crowding it over the yellow stripes as if to question its
right to venture from the safety of our cities.

By the time Vin awakened and I'd organized her meds for the morning, she was in good energy after a shower and a trip to the breakfast room. Waffles! Which Vin expertly cooked on the waffle iron and
doused with the real maple syrup she always packs from home. That
and good bananas made for a fine start of the day. Such simple pleasures. The breakfast room was mostly empty with only three tables
taken, a sleepy couple, a family with a toddler, and a large guy hunched
over his eggs and biscuits and brown gravy, muscular arms with sleeve
tattoos from wrist to shoulder, signaling a mythical tapestry of Gaelic
crosses and flags and hearts.

I wished we'd picked a table farther from his, but it was too late,
and as I stared he sensed my stare and looked up with a scowl. I was
at that instant sure he was our next-door neighbor with the stubborn
room key and the prodigious snores. But then he registered Vin's head
and his scowl turned to wide-eyed interest.

"Nice ink, lady."

Vin kept her neutral face, no acknowledgement that she had been
flattered. "Yeah, thanks."

Then, she and snoring man went back to their breakfasts without another word.

Our first stop was at the long-anticipated Wall Drug in the town of Wall, a vast emporium of touristy memorabilia. Vin loves browsing through key chains and lighters and dolls, but she doesn't buy anything, the mere experience of handling and fingering these treasures seems to satisfy her. *Nothing over* $1.99 reads the sign. Of course, we attract the attention of clerks who spot us as shoplifters of uncertain predilection. All in their minds: nothing on display here is worth stealing. But for Vin, the reward of pinching a small item is the prize.

And getting caught is one of the thrills of the journey. As soon as we stepped outside the store, a woman, perhaps in her seventies, dressed in a cowgirl outfit complete with short skirt, boots, and a sheriff badge called out.

"Excuse me, honey."

Vin turned to her and gave her a friendly smile. But we kept on walking.

"Now, don't you run away from me. You know I'm too old to catch you, and I would have to summon the assistance of a real sheriff."

"Can I help you?" At this point I knew what was going on.

"Well, thank you, young man. But my business is with your young lady."

"Sure, ma'am,'" said Vin. "What's the problem?"

"Would you allow me to take a peek inside your backpack?"

"I've been busted, Jordi."

"Yes, you have, darling," says the sheriff lady.

Vin took a deep breath and handed the backpack to the lady.

"Aha!" She reached inside and withdrew a small plastic replica of the corn palace, still bearing the $1.99 sticker.

Vin continues to be in love with the Corn Palace, its magnificent façade with turrets and balustrades studded with a million kernels, which by late summer have been pecked at by birds enjoying a bountiful buffet. In the half dozen times we've driven west she always insists we make it the first stop in our pilgrimage.

She gaped at the key chain as if seeing it for the first time.

"Maybe you have a receipt for this? Or are you going to tell me it just fell into your pack?"

"You know, that's just what I was going to say."

"Yes, you see, I'm way ahead of you."

"So, now what?" I said, pulling out my wallet and taking out a five.

"That would be the easiest way out," the sheriff shook her head sadly. "But Wall Drug takes a dim view of shoplifters. So, what I'm doing here is performing a citizen's arrest. I'm not a real sheriff but I will ask the pretty lady to accompany me to the manager's office while the law is alerted. There we will meet with Mr. Stinson who will decide whether to charge you with theft."

We waited at the manager's steel desk, enjoying a cup of coffee that the sheriff provided for five cents each, a promotional gift courtesy of Wall Drug. After about ten minutes, a portly man also in western clothes came sweating and huffing into the crammed office.

"Good job, Carla! I see you've got a couple of miscreants in custody."

"Just the lady, sir. The gentleman is her husband and protector."

"Well, between the two of them they can cover the cost of the merchandise. And I'll take their picture so we can be on alert the next time they come to Wall Drug."

And sure enough Mr. Stinson took out a camera from his desk drawer and had Vin and me stand in front of a white wall.

"You can smile if you like. One little click and you're free to go. Miss Carla will show you our rogue's wall on the way out."

The Wall Drug wall of shame was a cork board with about a hundred pics of faces smiling, either cheerful or embarrassed, hard to tell the prevailing emotions of this gallery of shoplifters.

Sheriff Carla walked us out to our car in the parking lot, as if to make sure we didn't swipe anything else on the way out.

"It's been nice meeting you, folks," she said. "You're my first collar of the day. And so glad you got sloppy. Catching shoplifters like you insures my job at Wall Drug. At my age if I wasn't showing results, I would have been fired years ago."

"Glad to help out, Miss Carla," said Vin as she accepted a hug from the sheriff.

We didn't dare laugh until I drove off the parking area and back on the highway, safely out of sight of Mr. Stinson and Miss Carla, who might not take kindly to Vin's hoots of delight. "We're Bonnie and Clyde!"

Lavinia

The Badlands.

Beyond where the prairie turns green and mountainous a hallucinatory landscape emerged. It called to us with sculptural peaks and crags in colors from gray to brown to golden to red to blue as the afternoon's waning light led us deeper. If God is in the details, then each promontory reveals his works in striations of color above the base and to the apex, all this repeated hundreds of times. At times it feels like an ocean frozen with peaks and waves rising in stone stillness. We came close enough to these rock formations to walk off the road and touch their warm surfaces.

It took us a couple of hours to slowly cruise the side roads into the park, without a word, so silent and awed were we, left with the inner chatter of our minds trying to comprehend this riot of color and texture. I wanted to know if Jordi was in tune with the God that makes this art happen, and whether other beings of the planet, eagles and coyotes and snakes and spiders have the consciousness to process this beauty, or is it purely a gift for humans. I turned to him to speak, but saw that he was absorbed, barely breathing as he took in the show.

We ended up at a nice hotel this time with quiet rooms and a fine restaurant. Later over wine and cheese we finally talked.

"The question is do we have to be at some level godlike to appreciate God's work?"

Jordi was skeptical. "You see a purpose in everything."

"And you think creation happens by chance."

"But not any less magnificent."

"Yes, darling, but it's the sense of mission in the created universe that gives it meaning beyond mere aesthetics."

"There's nothing 'mere' about natural beauty. It just has no purpose. It just is, and we give it meaning according to our needs."

I wanted to argue, but the tender evening was much too fragile to expose it to a debate. But, still, I like to get the last word, and he has to listen because, after all, I'm the dying one and I have insights. I said as much, with a smile.

Jordi can be stubborn. "An artist produces art that moves and delights. In many cases very far from any identification with God. Their work is motivated by ego and greed. Artists need approval."

"Yes, but the purest artist creates according to the divine touch of his soul. Even if they are not aware of it. Still, even Beethoven falls short of the magnificence of a good thunderstorm or the evening melody of a thrush."

"But even this divine touch is random. God can't be deciding that Picasso, with his narcissism and greed and misogyny, is more deserving than Norman Rockwell?"

"I don't know, Jordi. God knows."

"Do you picture some old man with a beard and a thunderbolt, or a beautiful woman with a telescope arbitrarily rewarding and punishing at their whim?"

"I'm getting tired of this conversation, my darling. I may find out after I die, but I'll be too far away to let you know."

What I know or imagine is beyond explaining and this conversation, a repeat of many we've had over the years, has exhausted me. My truth is my own, not easily shared. I follow a sound, a faint chime through different levels of subtlety, from the grossest to a whisper to a mere impulse, and I'm aware of a kind of solidity, a platform of energy that is the source of my thoughts, but empty of thought itself. It is a field of energy and bliss that is unconnected to the outward world. This formless void is intelligent and powerful and lies at the basis of the laws of the universe. It makes our clocks tick, our night and day cycle, our blood flow, our world turn, our hearts love, our stars burn. Through it our actions rewarded or punished. We understand all this to whatever degree our consciousness is clear of stress. Our only purpose as living entities is to clear the mirror that will reflect this field of pure intelligence back into our individual minds. It's this truth that sets us free.

"Free of what?" Jordi asked, and I realized I'd been mumbling my thoughts.

"I'm hungry," I said cheerfully. I poured myself more wine, even though I knew it would interfere or counteract or otherwise screw up the effect of the meds. "What's for dinner?"

"Whatever we want." Jordi lifted his glass. "Salud."

Jordi

We were rolling south through Colorado when Vin told me to slow down, that she was feeling sick. All morning since breakfast she had been queasy, and I was not surprised that the ride was not helping. The previous day she had insisted we stop in Yellowstone. Its underground energy in evidence as we walked the trail along the lagoons bubbling blue to green to golden, steaming sulfurous fog and soaring geysers.

We ended up at the lodge terrace for a view of Old Faithful, scheduled to blow its magnificent plume a hundred feet in the air within minutes, according to the official clock. The walk from one geyser to another had tired Vin beyond our expectations. Caffeine, iced and milky, reanimated her.

"The devil is restless today," I said, mainly to tease Vin, since neither of us has ever given Satan much credence.

"Ah, but he's a thing of beauty," she said. "Dangerous, though, I wouldn't want to step into his turf."

"Smell that sulfur," I inhaled deeply. "The scent of rotten eggs."

"The fragrance of sinners burning off their sins. Bosch's orgy of devils fueled my darkest fantasies when I was a kid. For about three years, between the ages of six and nine, I lived in fear that the slightest transgression would doom me for all time."

"How did you get over it?" I asked.

"Ysbel and I invented our own church. I was the priest and she was the repentant sinner. I prayed for her and gave her communion of cookies. I took it seriously, not so much as a game but as a way of currying favor with God. I had the power to save her and by doing so I was saving myself. God and I were tight," she crossed her fingers.

A crowd gathered close to the time that the big geyser would blow. Vin and I made our way to the edge of the terrace. Old Faithful knows how to play up the suspense, starting with some preliminary burbles and tremors and finally shooting a hundred feet up, a steaming column that keeps going and going, raining down in a wide circle at the base. When the energy eventually settled into a quietly bubbling puddle, we joined in cheerful applause. It made Vin happy to be part of the experience.

By the time we walked to the car, her vigor had flagged, so I had to put my arm around her waist to hold her up. She was making an effort to keep her head up and I was afraid she'd faint.

"Almost there, darling," I said at the sight of our car in the middle of the parking lot. She grew heavier and her legs started to buckle as if I were walking with a drunk. I held the door open for her and pushed the seat back so she could slide in, in a clumsy reclining motion. After I shut the door she lay her head against the passenger window. I got behind the wheel and reached across her to buckle her up.

We were past Colorado Springs when she awakened. She slept through city traffic, and once we started heading toward New Mexico the road grew twisty but traffic thinned.

"Did I miss Seven Falls and Hyde Peak and Garden of the Gods?"

"Yes, and a few more Colorado attractions, all yours for the price of admission."

"The whole state is a theme park," she said. "They've privatized God's creation."

This has been one of our habitual complaints about Colorado, so we don't usually take in the sights.

"Could we stop?" she said.

"Sure, a gas station is coming up."

"I mean, now."

"Something wrong?" I heard myself stupidly asking.

"Please," she whimpered.

I pulled over to the side of the road, and Vin opened the door and hurled a fountain of vomit. She retched until there was nothing but dry heaves. I gave her a bottle of water and dug out the Zofran. She drank thirstily and swallowed a couple of pills.

"Do you feel better?" I asked before getting back on the road.

"Sure, I feel empty." She wiped her chin with a paper towel and took a breath. "Where next?"

"We're inside New Mexico, and we'll stop before Taos and Santa Fe, into Ojo Caliente."

"Oh, yes. I could use a good soak. Maybe even a miraculous cure. Hot springs were popular therapies back in the day."

"Won't that give Dr. Dave a shock?"

This will be the third time we've stopped in Ojo during our years of road tripping across the southwest. Every time the soaking has been a balm to our body and spirit. The more fucked up you feel the better the bathing in the various pools, from warm to hot, with magic minerals like lithia and arsenic and soda, all clean-smelling with no sulfur stink like other springs. Once sacred to the original peoples, Ojo Caliente welcomes us with a deep sense of peace. Brief conversations hardly rise above a whisper as, white-robed pilgrims all, we wander from pool to pool, soaking and letting sweat bead on our faces, while the desert crags loom.

We reserved a private pool and stripped our bathing suits and let our naked bodies be gluttons for the gifts from the center of the earth.

Vin is shy of her nude body, belly swollen and the infusion port gaping just below her collarbone. This plastic opening the size of a quarter is the entry point, right into the big vein next to her heart, for all the shit that has to go into her body. A vast improvement over the needle sticks that she has grown sensitive to, each more painful than the last.

The solitude was wonderful and we touched each other under the water like children, caressing playfully yet feeling no real arousal.

Then, we headed to our room at the lodge and napped until dinnertime. Vin was not hungry, so she dug into two bowls of ice cream, while I feasted on pasta.

We went to bed early, but Vin had a rough night, and around midnight she had an explosive migraine that tormented her even after a dose of Imitrex. An hour later, she got up and rushed to the bathroom. There was nothing in her stomach, so she knelt at the toilet and vomited a thin yellow gruel. I stayed in bed to give her a measure of privacy, but I was startled by a series of angry cries.

"Fuck, fuck, fuck."

I rushed to the bathroom to find her sitting on the floor with nasty bruise below her hip down her femur.

"I fucking fell. I was standing and my knees collapsed under me, no support at all, like a rubber doll. Oh, darling, I am so sorry. I'm ruining the trip."

I helped her hobble onto the bed as she collapsed on her back. I wrapped ice cubes in a face cloth and pressed it against the bruise waiting for the howl of anguish that would signal a fracture. She responded with quiet moans that were more about impatience and disgust than pain. I rubbed the ice along the full length of her leg, trusting the cold to control swelling. After about twenty minutes, her breathing slowed down and she seemed to be resting easy.

"Well, that took care of the migraine," she said. "If your head hurts, break a leg."

"Let's try to sleep."

The next morning, she woke early and wanted to talk while I wanted to sleep.

"I'm feeling like shit, darling."

I finally sat up and reached for the medicine case on the night table.

"Poison is not going to make me feel better. You know that."

"It's what keeps you alive." I watched her as she dutifully gulped down the medicine, then drained the glass as she'd been told, pushing water at every chance to help dissolve the chemicals in her system.

"I can't go on."

"Don't be discouraged. You've been doing well."

"I mean, I can't go on with this trip. Please, can we just turn around and go home?"

"We can do anything you want. Let's get some coffee."

"Yes. There is clarity in caffeine."

She wasn't hungry for breakfast, so she nibbled on a pastry and slurped strong coffee in a foamy latte. I spread a map on the table and traced a route with my finger, north through Kansas, then into Missouri, then Iowa, then home.

"This is the quickest way back," I said.

"Not very exciting."

"The majesty of agriculture. Twenty hours of soybeans, with one stop around Kansas City."

"Let's go," she said, pushing back from the table and standing on her shaky legs.

There was a sense of urgency in her that I hadn't recognized before. I had the feeling that she was suddenly racing against some secret clock. She didn't say much as we loaded the car, but she was clearly reaching into some energy reserves. She strapped in and leaned the seat back and let out a sigh.

"I sure fucked up this adventure, didn't I?"

"We had fun, and when we stop having fun it's time to end it."

"Just like life." She takes another breath. "I'm so tired. You don't mind if I sleep and let you take us home?"

VI

Lavinia

I am bone tired. I never knew what that expression meant until now. I've been tired in my muscles and in my brain and in my eyes, but now it's my bones that plead for rest with a cold ache that goes from my rib cage to my hips to my thighs. It feels like they're filled with ice instead of marrow.

And so the song goes:

> *Dem bones, dem bones.*
> *Head bone is connected to the neck bone,*
> *Neck bone connected to the shoulder bone,*
> *Shoulder bone connected to the backbone,*
> *Backbone connected to the hip bone,*
> *Hip bone connected to the leg bone,*
> *Dem bones, dem dry bones gonna rise again,*
> *Now hear ye the word of the lord.*

I sing the familiar verses but as I glance toward Jordi who is fixed on the road ahead, I can tell he hasn't heard me, my singing is going on inside my head. What a waste, because I once knew the whole ditty and could sing it uninterrupted to the annoyance of my mother and father. Even as a kid I was obsessed with the rituals of the dead. I would sing and do the little skeleton jig. I could do it now in a heartbeat for Jordi's delight, if I wasn't so bone tired. Which is alarming because as far as I know my bones, last we checked, are fine and dandy. I've always had good strong bones, and even after I fell on my hip last night, nothing broke. Still, something for Dr. Dave to consider. Look at me, I'm the battlefield of a major invasion.

I'm glad I'm sitting back with my legs stretched out while Jordi speeds me home, because I don't believe I could take another step. I must've fallen asleep because I wake up as Jordi pulls into a service station. The place stinks of gasoline, which I don't remember ever noticing before and I wonder if there isn't a spill that's going to explode. Boom. Not a bad way to go, though I hope for Jordi's sake that we can fuel up and get out of danger.

My dear man still has a rich lifetime ahead of him. I want to wake up fully and open my eyes and see what is happening, but even my lids are tired and will not lift. I do hear him rattling around, sticking the pump into the gas tank, cleaning dead bugs off the windshield, and peering inside the car to ask if I'm hungry. I'm too tired to speak, although I hear his words and process the answer in my brain. And no, I don't want anything to eat. I may not ever be hungry again. But I am thirsty, and I want to wake up enough to ask for water. The most I can do to communicate is to open my mouth wide and stick out my tongue.

Jordi gets the message and I feel him nudging me, so I tilt my head and let him place a straw between my lips. I'm expecting water, but what I get is something cold and creamy and sweet. Ah, a milkshake. Vanilla. I try to say thank you, darling, but I'm hoping I have at least given him a smile of profound gratitude for this unexpected treat. And then he gives me water, which I drink thirstily, and pushes my head forward to place a pill in my mouth to swallow. I spit it out. I will not take any more poisons. I don't want to spend my remaining days in the torment of chemical aftershocks to my system. Nausea, diarrhea, head pain, cold sweats, hot flashes.

I feel him again pushing the capsule between my lips, which I have now tightened to not allow the slightest breach. I realize that without some kind of discussion about what I want, he's just doing what he believes is right.

And then I manage to speak. "No more shit, please."

"It's this shit that has been keeping you alive for three years."

"Yes, and I don't want to spend my last days sick as a dog."

"You can't just give up."

"Yes, I can."

Discussion over. I can tell I've made Jordi impatient. He starts the car and guns the engine to get back onto the freeway. The momentum pushes me back to a recline. I'm taking control of whatever life I have left.

A little later, Jordi speaks. "You are right, my darling. We'll have a talk with Dr. Dave when we get back."

I let myself fall asleep giving myself up to the smooth motion of the road taking me home. This sweet surrender washes waves of happiness over me. I have twilight dreams of my family's garden in Mexico, such an abundance of roses, zinnias, carnations, all brilliant colors gleaming with translucent beads as I wave a hose like a blessing fulfilling my responsibility to water the flowers.

I awaken suddenly and I'm sitting on a cold puddle between my legs. I groan with rage, and shame. Jordi turns to me, his expression of alarm questioning me.

"We need to stop."

"What's up?"

"Piss."

"Can you hold it for a bit? There's a rest area coming up."

"Too late." I'm sure Jordi can smell the urine wafting about me. One thing about the chemo, it turns my piss into a stinky brew.

He finally understands and I feel the car speeding up.

I sit in the misery of my own piss for about ten minutes. Next item on my shopping list: diapers.

Jordi curses when he sees the flashing lights of a patrol car behind us. He pulls by the side of the road and waits for the patrol to check us out on his computer.

The patrolman speaks into his loudspeaker. "Put your hands on the wheel, where I can see them, sir."

Jordi obeys.

"Passenger, I need to see your hands too."

I place my hands on top of my head. Interesting how TV has educated us on the procedures of the law enforcer. So, as we wait for the ritual that needs to unfold, I feel the piss burning between my legs.

By the time the cop comes to the side window, Jordi has calmed down. He's not going to make the problem worse by acting out his anger. He tells the officer that he needs to dig into his wallet for the license and registration. The cop can barely pay attention to the documents he is so involved with the tattooed lady in the passenger seat. He informs us that we were going twenty mph over the limit. Jordi explains as calmly as he can that he needs to get to the rest stop really soon because his wife is in some distress due to the side effects of cancer medication.

It never fails. The word cancer is the key that clears a path for whatever needs to happen: jump ahead in line, fast restaurant service, handicap parking, speeding ticket waved. Once more, the tyranny of the dying.

The patrolman, clean cut and rosy cheeked, seems shaken beyond his age of twenty-five or so. He tells Jordi to follow him and provides a noisy escort with the siren blaring. Jordi loves this and keeps up with the patrol car going ninety, swerving around the slow traffic on both lanes, under the protection of the law this time, which guides us to the parking spot closest to the restroom.

The patrol man drives off with a wave that Jordi answers with a quasi-military salute. I'm glad my small emergency has given him some fun. But he then focuses on the new problem at hand.

He pulls clean underwear and pajamas out of the trunk. He helps me slide from the seat, pulling me up to a shaky standing position against the side of the car. He is half carrying me with his arm around my waist and we do the three-legged walk to the men's room. He has figured in a matter of seconds that a man in the ladies' room would freak out women, whereas a woman in the men's room will not cause the slightest alarm. I glance at the row of urinals and feel a moment of penis envy, that men can so easily stick their thing out and piss standing up with all their clothes on. Clearly the superior sex, I'm ashamed to admit during this moment of weakness.

He leads me into a stall and pulls down my wet jeans and underwear. He wets toilet paper at the sink and sponges my legs. I reach for a wad and wash myself as best I can. Then he helps me into the clean clothes. He bunches up my urine-soaked clothes and stuffs them into a trashcan at the entrance of the rest room.

"Success," he says once we're inside the car.

"I am so sorry, darling," I say with a whimper. "You are good to me. I can't believe what I've been putting you through."

"You would do the same for me," he repeats for the hundredth time.

"Well, I wouldn't be able to carry you that's for sure."

Jordi

We make it home before dark, after a night of luxury in Kansas City, where we awaken in a king size bed, in a nice room in a nice hotel. We were due some comfort on this last leg of our truncated adventure. Room service fuels me with eggs and potatoes and toast. Just coffee for Vin and a spoonful of grape jelly she scoops out of the little plastic pack. I worry that she's starving herself but as long as she stays hydrated she'll be fine.

It's become apparent in the past few hours, leaving the hotel, stopping on the road, and now trying to get out of the car to walk to the elevator in our building, that her legs are giving out. And I'm not strong enough to carry her. I try to pull her out of the car but when I stand her up, she's dead weight in my arms. I lower her back into the car seat and make sure she's sitting safely and take the luggage up to our apartment.

When I return to the car, she's sitting on the ground, legs splayed, and she's weeping, her tears streaked and drying on her face.

"I thought I could stand on my own."

"Stay where you are. I'll borrow the wheelchair."

"Please, not a goddamn wheelchair."

"We don't have a choice, Vin."

I want to tell her that it's one more adjustment she needs to make, but I hold my tongue. She's had enough reality in the past two days without me adding to the burden. Still, it's hard to accept that a year ago she was still running every other day in all kinds of weather, cancer or not. It takes all my strength to pull her up and back into a sitting position inside the car. All we need now is for me to throw out my back, which has happened before, and we'll be two invalids in the team.

The building owns a chair for emergencies, but it takes me a while to track it down after office hours on a weekend. There is only one desk attendant on duty and she and I tour every secret corner of the building, from storerooms to offices and we end up finding it in the room devoted to residents' bicycles and scooters, and the occasional lost skateboard. Makes sense, a gathering of wheels.

I get back to the car triumphantly pushing the wheelchair and find that Vin has slouched back with a kind of grim resignation. It is hard for her to admit that she's not in charge and fully depends on me to negotiate the most basic actions.

I do feel quite in control now, easily steering the chair into the elevator and down the hallway to our apartment. I believe even Vin is relieved that we have solved the problem. So much is changing so very rapidly. She is off the poisons so that her appetite is back, and she can enjoy soup and cheese quesadillas and ice cream. Ysbel has sent us by FedEx a box of her signature brownies. I mash these down with milk and heat the mix in the microwave. They help her sleep when she wakes up restless in the night. She wants me to eat some with her, but I'm the one who needs to stay coherent.

Over the next three days the new wheelchair arrived, and Vin broke down in tears. Such a stark reminder of how helpless she has become. This whole process for her has been one of gradually losing things she was proud of: strength, with legs so weak she cannot stand up off the floor; stamina, she gets tired and sleepy early; beauty, hair gone, with a large belly and a puffy face with odd fat pockets. It has been happening gradually over the past three years, and yet she manages to cope, to adjust. The chair will give her mobility, give her greater access to things she enjoys. This has been so sudden that I'm still not fully used to her weakness and balance problems. Handicapped access, ramps, electric doors, parking permits are all new to me. Until now, handicapped people have been irrelevant, a mere nuisance because of their slow awkward pace in the rhythm of life. I'm realizing that assisting her in these final stages is going to be my main job.

Also delivered: a hospital bed that goes into the living room with various controls for back and leg and height adjustments. So if I need to help her out, all she has to do is raise the level and slide down the side to my arms. Getting to the bathroom is a challenge, so a portable toilet stands by the side of the bed for her to piss and shit into a bedpan, which I empty and rinse.

She still needs to take other meds, for swelling and pain and anxiety; I keep track and help her lift the back rest so she can swallow. I spend nights at her side on a recliner chair.

Anguish increases. Vin gets calls from Dr. Sarah and Dr. Dave expressing worry over her fall. I mean, are they surprised? Dave is concerned that the metastasis is growing in the brain, hence the unbalance, resisting Decadron, and the increased fatigue to the point that she got sleepy at 8:30 last night. I'm afraid of things rapidly getting worse. She's courting another episode like the first seizure, and we are helpless to do anything but wait. It keeps me sleeping in twilight. Alert to her every breath, every step in the night. When she sleeps her energy is so slow I can hardly hear her breathe.

A sudden noise in the laundry room startles me as Vin loads a washing machine and I dart out thinking she has fallen. A hospice team is coming to assess and educate and make a plan. This is freaking both of us out. They will come on Thursday, 1:30. Meanwhile, I feel the need to be more present. I insist against her wishes that I accompany her to the swimming pool. It turns out that she could not climb out on her own because her legs are weaker than the previous time she swam. My poor darling.

I'm also in charge of visits and phone calls and email. She tires easily and many times refuses to speak with her father and her brother, which means that I'm suspected of filtering out their calls. It doesn't help that one or the other calls every day. They end up talking to me, asking about how she's doing, her doctors' opinions, her numbers. I'm polite during these conversations. As obnoxious as they are, I need to remind myself that they love Vin, have known her all her life, and feel it's their right, and duty also, to keep track and offer support. They don't like me. And I don't like them much. But we are polite.

Vin is dearly loved, and she welcomes some visitors who now come with the unstated aim of saying goodbye. I can see it in their expressions, the way they knock softly and speak in whispers and reach a timid hand to her shoulder as if she were so fragile she might crack under their touch. There is a solemnity to these visits. Their conversations follow a ritual of reminiscences, chuckles over ancient gossip, promises of future plans once she gets well. We all know those plans will not materialize but that doesn't mean they can't be made. I'm as cordial as I can be, offer tea and cookies, show them how to manage the portable potty, thankful for the opportunity to escape the sick room and find some relief in solitude.

Vin asks if I've heard from Roberta, a young woman who was once one of her prized students and with whom she has stayed close for over ten years. Her absence now is unexplainable and Vin feels it dearly.

I send emails to Roberta that go unanswered. Things are not going well for Vin, I write. She asks about you. Stop by for a few minutes. We have magic brownies and strong coffee for special visitors. Nothing. I don't know what to say to Vin. She must be out of town, busy, dealing with her own turbulence.

I think to myself, not everyone can handle the end of life. It's a cowardly thing not to overcome your discomfort with death in order to offer comfort to the dying.

Susan and Martin, now in their seventies and friends for a lifetime of spiritual travels, drop everything and fly in from Chicago to see Vin. They pull chairs to the side of the bed, close enough to touch Vin's hand. They bring with them an aura of peace, sitting in silent meditation while Vin drifts in and out of awareness. Susan burns sandalwood, murmurs a pooja, lights a votive candle. Martin contributes his own kind of peace by nodding off. His unruly beard endows him with mystery and gravity, even as he sleeps. Susan elbows him awake and Vin smiles.

Together they bear a history of loss, parents, siblings, friends gone through the years. At their age, they are the last survivors of a long line of attachments. Martin whispers to me that the gods are playing a nasty trick on us by taking someone younger, it's the pathos of a parent losing a child, goes against natural law. He rambles on, muddying his waters so they'll appear deep. I'm at a loss on whether to agree or argue that souls mature at different rates. Vin has been preparing to die all her life.

"The gods know what we don't know," I murmur, feeling embarrassed about my lame attempts at spiritual discourse.

It doesn't take much depth to satisfy Martin. He nods solemnly, as if he has been given some profound insight. I'm hoping not to continue this discussion as I'm out of platitudes, so I hand him another piece of brownie and he settles back into the windmills of his mind.

Susan knows better than to try to figure out the ways of the gods. She has been following my small discussion with Martin and smiles when he clams up with the brownie working its magic. Her communication with Vin is eloquent and silent. She clasps her hand and lets tears well up in her eyes. Vin brings Susan's hand to her lips. I'm not sure who's comforting whom.

Vin calls Ysbel and leaves a voice message to say that she wants to say goodbye because she expects to die tomorrow. She tells me the same thing. I don't react much, just take it in. But this kind of talk creates panic and sorrow among her friends. I end up having to talk Ysbel down from her panic. Was this just too much pot talking? Or is Vin coming to terms with the fact that death could sneak in like a thief?

It exhausts me to see her fade. I am consumed by watching her for signs of life ending, expecting a turn for the worse at any time. We are talking more and more about her coming death, the love for life that she has, such sadness having to let go. I tell her that the way she has lived, without shame in her work, without flagging in her love for me, is a model of integrity. Tonight I massage her feet with lotion. I feel I'm worshipping her body, seeing divinity in the caring for her flesh.

Our last visitors of the day are a team from Dr. Dave's office. One is the nurse taking Vin's vitals and asking how things are going: *insomnia, pain, anxiety, nausea*? Yes to all. The other woman, trying for gravitas in spite of her youth and a sweet demeanor, seems to be working her way toward broaching a difficult subject. She adjusts her big glasses, purses her lips, and tells me her name is Andrea and that she's the hospice coordinator. I brace myself.

I can't believe two more weeks have passed. In that time the weakness in her legs is overpowering so that at times she cannot support her own weight even while standing. We have the hospital bed in the living room and her world has narrowed to the recliner, the wheelchair, the commode, and back to the bed. I can keep everything close together so that a transfer is a matter of two steps and a turn. The biggest challenge is the bath, and I have given her my last. I can't risk her falling and I'm not skillful enough to hold on to her, especially if her legs fail. A strong nurse comes to help. She straps a belt around Vin and uses it to help her into the shower for a gentle scrub.

Every day she fades a little more. She naps more frequently, sleeps more soundly, talks more softly, sometimes in a whisper. Last week she had a seizure as I was lifting her from the wheel to the big brown chair. Her head locked to the left, eyes vacant, blinking quickly. Result: 33% increase in the Decadron.

I am filled with small resentments. Ysbel comes to visit which makes more work for me, getting the guest room and bed ready, making extra coffee, extra food, extra entertainment. Others come to visit and Vin has me getting snacks and tea, back and forth from the kitchen to the living room. At night, I'm sometimes appalled at my anger at being the wash walla, the midnight brownie server, the shit catcher. I watch her on the moveable commode and pick up the wet tissues. All this is interspersed with foot rubs. I'm amused that I have for years eroticized all this. I am meant to serve women, a slave at their beck and call.

Andrea, the hospice woman asks, "How are you managing?"

I'm not sure what to say, so I respond with a shrug. Mute ambiguity can be the best of many possible answers.

She is not mollified. "How are you sleeping?"

"I sleep when Vin sleeps. She's up much of the night. I read to her. We take naps."

"How about the rest of the time? Hygiene, meds, food, errands, visitors?"

"Yep, hands full." She's gearing up for her main message, but I wait until she gets to it on her own.

"Can we go somewhere to talk?"

No way am I having any conversation regarding Vin without Vin being present. "Pay attention, darling," I say, "Andrea, our hospice coordinator, wants to do some coordinating."

"The system with its 24hr phone access will make things much easier. Potent meds are on hand, delivery of equipment is forthcoming."

"Sounds like she wants to take me away."

Time for Andrea to get to the point. Which she does, perhaps too abruptly. "I think it may be time for Jordi to be your husband and companion, rather than your nurse."

"I agree," Vin says, too readily. "I'm a handful."

"The good news is that a room may be opening up at Shanti House this week."

She means, I guess, that they're expecting someone to die any day now and free up the bed. I see from Vin's face that she has reached the same conclusion.

"It's a beautiful, comfortable place. And Jordi will be able to stay in the room. Full staff on call 24/7, all palliative meds available to make sure you're comfortable." She means mighty opiates. No addiction worries here.

"May I reserve a place for Lavinia?"

"Yes," Vin says. "Go ahead."

And that's it. No drama, no hesitation, no big questions. Simple words that mark the end of the road for my darling.

Lavinia

I wake up this morning with a definite sense of dread, not a new emotion for me these days but the darkness is darker, the cold is colder, the anxiety more gripping. Jordi is still asleep after a night of feeding me brownies and reading Moby Dick aloud. Queequeg thinks he's dying, and I'm keeping him company. I let Jordi sleep even though I have an urge to piss. No worries. The latest innovation from the nurse has me wearing diapers for the night. Depends you can depend on and let your husband sleep.

It's October and the light outside is dimly starting to emerge into our living room makeshift hospice. I sense that today is going to be a day like no other, and I'm a glutton for the objects that have given me a rich life for thirty years. I engage the backrest control and the bed buzzes into action so that I'm sitting up, waiting as familiar surroundings take shape. The Catrina in full festive regalia grins at me. Jose Guerrero's homage to the apple, Tres Manzanas Rojas, teases me with their perfect promise of crunch and sweetness. Anado's magical box, an altar with the bald deity at the center surrounded by jewels.

Jordi's phone buzzes and he's suddenly awake to pick up. He nods and nods, a bad habit of his as if expecting the person on the other end to be able to see his head emphatically signaling yes. After he disconnects he doesn't say anything. I watch his expression, as he thinks over the conversation he's had. I wait.

"That was Andrea, the hospice woman," he says finally.

"So, today is the day."

"Yes. We're to get a few things ready, toiletries, a few clothes, books, anything you want to have with you."

"It's Ok, darling," I say. "They won't have to drag me kicking and screaming."

He's at a loss for words. There's not much to say, so he busies himself putting things in my backpack. Yes to the Wall Drug T-shirt, yes to colorful socks, no to jeans and a knit hat. What's he thinking? I don't plan to spend any time outdoors. I sit on the edge of the bed and he pulls up the portable potty so I can piss, a common impulse when I'm anxious. Then he helps me slip on pajamas and my other favorite T-shirt with the skeletons. I like to dress for the occasion.

Jordi feeds me that morning's pills. The last of his nurse duties.

"Do you want some breakfast?"

"Just coffee. I want to be wide awake for this." While I've grown weaker, I've switched from tea. I like the energy jolt. Still, I wish coffee tasted as good as it smells.

Jordi keeps looking at his watch. That's one of his habits, always wanting to know what time it is. I've never cared; one reason I'm often late.

"Did they tell you what time they'd come for me?"

"Just that they were on the way."

I ask Jordi to draw the blinds wide open so I get a good view of the stone arch bridge over the Mississippi. I love this river, the Ganges of America. Jordi and I always expected that's where our ashes would go. No box, no hole, no stone. The apartment fills with light, as if to mark a holiday. I would have expected an overcast, rainy day, but the planet is in a celebratory mood.

I run my hand over my pate and feel its fuzz has grown in the past week.

Jordi always pays attention. "Want me to shave you?"

"I want to make a good impression," I actually hear myself chuckle.

He switches on his electric razor and within minutes he's polishing my noggin. He holds a mirror up for me, and I see the colors are up to full brightness.

They send two angels to get me, their muscular arms visible below the short sleeves of their green scrubs, their faces fixed in tight smiles. They could be twins they look so much alike. I name them Hans and

Franz. They seem worried, clearly expecting drama, which they seem relieved I do not provide.

Inside, I'm struggling to accept what is happening, the finality of it all. On the outside, I'm passive, expectant. I catch myself yawning as wild beasts do when masking aggression. One of them pulls the wheelchair to the side of the bed, and I make an effort to push myself to it. My arms and legs are suddenly unable to shift my body even a few inches to the edge of the bed.

"I'm sorry, I just can't."

"Don't worry, lady. That's what we're here for." The one I've decided is Franz has a dragon sleeve tattoo from his wrist to his bicep. He glances at my head ink but does not say anything. Still, I can tell I've earned a coolness point with him. Their voices are brassy, too loud for the close space we share. I find myself not liking them very much. It comes with being called *lady*. I've never thought of myself as a lady. A woman, yes. But then, I don't think I'd like for them to say, Ok, woman, time to go. Again, I let out a single chuckle, and that seems to put the two guys at ease.

"Just relax, lady, we'll do all the work."

There he goes again. But this time I don't try to help them. I close my eyes, take a deep breath, and become dead weight. And yet as they carry me on either side, I realize I'm as light as a rag doll in their arms. Meanwhile, I sense Jordi watching this operation nervously from the side. Whatever is happening to me from now on is out of his control. As they roll the chair toward the door, I realize I'm leaving my home, my world. I'm expected to steal one last parting look, but I've already surrendered. A dark curtain drops in front of my eyes.

They wheel me out of the elevator into the building lobby. There is nobody there, which disappoints me because I was expecting a sendoff. After thirty years I've made some friends. I think word got around that I was headed for my last stop, and people were a little embarrassed about waving me off. Beth, the desk attendant, bends down to give me a slight hug around the shoulders.

Hans and Franz transfer me from the wheelchair to a gurney, and strap me in, the bindings too tight around my legs and chest. I voice a weak complaint, but I realize that in their hands I'm an object rather than a living passenger. Still, I'm paying a lot of attention to all this procedure, you know, for the conversational material. They push the gurney in and lock it into the inside of the ambulance. Hans sits next to me and as they start to close the door, I realize that Jordi has been left outside.

"Wait," I hear myself grunt. "I want my husband in here."

"That's Ok, Lady. He'll follow us to Shanti House."

"Not Ok. He needs to be with me."

"Sorry, can't take a passenger. It's a liability thing."

"So an ambulance is not safe enough?"

He doesn't say another word, but shuts the door with a metallic thump that resonates with finality. As the vehicle rolls out of the parking circle and into the busy traffic I'm seized with a lonely vulnerability. It's the first time since I've been delivered into the rituals of medical science that Jordi is not with me. Granted there's nothing threatening about being driven to the hospice, but the fact that I'm strapped in and alone and voiceless makes it all clearer to me that this is the end of the line.

Jordi gets to Shanti House before me and is already standing by the front door. Seeing him there dissolves my anxiety. The guys pull out the gurney and unbuckle my straps and transfer me to a wheelchair. I can finally breathe. Hans or Franz starts to guide the chair toward the front door, but Jordi gently nudges him away and takes over.

"Don't leave me again, darling."

"Not a chance," he says as he pushes me into the main foyer of Shanti House. I register a few details at once. Peach walls and bamboo flooring. Flowers in vases everywhere. Dominating the salon is a ceramic bodhisattva draped in green and blue robes. Lifting his hand in teaching mudra, his piercing gaze seems to recognize me. A few people welcome me with smiles and soft greetings.

"Your room is ready, Lavinia."

The whole effect as I think back is that of a cloud of love that lifts me at every turn and into the room that has been set up for me. Peach seems to be the dominant color at Shanti House. I'm helped on to a bed and sit up to get a sense of the room. The covers are so smooth, maybe silk, a large window gives on to a lush flower garden, and at a small table Jordi has placed some beloved objects—a sugar skull, a Tibetan bell, a bronze Ganesh for the journey.

A switch on a cord rests on the bed, and I'm told I can push it whenever Jordi or I need help. It can be for any reason, not necessarily an emergency, but a nurse is guaranteed to appear within five seconds. For the rest, it's like a normal hospital room, private bathroom that I share with the adjacent room, remote TV, a water pitcher on a night table, a good light above my head for reading, or dim for sleep.

Nurse Lynn comes to check that I'm settled. She offers tea, snacks, something for pain.

"No thanks, I'm fine."

"Never be shy about asking for what you need. As long as it's legal," she winks. She means cannabis, which I have to find my own source for.

I activate the bed so that it rests flat, and Jordi helps me out of my clothes. I've always slept nude, and I don't see why that should change now. Still, I wonder if I'll get a diaper. No, he says, someone will help you to the bathroom whenever you need to go. I slip into the silky sheets, which feel like a balm on my skin as I move my legs from side to side.

I sense Jordi sitting on a recliner beside the bed, expectant to whatever I feel like doing, talking or sleeping or just resting. I don't feel like moving. Lying perfectly supine, arms and legs akimbo feels at once safe and vulnerable, somehow in hapless surrender to the new circumstances. In the afternoon the light in the room softens to a glow.

My gaze travels skyward as if expecting the sky beyond the flat white ceiling. Instead, I see a small black spider clinging upside down directly above me. I admire the precision of its hold, its six curved legs on either side of the round body poised for action. I wait for it to move, and within moments it scurries toward the wall, as if certain of its destination, only to change its direction abruptly. Ha, it's clearly lost. I wonder how it happened to get in the room, since the window to the garden is shut tight. But clearly, now that it's here, it has no idea how to get back to where it came from. So it darts in some confusion from one direction to another until it settles on the wall beside the bed, close enough that I could reach out and touch it if I wanted to. I want to exercise some telepathic energy on its behalf, but I have no idea how to guide it out of its predicament. I must've dozed off for a moment, because when I awaken the spider is gone. I sweep the walls and ceiling with my gaze but it's nowhere in sight. I wonder where it went and it makes me sad that I've missed the end of its journey. I get tea and cookies for my evening snack and Jordi helps me relax with a nibble of brownie.

I wait for the activity outside my room to settle down. As Shanti House quiets down the sounds of someone in the adjacent room keep me awake. I wonder if he has waited until night to make his presence felt. I say *he*, because his cough and groans and wheezes are those of a man's distress.

Occasional voices are audible through the door to the bathroom we share. A man is offering comfort. "Rest easy, be not afraid, Clyde." It's an old-fashioned name, you don't meet many Clydes anymore, so I picture an old man, still athletic as if from a farm background, large hands resting at his side, the back of the bed raised to facilitate breathing. The bathroom door to his room must be open because I hear people coming in and out, water running, toilet flushing.

Jordi, not using the room bathroom, which is exclusively for Clyde and me, has found one down the hall. He showers and comes back to find a cot has been made up for him next to my bed. I can't see him because he is below me, but when he reaches up I slide my hand to touch his.

Clyde has a wet coughing fit that goes on for minutes. Jordi can hear it too and I feel his fingers tighten against mine. Eventually his cough subsides and there is only his hoarse labored breath, and again a man's voice murmuring words of comfort.

Nurse Lynn comes into my room softly, asks if I'm doing Ok, if I need anything, offers a sleeping pill. I swallow it eagerly and she offers one to Jordi, who declines it.

"My neighbor is having a rough time," I say to her.

She does not reply, acts as if she hasn't heard my comment.

I'm immediately embarrassed. I know well that Clyde's distress is none of my business. But if so, why do I need to be witness to it? I guess I'm supposed to learn something, a foreshadowing of what's to come. I've never in my life been with someone who is dying. My whole experience has been in art, in film, in literature. Exit the King! And yet, I'm an expert on the Days of the Dead, I know all about the rituals of mourning and celebrating the life that has passed. I'm seduced by the poetry of the afterlife, though without any real conception of what awaits me. I'm not afraid of death, but curious. From Clyde's turbulence it's the process of dying that makes me uneasy.

Nurse Jill's pill doesn't knock me out, but instead puts me into a messy dream state, where the sounds of Clyde next door combine with images of a dark hungry bird, something like a crow or a raven, pecking out the eyes of a girl while she sleeps. She lies still, swaddled in a white satiny robe from neck to toes while the bird pecks and pecks. She is a beautiful child, with long blond hair and very white skin. I know the girl is not me and so I'm unable to scare off the bird. And then Clyde lets loose with a sudden stentorian series of coughs that drives the blackbird away and wakes me out of the dream.

I touch Jordi's hand and he presses my fingers to let me know that he is awake and aware of the turmoil next door. I'm not given to praying, but this time I do pray that a big someone out there should take pity on Clyde and help him on his way. As if in response, the coughing ceases, only to be replaced moments later by anguished retching.

Nurse Lynn comes in to check on me and stands by the bed, puts her hand on my forehead as if checking for fever. This time she nods toward the connecting bathroom door. "Sometimes, it's rough," she says. "But in the end, there's peace. Peace you earn."

She slips out of the room as quietly as she came, no sound of the door closing, and I wonder if she was really here, or if I imagined her comment.

"Jordi," I whisper. "Was Lynn the nurse in the room just now?"

He doesn't answer so I assume he's asleep. For a while, things are quiet in Clyde's room as well. The man who was sitting with him may have also gone asleep. I know Clyde's awake from his labored breathing. I wonder if he's aware of me even though I have been quiet. It's just him and me awake in the night. Still, dreams have weight, and mine must've provided some disturbance in the quiet, a shrieking bird, the sound of pecking, my own sudden cry of alarm. It's said that the only two times you're alone is when you make a speech and when you die. I want Clyde to know that he's not alone.

Shanti House is busy during the night. An occasional chime signals that a nurse has been called to a room, followed by quick steps, then doors opening and closing in response. Five seconds, and then all is quiet again. There are twelve rooms in the hospice and a person is dying in each one, all through the night, we are all gradually fading. The volunteers and nurses manage to conduct this ritual with strength and honesty. They have a limited vocabulary. One doesn't pass or transition or leave this world. We die. Sometimes it takes a long time. I like chatting with one of the day nurses, Lynn, and learn that the average is six days. That does seem awfully quick. There is one person, affectionately known as Mr. Jerry, who has become a long-standing resident after over two months. I have no idea how long Clyde has been here. Or how long I will be. No fucking rush.

I start to doze off when I'm shaken awake by a jumble of agitated voices next door. Clyde has company.

"Hello, Clyde. It's me, Father Mike."

Father Mike is very loud, as seems to be the practice when speaking to someone in a coma.

"Clyde, old buddy," the friend's voice chimes in. "Father Mike is here to comfort you and offer the sacrament."

"Clyde, my friend," it's Father Mike shouting again, "I'm ready to hear your confession, just signal with a nod."

Clearly, Clyde does not respond. As a comrade in dying, I have a clearer image of my neighbor than Father Mike or his old friend.

The priest suddenly jumps in with a singsong prayer.

"Eternal rest grant unto Clyde, Oh Lord and let perpetual light shine upon him."

Clyde suddenly shouts. "Fuck, no! Get this man away from me. Take your mumbo jumbo someplace else."

Father Mike is undeterred. "Grant your blessings to Clyde, your servant."

"I am nobody's fucking servant."

The other visitor in the room, the old buddy, quietly pushes Father Mike out of the room, followed by the door slamming.

Jordi

An extravagantly plumed bird, Ysbel sweeps into the room shaking off the black silk cape, peeling off long gloves and tossing a fedora on the nearby chair. She kisses me on the lips, and with her every move disperses invisible puffs of intense fragrance, vaguely redolent of jasmine and ripe oranges.

She wants to know. Everything. Cannot stop talking and talking as if a tumult of questions would somehow heal Vin. "How are you holding up, you fucking saint, you?"

I shrug off her drama. "We take the days and the hours and the minutes one at a time."

"Tell me everything. What does she know? Does she speak, weep, pray?"

"Not so you can hear."

Speaking takes a great effort for her now, and in any case, she doesn't have much left to say. But sometimes, while I doze beside her, she releases a long hum, something between a chant and a moan that seems to emerge from deep inside her chest. It's not predictable, and starts faintly so that I can only hear it when I place my ear next to her mouth and the sound emerges, a mingling of murmur and breath, low and resonant, warm and moist. It doesn't come from pain, but from some deep well of sadness. Sometimes, I hum along with her so that together we make a kind of harmony.

"If you will just shut up, sit with her, and listen closely, you will hear."

Meanwhile, people come and go, nurses and aides even the occasional MD pop in, although medicine has long given up on anything beyond managing her discomfort, such a bland word for pain and fear and anger. And in my contacts with these gifted caregivers I'm struck by their generosity. There is Jill, in particular, a small woman in her forties, light on her feet, quiet as a cat she glides into the room, dispensing serenity and morphine in equal values, hygiene and foot massages, words of comfort. "Darling," she says. She always calls Lavinia darling. I think she calls all her charges that, though to hear the word spoken to my darling makes the moment special.

"Darling, we need to put in a catheter because you are carrying a quart of urine and you're hurting. I can ease this hurt."

"No fucking violence," are the first words I've heard from Vin all day.

Ysbel wants to know what's going on.

"Lavinia is afraid of needles," I say.

"So, no needle then," Ysbel says.

"It's up to you," the nurse says to me, "but your wife is not comfortable."

"You mean she's in pain."

"Her bladder is full to bursting. Yes, that's pain."

I nod that yes, I agree to fear and suffering, to ease the pain you're experiencing. A tradeoff.

Ysbel leaves the room, unwilling to witness the procedure. I try to ignore the look she shoots me on her way out. Here less than an hour and already she's testing me.

As Jill approaches I can see fear cloud your face. The nurse senses it also and she approaches you gingerly, as if shy to touch the intimacy she must violate. Slowly she rubs the length of your legs drawing her hand over the sheets in long caresses from your ankles to your hips, taking the time to relax your muscles, calming your resistance.

Her lips grazing your cheek, she begs you to let her help you.

You shut your eyes to hold in the tears that burn not so much in pain or fear as from the shame of being made so vulnerable. You reach out for my wrist and clasp it tight as I face the nurse from the head of the bed.

Jill, hands gloved in blue, delicately raises the sheet to your hips and bends each leg at a time so that the ankle rests on the mattress. With the back of her hands she pushes your knees apart. She smears lubricant on the outside of your urethra and on the thin plastic snake that pokes its nose deep into the bladder.

You let out a faint moan.

"There, she whispers, that's all the pain. Relief will flow out of you like a spigot."

And, sure enough, the amber fluid starts to gush through the clear tubing into a plastic reservoir.

"Am I forgiven?" I speak into your ear.

You sigh and squeeze my wrist, which I take to be affirmative. Then you doze off and I take some pride that the break from the pain has enabled this rest. I pull my hand back and your fingers drop to the edge of the bed.

Ysbel comes back into the room and sits on the edge of your bed. She takes one of your feet under the sheet and starts to massage it, first the right, then the left. Your breathing lengthens but you remain asleep.

Ysbel weeps. "I can't help it," she half apologizes to me. "I'm such a drama queen."

"If there was ever a time for drama, this is it."

"You're so strong," she says.

"I'm saving my tears. Right now, my crying would not do her any good."

Ysbel stands up abruptly and says she's going to the room Shanti House reserves for friends and family.

"Is she gone?" Vin says after the door closes with a loud click.

"She's wiped out from the trip."

"Good. I don't want anyone watching me die, if that's what I'm about to do any moment," she adds with the first smile I've seen in days. "Just you, darling."

Dying is such an intimate private act, I'm starting to realize. She doesn't talk about it much, just a thought here and there at an unexpected time. So I have to be ready.

"I don' t know who I am. I don't know where I am. It's like being a foreigner to myself. Being echa bolas, all mixed up."

"You are my true and fully appreciated Vin, to me and to those that are here loving you."

"When am I going to die?"

"When you're ready."

"I guess I'll know, right? I don't want it to come as a surprise."

"Do you want to die?"

"Yes. But not right this very moment."

"You can go on living with the love you feel for me, for Ysbel, your mother and Luis and Roberta. This is the stuff that heals your soul, makes this bit of life you have left rich." She nods that yes, she agrees. I'm surprised when the guru kicks in and these bits of wisdom pop up. I hope I have the words she needs.

Then she adds a quiet grunt, and an invisible cloud of stink fills the room. She shuts her eyes tight, as if ashamed. I ring the call button, and within five seconds Nurse Jill enters the room. She quickly appraises the situation and shoos me out.

Dying is messy work for the body: A half dozen diarrhea BMs in twenty-four hours. Frequent pad changes and wipes of her bottom, which is raw from the process.

Ugly thoughts the past three nights. What if she doesn't die for weeks, but only continues to deteriorate? And meanwhile my life is on hold, no work, no sexual release, no distractions, and the money drains, while I accompany her day and night. Is it the Decadron and Keppra that are keeping her alive by holding the brain swelling down, and will they eventually be cut off? Not a question I want to ask at this point, lest I give my callous heart away. I feel resentful and fearful and ashamed all at once. I don't think there is any person I could confess to, this wish that she should get it over with and go. But then, day comes and I'm back with her, feeding her, watching her sleep, being in love with her. And I figure things will take as long as they take.

Ysbel

You're so strong, my friend, my darling. Even with your fading voice, its breath substituting for sound, your thoughts registering inside my head, as a word overheard out of the muddle of a crowd. Sitting here at your side, touching your hand, time stretches out beyond night and day, moments out of the past relived in the present, the time is now for you and me. I know what you want and I will stick with Jordi to make sure you have peace. And your peace becomes my peace.

It takes a mighty resolve to keep my devils at bay, and yours have the power of a mountain. They've been following me for years until now at this time, in this room, by your bed. They retreat to a corner, snarling, waiting to pounce, and even at a distance I get the reek of their gaping muzzles, red tongues flapping past yellow teeth. So many monsters. The lover you warned me about. The child you urged me to accept. The mother you saved me from, time and time again.

And now, here you are, letting peace seep through your palm to mine. As if this were your last gift to me, the fact of a quiet exit, the banishment of fear and resentment, gently going into that good night. I find myself thinking that I would happily go with you, if only to keep you from leaving me. It wouldn't take much doing—a handful of pills, a few drinks, last breaths inside a plastic bag. Would we still be friends out there in the void? I see us, free of these annoying bodies, intertwined in each other's presence, with not even a breath or a whisper to intrude into our intimacy.

You know all about the afterlife. The bardo, purgatory, nirvana, toloacan, elysium. Hell. That last one you never gave credence to. But in my mind, it's a real possibility. Because I have seen enough of it in this life to be ready for it. The only thing that would save me would be for you to hold on to me, carry me across rivers of fire and swamps of boiling quicksand. But give me a sign, a flicker or a press of your finger on my palm, and I will know what to do.

Lavinia

My neighbor Clyde is at it again. He is scared. I can hear him trashing on the bed, rocking back and forth, its frame actually hitting and banging rhythmically on the wall. In another context I would guess it was lovers at play. Here, I think he's trying to escape. I imagine he's been strapped down. I don't want that to happen to me. I tell Jordi that I don't want to be restrained. I will go gentle.

I just want him to hold my hand.

But Clyde has no one to hold him. I don't hear the calm voice of the man that brought the priest to see him.

He shouts a long guttural "No, no. Help me."

Nurse Lynn comes into the room, and speaks to him in her calm voice. I can't make out the words, but they have a soothing effect. Maybe she gives him Ativan.

"Call my friend Harry," he begs her.

"I have," she says. "He's on his way."

"I'm not going until I say goodbye to Harry."

Lynn turns on the TV to distract him with some game show. It actually seems to work, and he settles down.

I wonder what makes Harry special. He's the only person who has visited Clyde, no family, no other friends. But then one friend is all you need at a time like this, if it's the best friend, the one you love and trust.

In fact, Jordi is all I need. My room has been a gathering place for my family, unexpected and uninvited, and they have at times crowded around me, sucking the air and the energy out of the room.

I can hear them in the parlor talking loudly, excitedly, angry at Jordi. I asked him to let them in one at a time, but they overrun him. They keep accusing him that he has no right to keep them away from me. He tries to explain that the norm at Shanti is not to allow large groups of visitors. They tend to disturb the rest of the residents.

Suddenly there is a family invasion, with all of them entering the room at once. Jordi disappears with a shrug and I'm left with Father, Luis with his guitar, Mother, Aunt June with a bible. I haven't seen my aunt in years and hardly recognized her. I suppose I should appreciate her coming all the way from western Minnesota. Ysbel has trailed behind them and stands in a corner smiling at me with sympathy. I wonder if I'm expected to put on a performance, utter some last words. The truth is, I'm not ready to make my formal goodbyes just yet. But I am tired beyond words. So I wait for any one of them to break the silence.

Father goes first, since he's the patriarch and everyone seems to defer to him to set the tone of this impromptu intervention. "Greetings from our friends in Mexico, the Arreolas, the Jimsons, Ted Smythe. They all wish you a speedy recovery."

"That's ridiculous," I say. "Explain to them that I have no plans to recover."

"You have to think positive, Lavinia."

"Ok, Daddy, I'll keep that in mind."

Luis jumps in. "You don't have to be sarcastic. People are wishing you well. Accept that graciously."

I shut my eyes and take a deep breath as if to declare the subject finished. But Father can't let it go.

"It's been proven, you know," he says, "that a negative attitude makes things worse, health wise."

Mother speaks up for the first time. "I was just having lunch with Martha Velez. You know, the arts teacher at the International School.

Her husband has had lung cancer for years and it is suddenly in remission. Something to do with almond extract and chelation therapy, whatever that is. Anyway, she's doing fine. And sends her love, wanted to know if you've kept up with your poetry. I told her you had, though I haven't seen anything you've written in the longest time."

"Yep, mom, I'm still a poet. On Sundays. A Sunday poet."

"Well, you should send me something I can share with Martha. Anyway, this is nice, all of us together for a change. Luis should take a picture."

"No way," I raise my hand.

My brother pulls out his phone and aims it at me.

"Put that down," I snap, with newfound energy. I pull the sheet up to my face.

Ysbel comes to the rescue. "Come on Luis, you don't take a picture of someone who doesn't want her picture taken."

"Especially if she looks and feels like shit," I add.

"You look fine, Sis," he says, but puts the phone back in his pocket.

Father says, "come on, we're a family, let's show some harmony."

"I know what we should do," chimes in Luis. "Music is positive." He strums the guitar and starts a chord in an intro to Guantanamera.

Damn, I hate that song. I wish I had a dollar for every time I've heard it. But there's no stopping him. "Yo soy un hombre sincero, de donde crece la palma."

"Guantanamera . . ." I can't help but join in, like some conditioned reflex. And so we go on, a family singing together the old songs.

I glance at Ysbel who is resolutely not singing along. She can feel my distress and when I meet her eyes, she nods and slips out of the room.

Everyone is still singing when Jordi comes into the room with nurse Jill.

"That's great," she says with forced cheer. "Such a talented family. But sorry to break it up, Vin is due for some vitals and therapy."

I feel like laughing for the first time today. She hardly ever checks my vitals, assuming they are fading. And I don't know what therapy she's talking about. I smile in gratitude to Jordi.

"Jill is the boss around here," he says.

Mercifully they start to file out of the room, first is Father pausing by the bed to give me a kiss and a word. "We'll try to come again next week, he says."

"Thank you, Daddy, that would be great." How to say to him I won't be alive next week, without seeming rude?

Mother follows him, but she can't bring herself to say anything. She lowers her head to kiss me on the cheeks, and I feel the wetness of her tears.

My brother is still miffed that I wouldn't let him take my picture and that Nurse Jill interrupted the sing-along. Still, he presses my hand and murmurs "goodbye." I squeeze his hand back. Don't go away angry, I think to myself, but he's gone before I can speak.

Aunt June who has not said a word, is the last to leave. She shoots me a meaningful, somewhat scolding look, and purses her mouth as if to restrain some words. The tightly pressed lips seem to be her standard expression, regardless of the circumstances. She tries to hand me the bible but I don't take it. She waits a moment and instead places it on my lap. She leans in and I think she will also give me a kiss on the cheek, instead she whispers in my ear. I can't hear so I turn my face to her.

This time she is loud enough for her words to get out clearly.

"What are you going to say to Jesus when He asks why you haven't loved Him?"

"What the fuck?"

She's out of the room before she hears me. So I take the bible and throw it at the door with a bang that I hope she knows is meant for her.

Jordi rushes in, alarmed at the noise. He knows better than to ask me what's going on. He picks up the book and places it out of my reach. I've always been ambivalent about Christianity, but this is the first time I've felt such anger. Nice to have a parting moment with the faith.

Ysbel joins him and expresses the opinion that Aunt June is the devil's witch. We all agree and I marvel that anger has given me such a burst of energy just when all I wanted was a nap.

I hear some murmurings from the family as they leave. There are cheerful goodbyes, probably relieved their dutiful visit to the dying has been accomplished.

I appreciate this quiet time, and even the TV chattering away in the adjacent room doesn't disturb me. I hope my family hoopla hasn't bothered Clyde. I'm grateful to be alone with the two people I love the most. Jordi draws the blinds and lowers the backrest. I must've dozed off because I don't realize when they leave. I like them together, Jordi and Ysbel, and I know they like each other. I fantasize they will hook up when I'm gone. I remind myself to put in a word to the two of them.

So, goodnight, Jordi. Goodnight, Ysbel. Goodnight, Clyde. I turn the light off and it feels nice to drift off to sleep slowly, letting the thoughts in my brain settle, as if gradually lowering the volume in a noisy sound system down to a breath. If this is what dying will feel like, a slide into darkness and silence, then I'm not worried. I won't know it's happening until I'm dead, and then I don't know what I'll know. Time will tell.

My last waking thought is to remember to ask Jordi to read to me from *The Tibetan Book of the Dead*. Please guide all beings from this swamp of cyclic existence. Amen, sister!

It takes me a while to shake off a dream to the explosion of voices next door. Clyde is shouting as if lost somewhere. "Get me out of here," he yells. "I can't see, turn on the fucking lights."

Nurse Jill walks in and asks him if she can get him anything.

"Turn on the lights."

"Lights are on Clyde."

"Call Harry. Please, I need to see Harry."

"He's on his way. Meanwhile take this. It will make you feel better."

There's momentary silence and I guess Clyde is swallowing morphine or Ativan or both. Jill's little helpers.

"I don't need your goddamn poisons," Clyde shouts. "I need Harry. And turn on the light! I can't see my hands."

There is a moment of quiet. I hear the door close. Then, his friend's calm voice, "I'm here, Clyde."

"Step closer. I can't see you."

"But you can feel my hand, right? Now, squeeze. Harder, I want to feel your strength, man."

"Hold me. I'm on the edge of a black hole. One more step and I'm going to fall."

"I've got you, Clyde."

After several moments of silence, I hear Clyde's voice. "Harry, listen to me."

"I'm listening, friend."

"I never told you I loved you. You need to know that."

There's a long pause. "I love you too, Clyde."

"Thank you, thank you. I'm letting go of your hand now."

"Goodbye, friend."

I take the pillow and wrap it around my head. There are other sounds, of raspy breaths and moans. But I hold the pillow tighter because something profound and private is happening that I shouldn't be a witness to. Surely, Clyde and Harry are entitled to a measure of privacy. A few minutes go by in utter silence, and then I hear urgent chiming out in the hallway. In five seconds, guaranteed, Jill enters Clyde's room.

When I awake later in the morning I'm aware of a deep silence, an emptiness in the adjacent room, all the life has been swept out of the space. I tilt the backrest up and see Jordi sleeping in the cot beside my bed. He senses I'm awake and kisses me on the cheek.

"Café con leche?"

"Si!"

How quickly I've gone from tea to coffee for my morning fix. I need that jolt to establish that I am indeed quite alive. When he comes back with two cups, he announces that I have a surprise visitor out there who wants permission to enter.

I don't even ask who it is. "Please, no more visitors."

"You'll be glad to see this one. He brings apple pie."

"Ok, how do I look? I just woke up and haven't even brushed my teeth."

He hands me a brush with toothpaste and a glass of water. I swish and spit and feel cleaner just by that simple act. I reach for the coffee and place it on the side table. "Ok, darling, whoever it is can come in."

Dr. Dave enters the room and is all smiles. "Good morning, Vin, how's my favorite patient?"

I've lost track of time since entering Shanti House, but I can tell it's a Sunday, because Dr. Dave is wearing an obnoxious purple shirt. It's been ages since I last had a consultation with him. Once in hospice his job was done. No more scans or blood tests or MRIs. He's ready to send me on my merry way.

"Hanging in to complete the three years you promised me."

"You're doing great," he says. And because it comes from Dr. Dave, I believe him.

"Thanks. The patient next door died last night."

"It happens. But this morning you get pie."

He shows me two beautiful slices, golden crust and burnt sugar top that he places next to my coffee mug. "One for you and one for Jordi. He's earned a treat too."

"I didn't know you baked."

"Well-kept secret."

"I should eat it before I die, right?"

"No rush, believe me."

"Will I get some advance warning? The man next door knew it was happening for about two days. I could hear him."

"He was fighting it. You may just drift off."

"No. I want to be awake when it happens."

"Then you will be. The point is to be comfortable."

"You mean stoned."

"You're in charge."

Jordi jumps in. "We're almost out of brownies. Can you prescribe cannabis?"

"It's still illegal. I do have someone, a friend of a friend of course." He scribbles a phone number on a pad and hands it to Jordi. "Tell her to bring it to you at Shanti Hospice. That's all she will need to know."

"I'm on it." Jordi hurries out of the room.

For a few moments, I'm content to sit in silence with Dr. Dave. And he knows to just be with me, which is a switch from our previous hundred meetings when it was all questions and answers, numbers and predictions. Cancer treatment is a complicated thing, but now in the final days it's reduced to a simple process.

Still, I've never been short of questions. "Don't mind my saying this, but I think you're too nice a guy to be an oncologist."

"Meaning?"

"Sooner or later you end up killing all your patients."

"Sure. Most of them die on me. It's the one drawback of the job."

"You could've gone into OB-GYN."

"You won't believe this, Vin, since you consider me a good person. I don't like babies. I did get some practice in med school and residency. They're Ok after a few days, but the moment they're born they're disgusting. And all I can think of is that they're problems in the making. Little shits, juvenile delinquents, wife beaters, crooks, cheaters, religious nuts, phobes of different stripes. Even when I looked at them in an ultrasound, I wondered what I was bringing out in the world."

"And with oncology you're here when we leave this world. I think you like the competition, Dr. Dave. You vs. cancer, to the finish."

"Yep, they call it a battle."

"Is it one you ever win?"

"I win by trying. Tinker with this, tinker with that. The aim is not just to prolong life, but to offer a measure of quality along the way. There's a right combination for each person. No wonder pill. Sometimes a person can be cancer free for years."

"But it comes back, doesn't it?"

"Possibly. And sometimes you die of something else."

"Like getting hit by a truck."

"Actually, don't know of anyone who has been hit by a truck."

"I'm told it happens."

"The point is, in the world according to Garp, we are all terminal cases."

"And it's your job to supervise."

"It's a privilege. A person can be transformed by their knowledge of impending death."

"I can vouch for that."

"I don't help people die. I help them live with the knowledge that their time is limited. I've seen couples grow closer after they thought their love had cooled. Forgotten friends reunited. Siblings reconciled. Artists emerge. Adventures lived. Enemies forgiven. Faith recovered. Life is tasted more intensely when you know it's got an expiration date."

"Like cheese."

I wonder if they teach existentialism in medical school. This conversation has made me drowsy. I hear Dr. Dave's voice go on but I'm losing the sense of the words. But keep talking anyway, dear doctor.

Sleep sweetly calls me.

Jordi

After Vin falls asleep, Dr. Dave takes me by the arm and tells me I need to get out of the place. I'm hesitant to leave her alone, but I ask nurse Jill to text me if necessary.

"You need to relax. Try to let go of Vin for a while," he says.

"She's all I think about. I worry about her when she's awake and when she sleeps."

"Let's go for a walk. It will do you good to walk and breathe some air."

"She is sleeping a lot, off and on, day and night."

"She's doing what she needs to do."

"Is that how she's going to go, sleeping? No pain?"

"She's lucky that way."

There's a park near here and just being in the sun with trees and birds and kids at play feels good. It's also the only time I've been alone with Vin's doctor. All the other visits it's been the three of us. It feels awkward and I'm at a loss for words, as if we were to speak of Vin behind her back.

"How are you doing?"

"I try to sleep when she sleeps."

"You're in for a shock."

"Not a surprise. I've known it's coming."

"Don't kid yourself. I'll hook you up with support, a grief group."

"Misery loves company?"

"Sometimes."

I'm skeptical. But I don't wish to argue with him. I'll know what I need when it happens, not before. Right now, I need to be back with Vin, so I end the visit. I don't think I'll be seeing him again. He's cutting us loose, for his own good as well as ours. Until now, with Dr. Dave there's always been a sliver of hope. He's done.

"I'm grateful for everything, it's been a gift for Vin to have you with us."

"It cuts both ways. She has been a gift for me as well. She is a luminous being. I can see why you love her as you do."

We shake hands formally. He walks back to his car and I enter Shanti House.

First words this morning: "black and black." I waited for her to continue, but it wasn't the start of a conversation. Possibly the end of one in her mind. I couldn't figure out what she meant, though I can speculate. Will these be her last words to me? This is her first day without food. Her sleep is deep, with only brief breaks of wakefulness. While she hardly acknowledges me, I know she is aware of my presence. Still, I feel she is receding, leaving me behind. Suddenly, I'm relieved of responsibility for her feeding, pain relief, companionship. She is dying and I don't seem to have a role in either quickening it or slowing down. She is letting me go.

She's going. Feet cold, one more than the other according to nurse Jill, some discoloration around the mouth, which is now gaping open, bluish lips. I say her name and her eyes manage to open to slits. But little sense of focusing. I speak to her, tell her that I love her, that I wish her good rest, a good journey.

She seems to be resting easily with no signs of stress or pain. And for the last two to three hours she exhales with a loud hum. Nurse not worried, says she may be enjoying hearing herself. I started humming along with her a few minutes ago, and the result was something like a formless melody improvised.

A night of violent breathing, combining gurgles and moans so loud I couldn't sleep till around 5:00, and now the current state of her breath at noon, barely perceptible. She sleeps sweetly, peacefully, rapidly quieting down.

Nurse Jill is on alert. "Anything can happen at any time," she says.

I know better. Only one thing will happen.

I sit and sleep and meditate by the bed. I have nothing to do. After three years of sustaining my love, guiding her through anger and sadness and disappointment, to being the main caregiver for weeks, doing my tasks, and her tasks, and then every slight need she couldn't do herself—glass of water, toilet, feeding—now there is nothing else I need to do for her. Except offer her my companionship, my words of love and encouragement, and solidarity.

Vin continues her deep sleep with occasional whimpers. I think they are whimpers of sadness not of pain. So I need to help her die. I reassure her that as much as we love each other, it's time to let go. And in a sense I'm letting go of her. Her state in a coma makes for a very faint presence, not much for me to latch on to. And if she breathes her last while I'm away, so be it. We've said all we needed to say to each other. It's time we both fall silent. She in her mind, me with words.

Have a blessed journey, my love.

I hear her plaint and realize that the dominant emotion is sadness. She is not complaining of pain or fear. She is expressing the profound sadness she has been feeling about letting go, leaving me, and friends, and the life she has so enjoyed.

At 3:30 on Thursday Vin is in her fourth day of unresponsive coma, with no food or water. Her breathing is shallow and congested. She is dancing close to the edge, but not yet willing herself to tip over. As Dr. Dave put it, she will be doing this in her own way. What amazing control the dying have. Meanwhile, as I sit beside her, I go from numb to heartbreak and back again.

I sit in her room for a long time, very much hers after two long weeks of life struggle, and gaze upon her face, at rest now that nurse Jill has closed her jaw, which remained gaping after her last breath.

I collect a few objects that had belonged to her and stuff them in her favorite backpack. The small Ganesh. A single pearl earring, I don't know where the pair ended up. Her wedding ring, which I slip onto my pinkie lest I lose it. Her reading glasses. A sugar skull from Mexico. Her copies of Moby Dick, Don Qujijote, T.S. Elliot's Poems. With each one of these objects I feel her presence is being sucked out of the room.

And then it's just me and Vin in perfect stillness.

Nurse Jill knocks softly then lets herself into the room. She wants to know if I need anything, and tells me I can stay as long as I want.

"No hurry," she says, which is a nice way of telling me that there are things she needs to do.

"What's next?"

Our resident MD will complete the death certificate. The funeral company has been notified and will proceed with the cremation. But before they come, I will wash the body. Sometimes the company does it, but I want it done with care, soon, while her limbs are flexible. She pauses for a moment and looks at me directly.

"You may assist me if you want."

"Of course. Tell me what to do."

"I will leave you alone with her, so you can pull down the bed clothes, and remove any garments she's wearing."

And so, this is the last time I undress Lavinia. I pull off the bed covers and crumple them into a corner. She's lying supine, arms at her side, waiting for me to continue. I lift her back and pull up the hospital gown. Finally, the diaper she's been made to sleep with. There is greater dignity now that she's nude. Nurse Jill comes back with a pan of water, some lotions in small vials, and a stack of white towels and washcloths.

"We can use a fragrance if you like."

"Yes, Vin loved lavender."

She shakes a few drops of essential oil into the pan of water.

A small cloth goes over Vin's pubis. I appreciate the concern of modesty on her behalf.

"We're ready to start," she nods.

She directs me first to raise one foot so she can bend Vin's leg at the knee. She very gently wipes a wet washcloth from her hip down her thigh to her calf and foot.

"Now you do the other leg."

I lift it at the knee and marvel at how heavy it feels. I dip a clean washcloth in the warm water, and feel we are still taking care for Vin's comfort, don't want to bring a chill. I take care to run the cloth along her leg, marveling still at the runner's tone of her calves and quads, then the back of her knee, and on to her foot.

Jill and I are now moving as a team. Arms, from the shoulder down to her hands and fingers. Then her chest and belly and genitals, finally turning her over to one side to do her back and waist and anus. The scent of lavender is sweet on her skin. Finally, I take a moist cloth and lightly press it over her face. I marvel at it in repose, now devoid of pain and anxiety and fear. She has never looked more beautiful to me.

VII

Jordi

I've finally managed some coherent thoughts.

On Thursday, Vin took her last breath in the adventure of a lifetime of learning and loving and teaching. The past three years since her diagnosis of stage IV breast cancer were a rich time of travel and accomplishment. I will both miss and celebrate her presence in my life these past thirty years. Her friends and family are invited to gather for an evening of remembrance on November 2nd, her favorite fiesta, at 6:00 in our condo building's function room.

This my second night alone in the apartment and when I'm not distracted by book or screen, I am overwhelmed by the emptiness of the place, the utter strangeness of these rooms so apparently normal and yet haunted by her absence.

Up until now I have felt Vin was so close to me I could sense her shadow on my skin. And then she seems to have separated from me. It's forcing me to acknowledge her absence. I've removed my wedding ring, but kept hers on my pinkie. No longer a husband, but a widower. So I am aware of the missing ring and the new ring as my fingers unconsciously search for the familiar and notice the new. I don't have such an urge to weep, as Vin and I did enough of that in the past three years, crying at every crisis, every bad turn, every sudden realization that our precious time was limited, that things needed to be said, confessed, vowed.

Now, the organ of sensitivity, my heart, is in full bloom, by turns aching, at others swelling in the good fortune of having shared my life with her for over thirty years. I don't think I've ever been more alive to the sensations of my quickening heartbeat, my breath, the memories of the final moments and what I hope I did or said that helped her go gently into that good night.

I'll probably be here until next weekend. There's busy stuff to finish up. Then, we'll see where I go and what route I take. Much depends on the weather, but also on going by so many places that Vin and I loved. Even if I don't stay long in any one place, except Sedona where I would like to be a week, walking the spectacular trails that Vin and I knew well. Then California through December. Meanwhile, I feel for everyone who is also grieving.

I'm surprised that the expected offers of sympathy blowjobs from her friends have not materialized. The closest have been some meaningful looks from one of our favorite baristas, the ginger Kat. For the rest, sad women in need of a sad echo. Is this going to be my practice now? I'm too old and raw to actually look for another partner.

On Monday Vin ended her life's journey with a final voyage down the Mississippi. I walked down the steps of Boom Island until I touched the water. The envelope containing her ashes was a square of about 14x14", made of biodegradable material, a pale indigo with a cream ribbon. I pushed it out of the steps, its corner rising above the surface, like a ship's prow. It drifted until it began to sink, so slowly, a stream of air bubbles dotting the surface like pearls as the case filled with water. Even after it was completely submerged, the bubbles kept rising, shining in the sun, bursting and being replaced by new bubbles, and all the time I watched as her life seemed to ebb for the last time, now truly gone physically on the way to the Gulf of Mexico, to the shores of her country of birth. As I watched, my fingers found inside my pocket a single earring.

Then, on the walk home, a brilliant red bird, its plumage brighter and more intense than that of a mere cardinal, paused on the low branches along the path and allowed me to feast on its splendor for a long, long time.

≈ The End ≈

Acknowledgments

The poem "When I was eight" was written by Juanita Garciagodoy. Cover photograph is by Holly Wilmeth and is used with her kind permission. I'm indebted to Christopher Tradowsky for his editorial assistance. Rachel Holscher and her associates at Bookmobile have taken the novel from manuscript to design and typesetting with care and taste. Their work is much appreciated. I owe special gratitude to Rachel Fulkerson, my publishing consultant and dear friend, who provided valuable assistance in the publication of this novel.